DEATH BEFORE DISHONOR II: SECRETS

I0637657

Tanisha Renee'

Sky's The Limit Publications

Sky's The Limit Publications

P.O. BOX 10537

Daytona Beach, Florida 32120

This book is a work of fiction. Names, locations, characters and incidents either are products of the author's imagination or are used fictitiously.

Copyright © 2016 by Tanisha Renee'.

First Printing June 2016.

All rights reserved, including the right of reproduction in whole or in part in any form.

Cover Design by Miami Kaos

Manufactured in the United States of America

ISBN-13: 978-0-9906235-1-9

ISBN-10: 0-9906235-1-3

10 9 8 7 6 5 4 3 2 1

This book is dedicated to anyone who's ever believed, dreamed big and strived for greatness. Never give up on your dreams.

Acknowledgements

To my creator and Father thank you in abundance for every blessing and test. Nobody greater. To my sister LaQuisha, for always being my biggest cheerleader. To granny, thank you and I love you always. To my parents, thanks for everything. Love you. For the #teamcash, #teammoney #teampreme lovers everywhere thank you for your constant support. To the Secret Sessions members, we're linked forever. Love you all. To all reading this, may this book snatch your edges… lol.

DEATH BEFORE DISHONOR II: SECRETS

"Don't get crazy son." said Preme.

"I've been fucking crazy. I guess motherfuckers forgot! They want me back; well guess what, niggas... I'm back!"

The lights began to flicker off and on in the house, before the power going completely out. There was a loud rapid knock at the door. Chris paused ending the call, opening the nightstand drawer. He looked over at Sydney, who was sleeping peacefully. He grabbed the silencer from the drawer, closing the drawer back gently. The knocks continued downstairs, he walked over to Natalia's room, in the darkness, the wind howling outside her window. He turned the flashlight on his phone shining it on the room, looking in on her inside the crib. He turned the flashlight off, trying the light switch, nothing. He walked down the steps seeing flashing lights outside, he became uneasy, raising his gun. The knocking began again.

"Who the fuck is at my door?"

"It's Police, sir."

"What do you want?" he shouted from behind the door.

"There is a hurricane approaching land. This community has been asked to evacuate." Chris shook his head in disbelief, he looked again out the front accent windows, he realized besides the flashing lights the street was pitch black. He placed the gun in the small of his back, unlocking the door. There was a police officer and two firemen, Chris looked them up and down, unbothered.

"Sorry sir, to awake you. But, there's a hurricane approaching land and we are asking this community to evacuate, to a nearby shelter." Chris looked over to his neighbors outside with their dogs and children, piling into their luxury vehicles. He focused back on the police officer.

"I haven't seen anything about a hurricane on the news." He looked down at his iPhone and there was a weather alert flashing in red on the screen. Hurricane Amber was steady approaching.

"Do you have a place to go?"

"We'll be good." He closed the door abruptly, walking upstairs. He called Preme, he answered on the first ring.

"Hello."

"You see this fuckin' hurricane approaching. Our fuckin' power out. Forcing us to evacuate. What about yours?"

"I'm good. Y'all come over here. I'm having Julia fix up some fajitas."

"We on our way." Chris walked upstairs to awake Sydney, she immediately hopped up put on her clothes not asking any questions. She already knew the drill. She went over to Natalia's room and in minutes they were out the door, piling into their Range Rover, heading to Preme's. Once there Preme quickly pulled Chris to the side, they stepped into his office. Chris sat down as Preme went into his desk pulling out a gift bag. "I've looked into who has been calling your phone. It's not Ben. I have someone watching his moves. Maybe he might've had some fiend hit you up. But, no worries I know exactly where he is and what he is doing." Preme pulled a remote out of his desk turning on the television, the screen lit up showing different angles of Ben's house. The last screen showed Ben sleeping in his bed. Preme pushed the gift bag towards Chris.

"Here's a new phone for you. Toss the other. I'm having someone come and install a new security system in your house soon as power is back up. Also need to get you a generator. I haven't been able to get tabs on Money. But, no worries word on the street is he's off the grid. Besides, that nigga's time is limited on these streets. He's not dumb enough to try and fuck with me." Chris took the new phone out the box sliding it in his pocket. Preme smiled. "Enough of this bullshit. Let's eat." He got up from the desk, patting Chris on the back they walked out to the others in the living room.

A Year Later

It was a Friday morning around ten; Chris was up since 8:30 because Sydney had begun spring semester at University of Miami. She had been doing well in the Nursing program, and last semester had straight A's and two B's. She was upset by the B's messing up her average but Chris had gave her so many praises on her grades, he rewarded her with a weekend getaway to The Bahamas. Sydney had enjoyed the trip and came back replenished, ready to see Natalia. Chris felt some type of way about Natalia going to a daycare yet, so he enjoyed being home with her or taking her to his store. Dana and Vani had become the only people they felt comfortable with watching her, and on those seldom date nights they were always available to them.

Natalia was now a year old and as a cute as can be. Her hair which was dark brown and black curly locks, big hazel eyes, growing by the day she wasn't chubby as she used to be. Her one dimple and serious teething fetish always brought a smile to Chris' face. She was his twin. He didn't care that it seemed that Natalia was always with him. He loved having her with him, because that way he knew she was safe. She was sitting up on top of their bed, playing with her sip cup. Her hair wild and drool on her Hello Kitty onesie, she began to laugh clapping her hands. Chris heard her gold bracelets clinging together as she banged the cup against the remote control on the bed. Chris walked into their walk in closet, with a glass top island; he had his clothes sectioned off by brand. He went over to the Gucci section picked out a black V-neck shirt and jeans. He looked over his rows of shoes which sat on their own shelves, by brand as well, he pulled down a pair of black leather Gucci Hi-top sneakers. Once dressed he went back into the room seeing Natalia lying back on the bed looking at the ceiling. He picked her up walking towards her room.

"Now let's find you something to wear."

He kissed her cheek, placing her in her playpen as he walked into her walk in closet. All of her clothes had tags still on them. Sydney had everything in her closet decorated in pink and black, he glanced over the clothes finding her a Gucci denim ombre' dress and matching ballerina Gucci shoes. He gave her a quick bath and put on her clothes. His cell phone began to ring as he placed her shoes on her feet.

"What up."

"Hey, I'm gonna be at your store today. Those new Gucci pants come in?"

"Maybe..." Chris replied.

"You gonna do me like that, I'm your dad. You not gonna look out for me."

"I don't know... nah, I'm playing. I'm running a little late this morning with Tubby. So, I should be there around eleven-thirty, better yet give me thirty minutes."

"No rush, Chris. Do what you need to do. I need to talk to you, call me when you get up there."

"A'ight Pop."

"A'ight"

Chris was putting baby lotion on Natalia. He adjusted her necklace around her neck, a pink diamond cross pendant. She had two link bracelets and diamonds in her ears. Sydney had gotten them pierced when she was three months. Chris took her downstairs placing her in the highchair as he packed her bag. He fed her breakfast and attempted to fix her hair.

"Look your mom got me doing hair and shit."

He brushed her hair up into one ponytail, placing a ribbon head band in front to hold it down. He had learned that the headband worked wonders early, so anytime he had to attempt doing her hair it definitely would have a headband. He gave her a bottle, grabbing the bag heading out to one of his many Mercedes. He strapped Natalia in back heading towards his store, Reign.

Reign had become one of Miami's hottest stores. It specialized in having exclusive sneakers and designer clothes. The store had been featured in local magazines and continuous promotion on radio and television. Chris stayed out of promotion for the store, but his presence was known in the store. Reign's décor was upscale, everything white and gold, the back wall was lined with televisions showing music videos, and a VIP section for its celebrity clientele. He began to rhyme along with Mobb Deep's "Murda Muzik", Natalia made noises playing with her bear as the music bumped through the speakers. Chris glanced back at her through the rearview. Once at the store he parked into his reserved spot, walking over to the backseat to get Natalia out, grabbing her baby bag. He walked in through the back entrance, locking the door behind him. He heard Jay-Z blasting from the speakers. He shook his head turning it down, walking down the hall to the front.

"What the fuck are you doing?"

Nathan walked over to where Chris was startled. "My bad, Chris, I didn't know you were here." He put his hands in his pocket, moving nervously.

"So, I should be happy you're being honest with me? This is what you do, when I'm not here? Come pick this up!"

There were bags and boxes all over the floor. Nathan hurriedly pick them up, to please Chris. Nathan was young, eighteen years old, black with a low fade. He was the weekend help, but always seemed to be getting scolded because of his lack of common sense. He meant well half the time, but his lack of commitment, and drive annoyed Chris.

"Where's John?"

"He went to get something to drink from the store." Chris placed Natalia in her walker with her binky. "Hey mama!" said Nathan as he bent down to her. He touched her hand as she looked up at him. Chris walked over to the window display, shaking his head walking back to his office.

"I swear she looks just like you." Natalia began to smile as he made faces at her; she soon grabbed his chain pulling him. She laughed. The door chimed from the back door, John walked up with a plastic bag in his hand.

"Yo, Nate, I thought I told you to fix this display! You know Chris this close to firing your ass!" Chris came out of his office seeing John drinking a Brisk tea.

"What's up Chris?"

"What up."

He gave Chris pound as he put the drink down on the shelf. "We got some new shipments in back this morning."

"Let me see."

John was mixed, Puerto Rican & Black, low fade, about five foot ten, medium build and twenty two years old. He was Chris' ace and manager of the store. He kept everyone in check, yet was always reasonable when rules and guidelines were broken. He was definitely a playa, and ladies' man. He could be perceived as arrogant, but his charismatic personality and humor always made women want to know more. And right when they would let their walls down he would be everything they originally perceived him to be, a no good dog. He saw Natalia in her walker blocking the door. "Look at my little girlfriend."

Natalia smiled at him as he bent down to play with her. "Hi, little pretty," Natalia loved John because he always played with her, and gave her anything she wanted. She reached her arms up for him to pick her up. John walked away. Natalia began to whimper. "What you doing to my baby?" Chris yelled out from the back. John walked back over to Natalia picking her up. "You're too spoiled." He began playing with her throwing her in the air. She began to giggle. Chris opened up the boxes seeing this seasons women's collection from: BCBG, Michael Kors, Rocawear, Gucci, and Herve Leger. Chris skimmed over all the clothes.

"This BCBG needs to go out to the side display. Bitches will buy this shit faster than we can put them out."

"Nate!"

"Yo…" Nathan walked back to them.

"Come take this up front, to the side display, and do it how I told you." Replied Chris angrily. Nathan picked up two boxes taking them up front. They looked through more boxes finding the Dolce & Gabbana and Gucci shades that everyone had been asking about. Natalia began to reach for Chris.

"You gonna leave me, traitor."

Chris picked her up. "She gonna always choose Daddy." Chris kissed her cheek, as she laid her head on his chest.

"Aww… mami sleepy"

They began to put out the new items, as Chris sat behind the counter holding Natalia. He turned on the televisions that lined the wall behind him. John opened the doors and two black girls strolled in. They immediately saw the new BCBG and went over to the display. Chris began to feed her pureed peaches; her eyelids became heavy as she rubbed them. He handed her a sip cup of milk. The two girls walked up to the counter.

"Hi… one said to Chris, as she flipped her black Malaysian weave over her shoulder.

"How are you?" said Chris with a smile.

"We're okay." The girls replied in unison, blushing at him.

"Your daughter is too cute." said the one with the weave.

"Thank you." Chris looked down at Natalia, fighting her sleep. He repositioned her taking the cup away from her mouth.

"What's her name?" said the other girl with the short cut.

"Natalia"

"Oh, that's pretty." Replied the girl with the weave, she placed her hand on her hip, showing off her round ass. She had a Miu Miu dress in her hand. She was medium sized, wearing fake eyelashes that fanned as she talked, with a piercing above her lip. You could tell she had been with a few dope boys and her once cute appeal had metamorphosed into queen bee of thots. The door chimed and in strutted Sydney in an Adidas tank exposing side boob with matching tights which showed off her ass. She had her hair down flowing down her back, smiling as she saw Chris sitting behind the counter. She came behind the counter kissing Chris' lips. She bent slightly kissing Natalia on her forehead.

"What up baby how's your day?"

"It was okay. I have a big paper due, and a test coming up. I don't know any of the material. So, I'm gonna be on study mode hard these next couple of days."

"You'll be a'ight. I don't know why you stress over this shit and you ace it." He placed his hand on her ass caressing it as she leaned on him. The girls at the counter began to size Sydney up, looking her up and down. She picked Natalia up, she opened her eyes. "Hi, mama. Did you miss mommy?" she kissed her face as she cuddled her in her arms. Sydney walked over grabbing the baby bag off the shelf.

"You wanted to get those?" said Chris to the girls.

"Um… yea."

"Yo, Nate, come ring this up." Chris stepped from behind the counter walking over to Sydney. He smacked her on the ass again.

"Where y'all going"

"We're going by the store to get something to cook and going home so I can study."

"A'ight, don't be out all day with Natalia."

"Whatever." Said Sydney, as she rolled her eyes at Chris.

"You heard me."

Natalia looked at Chris sad to be leaving him. Chris reached over kissing her cheek. "Aww, daddy loves you tubby. I'll see you soon." She lay back on Sydney's chest, massaging her back. "See you later, papi."

"A'ight, He kissed Sydney's lips. I'll walk you out." Chris took the baby bag off her shoulder, holding the door as she carried Natalia to the car. Back inside the girls paid for their things. They watched Chris outside, almost foaming at the mouth.

"He is so fine!"

"I know! Did you see that girl all over him?"

Nathan smiled. "That *girl* is his woman. Y'all need to stop hatin'." The big booty one with the weave rolled her eyes.

"Was any of us talking to you?"

"Whatever Shanice, Chris not fucking with you, anyway" He laughed.

"Fuck you Nathan!"

Outside, Chris helped strap Natalia in. "Bye, mama." said Chris, Natalia waved back at him with a backwards open and closed bye. Chris laughed.

"Look at her, Syd."

"What?"

"Look how's she waving."

Sydney looked at her and smiled. "She's too cute. Good job mommy!" Sydney clapped showing her happiness. She reached in rolling down the window as she stood outside with Chris. "How long are you gonna be up here tonight?"

"Not long. I gotta go see Pop for a minute. Why what's up?"

"I'm just thinking... me and you need to go out for our date night, maybe the movies or something."

"We just went out Tuesday. Maybe, we need to take Tubby to the beach Saturday. We need to do things as a family. I'm not trying to have her at everybody house all the time."

"What are you saying? Sydney folded her arms. I do?"

"Don't get a fucking attitude! I'm just saying we are her parents. We are responsible for her and I don't want her in the streets all day."

"I don't need you to talk to me like I'm a child, Chris! I take care of my own daughter!"

"Yea... whatever Syd, see you later. I don't want her out in the streets." Chris looked in the backseat, she was sleeping. "Bye."

Sydney stormed around to the driver side, not looking back at Chris as she sped off down the road. Chris went back into the store. Nick stopped by after three, and Preme stopped in at five. He came in with his men, one posted inside the store and the other outside the door. Chris walked over to Preme, hugging him.

"Step in my office Pop."

Preme followed behind Chris. Once in the office, Preme looked around at the desk and shelf full of pictures of Natalia. Her toys were all over the floor. Preme smiled.

"Natalia is everywhere."

"Yea, she takes up half of my day." Chris laughed.

"Well, there are some things I need to clear up with you."

"A'ight, what's up?" Chris knew it had to be something serious for Preme to stop by the store. The seriousness in his demeanor had Chris' full attention.

"Well, I got news from Boston. They're reopening your mother's case. Need you to get the death certificate."

"Oh, what they find out on the murder?" said Chris sitting up in his chair.

"People had been calling in with new clues and shit."

"That's good!" Chris smiled.

"In New York, a lot of niggas falling off" Said Preme calmly.

"Why? What's going on?"

"I might have to go away for a minute. No biggie, I need a vacation."

"You're looking at doing some time?"

"Nah, I got a few offices coming at me. So, I'm gonna count on you for a few months, to carry the business for me."

"Where are you gonna be?"

"Maybe Rome or Belize, I'll be in contact with you."

"When is this happening? I need a while to set this up. Syd's gonna bug out if she finds out I'm even thinking about the game."

"Nah son, you're not gonna be on that side anymore."

"How so?"

"You're gonna set up the connects and maybe do a few drop offs. I'll have Darren help you out."

"Darren in the game"

"He's the one who schooled me to the game. Our whole family played a position in how I was able to reach this status, son. But, it will be a few weeks before all of this begins."

"Am I gonna be traveling a lot? You know I gotta be near Tubby." Preme smiled proud of Chris' growth. "You're not gonna be too far away from Natalia."

"A'ight"

"So, are my pants here?"

"Yea, they are up front near the window." Chris stood up dusting off his pants.

"I still can't believe my boy is engaged, becoming a man. Still no date? Have you even started planning anything?" Preme massaged his hands over Chris' back. "Yea, don't rush it pops. Shit, sometimes Syd make me wanna..."He took a deep breath. Preme laughed.

"Y'all will be alright. You gotta meet Laura"

"When am I gonna meet her? It's been months you've been telling me about her." They walked out to the floor of the store. The store had become packed with tourist and many locals, to catch the shoe sale.

"I told you she was in New York, finishing up some business. She'll be here this weekend."

"A'ight, I'll make sure I stop thru." Chris walked Preme over to the Gucci display. People began to point and stare at Preme like he was royalty or celebrity. Two men stared as if they were in awe that he was shopping. Preme paid none of them any attention. Chris acknowledged them. "Hey, how are you?"

"We a'ight." They replied. Chris leaned against the rack as Preme looked through the pants. Chris felt eyes staring at him, three women were approaching him. Two were Hispanic and one black. He turned to them. "Hi, ladies, how can I help you?" said Chris with a smile. One of the Hispanic women smiled, licking her lips at him. The black woman rolled her eyes at the others, moving closer to him.

"I'm fine. Can I try these on?" He looked into her face now realizing it was Angel, a notorious store groupie. She had been checking for Chris since she first laid eyes on him months ago. She held up a pair of 7 destroyed jeans and a pair of booty shorts.

"Yea, this way" she followed Chris to the fitting room. Once there he unlocked the door letting her in. Preme walked over to him with two pair of pants.

"I'm gonna take these." He placed a wad of money in Chris' hand.

"Nah, Pop you don't have to." Chris pushed the money back to him.

"Nah, that's you. I pay these crackers why can't I pay my son." Preme handed the money back to him. Chris accepted the money; he knew he wasn't going to win that argument with Preme. He put the money in his pocket.

"You can at least, get a shirt or two, pop."

"Bring me a few by the house."

"You need a bag?"

"Yeah" Chris walked over to the counter placing the clothes in a bag. Nathan walked up from the back he had been texting on his phone. When he looked up seeing Preme, he was in awe. He didn't know what to do. Should he speak, or shake his hand.

"Hi… Mr. Preme." He finally worked out nervously.

"What's up?" He replied. He took the bag in his hand.

"A'ight Pop. See you later."

Preme reached over and hugged Chris, he walked over towards the front door where his Rolls Royce Phantom was waiting outside. Nathan watched him go out the door with his security, as they opened the door and he got in back. The guys standing closest to the window smiled in awe, and began to praise Preme's swag and car.

"I didn't know Preme was your fam!" shouted Nathan excitedly.

"Yea… so." Said Chris smiling, John came out of the backroom with more new freight. He stood by chiming in on their conversation.

"Preme is like the king of Miami."

"So, what does that make me the prince?" Chris walked to his office to pick up Natalia's things. John laughed out loud. He put the boxes on the side of the counter, opening them with a box cutter. They were more glasses to go into the case. Angel came out the fitting room modeling the booty shorts, walking down the main aisle of the store as if it were a catwalk. She had Nathan and John's full attention, as they gawked at her body.

"Damn!" said John breaking the silence as they watched. Chris walked back out, standing beside John.

"C, check her out." Chris continued picking up Natalia's toys off the floor, throwing them into her toy bin. Feeling she wasn't getting everyone's full attention she walked over to the counter.

"Hi."

"What up." Replied Nathan and John in unison gawking at her body "Chris, can you ring this up for me?" she replied looking directly in his eyes, with a flirty smile on her face. Chris turned around, going over to the register. He looked around the counter for the merchandise, she was to buy.

"Where is your pretty little girl?"

"At home." Said Chris bluntly, he knew where this conversation was going and he was in no mood to play cat and mouse with her. Angel leaned her breast over the glass counter, licking her lips enticing John and Nathan. They stood frozen, lusting over her body and wondering what her mouth game was like. Her full attention was on Chris.

"She's too cute, tho. Just like her papi."

"What are you buying?"

"These." She arched her back, lifting her shirt showing her belly piercing. She ran her fingers slowly across her washboard stomach, revealing a strawberry on her lower abdomen. She looked over her shoulder down at her ass in the shorts, which barely covered her round derriere. "Can you get the tag for me?" Chris walked around the counter to her, she leaned her body over the counter, poking her ass on his body. Her ass ate the shorts, showing everything about her love below. "Can you reach it better now?" Chris pulled the tag out of the shorts taking a quick glance at her apple bottom. "Yo, I gotta go." Said Nathan shaking his head staring at this girl throwing herself at Chris was getting him more than erect. "I got it." Said Chris he couldn't help but lick his lips as he glanced again at her. She smiled finally getting the reaction she wanted. She got up slowly from the counter, running her fingers through her hair. Chris rang up the shorts. "Oh, wait and these!" She bent over to the stool seated beside the counter that she had rested her pants on. "You like bending over huh?"

"Something wrong with that," she said licking her lips again.

"Nah, nothing at all."

"Yea... I like doing other things too." She took her card out of her Chanel wallet, paying for the items. Chris handed her the receipt and bag. She placed the card and receipt in her wallet. "Bye...Chris" she replied with a smile this time saying, I want you now. Chris smiled, looking into her eyes. "Have a good day." She turned towards the door twisting her hips for all of the onlookers' entertainment. John grabbed himself, "Damn, Angel be sweating you hard."

"I know right." Said Chris nonchalant

"Did you see when ma bent her ass over? Listen, if you not gonna get at ma, I will, she's fine as fuck."

"How many times I gotta tell you... I'm not fucking with these broads!" said Chris laughing. John walked over to the front of the store closing down the shades.

"You know they come in here to see your ass. Chris this... he mimicked a female's voice, where's Chris?"

"They're paying money. I don't give a fuck if they trying to see me all day every day. I'm getting money." Chris laughed. "You wildin' son"

"Shit, I got a daughter to feed and house to take care of. I'm trying to do shit the right way. So, if they want to pay to look at me all day, they can look all fuckin' day!" John laughed again waiting for the last customer to leave out the door, so he could lock it. Once locking the door and walking back to the register where Chris was posted. "So, you saying if you wasn't with Sydney, you wouldn't get at Angel?"

"I ain't sayin' all that... Chris replied smiling taking the money out of the register placing it in a bank envelope.

"You would! Shit, I pull hoes on the regular and I could get Angel."

"So, what you saying" Chris said defensively.

"I can pull more hoes than you, married man."

"Nigga please." Said Chris

"Wanna bet?"

"A'ight, what we betting"

"Uh... whoever win, buying courtside tickets for the Heat game." Chris smiled thinking that was a small bet for him, frankly any bet he would've stated would have been nothing for him to obtain. But John was his man and this bet would be all in competitive love showing who was the man and would have bragging rights. "A'ight, whatever. Whoever gets the most numbers tomorrow by closing wins."

"A'ight, bet." They shook hands, sealing the bet.

"Trying to get me fucked up huh?" Chris laughed out loud, placing the envelope under his arm.

"Nah, give your numbers to Nate punk ass. You know that nigga need them."

"Yea... Syd will come in here beefing like a motherfucker. But, we'll see what happens when you buy our tickets tomorrow."

"Nigga when you buy my ticket." Chris handed John two grand. "Here I might need you to open again; I gotta take mami to the doctor tomorrow."

"No problem, it's what I fucking do, part of being a manager right. Ay, remember the girl I told you came and applied for the new closer position. You want her to come in for an interview with you tomorrow?"

"Yea, is she professional? I don't need any more hood rats, Brandy is enough."

"Ma is a fucking dime, small waist, big ass, and big ass tits. She's mixed with something, bitch sexy as hell." Chris shook his head at John. "Once again, is she professional?"

"Yea, she's good people. But, we need someone soon because Brandy saying she may only work weekends, because of her classes and shit."

"Tell Brandy to come here around one tomorrow, and we can talk about this."

"A'ight, what time you want the interview?"

"Around one-thirty or two"

"I'll call her on my way home."

"A'ight" Chris and John walked out the backdoor towards their cars. Chris looked over his shoulder and around the car before he got in. Some habits are hard to break, and although he didn't feel threatened or that anyone was after him, he always had to be two steps ahead. His phone began to vibrate and ring loudly in his pocket, he pulled it out looking at the screen, and it was Sydney.

"Hello"

"Hey, where are you?"

"I'm leaving the store. Why, what's up?"

"I need you to go by the store and get Tati some more wipes, and juice. I gave her the last juice a minute ago. Also, she has a slight temp."

"She a'ight?" Chris stopped in his tracks. "Yea, she's okay. It's a slight temp. I want to keep her hydrated." She replied trying to soothe Chris' worries. "Well, since you have a list, why don't you get ready and I'll pick y'all up and we can go together. I have a few things to pick up myself."

"Where are we going Walmart?"

"Yea, I'll be there in a minute."

"Okay, bye." Sydney hung up the phone changing Natalia's diaper on her expensive changing table, she had told Chris they had to have. She basked in the ambience of their home and life they had started together. She loved spending time with Natalia alone, she grew to love the little things, like the scent of her Johnson's Lavender scented lotion against her skin. Motherhood had always been a dream of hers, but more than often she felt this new life was too much to handle. A part of her hated this new responsibility and longed for the fast life Miami offered. The drama free lifestyle had been everything to her. But, inside she felt unhappy, longing for a change. Her mind began to wander as she threw away Natalia's soiled diaper, she looked down at her. "Dada." Said Natalia clearly. Natalia had yet to say mama, her only words were dada, baba and no.

"Oh, no you don't!" replied Sydney becoming angry. Natalia looked at her with a smile on her face clapping her hands together, repeating it over and over like a song. Sydney's eyes pierced into her child, filled with jealousy. She pulled up her clothes placing a binky in her mouth as in to silence her. She placed her on their bed as she looked in her closet to change clothes. She pulled out a pair of Dolce & Gabbana jeans with a matching shirt, and matching wedge heels. She placed her diamond necklace around her neck, grabbing her phone and purse off their custom armoire from France. Her phone rang loudly, Natalia smiled moving to the ringtone. "Hello"

"Hi Syd,"

"Who is this?" Sydney replied trying to figure out the woman's voice. She picked Natalia up off the bed. "Dada, she whimpered." Natalia began to hit Sydney with her binky as she continued to whimper. Sydney tried to adjust her on her hip. "Tati, please... she pleaded."

"Dada! Dada..." She continued ignoring Sydney's request. Sydney put the phone back to her ear. "Hello?"

"Syd, I'm still here, it's me Nadine." She replied sympathetically.

"Oh my god, Nadine, how have you been?"

"Girl, I'm good. How's the baby?"

"Being a crybaby, working my last nerve." Said Sydney as she chuckled half seriously.

"Aww... how are you doing? How's life?"

"I'm okay. School is becoming so stressful, but I'm hanging in there."

"Girl, hang in there. You can do it." Sydney smiled at Nadine uplifting words. She needed to hear that sometimes. Natalia began her fit again. "Dada... Dada..." she screamed in Sydney's ear. "Aww, is she talking now?" "Yea, she wants Chris, she just loves her daddy." said Sydney sarcastically. Sydney went to Natalia's room getting her sip cup and brought her back and sat her down on the bed. She gave her the cup propping her head up on a pillow. Natalia looked Sydney in her eyes throwing the cup across the room. Sydney glared at her as she went to pick the cup up off the floor. "Tati, stop it! Now your daddy's not here. Knock it off!" She shouted. Natalia began to cry loudly. Sydney heard Chris pull up outside, Nadine sat on the line listening and waiting patiently. The front door opened and the alarm chimed, Chris heard Natalia upstairs calling for him. DADA... DADA. "Mama... what's wrong?" he yelled from downstairs. He walked up their sprawling stairs, glancing at their pictures on the wall. As he got closer he could see Natalia sitting up on their bed tears streaming from her eyes.

"Aww, you missed your daddy mama? I'm sorry." He picked her up cradling her in his arms. He wiped her tears from her face, kissing her cheeks. He looked over and saw her cup on the floor; he reached down handing it to her. She sipped it quietly looking up into his eyes. "She's so spoiled. You need to stop picking her up every time she has a temper tantrum. She thinks that shit is okay."

"I'm not neglecting my kid, Syd."

Sydney rolled her eyes looking over at Chris. "Whatever, she's not going to get her way all the time. I'm not having it." Natalia was drifting off to sleep in Chris' arms. She massaged her tiny fingers across his chest as her eyelids stopped fighting and she drifted to sleep. Chris looked down at her. "Look at my mama." He kissed her forehead, rocking her slowly. He waited a few seconds before placing her on their bed. He placed her up on the pillow, placing a blanket over her. She began to whimper, opening her eyes. "Go to sleep" said Chris sternly. Natalia looked into his face and knew he was serious. She laid back down closing her eyes. Chris went into the closet changing his clothes to a black Versace shirt, jeans and Timbs. He went to the mirror checking over his appearance. Sydney walked into the bathroom, which was his and hers. She sat on the side of their Whirlpool custom tub, which had Versace golden heads on the side. Chris saw that Preme had one and he wanted the same, so Preme had it custom made and was wrapped in a bow when they arrived.

"He gets on my nerves." She whispered to Nadine.

"What he do?"

"Well, he's definitely changed is all I can say."

"Is that a good or bad?"

"Well... it's good for everyone else but me." Sydney leaned over looking towards the door to see if Chris was nearby.

"Well, I got something to tell you."

"What?"

"We're all coming down in a few days, we got a room already, and I can't wait to see you."

"What! Oh my god! You didn't have to get a room; you could've stayed with us."

"Well, thanks but it's too many of us to impose. It's going to be me, Tori, Mercedes and her friend Kiana coming down."

"Mercedes?"

"Yea... if you don't want her coming, she won't come."

"I don't want her here."

"Okay. We'll be there Thursday."

"Okay, call me when you land and I'll pick y'all up from the airport."

"Oh, cool. I can't wait to see my god baby."

"She's a handful." They both laughed.

"Well, I can't wait to see you. It's been months, I've missed you." Chris walked into the bathroom, the whole room was filled with his cologne. "Are you ready?"

"Yea, I'm ready. Sydney ran the brush through her hair quickly. Chris turned around walking out the bathroom. Well, girl... I gotta get off the phone. I'm going to the store with Chris."

"A'ight Syd, talk to you soon. Kiss Tati for me. Love you."

"I will. I love you too, be safe. Bye." Sydney hung up dropping her phone in her purse walking out to Chris. He had Natalia swaddled in his arms with her baby bag on his shoulder in the hallway. "You got her binky and diapers in there." "Everything is in there. We've been waiting on you." Chris looked affectionately at Sydney. She looked back at him. "What?" "I'm just looking at you." She walked by him and he smacked her across her derriere. Sydney looked back at him again. Her eyes seemed weary and she looked stressed. "Give me a kiss."

"What?"

"You heard me?" She came over to him kissing his lips. She pecked his lips, He took his free hand cuffing her chin drawing her into him, kissing her long and slow. Natalia remained sleep in between their embrace. "I love you." Said Chris looking into her eyes, he knew that Sydney had been feeling some sort of way since Natalia was born. This past year he had begun to notice changes in Sydney's behavior and her actions towards him. He knew something had been troubling her, but he continued to put it off, not wanting to press the issue while she had been stressed with college. She looked back into his eyes, which were sincere, he was her everything. "I love you too." She said with a smile. Chris walked downstairs to the Range Rover. Chris strapped Natalia in. Sydney followed behind placing the alarm on as she locked the front door. She walked over to the passenger seat sliding inside. He started the car immediately switching thru his different catalogs of rap albums covers on the screen. "I don't want to hear that. I want to hear some R&B." Sydney reached over to the touch screen display changing to Pandora, top hits. Rihanna came through the speakers; Sydney immediately turned it up singing along. Chris cell phone rang; he looked down at the phone smiling as he answered.

"What up, nigga!"

"Yo, what's good? What you getting into tonight?"

"What you got planned?"

"Well, we having a poker game at my other crib in Lauderdale tonight. You down?"

"Yea, I'm down to take niggas money."

"A'ight, we starting around 8:30, but I'll hit you up later to see what's up."

"A'ight nigga, we gonna get some money tonight."

"We can blow this shit tonight on some shoes." Chris laughed.

"Hell yea, buy my baby some new toys, her piggy bank money."

Nick laughed as he and Chris ended their conversation. Their poker games stakes would get high, but some of their niggas who would come through couldn't keep up so they would take their money for fun. Last time they had a poker game, one of Nick's people, Olie, tried to keep up putting twenty five grand on the table. He was upset when he lost his re-up money. Chris took the money after he won throwing it in the air, throwing it in his face verifying that he wasn't on his level. Chris never liked him he got a vibe from him; Chris poured his gold bottle champagne all over the money. Olie cringed as he watched Chris make a mockery of his hard earned cash. He got up storming away from the table. Chris taunted. "Come on nigga, don't be a sore fucking loser. Somebody's in their fucking feelings, about some pocket change. You believe that shit?" said Chris as he laughed at Olie. He never returned to another one of their card games.

They pulled into a parking space at Walmart. Chris looked in the rear view mirror looking to see if anyone had followed behind or was lurking around the car. Sydney interrupted his thoughts. "Who was that?"

"It was Nick."

"And you are going out tonight?"

"I'm not *going out*, I'm going to play cards for a minute."

"Hmmph" Sydney scoffed as she rolled her eyes getting out the car. She slammed the door behind her, which awoke Natalia. She went into the backseat unhooking Natalia from her seat. Natalia looked around confused; she put her arms around Sydney's neck, not wanting to wake up. Sydney grabbed her baby bag throwing it across her shoulder. Chris stormed over to Sydney, his mood annoyed.

"What's all this huffing and puffing for?" He grabbed an available cart, placing the baby bag in it. "I'm saying it's crazy, we can't do anything together, but you can go chill with your niggas."

"That's different. I'm not dropping Tati off with anyone; she's staying home with you."

"Who says, I'm staying home?" She snapped back at Chris. She placed her hand on her hip, giving him full attitude. She glared into his eyes, not backing down from the unit on his face which said don't try me Syd. He clenched his jaw trying not to give Sydney a reaction. "Where you going?" He replied calmly. "Don't worry about it. Natalia will be with me."

"Whatever Syd, you going to take the stroller" Sydney turned up her nose at the raggedy cart Chris had picked out. "Yea, I'm not placing her in that dirty ass cart." Chris reached in the trunk and got out Natalia's stroller. He cleaned out the inside, placing her blanket inside of it as a liner. He took Natalia out of Sydney's arms placing her in the stroller, his chrome reflected against his back as he bent into the stroller. Sydney reached in cleaning her dirty nose and face with a wipe. She began to cry, she hated having her face cleaned. Sydney smiled. "Oh stop it." A black family walked by admiring their family as they walked into the store. Like many before them saying Natalia looked just like Chris. Sydney hated when people said that, and although she agreed on several occasions, she started to loathe random spectators' admiration for Chris. It made her feel like they didn't see her, as in you are cute, but your man and baby are gorgeous. Her feelings lately had begun to take over her thoughts. It made her attitude change about everything. She then pondered why she invited Chris to come anyway.

As they walked into the store, Sydney began to smell something foul. Nothing was unusual about that in Walmart, because it could be anything or anyone. She stopped pushing Natalia and leaned into the stroller, to get a whiff of her. She was definitely rotten. She told Chris she was going to take her to the bathroom up front and she would meet him in the food section. Sydney walked past the front of the store, like always it was a scene. Handfuls of people with baskets overflowing with groceries and only a few registers open. The self-checkout was backed up and she felt all eyes were on her. As she got closer to the bathroom she saw a group of men at register fifteen with a cart full of soda, beer, and charcoal. She turned her head trying not to have eye contact with them, knowing it would be a problem if she gave them the slightest bit of attention. Sydney glanced over at the guy on the end. He looked either Jamaican or Bahamian, wearing Polo by Ralph Lauren shirt which was red and white, over slim fit jeans and the latest J's on his feet. He had two huge ropes on his neck. He felt eyes looking at him; he turned locking eyes with Sydney. "Damn, look at her." He tapped his nigga on the shoulder. "Hell yea, she bad." She hurried towards the door. Sydney rushed into the family bathroom, changing her diaper. When she walked out, she saw the guy in the red Polo.

"Sup ma." He said surveying her body.

"Hi." said Sydney, walking swiftly away from him. He caught up to her, forcing her to slow down as people stared at them.

"This yo' little girl" His accent, a southern drawl, his bottom teeth of his mouth were gold, his mouth shined when he spoke. He had a bald head and He smiled at Sydney taken back by her exotic beauty. Sydney didn't respond. He bent down looking in at Natalia in the stroller, a smile on his face. "Hey mama" Natalia looked at him as in *who the hell are you.*" After not getting a reaction from Natalia, he focused back on Sydney. "She's pretty just like her mama. He said almost sounding perverted. So, what you doing in here by yourself shawty..."

"I'm not. I'm with my fiancé." Sydney's eyes surveyed the lines looking to see if she saw Chris anywhere.

"Oh, that's cool. So you're not looking for no new friends?" He continued, ignoring her blatant non interest. "So, you happy with ole boy, huh?"

"Yes, I'm very happy."

"Well, you are sexy as hell. I had to speak to you, my name is Yogi. He smiled at her again, this time she felt his eyes undress her top as he licked his lips. She became disgusted. Holla, at me when that nigga fuck up, I know I'll see you again." "Bye." Sydney replied cutting him off as she almost power walked to the grocery section. She didn't dare look back, but she felt him watching her the entire time. She exhaled deeply, happy to have ended a possible situation. Because if Chris would have come to a register and seen Yogi, she played a massacre scene in her mind. She shook the thought out of her mind, thinking of how good Chris had been doing lately. When she looked down aisle six she saw Chris picking different boxes of cereal.

"It took you long enough! I've went through half the aisles." Sydney sighed. Not wanting to start a possible argument with him. She looked into the cart, skimming over all the items. Chris had all of his favorites. They walked over to the juice aisle, Chris immediately went over to the Juicy Juice, and he picked up six bottles. Sydney looked at him in dismay. "She needs more snacks."

"It's on the next aisle." They walked over to the baby foods. Chris looked over the jars as Sydney leaned her body on the cart. As she daydreamed she looked at the others on the aisle, who were eyeing them. She rolled her eyes, ignoring their stares. Chris grabbed a handful placing them in the cart. Sydney leaned in looking at the jars. "She doesn't like carrots, Chris."

"I didn't get carrots." He replied.

"Yes, you did." She reached in trying to grab the jar, Chris stopped her. "This is turkey and one is chicken and the other is some banana shit. I know what I got." Sydney continued to grab the jars to confirm.

"Yo, you wildin', I told you I didn't put no fucking carrots in here." The people on the aisle looked over at them, quickly before looking away. Not wanting any problems.

"I'm just checking. Geez, is that a crime." She replied nastily. Chris ignored her pushing the cart, as they walked towards the next aisle. As the cart reared out onto the main aisle, a group of men were coming towards them. Chris walked ahead to the diapers, Sydney tailed behind him with Natalia. She looked over realizing it was Yogi and his friends. She quickly turned away. Chris had piled diapers in the cart.

"I keep telling you not to let them get low. Always have at least one box ready."

"I know. But you forgot that she was sick last week."

"Oh yea, but she still should've had plenty left." Sydney bent down picking up some Johnson's baby products and placing them in the cart. Yogi stopped at the end of the aisle admiring Sydney's body. He licked his lips, as he imagined her naked body on top of him. Chris felt as if he was being watched he looked over seeing Yogi watching them. Chris bit his lip thinking maybe he was looking at someone else, cause he just knew he didn't have the audacity to fucking stare at him. He looked around realizing they were the only ones there. He was furious.

"You fucking know me?" Chris shouted. Yogi looked past him, his eyes scanning over Sydney again. "Fuck is he gawking at, like he fucking know me." Yogi walked away. Sydney massaged his back, trying to calm him down.

"Baby, it's okay"

"Nah, I don't like how that nigga was eyeing me. Like I'm with his girl or some shit." Sydney let him vent she knew that if she tried to calm him down. The situation would have escalated quickly. After a few moments he calmed down. They shopped for twenty more minutes before heading to checkout. It was about time for Natalia's bottle; Sydney took a new nipple out of her bag, and placing it on the bottle. She handed it to Natalia and she threw it. Chris looked over at Natalia, shocked that she was behaving this way. He picked up the bottle handing it to her. She reached up for him. "DaDa" Sydney rolled her eyes at how she had Chris wrapped around her finger. Chris obliged and picked her up out of the stroller.

"Hey mama, you can't be throwing this bottle." She looked at Chris and smiled grabbing his chain on his neck, playing with it.

"She is so spoiled, and it's all because of you."

"Whatever, it's not because of me." He smiled kissing Natalia's cheek as he put her in the air. A few women came in the line behind them and they began to eye Chris and Sydney to see why he was with her. Although Sydney was gorgeous, but to many girls wanting to be Chris' wifey she could be easily replaced in their eyes. The total came up to six hundred dollars. Chris pulled out his rubber band of money. All fifties and hundreds, he looked at the twenties that had gotten in his stash. He handed the cashier hundred dollar bills and she ran the marker over his money. The drawer opened and she began to make change.

"Give it to her." Said Chris as he walked towards the exit, the cashier handed Sydney the change she placed Natalia on her hip and slid the money in her back pocket. The cashier smiled at Natalia. "You have such a pretty baby."

"Thank you." She replied, placing Natalia in the stroller. Chris was all the way at the car. She waited until cars passed and walked across the street. As she walked through the parking lot she noticed a candy orange box Chevy with oversized tires orange leather bucket seats. Yogi and his friends were inside watching her. Sydney looked away not wanting any eye contact with him. She reached the car, which conveniently was parked right in front of Yogi. She opened the backdoor strapping Natalia in her seat. Natalia began to whine, Sydney handed her a binky and turning on the television monitor in the backseat, Disney's Frozen. Chris was at the trunk putting the bags in; she smiled as she folded up the stroller handing it to him. He made room for it in the back. He was almost done as she came over to him, watching him put the bags inside. Sydney placed her arms around his body, resting her lips on the nape of his neck. "Christian, I love you." He smiled turning to face her. She smiled showing her perfect white teeth a smile that would always make Chris weak. He looked into her eyes.

"Oh you just felt like telling me that."

"Yes, you love me?" She replied seductively.

"Of course, I do." Sydney smirked at his nonchalant yet cocky response.

"Well..." she replied with her arms folded firmly across her chest. Chris smiled; he placed his finger in her belt loop pulling her close to him. He hugged her body, kissing her neck slowly sending goose bumps up her spine.

"I love you ma." He looked into her eyes, grabbing her chin kissing her lips. She smiled, knowing that they had an audience.

"That's better." He laughed closing the trunk. They walked around getting in the car. Sydney put her feet up on the dashboard, as they pulled out of the parking lot.

"I'm going to visit my dad in LA soon."

"When"

"Maybe next month, sometime"

"So, are you planning on taking Tati?"

"I don't know if I want her to be on a plane, just yet."

"That's up to you."

"Well, maybe I'll let her stay home with you. " Yogi watched their car as it sped out of the parking lot. Although he couldn't see behind the darkened tint, the scene they had just displayed made his skin crawl. His eyes burned green with envy.

"You see that nigga? Who that?" his friend in the passenger seat looked around to see who he was looking at. He shrugged. "Who?"

"In the Range"

"Oh, that's that nigga from the shop on Collins."

"What shop?"

"You know that store, Reign, that everybody been going to, he owns it."

"What else he doing, who he know?"

"I don't know a lot about him. I hear people in the store saying he got bread, got some ill connects, know what I mean. He's from up north."

"Yea, I figured that, I could tell how his punk ass talks."

"Yea, we need to stop by that store and pay him a little visit." He nodded his head agreeing with Yogi.

"That nigga linking up with somebody, that's what we need to know"

"Yea you're right, because that nigga definitely got some bread."

"Speaking of connect, I need to see if I can get in with Preme. I'm definitely trying to get on that nigga team."

"Hell yea. Preme the man, he on that presidential shit ain't, nobody fucking with his team. Nigga been getting money forever, you get with him you fuckin' made it" Yogi looked off brainstorming a plan of action.

Chris and Sydney arrived home; Chris came back out getting the bags. Sydney had taken Natalia upstairs for her bath. Once she was done she laid her across the bed wrapped in Hello Kitty robe rubbing baby lotion over her body. Chris came into the room pulling up his shirt lying across the bed beside Natalia. She began smiling playing with his arm. He turned over playing with her. Sydney put on her diaper. Natalia rolled over and sat up on all fours crawling across the bed.

"You see her! She's gonna be walking soon" said Chris as he sat up admiring his princess.

"She's so strong" Sydney admired her a while longer as she made a mess of their duvet on their bed. Sydney went over to Natalia's room to get her pajamas, which was by Armani. It was pink with white flowers all over. They went downstairs to the kitchen. Chris plopped down in the sitting room which was decorated in vintage Versace, Natalia sat on his lap. He turned on their 90+ inch television; he went into the security app checking over all the different angles that looked outside of his home. Once all cameras were to his approval he turned to MTV 2 watching *Martin* re-runs.

"Baby, are you hungry?"

"Yea, what you cook?"

"I made some baked chicken, mashed potatoes and broccoli and cheese. Also a salad."

"Yea, you gonna make me a plate?"

"Of course"

"Thanks ma"

Ten minutes later, Sydney came out to Chris with his plate and a glass of Sprite. He sat up taking the food; she went back in the kitchen to bring Natalia's food and bottle. She came back sitting beside them. Natalia came over to Sydney seeing the food in her hand. Chris began to laugh at Martin in episode: No Justice No Peace. Sydney looked up at the screen laughing with him. "Damn, this food is good, baby."

"Thank you."

She put Natalia in her walker, and fed her peas and chicken. She looked over seeing Chris' plate was empty. She shook her head. His plate was running over and he was already done. "Yo, I'm full now. I need to take a fuckin nap." He got up taking his plate to the kitchen. After Sydney was done feeding Natalia she placed her in her playpen. She went upstairs to get her laptop and books. She tried to situate her items on the table as she pulled out her pen and paper; Chris came back to the couch lying down on her lap. "Baby, I need to study."

"I'm not bothering you." She placed the laptop on the edge of the couch, continuing to read her book. She looked down at Chris.

"When are you going back to school?"

"Me? I'm not a college bound nigga."

"Don't say that. You should go, you have so many other talents you should use them and you're smart."

"Nah, I don't know about college."

"Just think about it." She looked down into his eyes. He looked at the television, thinking what he would look like in a college. His attitude and reputation preceding him on the campus, made him laugh. But it warmed him to know that Sydney saw so much more for him, he admired the fact that she believed in him. She nudged him. He simply replied. "I'll think about it."

"I have a math test. I fucking hate math, and my professor didn't even go over any of this new material."

"Let me see." Sydney pulled out her math book showing him the problem. He read over the question and sample. He began to figure it up in his head. "It's not hard, Syd. You have to find the square root of this number first." He took her pencil writing out the problem of one of the even problems, he circled the answer he got. Sydney looked over his work flipping to the back of the book for the answer.

"You're right baby, how did you do that? I mean no calculator or anything?"

"Well it's easy. He sat up showing her how he got his answer. She listened carefully as he gave her a detailed breakdown. It's easier doing it by hand then trying to calculate." Sydney was in awe, she couldn't get over how serious he was about this problem. "You are seriously too smart Chris. You need to go to college, have something to fall back on. Your mom would be proud of you." Chris smiled.

"You really want me back in school huh?"

"Yes! You are smart, baby. I mean, I want you to be happy in whatever you do. But, with a degree It would help more in the business area, you know help you with future business plans. I mean why short yourself, it's not like you don't have the knowledge." Chris ran his fingers through his hair taking in all of Sydney's points. He then thought about his discussion with Preme.

"We'll see Syd." He got off the couch glancing over at Natalia in her playpen. She was playing with her teething ring drool everywhere. He thought about what her future would be like. The only thing that continued to replay in his mind was that she would never struggle like he did; he would make sure she had everything she needed and more. That was a promise.

He walked upstairs to take a shower. Once done he called Nick, to see was the card game still on. Nick said that they were all heading to his house now; they had stopped to get a few bottles. He told him to come thru whenever. Chris told him he would be there within next forty five minutes. Chris went into his closet picking out an Alexander McQueen black shirt, jeans and matching hi-top sneakers. He looped his belt as his looked at his reflection. He went over to his jewelry putting his black diamond bracelet on his wrist, Cartier on the other. He grabbed his Jimmy Choo cologne, spraying it quickly over his body. He went through the main safe grabbing a brick of cash. He walked back down to Sydney and Natalia. Sydney had her hair pulled up in a tasseled ponytail, with pencils as her hair clip.

"Baby, check this for me?" Chris came over to her looking over her paper. Sydney looked him up and down; she smelled his cologne that she loved enticing her. His muscles, and caramel skin looked good in his fitting shirt. As he leaned over her body, she looked at his washboard stomach that sat in her face. She bit her lip, thinking of him on top of her, she wanted him.

"You good, ma, you got it."

"Really, they are right?" she replied excited looking over her answers.

"Yea." He looked down into her eyes. She tugged on his shirt, for him to bend down. He smiled at her, "What?" His eyes were now in front of hers. She pulled him down closer kissing his lips. She leaned back onto the couch dropping her books to the floor, pulling Chris on top of her. She wrapped her legs around his body as he kissed her lips and ear, which was Sydney's spot. She began to cream in her panties.

"You know, I love that cologne on you. Why you have to be all fly and shit for your boys?" He smiled at Sydney, knowing that she wanted him right now.

"I'm always fly, Syd."

"You sure, you're only playing cards?"

"Yea why?"

"Just asking, you look like you're going to do more than play cards." Sydney replied rolling her neck as if she was pissed. Chris could feel her attitude getting ready to explode.

"Whatever, I'm going to play cards. I'm gonna get out of here, before you have any more ideas."

"Yea, whatever" She replied rolling her eyes. Chris walked over to the playpen picking up the baby. He kissed her throwing her in the air. "Bye mama. Have fun at home with your mommy tonight." Natalia giggled grabbing his face.

"Yea... we're not gonna be in all night." Chris turned to look at Sydney, his eyes piercing. "Where are you going?"

"Visit Vani maybe" Chris put Natalia back down into the playpen. She laid down, looking at her father.

"You can't stand that I'm gonna be out huh?"

"Whatever Chris"

"I'm gonna call you, don't be out all night." Said Chris his demeanor serious and eyes piercing through Sydney's glare.

"Don't you be out all night with your friends" Chris ignored Sydney's comment feeling his blood starting to boil; he decided it was best he go. He walked outside to his latest cars, and hopped inside his Maserati speeding off into the night. Sydney got up from the couch, picking up Natalia. She was furious.

"Hmmph. He wanna go be with his stupid ass friends, I'll go be with mine. Think he's gonna keep me in the house all fucking night while he's out in the streets. He's got me fucked up." Sydney went upstairs changing her clothes. She placed Natalia on the bed as she rummaged through her closet. She pulled out a racer back black top that revealed major side boob and Moschino tights that showed her every curve. She looked at her coke bottle figure in the mirror; her ass sat high and juicy, she smiled in approval. She put on a matching belt and peep toe boots, and placed her necklace on her neck. Sydney brushed out her hair, applying MAC lip glass on her lips.

She went into Natalia's room grabbing something for her to put on. She put her on a pair of socks, Armani booties and a sweater. She proceeded downstairs to refill her baby bag with bottled water, and juice. Her phone rang halting her pace, she glanced down at her iPhone seeing Vani's name on the screen. "Hello"

"Hey Syd, what you up to, I'm bored as shit."

"Getting ready to come to your house." Sydney replied with a chuckle.

"Well, come over then. I was just about to ask you that."

"Okay, I will see you in about twenty minutes, walking out the door now."

Sydney grabbed her bags and Natalia on her hip heading towards the door. She went out to one of the garages putting the alarm on the house. She decided to take one of the Mercedes' driving off down the road. Halfway down the road she realized she wasn't gonna make it. She was out of gas.

"Shit! She hated getting gas with Natalia in the car. But, she knew she would have to. She pulled up to the station seeing it was a lot of people there. She wasn't about to leave Natalia in the car. She looked into the rear view mirror and checked all around. Something she learned from Chris, always be aware of everything. She grabbed money out of her purse realizing she left her wallet in the house. She quickly took a hundred dollar bill out of her purse, placing her purse behind the passenger seat. She got out of the car; she held her head up high her hair flowed in the night's breeze. A Mercedes pulled up behind her as she walked around to the backseat to get Natalia out. Two men at the opposite pump looked over at her.

"Damn! Shorty fine as fuck!" one yelled out. She ignored them, taking Natalia out, as she closed the door she saw Nick walking beside the car to the store.

"What's good Sydney?"

"Hi, Nick." She replied with a smile, cupping Natalia's butt in her arm. He came closer, smiling seeing Natalia.

"Hey, mama, you miss your uncle Nick." She smiled at him. Sydney put the alarm on, as they walked towards the store. Onlookers stared at them.

"Don't get Chris in trouble tonight."

Nick laughed. "We gonna be good. I don't know what you talking about, we stay out of trouble." They reached the door;

Nick held it open as Sydney walked in. He glanced at her body as she walked in.

"You be good aight, Syd. Don't be out too late." He replied looking once more at her outfit shaking his head, as he walked in after her. Once she paid for gas walking back out to the pump three new cars were outside.

"Damn, ma"

"Ay, little mama hold up" Sydney ignored their calls. She unlocked the door, putting Natalia inside letting the window down so she could see her. She began to pump gas, one of the men came over.

"How you doing beautiful?" Sydney looked at the man, rolling her eyes. He was dark skinned wearing a white tee, True Religion jeans and gold grill in his mouth. "Dem' tights looking right on you, baby. Damn, I had to come, holla at you." Sydney looked away thinking to herself would he stop talking to her.

"So, what's your name?"

"Taken." She replied bluntly.

"Damn, he must not be doing you right, you out here dressing sexy for me."

Nick had come out of the store, a red bull in his hand. Sydney cringed inside; she wanted this clown to go now. She knew that Nick would tell Chris about this encounter and the last thing she needed was to hear him beef about this bullshit. Nick was now in ear shot of them, he smiled looking directly into her eyes.

"So, can I get your number?" Nick looked directly into the man's face, not believing this pussy had the nerve to talk to his ace's old lady.

"Um, no, I'm married." He took the nozzle out of her hand.

"Let me pump that for you beautiful. You don't need to be getting those pretty hands dirty on this shit." Nick laughed out loud getting inside his car.

"That's okay. I'm done." She replied sharply taking the nozzle back. She was finished, she walked to the driver door getting in locking her door and rolling up Natalia's window, the guy stood at the back of the car, disappointed. Nick was still at the pump inside his car watching them.

"Ain't that fucking Bolo punk ass?" His passenger, Smoke laughed. "Trying to get at Chris ole' girl"

"Yeah, he laughed, Chris would've killed ma if he saw her in them tights."

"Oh, hell yea"

Sydney sped off down the road silently beating herself up thinking why did Nick have to be there. She knew he would tell Chris she imagined the scene in her mind. But a part of her didn't care what Chris had to say. She pulled up to Vani's complex which was a condo. She pulled in the parking space in front of the door she saw the door open as she got out getting Natalia. She grabbed her bag walking up to the door. She looked up seeing a man about six feet tall, muscular, wearing shorts and a wife beater he reeked of weed. She assumed this had to be Mark, she decided to speak not wanting to disrespect Vani.

"Hi, how you doing?" he looked up looking into Sydney's eyes; stopping in his tracks his eyes scanned her body.

"How you doing, he smiled, this must be Natalia." He touched her arm before walking towards his car. She proceeded into the house. Vani came over immediately picking up Natalia, and playing with her.

"So what happened that you are out tonight?" Sydney sat down, resting the baby bag on the floor.

"So, that's Mark?"

"Yea, he came in here on that bullshit, I told him take that shit back where he came from. They both laughed. So, what happened with you?"

"Well, Chris decided he was going out with his boys to play cards and I'm supposed to stay in the house all night. Ever since we've had Natalia he is this other person."

"What do you mean?"

"He's changed. He treats me like I'm his fucking child and I mean I am happy that he is an excellent father to Natalia. I mean, just because I'm in school trying to better myself he treats me like he's the parent of the year, because I'm not there all the time. But is this what I have to look forward to years from now? I'm sick of him demeaning me and treating me this way."

"Wow, I do think Chris is a good nigga. I mean, I think y'all need to come to some sort of agreement about how you want your family life to be lived. If you plan on marrying him, y'all definitely need to talk. Years later in the marriage it's going to be ten times worse."

"Vani, talking to Chris sometimes is in vain. We'll argue. He'll talk shit, I'll talk shit, and it will almost come to blows. I don't want to go there with him. I just never knew when the baby came he'd change this bad."

"Well, he did and the point is now what are you going to do about it? Anything you choose you know that I'll always have your back."

"I don't know what I'm gonna do. It's like when we are good, were good. I love him, with every ounce of me, Vani. But, then sometimes, like today I asked him to take me out, ya know just me and him. She mimicked Chris. *We just went out! We're not gonna keep dropping Tati off with people. We are her parent's, that's our fuckin' responsibility!"*

Vani's mouth dropped, not believing what Sydney was saying to her. "He said that?"

"Yea, I'm always trying to get in the streets" Sydney replied throwing up air quote, hand gestures.

"Oh, hells no, fuck him! He better stop fucking tripping before you leave his ass with the baby! He's got some fucking nerve." They both laughed.

"And to make matters worse I just saw his homeboy at the gas station, and some nigga was trying to talk to me."

"What, wearing that?"

"Yea, I know he's gonna tell Chris."

"Hell yea, he's gonna tell him. You know niggas gossip more than bitches." Natalia had drifted off to sleep in Vani's arms. She laid out her blanket over the couch making her a space, placing another blanket over her body.

"Oh yea, my girls are coming down Thursday! We are going to have to show them to the best clubs and shit."

"That's cool. But, you not gonna be going out every damn night!" Vani replied in her best Chris impersonation.

"Whatever, I do what I want!" Sydney got up from the couch going to the fridge for a drink. Vani looked at her ass as she passed.

"Oh, you were working it tonight. I know niggas was all over you with all that ass out tonight. Hell yea, he told Chris. They both laughed again. Sydney grabbed a lemonade walking back to the couch. Vani adjusted herself on the couch resting her leg on top of the table. Oh yea, I meant to tell you Tina was in Chris' store the other day and said that bitches be in there all day trying to get at him. Be all over his ass flirting and playing with Tati and shit."

"WHAT! He has those bitches in my baby face?" She repeated not believing Vani. She sat up on the edge of the couch.

"That's what she says, and Tina knows every fucking body. She said that it be mostly hoes in the store, trying to get at Chris. I believe it, 'cause I know some of them broke hoes she told me about can't afford most of that shit in there."

"We'll see about that." Sydney replied calmly. She didn't want Vani to see the rage that was boiling inside of her; she sat back on the couch sipping her drink.

In Coral Springs, they had begun their card game. In true Nick lavish fashion he hired a personal chef to prepare some wings, fries and steak. He had a fully stocked bar. Hennessey and Remy sat in the center of the table, which was his favorite choice of drink. This house was his secondary house which he used for leisure activities. Around the Mahogany table sat: Nick, Chris, Damien and Cedric and Russ.

"Yo C, how your baby doing nigga?" said Damien as he poured himself a cup of Hennessey.

"She good." said Chris.

"Yo, when y'all getting that new True Religion shit in. I heard they got new all black shit?"

"Yea, that's been in there about two days now."

"Damn. I gotta stop thru, and get that." Chris nodded his head in agreement. He wasn't trying to talk about the store he was a true competitor and was all about winning, even if it was small money to him, he loved the bragging rights. The first hand Chris won, which was eight thousand dollars. By the fourth go around Chris had won two and Nick had won the last. Cedric was fuming. He was about twenty two years' old, medium build and brown skinned. He was originally from New York, but had been in Miami about six years and quickly networked with a few key players with his promotion company/weed business. He never liked Chris too much; he thought Chris was too arrogant and shined too much with his money. He felt that his cockiness always said no matter what you do nigga I'm still better than you. So, the thought of Chris considering his hard earned money pocket change enraged him. Cedric's nickel and dime money was mediocre to Chris and Nick's stacks. As Nick began to deal the cards for the fourth round he looked over at Cedric quizzing.

"You in this round? You're getting a little low over there nigga." Nick chuckled a bit.

"Man fuck you, I'm getting money."

"Yea pocket change, don't be putting all your rent money in this card game. You know it's close to the first." Chris chimed in.

Cedric sucked his teeth placing three thousand dollars on the table. "Now raise that!"

"Are you serious?" Nick replied with a laugh.

"That's, my shorty toy money. Get the fuck outta here, with that shit." Said Chris taunting Cedric. Nick took out ten thousand dollars slamming it on the table.

"Top that!"

Damien pulled out. "Y'all niggas wildlin' I'm out. Russ soon followed after. Chris took out sixteen thousand dollars.

"Damn." Everyone looked at Cedric to see what his response would be. He began digging in his pockets. Soon ones, fives and tens lay on the table. Looked as if this was his last stash of money, it came up to twenty one hundred and fifteen dollars. He took off his chain and watch placing it on top. Nick laughed out loud.

"Man keep the fifteen dollars, so you can get something to eat later."

"Fuck you" As everyone looked over their cards, Chris began to study his hand. "Oh C, did we tell you we saw your ole girl at the gas station."

"Which one"

"On Eastside, by the crib. You should've seen Syd tonight. You would've been vexed nigga."

"Why, what she was doing?"

"Dressed in one of them tank top jump-offs with her fucking titties out on side and shit, some tights that showed every fucking thing son! You need to check on ma." Chris cringed not believing Sydney left the house.

"She'll be a'ight." He replied simply brushing the image out of his mind. At the end of the game, Chris won. He took all the money stuffing it in his pocket as if it meant nothing to him.

"You gonna take all my pocket change for tonight, a'ight nigga. Just fucking with you, good game." They gave dap as Chris stood up from table. Cedric was pissed you could see the steam beaming off his forehead. Russ and Damien looked over at him.

"You should've stopped, Ced." He didn't say anything watching Chris pack up his money. Chris looked down at his chain and watch he just won. Chris pulled out his iPhone.

"We gonna play again C?"

"Nah, I gotta go"

"A'ight, we gon have a rematch soon my nigga. You just got lucky tonight nigga" Chris laughed at Nick grabbing the bottle of Henny and taking it to the head.

"You good Chris"

"Yea just needed a drink for the road, you know I'm good"

"A'ight, I'll see you tomorrow."

"A'ight, y'all, be safe. Thanks for the pocket change, Ced."
Chris replied with a smile. He walked out the door calling
Sydney's phone. He took the watch and necklace throwing it
across the driveway. What was he gonna do with that second
rate shit? No answer.

Meanwhile, Sydney was still at Vani's she looked down at her
phone on her lap. They were still up watching a movie as
Natalia slept on the sofa.

"That him?" said Vani.

"Yea, I better head home." Said Sydney sighing as she got off
the couch. Chris had sped down the road. Almost thirty
minutes later and Sydney hadn't made it outside yet. Chris
drove by Vani's apartment complex. He looked around for one
of their cars. He saw the Mercedes parked in front of the door.
He looked down at his phone it was almost two thirty in the
morning. He was pissed. He sped away. Sydney came out of
the house minutes later. Natalia was wrapped up in her arms in
a blanket. Vani walked them out to the car.

"Hey Syd, come by the shop tomorrow. I wanna try this new
color on you."

"Okay, I'll call you." Just as she was getting in the car, Mark
pulled up. Vani rolled her eyes going back into the apartment.
Sydney sped home, almost running through several red lights.
She opened the garage pulling in. She looked for Chris' car,
she saw the lights were still off. She hurriedly grabbed Natalia
and her bag. She ran upstairs to their bedroom, almost tripping
over the last step. She placed Natalia on the bed stripping off
her own clothes and placing on a tank and boxers. She placed
Natalia's bottle and binky on the nightstand. She stripped off
Natalia's clothes to her onesie and socks. She ran down to her
room throwing her clothes towards hamper missing falling to
the floor. She placed Natalia in her arms lying down beside her.

Thirty minutes later Chris came home with a foot long sub and soda. He walked down the hall peeking into Natalia's room. No baby. He turned the bedroom light on seeing Sydney and Natalia in bed sleeping. Natalia was completely knocked out her arm in Sydney's face. He looked at Sydney as in "*your ass ain't sleep.*" After he was done eating he went downstairs to throw the trash away, he came back upstairs going to the bathroom to shower. He saw Sydney's evidence of apparel skewed across the floor. He picked them up examining the tights. He knew those well, when they had come out a few weeks ago at his store, he had to get them for Sydney. He liked the low cut and how it accentuated her every curve. When she tried them on they looked painted on her body. He threw them on the floor, as he proceeded to the shower.

The next morning Sydney woke up in a panic looking around for a clock to see the time. It was eleven thirty. Natalia's doctor appointment was at ten. She got up out of bed seeing both of Chris' phones on top of the dresser. She knew he would never forget his phone, so she knew it was on purpose. She walked down the hall to Natalia's room, seeing it was clear. She walked back to their room going to the bathroom, seeing her clothes on the floor. She couldn't believe she left them there. She shrugged it off, stepping into the shower.

She began to wash her hair and body, thinking about what Vani said last night. She then thought of Natalia's appointment, upset she missed it. Twenty minutes later, when she was done she stepped out wrapping a towel around her hair, and body. She could hear Chris in the room talking loudly on his phone. She walked out to the bedroom, looking at Chris. He was sitting on the edge of the bed in Dolce & Gabbana all black, new Jordan sneakers and diamonds on his neck and wrist. Sydney walked past him going to the closet. Natalia lay on the bed sucking her bottle, a small bandage on her leg. Sydney walked over to examine her leg.

"They give her a shot?"

"Yea, she's good. My mami didn't even cry." Replied Chris as he hung up the phone, ending his call.

"Aww, so what did they say? Is she okay?"

"Yea... doctor said she's healthy and on point with everything." Sydney picked Natalia up, kissing her cheek. "I'm so mad that I overslept and missed, my pooh bear's, appointment." She placed Natalia back on the bed, adjusting her towel. She began to walk back towards the closet. Chris grabbed her arm. She turned around quickly, glaring at him. The grip he had on her wrist forced her to come into him.

"WHAT?" She barked defensively.

"You went out last night huh?" He released her wrist.

"What are you talking about?" she replied her hand on her hip.

"So, I'm speaking fucking French now? You heard what the fuck I said." Sydney stood in front of him, unbothered. She adjusted her towel again. "Yea... and so did you."

"We're not talking about me. What time you and Natalia come in last night?"

"It wasn't late Chris. It was about ten or eleven."

Chris became enraged by her blatant lies. He stared into her eyes, biting his lip trying to compose himself before he lost it. He couldn't believe she would look him in the eyes and lie to his face.

"Ten or eleven huh." He got off the bed. Sydney glanced at him rolling her eyes walking to the closet. She picked out lace panty and bra set, putting them on. She picked out a short BCBG dress that was V-neck in front and white. Her breasts spilled out of the top. Chris came out of the bathroom with Sydney's clothes balled up in his hand.

"Why the fuck you wear this little shit last night? You thought this shit was cute!" He yelled as he threw the clothes at her hitting her in the face. She fixed her dress walking over towards him.

"I'm my own person. I will wear whatever the hell I want! I'm not trying to dress to impress you or any of your fucking friends."

He glared at her.

"Nah, but you want to walk around with a baby looking like some fucking hoe in the streets! Sometimes I swear you do shit to make me vexed."

"Yea, sure, she walked away from him rolling her eyes. And you keep them hoes you talk to in your *whore* store away from my baby. Let me find out you had the next bitch in my baby's face!"

"I don't know what the fuck you talking about! I don't have Tati in the fucking streets around any and everybody, I'm not always in the fucking streets showing my ass or bullshitting half the fucking day and I damn sure don't have a one year old baby out til' two in the fucking morning! That's what the fuck you need to be worrying about."

Sydney's mouth dropped as tears welled up in her eyes. "FUCK YOU!" Sydney threw her shoulder roughly against his chest as she stormed past him, slamming the door behind her as she walked into the bathroom.

Chris smirked. "Yea, go sit on the fucking toilet and feel sorry for yourself. You do dumb ass shit, you get treated like a fucking dumb ass!" Chris placed pillows around Natalia before he walked out of the room. Sydney fell to the bathroom floor crying, she hated feeling like this. She felt stupid, embarrassed, like a child who had been scolded by her parent. She placed her knees in her chest as she let everything that had been building up inside of her for months pour out on the floor. She stayed in the bathroom for ten minutes. Chris came to the bathroom door opening it. She was startled, she wiped her face quickly.

"What the fuck are you about to do?" He barked at her.

"Don't talk to me like that! I'm not stupid or a fucking child!"

"Yea, sometimes you act like you don't have one of those either." He replied sarcastically.

"I'm not your fucking problem! You're the one that asked to marry me. Can't see your fucking life without me bullshit! You're the asshole that couldn't wear a fucking condom! No, I didn't ask for a baby... but I love her more than anything and just because you sit on your ass all day with her while I better myself doesn't make you a better parent than me. So, don't say that shit to me!" She jumped up from the floor and was inches away from his nose. He didn't flinch; he looked down at her unfazed.

"Nah, its shit like what you did this morning, make me wonder where the fuck your head is at. It's not about you anymore. Grow the fuck up!" Chris turned away from her, walking out the bathroom. She took off her engagement ring throwing it at his back. She rested her arm against the counter, as tears fell from her eyes again. This time hot and salty as they pierced her cheek, rage bubbled inside of her. Natalia began to cry in the room, being awakened from their loud voices and commotion. Sydney continued to cry as she walked out to pick up Natalia. Natalia sat up in the bed looking at her skeptically. "DA-DA" She screamed as Sydney picked her up.

"Stop It!" Sydney yelled. Sydney put her firmly in her arms. She shoved the binky in her mouth. Natalia began to whine. Anger built up in Sydney as she looked down at her baby girl. "Stop it!" She replied sternly to her. Natalia looked up at Sydney seeing the seriousness in her face she became quiet. Sydney went back to the closet and she picked out a pair of Moschino shorts that barely covered her ass, matching belt and heels. She sat Natalia on the bed and she bed played with

Sydney's cell phone. Sydney quickly changed clothes. She sat on the bed massaging lotion over her legs. She placed Natalia on the floor as she went over to the mirror to apply her makeup. All of her makeup was aligned by color and brand. Chanel, MAC, NARS, Dior and Bobbi Brown lined the drawers of her vanity mirror. She looked at her reflection as she applied red Chanel lipstick on her lips, Chris loved red on her. She brushed out her hair letting it flow down her back.

Sydney walked over to Natalia's closet picking out a similar outfit to hers; she put her hair in two ponytails letting her long curls flow over her shoulder. Chris came up the stairs seeing Sydney standing in the center of the bedroom admiring her body in the mirror. The shorts barely covered her full ass, her legs oiled up and full breasts. He looked away from her, not wanting to give her any attention. He picked up Natalia who was sitting on the bed. He looked at her outfit. Sydney continued to brush her hair to one side as Chris smirked at her flawless appearance.

"You wearing that today?" He finally worked out.

"Um… yes. And if I must say, I look pretty damn cute." She walked past him looking into Natalia's baby bag to see what she needed to add. Chris placed Natalia on the floor, on top of their Versace rug. He saw Sydney's engagement ring sparkling on the floor. He picked it up.

"What's this supposed to mean? You're done with me?"

Sydney turned around looking over at him. He was holding the ring in his fingers. She looked past him and the ring placing a blanket and change of clothes in Natalia's bag, ignoring him.

"So you can't talk to me?"

"Chris, you can't control everything. Ever since I had Natalia you treat me like shit."

"HOW, I FUCKIN…"

"See, look at you, you're about to blow up now."

He sat on the bed, clutching the ring in his palm. "I know I got some issues with my anger and attitude. But, I've changed a lot of shit for you and the baby. So you can't sit there and say I haven't changed and try to do fucking better. I mean its pisses me off because I feel you should do more than you do. But that's why we should be able to talk about shit."

"You want me to be a housewife in the house all night. It's not about to happen. I'm young and I want to enjoy my life. I can take my baby wherever and do whatever I want. I mean, I don't see you not hanging out with your friends or doing whatever the fuck you want to do. I'm not marrying you for you to control my life or Natalia's life. I refuse to live my life that way! So, maybe you need to change some of your ways, before we decide to make this forever."

"So, this is you? Is what you're trying to say?"

"Yes, this is me." Chris looked at her again; he flicked the ring on the bed.

"Well, do you." He placed his shades over his eyes, getting up from the bed walking out of the room. As she heard the front door slam downstairs she smirked. "Whatever" Sydney took Natalia downstairs to put juices and snacks in her bag. She sat Natalia in her walker on the kitchen floor. She began to clap her hands. She smiled looking over at Sydney. "MA-MA" Sydney stopped looking over at her.

"What did you say baby?"

"MA-MA"

She replied with a smile. Sydney smiled back at her tears filling her eyes. She bent down picking her up again. "Mama, that's right. Good girl. She kissed her cheek. Natalia continued to say it over and over again. In this moment those words were everything to her, tears streamed down her cheeks. She was blessed, she was a mother. She wanted to call Chris and tell him about it, she then realized that she wasn't done with him yet. She thought about her actions and yes, she may have been wrong for being out all night with Natalia, but he was wrong for belittling her and trying to control her. They were young and maybe they moved too fast getting engaged. They definitely needed to talk, but she felt it was best to give him a little time. She walked out to the Porsche' Cayenne, driving towards Vani's salon.

It was around one in the afternoon when Chris arrived at his store. John was working on a few boxes, Chris walked through the front entrance. A few girls had come in and awaiting his arrival. He acknowledged them. "What's good? How are you ladies doing today?"

"We're good." They replied in unison with bright smiles on each of their faces.

"Let me know if you need anything."

"Okay" Chris walked towards the back. John soon came to the back with him.

"What's good?" said John as he approached Chris giving him dap. Chris began to open a box that was on the floor. As he opened and realized it wasn't merchandise he looked skeptically at John.

"They're some promotional shirts they wanted us to give out for the big concert this weekend."

"Who brought this shit here?"

"Record label, street team. Brought it through with these flyers, and posters."

"I don't want this shit! Tell Nathan and Brandy they can give this shit to their friends." Chris walked towards the counter, John followed close behind.

"A'ight, I'll let them know. So our bet still on, nigga?"

Chris laughed. "Yea, we on. You ready to lose nigga? You just have the bread for our courtside seats."

"It's nothing. I does this shit. He replied loudly, massaging his handsome face. Anyway, the interview chick will be here at one-thirty. Brandy should be here at two-thirty."

"A'ight." Chris replied nodding, he looked over the merchandise as John took the promo items to the back. Chris turned on the television screens. Chris Brown's *Loyal* came through the store's surround speakers. The song was rather symbolic with the morning he was having, he immediately bopped his head to the beat. As he cleaned the counter. He felt someone approaching his personal space. He glanced up from the counter, staring into double d's. Chris quickly looked up to her face. She was stunning. She was wearing a black blazer, v neck white top and black pencil skirt. She had a pair of Gucci pumps on her feet, he scrolled back up to her face. Her full Ruby Woo lips, honey skin, dark hair and seductive eyes, had definitely captured Chris' attention. "Oh, hey... Chris this is the 1:30 interview... um..."

"Tatiana." She interjected with a smile.

"I'm Chris, the owner. How are you? He replied with a smile, and extended hand. They shook hands. Step into my office." She followed him down the hallway to his office. He opened the door to his office, she took a seat on his Versace plush chair. As he took his seat behind the desk. He moved his phones off his desk, tossing them inside. He went into his desk looking for her application, that John said he placed on top. Tatiana looked around on his desk of pictures he had of Natalia, and Sydney. She looked down to the floor and saw a case of Mott's apple juice and a case of diapers. "I'll be right back."

"That's fine." She replied with a bright smile, exposing a dimple in both cheeks. Chris walked out to John to ask him about the location of her resume'. Once he had it he walked back to his office. "I apologize. I'm usually a little more organized." He replied with a smile.

"It's cool. She replied softly. Is that your baby?" She pointed to Natalia's professional picture. "Yea, that's my daughter." He replied proudly glancing over at the picture.

"She's adorable."

"Thank you. He looked over her resume'. So, Tatiana how did you become interested in the position?"

"Well, I've been in this store a few times, I love the style and what it represents. John said that you would be looking for part time position opening soon, and since I'm trying to continue with my modeling career. A little extra cash couldn't hurt."

"We are looking for a part time sales associate, possibly leading to full time. We may have an employee leaving and need that position filled immediately. Would you be interested in that position?"

"Yes, that would be great."

"Do you have any sales experience?" He skimmed over her previous jobs mostly were modeling gigs.

"Yes, I worked for Victoria's Secret for two years."

"Okay. Well, here we are laid back. I don't ask for much, working your shift, a certain level of customer courtesy giving each customer a five star experience. Making them want to come back and showing them why we are one of Miami's best stores. In the morning I am usually here with my daughter, our team here is more as a family than just coworkers. We also have contests each month for designer products we are sent in or from celebrities that come thru, as well as cash prizes for highest sales. No family discounts or any for that matter. Our starting pay is 11.25. The hours we are looking for are Tuesday thru Saturday, twelve to seven. Are those hours good for you? Did you have any questions?"

"No, that's great. I don't have any questions." Tatiana normally the thorough queen, couldn't help but be mesmerized by his presence. He looked over her high school information. "You're from Boston? Me too."

"Really?! I've been here almost three years now. How about you?" She normally would get into old stomping grounds and what part he was from, but she had to calm herself and remain professional.

"Well, I moved here from NYC. But, I was raised in Boston."

"Do you miss the weather yet? I mean those brutal winters." She replied sarcastically.

"Hell no! Glad to be away from the snow. I would like my baby to experience it though, you know. Good memories. He replied lightening the mood with a smile. She nodded her head agreeing with a smile. If you don't mind me asking, are you mixed?"

"Well, my father is Peruvian. My mother is Trini and Costa Rican."

"That's cool. Me too."

"You're Costa Rican?"

"Nah, Peruvian and black."

She laughed out loud. "I was going to say."

"Say what?"

"I was going to say, I haven't seen many sexy Costa Rican men and definitely not out of Boston." They both laughed out loud. He continued to review her resume' but in his mind her personality had already won him over.

"Well... Tatiana you seem good."

"Oh, one thing... call me Tati, everyone calls me Tati."

"Okay. That's my daughter's name."

"Really?"

"Yea, it's her nickname, her name is Natalia."

"Aww… that's cute."

"Yea… so, I will definitely remember you." He replied with a smile.

"Well, I guess that's good for me." She replied with a flirtatious smile.

"But, you're good Tati and we would like to have you here."

"Really?! Thank you!" She shook his hand.

"You will need to get with John and he will set you up for training and your schedule. You will start next training most likely next Tuesday. I will have John contact you."

"Okay. Do I need to bring my documentation then?"

"Yes. Any other questions?"

"No, I'm good." Chris stood up from his seat, she proceeded to stand up as well. She adjusted her skirt as he walked past her to get the door. He glanced over at her round apple derriere.

"Welcome to the team. I'll see you Tuesday." He held the door open to allow her to walk thru. She walked past him a smile on her face as she switched her hips. She flipped her flowing curls over her shoulder, as she turned heads walking out the front double doors. John watched her every move from the register. He heard Chris' footsteps coming from behind. "Yo, C… you better had hired her."

"Yea, she's good people. Good personality."

"So, she's hired." He replied impatiently.

"Yea. She starts Tuesday. Have the paperwork ready. Twelve to seven."

"Hell yea. I'm not gonna mind seeing that ass every day." Chris laughed at John's bluntness. "You wild son."

"Real talk. You know she was fine."

"She a'ight." Said Chris nonchalant, changing the channel on the screen.

"Yea, you just saying that cause Syd got your ass on lockdown. She's bad, you buggin'." Chris walked off becoming engrossed in his own thoughts, tuning John out. He thought about how cool Tati was and how they immediately hit it off, she would definitely be an asset to the store.

*　　　　*　　　　*

Meanwhile, in Hollywood, Sydney was at Vani's salon getting her hair blow dried. The salon was packed, like always. Vani definitely kept a loyal clientele. It also didn't hurt that Dana was known as the best in nails, for her original designs. Women loved the fact she was always booked to capacity, and her being unattainable kept them coming back.

"What did Chris say this morning when you came in?"

"We had a big argument! He yelled, I yelled. We called each other names. I threw the ring."

Vani dropped the blow dryer, turning Sydney in the chair so she could see her face. Vani was always overly dramatic, but Sydney needed that today to fuel her ego. "What! Not the fuckin' Tiffany?!"

"Yea. I don't know, this new attitude he has, and I'm really thinking I've had enough of it. I am seriously thinking we need a break." Vani looked at her through the mirror seeing the hurt in her bestie's eyes. Over the past few months she had started to see signs of turmoil in their relationship, but she never thought Sydney would consider a break.

"A break?" Vani finally replied.

"Yea. Not to see someone else. Maybe just to get away. Get back to me, doing what I love. I feel like I've lost me. Everything has become what he wants, the baby...you know?"

"I mean if that's what you want cousin, I have your back, no matter what. But, you know that the streets are always talking about Chris. Almost every bitch that sits in this chair has been checking for him. The minute they know there is a little bit of fuckin' friction, bitches come out like fuckin' vultures. You feel me?"

"I don't give a fuck about those hoes. Because not one of these hoes is like me." She replied confidently, as she eyed a few onlookers waiting up front. Vani laughed at Sydney's outburst. She was proud of her cousin's confidence, but she knew Miami all too well. Everybody was looking for a come up, and the moment word got out that Chris was a free agent, bitches would be lining the store floors.

"You're a mess." Vani replied.

"You know maybe I'll take a trip to LA. My dad has been begging me to come out. That will be the vacation I need, to evaluate some things."

"When, do you plan on doing this?"

"Maybe two weeks."

Two girls walked in half dressed. One in a crop top which said fashion killa with denim shorts that barely covered her bottom, Jordan sneakers on her feet and her hair pulled up in a bun. Showing off her bamboo hoops. Her friend was wearing a bandeau top, high waisted skirt, with a pair of Jimmy Choo sandals. She flipped her hair as she pulled her iPhone from her clutch and snapped a selfie. The other girls looked them over doing mental calculations of their outfits.

"Your skirt is cute. Where did you get it?"

"Reign, on South Beach." Vani looked over at the girl. She and her friend were about eighteen, they came faithfully every week for a touch up. They so badly wanted to be a part of the fast life.

"Oh, I heard of that place. It's owned by a guy named Chris right?"

"Yea, that's it."

The friend in the crop top smiled. "With his fine ass!"

"Ay, don't be talking about my man!" said bandeau top with a flirty smile.

"Whatever, Angel." She nudged her.

"Girl, I was in there a couple of weeks ago. He was wearing this Tom Ford shit. He had a diamond chain on. Nigga was fresh head to toe, n'ahmean. His swag always on a 100, bitch."

"Ooh, I know he looked good. He can be wearing simple shit and look sexy as fuck."

"He was like, *can he help me?* I was like nah, I need to be helping you showing you what this mouth do. Shit, I've been thinking of getting a job in that bitch." She laughed. The other girls laughed chiming in.

"Yea, he is fine."

"Okay! I think every bitch go in there just to look at his ass." Sydney sat up in the chair, doing her own evaluation of each of the girls. They were all no competition to her, except Angel. She was attractive, and she knew her man, she would definitely be his type. Natalia began crying. Sydney had almost zoned out that she was sleeping in her stroller. She stood up from her seat, and picked her up, handing her a sip cup. Sydney ran her fingers through her curly mane as Natalia wiped her eyes, angry that she was up early from her nap.

"Aww... she's adorable." Said Angel marveling at the Natalia's long hair and cute outfit.

"All that hair! She's a cutie." Said her friend.

Sydney sat back down so Vani could finish her hair. Natalia calmed down looking up at her mother, she placed her hand on her chest, resting her head on Sydney's bosom. Vani had turned Sydney away from the mirror doing final touches to her hair. "Chris is gonna go crazy, when he sees you like this!"

Sydney smiled. "Hopefully, I'm still cute."

"Girl, don't play with me. When have I ever had you out here lookin' crazy?" Vani spun her chair around so she could see her reflection in the mirror. "OMG!" Sydney shouted as she looked at her reflection in the mirror. Vani took Natalia out of her arms, so she could examine her hair closer. Her hair was honey blond and straightened. Sydney hadn't had her hair blown out in years, her hair fell down to the middle of her back. Her hair was parted down the middle, and Sydney felt she looked like a goddess. "I love this color! This is amazing!" Sydney stood up, running her fingers through her hair. Angel watched her sizing up everything on her, even the manicure on her fingers. "I can't believe my hair is this long! Oh, guess what? Tati said mama today!"

"Aww... for real. I know you were on the verge of tears. You big water bag."

"Girl, you know it. She said it in between me and Chris' argument. Sydney touched Natalia's arm. You gonna say it for cousin Vani? Ma-ma..." She said slowly as an attempt for Natalia to repeat after her. Natalia smiled, covering her face.

"You're not going to say it for me, Natalia?" Said Vani tickling her. She giggled in her arms.

"Da-da." She replied clearly. Sydney and Vani burst into laughter.

"She is definitely Christian's daughter. Always has to be difficult... do things on her own time." Sydney walked away towards the bathroom. The girls glanced over to Vani, Angel glanced at the baby, she just knew that the baby couldn't possibly be her man crush Monday's baby. She asked her friend, she examined the baby as well, and concluded she wasn't sure. Natalia began to rub her eyes again. Dana came in through the back with her suitcase. "Hey, Vani."

"Hey, girl. You have about three clients came in early."

"Okay. She walked over to Vani, so she could pick up Natalia. Hi, pretty mami. Looking just like your daddy." She kissed her cheek. Sydney came out of the bathroom. "She doesn't look like him."

"Someone in their feelings. Sydney hugged Dana. Check you out Syd! That hair is slayed honey." She snapped her fingers, before she ran her fingers thru Sydney's hair. "Vani, you did that!"

"I know. Vani replied proudly. I told you this color would be cute on Syd."

"Yea, you did. So, Mrs. Sydney where is your husband?"

"He is at Reign today."

"Oh okay, I need to come thru. I heard y'all had a lot of new things come in."

"Always. Stop by. Dana looked down at Natalia kissing her once more before handing her back to Sydney. I better go, she's probably hungry."

"A'ight, Sydney. Call me later."

"I don't know I may have some apologizing to do with my baby." She laughed.

"He's your baby now huh? Last night he was an asshole." Said Vani.

"Yea. But, he's still mine. I can call him what I want. I don't need you pointing out what I said!" said Sydney hitting Vani playfully. Sydney said her final goodbyes before heading out the door with Natalia in her stroller. All eyes followed her as she walked out the doors. She strapped Natalia into her seat, she folded up the stroller placing it in the trunk before climbing behind the wheel. She started up the car to let the air circulate, as she pulled her iPhone from her purse, texting Chris.

Hi, baby. I'm sorry. I love you.

She snapped a quick picture of Natalia sleeping in the backseat. She looked down at the picture, immediately feeling embarrassed and stupid for feeling jealous of Natalia saying daddy first. She thought of all the petty things she had let get under her skin, and began to contemplate what had she been doing. Natalia was healthy, they were living a good life and Chris had made sure that their family had wanted for nothing. What was she complaining for? In that moment she realized she had become ungrateful. What a blessing it was that Natalia had both parents, which in itself made her smile. Sydney quickly detoured home. Once there, she brought Natalia inside placing her inside her playpen as she ran upstairs. She looked over the floor, for her ring. She found it sparkling on the bed, she slid it back on her finger. She went into the safe in their room, and grabbed some extra stacks. On her way out the door she grabbed Natalia some snacks, as she carried her back out to the car and strapping Natalia back in her seat, her phone beeped loudly alerting she had a text. She walked around to the driver side, reading the message out loud.

You love me. But... You can't talk to me.

She quickly responded. *Don't act like that! You know I love you.*

Natalia began to eat her cookies as she looked out the back window. Moments later they were in the mall parking lot. Sydney parked, pulling out the stroller. As she cleaned it off and placed her bag in the bottom of it. She could hear Natalia screaming in the backseat, I'm right here baby. She replied to her cries. She screamed out Ma Ma. Sydney smiled opening the back door to take her out. She stretched her arms out yearning to be released from her seat. Once in Sydney's arms she calmed down, she decided to walk for a bit before forcing her into the stroller. As she approached the entrance of the mall, Natalia continued to call her. Sydney took out her phone deciding to record the moment. She realized she had a text from Chris she opened it once she was done. It said:

So, are you leaving me? What's goin' on?

She smiled, taking a picture of her ring on her finger. She quickly responded. *What does this mean? It's me and you forever babe. I'm sorry. I love you.* She sent him the video of Natalia talking, tossing her phone in her purse.

Meanwhile, at Reign it was packed. Chris had been out on the floor, assisting however he could. He was assisting one of their VIP customers, in the private suite. She was an up and coming vocalist, Ana Ray, who had been featured on at least five current radio hits. She was a hometown star and she always showed love to Reign. Her style was edgy and she was a sneaker head. John had made sure to keep her informed on exclusive releases and for that she was loyal to promoting and supporting Reign. Chris was finishing up with her and her dancers, each were getting two pairs of designer sneakers. She and her girls took their last sips of wine before slipping out the back door to their awaiting SUV. Once he saw them out he walked over to the counter to check sales. He felt his phone vibrating in his pocket. He took his phone out seeing Sydney's message. He opened the message, Natalia's voice rang out loudly saying "Ma Ma." Chris smiled knowing that Sydney was overjoyed with the thought that Natalia had finally said her name.

John heard the video he looked down at Chris' phone. "Is that the baby?" He replied with a smile.

'Yea, she called Sydney mama today." He handed the phone to John so he could see the video. "Wow, man. I know Syd happy."

"You know it. That's why she sent me this shit to brag." They both laughed out loud. The store doors opened in walked Angel and her friend, with freshly manicured nails. She immediately saw Chris sitting at the counter. She smiled, reapplying lipstick to her lips. She walked over to sunglasses which were placed in the glass beside where Chris was located. He looked up.

"What's good Angel? How may I help you?" said Chris. Angel smiled happy to have his full attention. "I came in here for those new Gucci shades." She replied as she leaned onto the glass counter, arching her back as she flipped her hair. Chris reached into the display handing her the glasses. She placed them on her face, checking out her reflection in the mirror.

"Where is your little girl?"

"Home." He replied nonchalant as he waited for her to make a decision on the shades.

"I think I saw your baby today with your sister, at the salon." Chris laughed at how forward she was.

"I don't have a sister. That's my wife." He replied bluntly. Angel smiled. "I'll take these. Hmm, she's your wifey but I don't see a ring on your finger. She pointed to his hand. So, you're still available." Chris laughed out loud. John rang up the shades for Angel, as Chris walked back to his office. Angel watched him walk away. "He is so damn sexy. One day he gon' stop playing these games and be in my bed."

Meanwhile, at home Sydney had begun cleaning up the house. She was in the laundry room starting a new load of Natalia's clothes. The music was blasting through the house, J. Lo's "Booty". Sydney went into the kitchen to check on dinner, she was making shrimp Alfredo, asparagus and breadsticks. Natalia was in the playpen in the middle of the living room, dancing to the music. She clapped her hands loudly and began to shake to the rhythm. Sydney laughed as she shook her own hips to the music. Natalia laughed watching her.

The house phone rang interrupting their party. Sydney looked at the caller id seeing it was an Orlando number.

"Hello." She replied catching her breath.

"Hello, mama! This is Darren. Is Chris there?"

"Hey, no he's at the store"

"Oh, okay. How's the baby?"

"She's good."

"And yourself?"

"I'm good. How's your family?"

"Were good. Probably heading to France soon."

"Oh, that should be exciting."

"I told Chris, that you guys should join us. We always have a good time."

"Oh, well I will let him know."

"A'ight, I'm gonna try him at the store. Good speaking to you Syd."

"You too."

Sydney ended the call, placing her phone on the counter. She grabbed the remote to the stereo system turning back up the music. Nicki Minaj's "Pound The Alarm" came blasting through the speakers via Pandora. Natalia immediately threw her hands in the air, clapping them together. Sydney laughed out loud, watching her mini muse dancing to the music. She began to flip her hair over her shoulder, trying to mimic Sydney. "Are you dancing mama?" said Sydney as she swayed her own hips side to side. Natalia laughed out loud, repeating the oh's along with the song. Sydney walked over to Natalia speaking to her in Spanish. Natalia smiled at her covering her mouth, knowing that Sydney was waiting for her response. Sydney was firm on incorporating Spanish & Portuguese in Natalia's language, and everyday conversation. Sydney knew how much that meant to Chris, and she knew he would be happy to know his baby was fluent. Sydney wanted her to embrace every part of her heritage. The many mixtures that made up her family was present in their home. After working up a sweat, she grabbed a glass of water sharing it with Natalia. She turned the music off carrying Natalia upstairs for her bath.

It was almost six p.m. Sydney tossed a few of her toys in the tub, the bubbles began to form touching Natalia's hands. She let out an excited yelp. Sydney smiled admiring her baby, it felt good to be home spending time alone with Natalia. Her bath time had become one of Sydney's favorite bonding time with her. As she took down her ponytail, lathering the shampoo in her hair. Natalia laughed splashing water with her feet.

Chris had left Reign and was pulling up to Preme's gate. He entered the code, once allowed entry he parked in the circular driveway next to Preme's white Bentley Continental, which sat in the driveway. He reached into the backseat grabbing the bag, before walking up the steps to the front door. Preme greeted him at the door, they embraced as they stepped inside and Preme locked the door. Chris handed him the bag as he glanced over his foyer. Preme peeked into the bag. "What's this?"

"Your shirts and a few jeans." They walked back to his office. Chris took a seat at his mahogany desk. Preme took a seat behind the desk, turning off his iMac.

"Darren called huh?"

"Yea, he was talking about you going away and everything. Talking about me being in charge and taking road trips."

"Yea, I'm going to need you to take a few meetings for liquor stores and franchising. As far as the streets I'm going to need you to see what's goin' on in Atlanta, Connecticut and Virginia. In Connecticut, I need you to check on Domino and his team. He needs some work. He already knows I don't fuck around, so you shouldn't have a problem. Now I got some other meetings in Houston and Chicago. I'll have Darren get with you on my itinerary on that. I'm thinking of producing my own Vodka, while I'm across the pond, take a few meetings."

"Yo, that will be hot pops. I always wanted to do something like that, how does startup for that work? I mean."

"I never knew you were interested in that. I can get with you and we can go over ideas for branding. We can make you the face, I will be silent investor, or partner. What you think?"

"Damn pop. Hell yea, we can do that."

"Good, it's handled. We're partners, I will get with the lawyers and set up some meetings."

Chris sat in awe. Preme never seemed to amaze him with how quick he got things handled and was about his business. "I mean Pop I want to be invested in this thing too, n'ahmean. I'm serious about this."

Preme smiled. "I got you."

"Now, how long is all of the traveling going to be? I mean, am I going alone? Or taking Darren?"

"Maybe a month or so."

Chris immediately felt a wave of guilt and uncertainty. He didn't know how he felt about being away from Natalia for any long periods of time. He wanted to always be present. Preme saw the worry on his face. "Don't worry you won't be away from her that long. I can assure you that. Said Preme reassuringly. I don't want you in NYC. Ben may still have plans up his sleeve, and I don't want you getting caught up with any of that bullshit. You feel me?"

"I'll stay out of NY."

"I'll be leaving next weekend. When Darren gets in town we will iron out all the details."

"A'ight, that's cool."

Preme reached under his desk handing him a Louis Vuitton Bag and an envelope. Chris looked into the bag seeing stacks of money. He looked up at Preme. "What's this for?"

"You working right? I'm paying you." Chris proceeded to hand the bag back. Preme pushed it back to Chris.

"Pops, you do enough for me. I should be able to things for you."

"Take it. I'm not hearing it. I haven't been there for you when you were growing up. I'm trying to be there for you now. I know money isn't going to make up for time, but maybe it can go towards securing you a better future. N'ahmean."

"Nah pop."

"Damn, you're stubborn. Just like me. How about say its payment for Natalia's college tuition. Put it in her piggy bank and put the rest away for you." Chris decided to keep the bag. Preme smiled, knowing that Chris would keep the bag if he involved Natalia. Chris looked down at his iPhone, it was seven thirty. "I guess I better head home." He and Preme walked out of the office, walking through the foyer towards the front door. Chris proceeded ahead to his car, Preme watched on from the door.

"When you going to bring my granddaughter over?"

"I'll bring her by whenever you want. You can keep her all day." Said Chris with a smile.

"Bring her by this Friday."

"A'ight. You going to be ready to babysit? No shade, but it's been a minute."

"I'm good. What you tryin' to say, I'm an old nigga? I got this. Kids love me."

"Okay, Pop. Chris laughed. I'll bring her by."

"Better yet, bring her Wednesday. I'm going to see Ma in Coral Springs, I know she has been wanting to see her. She's been asking about seeing you too. Whenever you get some time, just go by and see her."

"I will."

"Be safe, son." Chris saluted Preme as he slid in behind the wheel.

Once home Chris pulled into the garage, checking over the car as he walked up the steps into the house. He was greeted with the aroma of Lemon cleaner, Febreze and food. He looked around the house it was spotless as he made his way to the living room, moving towards the smell of food in the kitchen, glancing into the pots on top of the stove. He took down a plate from the cabinet, making himself a plate. He grabbed a can of Sprite walking upstairs to the bedroom. Sydney was lying across the bed on the laptop. The baby monitor beside her listening in to Natalia sleeping in her room. She looked up at Chris. "I got your text of Natalia."

"Wasn't she cute?"

"Yea. I know you was sending that shit to brag." He replied with a smile. Sydney laughed. He grabbed the television remote checking the security cameras, he looked in Natalia's room. He turned to ESPN. He became fascinated with the 30 for 30 series. Once finished and stuffed he took the plate downstairs and placed it inside of the dishwasher. Sydney slipped away to the bathroom. Chris came back and laid back against the headboard massaging his hand over his full stomach. Sydney emerged from the bathroom in one of Chris' white t-shirts, pair of La Perla black lace panties and a gift box in her hand. She climbed into bed sitting beside him on her knees. "We can't continue to get mad with each other without talking it out. I think this is one of our biggest issues. Our anger." Chris looked over at her looking into her eyes. He moved his eyes over her face, he touched her hair. "You dyed your hair?"

"Yes. But…"

"Yo, I like this." He twirled her hair around his finger.

"Baby… you're not listening to me. I don't want to fight with you every day. I'm sorry for having Natalia out late, and not considering your feelings. But, I don't like you controlling me and telling me what I can and can't do. Or telling me what to wear." Chris let go of her tendrils looking into her eyes again.

"Syd, I never said you couldn't go chill with your cousin. It's the slick way you went about it, then for you to lie to my face. You pissed me the fuck off. Why lie to me? If you would've been real with me, I could've accepted it. Probably still would've been vexed, but I would've accepted the truth."

"Okay, I understand. Anything else you want to say?"

"I'm sorry. I went over the edge and got vexed about it. But, you know I have a crazy temper."

"So, that makes it right? I changed a lot of things for you too baby. Instead of going over the edge, why can't you talk to me, calmly and respectfully? I mean if we can't communicate how are we ever going to make it married?

Chris sighed. "I hear you. Just stop making me mad."

"Baby!" Sydney hit him playfully He rolled over on top of her. He looked into her eyes, kissing her lips. "I like this color on you. It's sexy."

"Really. Vani did it today."

"I like it. It looks good straight."

"Thank you." She looked into his eyes, kissing his lips. Chris got off of Sydney, sitting up on the bed. "Just don't wear that shit again without me, and we good." Sydney laughed. She couldn't help but laugh at his demand, but she would respect it. She nodded in agreeance.

"Fine, I will wear the pants with you, and wear my string bikini when I'm at the beach with Vani." Chris glared at her. "I'm playing baby. She laughed laying on his chest, kissing it softly. I have something for you."

"What?" said Chris. She reached under the pillow grabbing the gift box. She sat on top of Chris' stomach. She opened the box. Inside sat a Platinum band, covered in rows of diamonds, 8 carats to be exact. "Give me your hand." She took Chris' hand, sliding the ring on his ring finger. "Will you marry me?" Chris looked down at the ring, he then looked up at Sydney. "No! Because you're fuckin' crazy. I'm not having my daughter in this lifestyle." He replied in his best Sydney impression. She hit him on the chest.

"Christian!"

"Of course, I will marry you." Sydney kissed his lips. Sydney got off of him placing the box on the nightstand. "When did you get this?"

"Don't worry about it. I bought it for you."

"It's hot. I like it. Thank you." He reached over kissing her cheek again.

"It matches mine." She put her hand up to his. "I see." Chris' phone rang loudly interrupting them. He glanced over on the nightstand, he didn't recognize the number. He picked the phone up, answering the call.

"Hello."

"Hello, is Jay there?" said a woman thru the receiver.

"You got the wrong number." He ended the call placing the phone back down on the nightstand. He got up going over to Natalia's room. He came back into the room with Natalia's life size Hello Kitty bank. Sydney had purchased online. He dumped out the contents of the Louis Vuitton bag on the bed.

"What are you doing?" Said Sydney, looking over the stacks of money all over their bed.

"Pop gave Tubby money towards her college tuition. Start my baby college fund." He began separating the stacks of money. It was over forty, ten g stacks, wrapped in gold straps. He pushed a few over to her. "You add that up."

"Baby, you are not putting this in there?"

"I'm putting twenty in here."

"That's too much to have in there." Sydney stacked the money up. Unbothered by the amount, this wasn't the first time Chris had asked her to count along with him. It was well over four hundred thousand dollars across the bed. She walked over to their safe, which was hidden in the island in the center of the closet. She placed her thumb and index finger on the mirror which set in the center of the island. Which, many wouldn't think of it as anything more than a mirror. The island opened and the safe rose out of the top of it. Sydney typed in the code and the safe opened. This was one of many safes located around the house. This is where as Chris called it, "Retirement money". Chris came in after her looking at the piles that already lined the inside along with gold bars. He handed her a few the others. "Baby, that is too much to put in that piggy bank. Besides its plastic. What if someone steals it?"

"First of all, I'm not having any shiesty niggas I can't trust in my house. Besides, no one is going to know it's in there, but me and you. You can't see thru this shit."

Sydney realized her logic was going nowhere with him. She decided to dead the conversation for now, and later when he wasn't home to remove the money from the bank. She closed back up the safe walking back to the bed. Chris carried the kitty bank back to Natalia's room. When he walked in the room, Natalia was sitting up in her crib looking at him. He placed the bank back in its place, smiling at his princess. "Hey Tubby. Have a good nap, mama?" He walked over picking her up out of the crib. She laid her head on his chest, as she rubbed her eyes. Chris walked back into the room, Sydney touched her back. "I better get you some milk." Chris sat down on the bed cradling Natalia in his arms. She began to cry. Chris looked down at her sleepy face. "What's wrong?" He grabbed the pacifier which was on the nightstand, cleaning it off and placed it in her mouth. Natalia took the pacifier out of her mouth, throwing it on the floor. She screamed louder.

"Oh, you gonna do Daddy like this?" said Chris as he laughed. Sydney heard her screams as she came up the stairs. "I'm coming baby. Mommy's coming." Sydney came into the room armed with the bottle, she took Natalia in her arms to feed her the bottle. She stopped crying, looking into Sydney's face. Chris watched as Sydney rocked her gently in her arms.

"Damn, we got any ice cream in the fridge?"

Sydney laughed at his random request. "No, I threw the carton out today. It was old. But, I can go for some ice cream too. Why don't you go get us some Oreo ice cream?"

"Why do I have to go to the store? When did this become us, I said I want."

"Because I asked you nicely and I love you. I'd do it for you." Chris looked over at her, as she flashed a flirty smile with puppy eyes. He wasn't falling for it, he knew Syd would never leave out this time of night for ice cream.

"Yeah right, you'd go to Walmart to get me some ice cream. But, because I'm a nice, standup guy I'll go get the ice cream. While I'm in there get me a PlayStation or some shit."

"I need an iPad."

"Why?"

"Because sometimes I don't feel like carrying my MacBook to school and I can put my notes on there, instead of carrying a notebook around." Chris nodded his head as he walked over to the closet grabbing a black shirt, Givenchy jeans and pair of Timbs from his rows of shoes. He put a Black Yankee fitted on his head. Natalia sat up watching him, knowing that he was leaving. She spit the bottle out reaching for him. Sydney smiled at her. "Look baby…"

"You want to go with me Tubby?" Natalia began to whine as he picked her up.

"Baby, don't take her out in her pajamas."

"A'ight Syd, I will change her clothes." He walked down to her room, going into her closet picking out a Dolce & Gabbana long sleeved onesie with the matching joggers. He came back into the room with a pair of socks and a pair of UGG boots.

"One thing I can't stand is a baby in the store, with no fuckin' shoes on." Sydney nodded her head.

"Let me brush her hair up real quick." Chris sighed, becoming annoyed. "You can put the headband on there. Shit, works wonders I do it every day."

"We know." She picked up Natalia brushing up her thick mane into a ponytail, her curly baby hair was still out around her edges. Sydney tried to pull them behind her ear.

"Can we go now?"

"Yes. Wait, one more thing. She went over to her closet picking out a Burberry diaper bag, she threw a baggie of wipes and diapers inside. Chris finally walked downstairs and he and Natalia were off to Walmart. He grabbed a cart inside placing her cart cover over it before placing her inside. He walked over to the ice cream aisle and grabbed two cartons of Breyer's Oreo cookies and cream ice cream. He browsed the grocery aisles picking up a few more items. He stopped on the juice aisle. There was three black men talking loudly amongst each other, Chris glanced over them as he walked past going over to the Ocean Spray Cran Mango, had become Sydney's new favorite drink so he grabbed a few.

"Yo, we need to handle this shit down here and be out." said one of the men.

"I hear you. But, we can hit up a club or somethin' tonight. We been here three days."

"A'ight, we can hit up a club tonight. But, I'm telling you I don't fuck with these fuckin' southern niggas. Be on that back wood shit." They all laughed walking towards Chris to grab a drink. The loudest grabbed a drink, he glanced over at Chris, doing a double look.

"Chris?"

Chris turned around, looking the man square in the eyes. His demeanor changed, he smiled. "Tarik?"

"Yea! What's good nigga?!" shouted Tarik. They laughed embracing each other in a hug and grip. Natalia sat in the cart watching their interaction. "Damn, how you been?"

"I'm good. How you been nigga?"

"Man, so much has happened. It's good to see you though. Wait a minute… is this the baby?"

"Yea, this Tati." Tarik smiled waving at her. Natalia looked at him unbothered, by his Kool-Aid smile.

"She looks just like your ass, son! He laughed. Who would've thought? You still with um… Sydney?"

"Yea. We still together. I locked it down." Said Chris shaking his head jokingly.

"What?! Congratulations, when that happened?"

"Yea, we've been engaged about a year."

"So, what happened to my pictures and shit?"

"Yo, when I left New York, I left everything and everyone there. I haven't talked to anyone since I left. But, what you doing down here?"

"You know I'm still in the game. Finally got my own crew came down here for a few things, n'ahmean."

"A'ight. Chris looked over at his friends and then back at him again. I see you shinin'" Tarik was wearing a black Yankee fitted, white Gucci shirt, jeans and tan construction Timbs on his feet. Two chains on his neck, a link bracelet on his wrist. It was mediocre to Chris, but more of the come up starter kit.

"Yea, a little bit, just a little. He replied taking the attention off himself. You know I always told you I was trying to make it like you and Money back in the day. One day, though."

"Yea, that was the old me. I'm not into the game, hard like I used to be. Priorities and shit change, I'm a changed man son." Tarik's crew looked over Chris' attire, although he was dressed simply. He was clean. The black diamond bracelet on his arm, and diamond rosary on his neck screamed he wasn't just another trap nigga.

"So, you opened up your club?"

"Nah, I opened a clothing store on South Beach"

"That's good, you said you was goin' to do that shit. I'm happy for you. We didn't have a clue what happened to you. But, give me your number son, so I can get up with you before I leave."

"No doubt. Chris gave him one of the numbers to his burner phones, he rarely used. Good seeing you 'Rik." They dapped each other up once more. Natalia interrupted their moment, tugging at Chris' shirt. "Da-da." Chris smiled at her picking her up out of the cart. She rested her head on his chest, rubbing her eyes. "Damn. Look at you, family man. Oh, my bad this my niggas Junior and Vito."

He acknowledged them with a head nod. Chris placed Natalia back in the cart. "Well, I'm gonna let you and little miss finish y'all shopping. I'll get at you tomorrow."

"A'ight Rik." Chris walked on towards electronics. As he glanced over the aisles he shook his head thinking how crazy it was, that he saw Tarik tonight. It was definitely a small world. He walked over to the game cases looking over the PlayStation 4 games. Which were locked in a glass casing. A white female associate walked over to him in blue vest, khakis and purple Chuck's on her feet. She looked to be about eighteen. "Hi, may I help you?"

"Yea. I want a PlayStation four and a few games."

"Okay. She took the keys opening the case. She waited for Chris to tell her which games he wanted before she handed him the game console. Chris reached in picking the games out himself, he began throwing them in the back of shopping cart. He had thrown over ten new release games inside. The girl smiled nervously. "Playing a lot of games huh?"

"Something like that." He replied nonchalant.

"Umm… well… you do know that you have to pay for these at my counter?"

"A'ight. Whatever. Are you gonna get the PlayStation out of there too? I also need an iPad. Where are those?"

She placed the PlayStation console in the cart. "The Apple items are over here. Any one in particular you looking for?"

"I don't know. It's for my wife. Which one is the best one?" She showed him the Apple display and began to explain the features of each one. Chris decided on the iPad Mini with 128 GB. The associate then talked him into Beats by Dre, Studio headphones. He threw two of those in the cart. He followed the associate over to the register. His phone rang loudly in his pocket. He reached in his pocket, grabbing the phone glancing at the display. "Hello."

"Chris, I'm going to be running late tomorrow. My sister flying in from New York. Told me at last minute. I won't be able to open."

"A'ight, what time you going to be there?"

"Probably around noon."

"A'ight, John. I got it." The woman began scanning the items making loud beeping sounds for each item.

"Where you at?"

"Fuckin' Walmart. Getting a PlayStation, been in this store too long." Chris laughed.

"Hell yea, that's how it always happens in that bitch. You go in for soap, you come out with a cart full of shit."

Chris laughed. "Hell yea. But, I'll see you tomorrow." Chris hung up the phone handing it to Natalia. She smiled looking at the light on the screen. He looked behind him a line had formed. Two teenaged girls were behind him, they began to blush and make comments about how cute Natalia was. The total came up to 2258.54 after tax. He went into his pocket, he counted off twenty three, hundred dollar bills. The girls behind him looked over in awe at the money the cashier had sprawled over the register. She began to run the counterfeit pen over each bill. "He's ballin, bitch." Said one of the teenage girls. His phone rang in Natalia's hand startling her, he chuckled as she quickly handed it to him.

"What up nigga?"

"Yo, what you doing?"

"In Walmart. What's good?"

"I wanted to see if you wanted to ride with me to Daytona tomorrow?"

"Why you going there?"

"I need to check on some business."

"Yea, I'll ride with you. Hit me up tomorrow with the details and shit."

"Bet."

"I need to get at you about a few things anyway."

"A'ight. I don't want to hear tomorrow, that Syd beefin' and you ain't goin." Chris realized that the cashier had never gave him his change.

"Yo, hold on. Aye, what's taking you so long with my change?" said Chris angrily.

"Um… I'm waiting on a manager."

"For what?"

"I typed in the wrong amount."

"So, you telling me you work a fuckin' cash register and you can't add and subtract?" replied Chris sarcastically.

"I'm soo sorry, sir."

"Look… I gave you twenty three hundred dollars… the total was what twenty two fifty eight… you owe me, forty one dollars. Fuck the change. Chris picked up the phone. Yo, Nick I'll talk to you later." The manager came over, seeing the line and frustration on everyone's face.

"What's the problem?"

"Your employee can't count fuckin' money." Natalia began to rub her eyes and yawn. The cashiers face turned beet red, with embarrassment.

"He gave me twenty three hundred dollars and this was the total. I typed in the wrong amount." The manager grabbed a piece of paper, subtracting the amount. Chris sighed. "This some bullshit. It's forty one dollars."

"He's right. Said the manager. She opened the drawer counting out the change. He snatched the receipt and money. "All this over fuckin' forty dollars! Here take this shit." He handed the change to the two teenage girls behind him. One of them was too shy to take it, her friend took both twenties with a smile. "Thanks cutie." He pushed Natalia out of the store. Just another night in Walmart.

Once home, he brought Natalia up to Sydney, he put the ice cream up downstairs bringing the bags upstairs to their bedroom. Sydney looked into the bags, inspecting what he bought.

"Guess who, I saw in Walmart?"

"Who?"

"Tarik."

"New York Tarik?"

"Yea, he down for a few days. Seeing him, brought back a lot of memories." Chris sat down on the bed taking off his shirt.

"Are you going to spend time with him?"

"I gave him my number, to that burner phone. So, he can hit me up. We'll see what happens." Chris stripped down to his boxers throwing the clothes in the basket. Sydney looked over his body. He sat down on his side of the bed going thru the bag. He handed Sydney the iPad, and pink Beats earphones. "You got me the iPad! How sweet?" she replied excitedly. She kissed his lips. "Thank you baby." "You're welcome. Next time I'm sending you in that store. Shit, took all night." Sydney opened the box, beginning the registration. An hour later they were all knocked out.

The next morning Chris woke up it was ten thirty. He looked over at his phone on the nightstand, no missed calls. He walked over to the bathroom, hearing Sydney's voice downstairs. Chris took a shower, putting on a wife beater and Jordan shorts. He walked downstairs to Sydney and Natalia. Natalia was in her playpen, her hair up in a ponytail with a white bow. He picked her up kissing her face as he threw her in the air. She giggled loudly. He walked over to Sydney kissing her cheek, she smiled kissing him back with her phone perched to her ear. "I know" she replied with a laugh. He grabbed some grapes from the fruit bowl Sydney had placed down on counter. He sat down on the couch watching Doc Mcstuffins with Natalia. Sydney hung up shortly, walking out to the couch taking a seat on Chris' lap. "So, my mom wants to know when we are coming to Connecticut."

"Soon. Maybe a few weeks. I have to go to Atlanta in a week or so anyway."

"Why?"

"Business. Meet with vendors. No biggie."

"What business?" said Sydney looking down at Chris seriously. Chris glared back at her his face saying, why are you questioning me.

"I just told you."

"Who are you going with?"

"Nick."

"Hell no. I don't like you going out of town with Nick."

"Why not?" He caressed her derriere.

"Because every time you are with Nick, you always get into some shit."

"What?" said Chris as he burst into laughter.

"What my ass! Every time you go out with Nick, you get crazy and forget all your responsibilities."

"Name one time, I got reckless."

"Really? When Tati was four months and you went to the strip club with Nick, and y'all got into some brawl."

"Nah, see what happened was, nigga thought he was gonna disrespect me on that sly shit. Fuck that. I was supposed to just sit there and let him disrespect me?"

"You could've walked away. Besides, what about that time we went to Wet Willie's and you and Nick got pissy drunk and you decided to threaten the bartender. Or the time when we all went to Hard Rock and you got into it with some random guy, because he was talking to you."

"Whateva. Why you bringing up old shit anyway." Said Chris with a smile, he kissed her neck.

"Because you and Nick is never good together, and remember the game is over for you." She grabbed his face kissing him.

"Yea, I know." He looked into her eyes, a million thoughts rushing through his head. He ran his fingers through Sydney's hair. "I love this color on you. I definitely don't want to hear about you out in the street with that tight shit, like this."

"I'll wear whatever I want." She replied playfully.

"A'ight ma. Wear what you want. If I see or hear you out showing all of this, I'm coming wherever you are and actin' fuckin' wild."

"You wouldn't."

"A'ight. Remember who you talkin' to. You know I don't give a fuck." Sydney got off of his lap. "Don't curse in front of Tati."

"My bad, baby."

"I know, she's heard worst at your whore store."

"You buggin'" replied Chris. Sydney walked into the kitchen taking the last pieces off the griddle. She mixed up peaches for Natalia. She made a plate for Chris, calling him over to the table. She brought Natalia into the kitchen sitting her down in her high chair. Chris realized that he was to open the store. He called John. He said that his sister ended up missing her flight, so he was on his way to the store. John was definitely a lifesaver, Chris had completely forgot. His phone rang, Nick displayed on the screen.

"Yo."

"What's good playboy?"

"Chillin' about to eat breakfast with the fam."

"We still on for today?"

"Yea. What time you want to head out?"

"I'm ready. Just getting the car cleaned down here at car wash."

"Well, come thru."

"A'ight, I'll be thru in about thirty minutes. I'm almost done here. Ask Syd if she got some food for me?"

Chris put the phone away from his ear. "Nick, said you got enough for him?" "I have enough for him. Tell him I need to have a little chat with him." "We got you. Come thru." Sydney sat down feeding Natalia. Chris began digging into his plate. "Pops, wants to get Natalia on Wednesday."

"I'd love to see that. She replied as she wiped peaches from her mouth. What are we going to do for Tati's second birthday? I was thinking that we should take Tati to Disney for her second birthday. Have you ever been to Disney?"

"No. have you?" said Sydney. Chris looked at her, his eyes saying *when the fuck would I have been to Disney.*

"I guess that's a no."

"That's a definite no."

Sydney laughed. "What do you think?"

"We can do that. Make the reservations and we can go." Sydney nodded. The gate buzzed. Chris looked on the television screen seeing who it was. "I know y'all see me!" Sydney got up pressing the button to open the gate. She handed Natalia a cup of Juicy Juice. He got up to unlock the door. He walked down the hall to the double doors. Sydney took Natalia upstairs to get cleaned up. "What up?" He and Nick dapped each other, as he locked the door behind them. Nick was wearing a Crooks & Castles black and white jersey paired with dark jeans and black Versace high- top sneakers on his feet. Nick followed Chris into the kitchen, Chris sat back down to finish his plate. "Help yourself." Nick washed his hands before fixing a plate.

"You know Ced still vexed with you about that game?"

"Fuck Ced. Shouldn't play a man's game if he gonna bitch about a few coins."

Nick laughed. "You know that nigga missing rent money, car probably gone be repoed. He been on the grind hard." They both laughed. Sydney changed into a Moschino white tank over a pair of skinny distressed jeans, Christian Louboutin studded sandals on her feet. Her hair up in a bun, diamond studs in her ear. Natalia in a Roberto Cavalli ruffled logo dress, with ballerina flats to match. Sydney placed her in the playpen. Nick sat down at the table. "Good morning Sydney."

"Good morning Nick. Don't get Chris in trouble today." Sydney grabbed one of the sausage links off the plate, staring into Nick's face.

"Why you always calling me the troublemaker?"

"Because, you're always at the root of every situation." Chris got up from the table dumping his plate in sink, before heading up the stairs. When Chris was out of sight, Sydney walked over to Nick slapping him across the back of his head. He grabbed his head. "Yea, that's for runnin' your mouth the other day and don't get Chris in trouble. I don't want to hear he locked up somewhere."

"A'ight Syd. I'll make sure we good, like I'm the bad influence." Sydney walked over to Natalia picking her up out of the playpen. "Baby! We're leaving." Chris emerged at the top of the staircase in a black Givenchy star shirt, black Givenchy jeans and Timbs on his feet. He had a bottle of Lubriderm lotion in his hand, massaging it on his arms as he walked down the stairs. He looked down at his tattoo, he immediately thought of Dre'. He shook the painful memory of his fallen lieutenant out of his mind. When he reached Sydney at the bottom of the stairs he kissed Natalia on her lips, before kissing Sydney. "Be good baby." She replied softly in his ear.

"I'm always good." He smiled.

"I'm serious. Don't forget your promise, the game is over for you."

"I know ma." He kissed her lips, this time long and slow. Natalia sat on Sydney's hip, she smiled at their embrace. "Damn, I love this color on you."

She smiled. "You be good today, and you can see it later over my naked body." She licked his ear lobe and neck. Chris bit his lip, clearing his throat.

"Yo, Nick lets go. Love you." Chris walked towards the front door.

"Love you too. Say Bye daddy. Said Sydney to Natalia as she waved her hand. Natalia mimicked waving her hand making a backwards wave. Chris smiled. "Bye, baby."

"Thank you for breakfast Syd."

"You're welcome." She followed behind them out the door so she could lock it. Chris proceeded over to the passenger side of his Nick's S class Mercedes, moments later they were on 95

North in route to Daytona Beach. In hour into their ride Chris decided to hit Nick with his proposition for coming along with him to Atlanta. He turned the music down looking over at Nick. "Preme want me to handle some things for him..."

"Wait a minute, you getting back in the game?"

"Well... I gotta do what I gotta do. You know fam' comes first with me, always. So, I was wondering if you wanted to ride with me to Atlanta. Have a few things to handle."

"Yea, you know I got you. I'm down just let me know."

"It's just the game bring back too many memories. Ever since I've been out, a part of me questions my decision. Did I really leave for Natalia or was I running from my past. I've never ran from shit my whole life. I saw my homeboy from NY, in Walmart the other night. I haven't talked to him since I left. When I saw him I was thinking, this nigga still on this same shit. I'm like where is the fuckin' boundaries in the game. I have fuckin' liabilities now you feel me, and getting' back in this shit. I see myself possibly slippin' back to that dark shit, anyone test me on some bullshit, I'm layin' niggas out on site." Nick looked over at his ace, he was looking out the window, and he could tell this decision had been weighing heavy on him.

"Yo, just make those moves keep shit movin'. I got your back nigga." Chris looked over at Nick, he appreciated his support. But, Nick saying he had his back wasn't security enough for him. Nick had grew up a privileged life under Mart and Preme. He had never witnessed the dark struggles and demons that Chris carried from his past.

"I still have a lot of things I need to put to bed. My mother's death, Dre' and my whole life. I need some answers. It's funny every time I get used to the good life, something pulls me back. He chuckled. I'm starting to wonder if this all I'm here for." Nick sat quiet, he didn't know what to say to give some sort of empathy to his ace's thoughts. He couldn't relate to what Chris had been thru because all his run ins on a street level, were all handled by his father's muscle, he rarely had physical altercations. He was more mouth than bite. But, when with Chris he felt he had to put on to gain his respect, because he knew Chris could see thru his façade. Chris became lost in his own thoughts again. If he was to survive this time in the game, everything would have to change. No bullshit.

They arrived on International Speedway in Daytona Beach around five p.m. Nick had received a text and the exchange was to go down on Mary McLeod Bethune Blvd, at an abandoned building behind a carwash. They decided they would stop by the mall to get something to eat. Chris looked down at his phone it was a text from Tarik, saying that should meet up for drinks. Chris responded he would get back to him later. They both stepped out of the car, Chris watching his surroundings they walked into the mall entrance, which was the food court. Chris headed over to Chick- fil-A, he decided to call Sydney to check on the baby, as he was scrolling thru his calls to call her, his phone rang it was Sydney.

"Yo."

"Hi baby."

"Ma, I was just about to call you. You read my mind huh?"

"Aww, you were thinking of me?"

"Of course. Always, that shouldn't even be a question."

"Aren't you sweet today? What are you doing?"

"Getting some food. What my baby doing?"

"We're at the beach and she's making a mess of her hair. Baby, you should see her in this bikini."

"You got my mami in a bikini? I didn't approve that." He replied sarcastically.

"I'm going to send you a picture of her. She's adorable."

"A'ight. What you wearing?"

"My bikini." Chris sighed. "On that note, y'all have fun. I will see you later."

"Okay. I love you baby."

"Love you too." Chris ended the call, sliding the phone down in his pocket. Nick tapped him telling him he was walking over to Sbarro for a slice of pizza. A woman tapped him, letting him know he was next to order. He thanked her and proceeded to order his food. As he was waiting on his food, he glanced inside H & M on the corner. The cashier gave him his order, and Polynesian sauce, he threw it in the bag. Nick walked over to him. "They ready."

"A'ight." Chris took a sip of his lemonade. As they headed out the door a group of girls, early twenties, walked behind them. They began to tally up everything they were wearing from head to toe. "Red, in that black cute."

"You can tell they not from here." The friend replied as she applied lip gloss to her lips. Chris looked over his shoulder to put a face to the chatter that was behind him. One of the girls was wearing a silk bonnet on her head, flip flops on her feet and her top row of teeth was gold. The others were decent, but looking at bonnet girl, Chris couldn't help frowning up his face at her.

"Oh, hell nah, Tika, no he didn't shoot you a unit."

"Okay... fuck him. He is not all that!" Nick turned around and looked at the girls, he looked over at Chris. They burst into laughter. "That fuckin' bonnet though. I mean I can't even take her serious with that shit." They ate their food on the way to the location, Nick had been to Daytona a few times before with a crew, this was his first time solo but he remembered his way around. When they turned on to Fulton Street, Nick took off all of his chains, placing them in his center console. "What you doin?!' said Chris disgusted.

"Shit, some of these niggas grimey. Ain't no nigga jackin' me for shit!"

"Ain't no nigga putting fear in me! I do what the fuck I want. N'ahmean, fuck these niggaz!"

"Well, you do you." Nick adjusted his chrome on his waist. His cell rang as he pulled up to the building. "You there?"

"Yea."

"A'ight, I'm coming out." Chris looked at the wooded area surrounding the building, the car wash was packed in the background. Nick reached into the backseat grabbing a black duffel. Chris sat up to see who would emerge from the building. A dark skinned, slender man with dreads and gold teeth emerged. He had a black duffel in his hand. They greeted and exchanged bags. Chris looked around for dreads protection, he knew his team had to be lurking somewhere, what nigga with sense would come to a drop alone. He focused back on Nick's expression. He could tell he was pissed. Nick looked into the bag. "Do I look like a fuckin' joke to you?!" shouted Nick. He dropped the bag, pulling out his gun hitting the man with the barrel of the gun, the guy fell to the ground holding his face. Nick became furious stomping on his body. Chris jumped out of the car. "What the fuck goin' on?" He walked over to them.

"This fuckin' clown tried to play me." Chris looked over the counterfeit money that was scattered on the ground. Now, inches away from dread he realized he was about 40 years old and definitely used. He used his gun to skim thru the money in bag, it was all fake. "Make that nigga give you your fuckin' dough." Nick picked the guy up. He placed his gun up to his mouth. "Where the fuck my money?!"

"Look, I'm not dude. He pleaded as blood spewed from his gold grill. They forced me to come out here. Please, I was just to bring bag." Chris became annoyed by his pleas, he pulled out his own gun. "Who the fuck is they? You better tell me somethin' or I'm gonna blow ya' fuckin brains out."

"They told me to bring him the bag and meet them in PPU apartments, in fifteen minutes."

"Let's go." Said Chris he signaled for Nick to bring him to the car. Chris slid in behind the wheel. Nick sat in the back seat with a gun to dread's head. After dread lead them over to where he was to meet the crew Chris pulled on the side of the buildings on the street. The apartments were single level, red brick buildings. "We going to go in here, and get this fuckin' money. What the fuck this nigga name?" said Chris pointing his chrome in his face.

"They call him Al."

"Looks like its two doors to these shits. You and him go knock at the back I'll be at the front." Chris stepped out of the car looking around as he walked over to the front door. Nick walked dread to the back door at gunpoint. He pointed the gun at dread's head as he stood on the side of the wall. Dread opened the screen door, knocking on the metal door twice.

"Who is it?"

"Reggie." He replied nervously. The deadbolt was removed from the door and the aroma of weed filtered out of the apartment. You could hear a group of people talking inside of the house. Reggie put the bag up in the air. The guy grabbed the bag turning his back to Reggie, walking back thru the kitchen to the living room. Nick pushed Reggie into the house, coming in behind him. "Reg, got this work from this pussy Miami nigga." There was three men in the living room, they had been counting money on a card table, weed and pills sat in the center of the table. The cinderblock walls were covered with Scarface pictures. "PUSSY THIS, MOTHAFUCKER!"

Nick began firing, everyone ducked. Reggie fell to his knees. Al who opened the door was hit in the back, a friend on the couch. Chris came through the front door firing two into one of the mens stomach. Chris shot another in the face. The three men lay out on the floor.

"Thought you could play me. Huh? said Nick as he kicked Al as he tried to slide his body down the hall. Nick shot him again in his side. Al shouted in agony. "Where my fuckin' money?"

"Closet shelf in the bedroom... the refrigerator." Chris walked over to the fridge throwing everything out. There was Walmart bags in the freezer, he cut open the bags seeing stacks of cash. "It's here son. Chris grabbed a garbage bag from the top of the fridge tossing all of the bags inside of it. He came back into the living room to watch Al while Nick went into the room. Nick came out with a duffle bag on his shoulder. "I'm nothing to be fucked with nigga!" Nick fired off two more to his head. Reggie sat shocked in the middle of the floor. He was covered in brain matter from Al, and his own blood soaked in piss. He looked around at the bodies that surrounded him on the floor. Chris walked towards the door. "Let's go." Nick looked down at Reggie. Chris threw the bag in the back seat. He heard two gunshots ring out from the apartment, he climbed in the passenger seat. Nick soon came out of the house, he tossed the bag in the backseat, soon speeding off down the road.

No one spoke until they were outside of Orlando on 95 south. Chris decided to break the silence. "That was a bullshit ass deal son. You don't ever do business like that. What if I wasn't there? What would you have done?"

"I don't know." Nick replied solemnly.

"This game is fuckin' serious! You can't be having fuck ups like this, you feel me? You could've been stretched out like them niggas. You too fuckin' trusting and careless son. You could've got all of us bodied out here today! From the moment you stepped out the fuckin' car I knew this shit was goin' south."

"I know, I slipped up. I'm usually on top of my shit." Nick shook his head.

"I have a fuckin' daughter and a fuckin' fam to look after. I'm not trying to be fucked up over someone else dumb ass shit. You feel me?"

"Yo, my bad, sorry I put you in this shit."

Chris' cell rang, he looked down at the screen a part of him knowing who it was already.

"What up pop."

"Where are you?"

"On 95. Why what's up?"

"Come by when you get here."

"A'ight."

"Tell Nick to be here with you."

"Yea." Chris ended the call looking over at Nick. "Pop want to see us." Nick took a deep breath, not wanting the wrath of Preme. They arrived in Miami at one in the morning. Chris had Nick to drop him off home, so he could get his car. He walked upstairs to his bedroom. Sydney and Natalia were sleeping in their bed. Natalia snoring, stretched out over Chris' pillow. He kissed Natalia's face, before walking over to the closet to change his clothes. Sydney moved in the bed. "Hi baby." She sat up turning on the lamp on the nightstand. Chris froze in his steps. "Hey, ma." He replied walking over to her, fully dressed.

"Where are you going?"

"Going to chill with Tarik. I'll be back." Sydney wiped her eyes. Chris came over kissing her lips. He sat down beside her. She looked over his face, her eyes quickly focused in on a scratch on his neck.

"Be careful, baby. It's late."

"I'll be a'ight. Just going to get a few drinks." She touched his neck running her finger across the welt, which had formed on his neck.

"What happened?"

"Oh, I was out playing with Nick and fuckin' dogs."

Sydney looked at him her arms folded, attitude beaming off of her. "Christian, don't do anything crazy."

"Ma."

"Listen to me, don't do anything crazy. I love you." She grabbed his chin, kissing his lips again.

"I love you too." He got off the bed walking downstairs. He grabbed a Lipton Peach tea out the fridge before placing the alarm back on the house as he left out the front door. He climbed behind the wheel of the Range Rover heading over to Preme's house. Nick met him at the gate, they parked exiting the vehicles, Preme greeted them on the steps. A look of utter disgust plastered across his face. Chris walked into the house first Nick trailed behind him, not wanting eye contact with Preme. They walked over to the kitchen. Chris took a seat on one of the barstools, Nick stood beside him.

"What the fuck was that in Daytona?"

"I don't know... I slipped up Preme." Nick interjected.

"Who set that shit up?"

"My people set it up. I take full responsibility."

"You could've got both of you killed, and I would've had to merk everyone in your fuckin' family, for my loss. You can't have fuckin' slip ups. I know we raised you better than this!" Preme shouted as he threw a Versace vase off the counter it came inches from his head. He moved quickly as it shattered into the wall. He walked over to Nick's face standing inches from his nose.

"I know. Said Nick apologetically. I fucked up."

"You fuckin' right, you fucked up. Mart is lit with your dumb ass right now." Preme pointed to the scar on his face, which ran across his right cheek. You see this shit comes from fuckin' slip ups, dealing with family. Family not having they shit together. Why should I have to bury my son over your dumb ass?!" Preme hauled back with everything in him, punching Nick square in the face. Nick fell back to the floor, blood spewing from his nose and mouth. "Don't let that shit happen again." He kicked Nick in the chest, stepping over his limp body. Nick lay on the marble floor trying to regain his composure, he couldn't breathe. Preme patted Chris on the back. "How are you?"

"Pop, I'm good."

"What the fuck went down, my people telling me a few bodies?"

"Yo Pop, when we get there shit wasn't right. I just could feel that shit. I sat in the car, he went to do the exchange. I could tell by the way he was moving some shit had went down. Nigga gave him fake fuckin' money and he wasn't even the real nigga he was to meet up with. It was a fuckin' set up."

"What?! So you made him give you the dough right?"

Nick finally composed himself, attempting to stand up while trying to catch the blood that was dripping from his mouth and nose.

"Hell yea. So that's when we went to the stash house and did some work."

"Whose idea was that?"

Nick wiped his mouth. "It was Chris."

"Good looking out. Shouldn't have deals end like this. You need to make sure you know everything that is going down before you start doing business. You have to be two steps ahead of the next nigga. I always told Mart you wasn't built for this shit. You not ready to handle distribution or do anything on your own. You better off working in the lab, you not built for these streets."

"I promise Preme, I will get it together and I'll show you."

"Don't make empty promises. You can't do shit. You gonna have to prove we can trust you with work again. You are now at the bottom fuckin' nickel and dime nigga. Maybe treat you like some bum nigga, you will man the fuck up!" Nick nodded his head in agreement, embarrassment all over his bruised face, symbolic to his bruised pride. He was hurt that he let Preme and his dad down, especially Preme, one of the greatest in the game. He knew his Dad's wrath would be brutal. He cringed thinking of part two of his punishment.

Preme looked over Chris, making sure he was okay. He noticed the present scratches on his neck. He ran his finger across it touching the dried blood. "You a'ight?" "Yea, I'm good."

"Go, clean your neck in the bathroom. You got some blood there."

Chris touched his neck, to see if any blood came off on his fingers. He got up from the stool walking down the hall to the bathroom. Five minutes later he emerged walking back to where they were seated. He wiped an alcohol swab over his neck. He looked around for Nick, thinking *I didn't hear any gunshots.*

"Where is Nick?"

"I sent his punk ass home. I want you to be careful that nigga. He's bad business." Preme said sternly.

"Nick's a'ight. He's just not a street nigga, n'ahmean."

"He's in the wrong fuckin' business. He's fuckin' reckless and he's soon to be in a morgue somewhere. Listen, I don't take this shit lightly, that bitch will fuck up everything we have built and what you have built for yourself. Keep that pussy at a fuckin' distance." Chris sighed, throwing the swab into the garbage. Although, Nick fucked up today he knew that it would be hard to cut him off. Nick was family, but he respected Preme's advice. "I hear you pop."

"I mean if you choose to continue to be friends with him. But, business should be a wrap with him." Chris nodded his head agreeing to end the conversation. He didn't know what he wanted, but he knew that it wasn't going to be easy. Chris looked down at his phone, the screen displayed two thirty in the morning. Preme walked towards the kitchen opening his Sub Zero Refrigerator he grabbed a bottle of water. "Where's the heat?" Chris pulled the gun from his waist placing it on the counter. "I'll get rid of that. Go get a new one." Chris walked out of the room going to the basement, which was a movie theater. Black plush velvet seats for twenty. He walked over to the shelf, he picked up small globe running his finger along the base. The base beeped loudly. The globe opened slowly displaying a scanner, Chris looked into the scanner letting the scanner, scan his pupil. A green light flashed in the globe. The shelf slowly opened revealing a golden door with hand pad. Chris placed his third finger in the hole, the golden door slid open. The room, equal to a guest room, slowly lit up displaying an arsenal of guns and weapons inside of glass casings all around the room. Chris grabbed his favorite choice of weapon, 9mm, exiting the room. He walked back up to Preme, the gun on the counter was gone. "I better get home, before Syd gets suspicious. I don't feel like hearing her fuckin' beefing tomorrow."

"Yea. Before that shit be all over the news. You left any witnesses?"

"Nah, I think everyone's done. I left out to let Nick finish, I heard two last shots."

"A'ight, I'll look into it. You good." Preme walked over to him patting him on the back.

"A'ight Pop. I'll holla at you tomorrow." Chris headed towards the door, the only thing on his mind now, is his California King bed. Chris arrived home at three-thirty. He walked upstairs stripping off his clothes to his boxers, throwing them across the ottoman at the end of the bed. He placed the new gun in the safe. He checked the security cameras around the house on the television, before sliding into bed. Natalia moved, feeling his presence. She moved over laying her head on his chest, snoring softly. He looked down at his princess, he kissed her cheek massaging her back. He thought about what transpired today. The gun shots rang out in his thought, he heard the shouts and could see their blood soaked shirts. He said a prayer, looking down at Natalia again, closing his eyes.

The next morning was Monday, Sydney woke up early heading to class. Chris overslept, waking up at noon. His phone displayed ten missed calls. Tarik, the store, and Sydney. He looked over seeing Natalia sitting up on Sydney's side of the bed, Despicable Me movie playing on the screen. He picked her up. "Hey mama! Daddy sorry." He knew her diaper was probably soaked he carried her to the bathtub. He sent Sydney a text saying he overslept, and she replied she was on her way home. He called Tarik back and they agreed to meet up at Mama's restaurant on Ocean, it was a new soul food restaurant that he loved. He took Natalia out of the tub wrapping her in a towel, he tickled her neck as he adjusted her gold necklace with heart pendant. He kissed her cheek, gazing into her bright hazel eyes. He couldn't believe how she had changed everything in his life, she was his everything. He carried her down the hall to her room and into her closet. He changed her into a denim romper, and Gucci thong sandals. Chris picked up the brush attempting to brush her hair, he gave her a top knot with his faithful headband. Chris examined his work, smiling at the good job he did. He went downstairs and grabbed her some goldfish snacks sitting her on the bed, as he went into the bathroom, leaving the door open.

Sydney came in downstairs, she walked up stairs carrying her black Louis Vuitton Michael backpack across one shoulder, her iPad in hand. She could hear the shower water running. She hurried upstairs, seeing Natalia sitting up with sip cup and snacks. She smiled seeing Sydney. "Hi baby." She placed her things down on the bed, picking Natalia up. She walked into the bathroom, now covered in steam. She knocked on the glass door, Chris turned around soap covering his body. He opened the door. "I was just telling you I've got Natalia." "A'ight. How was school?" He leaned in kissing her face.

"Good." She looked over his chiseled naked body. Natalia too preoccupied with her cup was more fascinated with the water. Sydney scanned her eyes over every part of his body. Although, her eyes couldn't help locking in on his inches as the water trickled off of it.

"You good? I see you eyein' the kid." He replied with a smile.

She bit her lip. "Whatever. I'm just making sure everything is correct." Chris laughed rinsing off his body. Sydney closed the door leaving the bathroom. She went down to the kitchen to make herself a sandwich and she made Natalia some spaghettiOs. She placed her in her walker turning on the television to Keeping Up with The Kardashians. Chris came downstairs, in jeans. Sydney looked over at him as he walked into the kitchen. "Chris, what happened to you yesterday?" He grabbed a drink from refrigerator walking over to her. "What are you talking about?" He replied annoyed with where this conversation was going to lead.

"Your neck! What happened?" She yelled almost dropping the bowl of food to the floor.

"I told you we were out with the dogs." He replied calmly walking over towards her.

"Chris, you better not be letting Nick fuck up what we have. I'm not fuckin' stupid."

"Syd, I told you that shit is behind me."

"I know what you said, but that doesn't mean shit. I know you."

"So, you don't trust me?"

Sydney turned her neck, grimacing at Chris. "Don't go there Chris! I trust you enough to know the littlest thing that your fam' needs you for, you will risk everything to do it."

Chris swallowed the lump in his throat, rolling his eyes. "I told you I'm not into that shit no more. End of discussion." He turned to walk back upstairs.

"Baby... wait. He stopped turning around looking into her face. I just want to say this last thing. I love you, baby. But, I refuse to go thru that again seeing you laid up in a hospital on breathing tubes. God forbid next time there is no visit, next time could be me identifying your body in a morgue."

Chris sighed, thinking in his mind Syd had took it too far and was being dramatic saying she would be identifying him in a morgue. He smiled to himself, *she identify me in a morgue that nigga will be in that bitch too.* He finally replied, "I'm good Syd. We're good. No worries." He walked over kissing her on the lips. She looked into his eyes as she caressed his face in her hand. "You just think of Tati."

He looked down at Natalia who had food all over her mouth, fighting her sleep as she rubbed her eyes repeatedly. He touched the top of Natalia's head before walking upstairs. He came back down fifteen minutes later fully dressed, Sydney was cleaning up Natalia. "I'll be back."

"Where are you going?"

"To meet up with Tarik at Mama's"

"Okay. I love you."

"I love you too Syd." He kissed her again before leaving out the front door. Tarik had sent him a message saying that he was ten minutes from restaurant. Chris hopped into his black Lamborghini Aventador. He arrived there first, the waitress who recognized him the moment he walked in the door quickly whisked him back to their vip section. She was brown skinned, black hair with silver highlights styled neatly in a bob, and slender. She handed him a menu. "May I get you something to drink?" "Yea, let me have a sprite for now." He looked up seeing Tarik walking back to the table. He was wearing a white tee, jeans, Cazal frames on his face and Timbs on his feet. Chris stood up and they dapped each other as Tarik sat down. The waitress came back with Chris' drink and quickly took their orders. Chris looked over at Tarik the numerous chains hanging from his neck. Tarik looked down at his phone, as he rested it on the table. "So, what's good Young?! How's the family?" Chris sipped from his drink, thinking how long it had been to hear someone call him that.

"Everyone good. How about you? What's good in NY?"

"Yo, so much fuckin' shit man. You remember that um… girl you was fuckin' with… what was her name, Gisele?"

"Yea. What about her?"

"She was merked a few months ago."

"What?" Chris sat up not believing the words out of his mouth.

"Yea. They found her naked chopped up in a fuckin' dumpster in Queens." Chris shook his head in disbelief. He couldn't wrap his head around Gisele going out that way, although she did him dirty, never thought of popping her. Well, he contemplated shooting her but never ending her life.

"You sure Gisele?"

"Gisele? I meant the one Money was fuckin' with, her sister right? Gabby." Chris exhaled a sigh of relief. "They sayin' Money did that shit. News saying no leads, of course niggas ain't saying shit. Money got the streets shook right now."

"What's going on?"

"Man, since you left, niggas been asking what happened to you and shit. Shit, niggas said that you were popped at your place and niggas torched you in that shit."

"Hmm..." said Chris digesting the fact that everyone thought he was dead. Something about that didn't add up to him, but he wasn't going to question Tarik's loyalty at this moment. He was good, no worries in his life, fuck what niggas thought.

"I had been calling your numbers. Went by your crib seen the cars all burned up, I was like what the fuck. I asked Tone about you, I even asked Money, fuck ass, no one knew shit. I even called that nigga Lewis and he didn't know shit. What the fuck else I can do, n'ahmean."

"Well, I had to get away from all that shit. I have a family now, n'ahmean, shit change. I had to leave all that shit behind and move forward for my baby. Change been good, I can't complain."

"I hear you. Man, if I could I would too. He replied. The waitress came back with their food. Chris had ordered southern fried wings and shrimp, with red beans and rice. Tarik had ordered a ten piece wings and fries. But, Money fuckin' crazy now Young! After you left, nigga just started poppin' niggas left and right. He got rid of his crew. Nigga be in the streets dolo, with a fuckin' machete and sawed off, n'ahmean. Ben can't tell him shit. He told me he thru fuckin' with Ben. Tarik stuffed a piece of chicken in his mouth. Son, heart gone. He out there."

Chris had dug into his food, savoring the flavor of rice. "Well, maybe he can get his weight up. He always bitched that niggas was always slippin', now he can get shit done." Chris replied with a smirk.

Tarik laughed. "Yo, you remember Malik? With the bum ass explorer?"

"How can I forget that pussy ass nigga." Said Chris as he wiped his mouth with a napkin.

"Money popped that nigga in the club in front of everybody."

"Word? He dead?"

"Nah, he popped him in the stomach. Last I heard he was in a rehab. Niggas say that Malik had been plotting to pop Money. Money got wind of that shit and deaded that shit. They say Malik gonna be fucked up for life. Money ass be ghost for real, daylight that nigga gone. All night niggas say he be out the block lurking and shit. Nigga got that thick ass beard going now, lost madd weight you see that nigga you wouldn't know who the fuck he is." Tarik laughed out loud. Chris chuckled as he sipped his drink. At first he was amused by the Money conversation, but now he was bored. Fuck that bum ass nigga he thought. He decided to change the subject.

"So Tarik, what's up with you?"

"I got a little crew. I got one girl I'm with now."

Chris smiled. "You got one woman now?"

"Yea, I know. Fuckin' changed up. She been cool, holding me down, since I've been out the city. I've been on the low, may have an ass of warrants."

Chris looked down at his phone. He had over ten text messages. He scrolled thru them as Tarik continued on. He realized one of the texts was from John, saying call Reign. Chris interrupted Tarik to tell him he had to make a call. He called the store, John answered. Tarik listened in to his conversation. "Yo... what's good? Nah I'm not coming in today. How's it looking in there? Oh, she start tomorrow, make sure no bullshit. Hit me up." Chris hung up the phone. "My bad. Tarik."

"Oh, we good. He was done with his food he sipped his Patron. Did I tell you your cousin Nia fuckin' with Reese now?"

"What?"

"Man, he turned shorty out. She look like a fuckin' hood rat for real now. She be carrying work for that nigga, doing hits for that pussy. You see her you wouldn't even recognize her. She pop fuckin' pills." He shook his head. "Damn, who would've ever thought Nia be a hood rat." Chris phone rang, he looked down the phone displayed Nick. He answered. "Yo."

"You busy?"

"Why? What up?"

"Pops is fuckin' wildin' man. He snuffed me this morning. Took my fuckin' whips, fuckin' everything. I'm out here looking like a bum ass nigga." Nick shouted.

"Well... son, you are a bum ass nigga right now. You gotta prove that they can trust you again. You fucked up."

"I don't think you get what I'm sayin'. I have nothing. No clothes, no dough. I'm ass out!"

"What?"

"Pops went to my cribs took all my clothes and shit and torched that shit. I don't know what the fuck he did with my whips. Took all my stashes. Bullshit man!"

"Damn. That's fucked up, son. But, you did this shit to yourself. Man up, and get on your fuckin' grind instead of bitchin' over the fuckin' phone. If this petty shit was everything to you, maybe they was right to jack your ass crying about this fuck shit." Nick sighed.

"I can't even buy a fucking shirt. All I got is my fucking sweat pants I'm wearing."

Chris had become annoyed with his tantrum. "Look, come by the store. I'll give you some clothes. But, you better get your fuckin' shit together. You gotta prove to pops and Mart you can do this shit. I'll give you one fucking outfit. I don't want to hear shit else but you out there grindin', shit I'm not even supposed to be associated with your ass after that bs."

"I know, I appreciate it C. I'll come by the store in an hour."

"A'ight." Chris hung up the phone. Tarik looked over at him.

"Damn, you stay busy huh?"

"Yea, always something going on. Chris looked for the waitress to receive the check. But, I'm going to head out of here and handle a few things. It was good seeing you. He dapped up Tarik again, as he reached in his pocket he pulled out a hundred dollar bill. The waitress came back with the check he put the money in her hand. "Keep that. I don't need any change." The girl smiled brightly thanking him repeatedly.

"Damn, it's been good seeing you too Young. Maybe we can link up again someday."

"Yea, maybe we can meet up at Hard Rock or some shit next time. A'ight." Chris grabbed his phone off the table, heading towards the door. Tarik watched him as he walked out to the curb, getting behind the wheel of his Lamborghini. He hated to admit it. But, it was clear, Chris had changed and he knew they would never be what they were in the past. Chris had matured was living a hustler's dream. Tarik felt he was still that thirsty bottom nigga, below Chris, and it seemed impossible to catch up. The paper he had been making building with his crew was nothing, compared to the paper, he could tell that Chris was making. He noticed that he wore one diamond necklace on his neck, one ring and Cartier watch on his wrist. Chris style was simple and clean. Whereas Tarik's was loud and gaudy, felt he looked like a nigga on the block. Tarik's phone rang interrupting his thoughts. He looked at the screen it was a private number. He answered hesitantly. "Yo."

"Yo Tarik, this is Preme."

"What's good?" He replied nervously.

"What's good is I know you just met up with Chris. Let me make myself clear. I know you have come up on a few pennies, you small time pussy, and you think you hot shit cause you got those cheap ass chains on your neck. Tarik looked around. If anyone finds out where the fuck Chris is, I'll make it my personal duty to watch you take your last fuckin' breath at my hands. You understand? You fuck with my family well-being, I will personally come to Connecticut and blast you and every pussy ass bitch you got living in that sardine can on Ferguson. So, anything you got planned try it. I want you to, been a minute for me, but I've been inching to use my new toys. And I know about the murder attempt. Try me nigga." The call ended Tarik was shook. He immediately looked towards every exit, seeing if anyone was lurking. He dropped forty dollars on the table, scurrying quickly out of the restaurant.

*   *   *

Chris had arrived at Reign after going home to switch cars. He got out of the car, walking up to the door. Once inside, he walked down the hallway up to the front register. John was working the register and there was three people waiting in line. "What's good boss? We've been busy all day today." "I see…" Girls looked over to the register realizing Chris had arrived. "He's here." One replied. Chris walked around the sales floor, to greet the customers, and fix the displays. Chris enjoyed being in the store this was his investment, he was dedicated to making it a success, and being active in daily operations. His phone rang in his pocket, he pulled it out seeing Nick on the display. "Yo." He answered. "I'm outside." Chris grabbed a

Crooks & Castles shirt off the rack, with matching joggers. "A'ight." Chris ended the call walking out the back door. He was greeted by Damien's Yukon SUV. Nick emerged from the backseat, his face beaten and bruised. His lip busted. Nick looked as if he had jumped in a gang fight, he looked bad.

"Damn! You a'ight nigga?" said Chris handing the clothes over to him.

"Yea, I'm good. Thank you." They dapped each other.

"So, what you about to do for bread?"

"Damien, got some work, I can work on." Chris looked around. He went to the trunk of the Benz getting the duffel bag out from Daytona.

"Use some of this to get you started."

"Yo, thank you C. I owe you nigga."

"Yea, nigga. I'm not gonna forget that shit either. Chris handed him the bag. You better be out here grindin' all fuckin' day nigga. You know they're watching your every fuckin' move."

"I know. Let me get out of here 'tho, before someone see me."

"Hell yea. I don't need you out here scaring away my customers."

Nick laughed. "Fuck you, son."

"Nah, get money playboy." Nick gave Chris dap one last time. Damien stuck his head out the driver side. "What's good C? When we playin' cards again nigga?"

"Soon, nigga. Let Nick get his weight up, before I take his bread again." Damien laughed.

"He look like shit don't he." Nick threw up his middle finger as he headed back to the backseat of Damien's SUV. Chris walked back inside the store, his phone rang again it was Sydney. "Hi baby."

"Sup ma. What you doing?"

"I'm at the park with Dana and Tati. I was calling you to see if you wanted to go out for dinner. I don't feel like cooking today."

"Where you want to go?"

"Benihana? Applebee's? Olive Garden? I mean nothing fancy, I'm pretty sure Tati will be asleep halfway thru dinner."

"Olive Garden sounds good."

"Well, we are almost done here. We'll meet you at the house in about twenty minutes."

"A'ight. Love you."

"Love you too."

Sydney ended the call sliding her iPhone into her black Birkin bag. Dana continued to bounce Natalia up and down on her lap. She laughed as Dana tickled her tummy. "So you're going out to dinner with your boo thang." Said Dana playfully.

"Yes. We need to get out of the house. Hell, I think we need a vacation." Sydney laughed.

"When are you gonna visit your mom?"

"Well, I'm supposed to go out to LA to see my dad in a few weeks. But, I don't know if I can deal with his million questions about me and Chris' relationships and unsolicited bullshit. You know he hates Chris, and I have not told him that we are engaged."

"What?! You're lyin'? When are you going to tell him?"

"When he is walking me down the aisle. Hell, if that even happens." They both laughed taking in the sun. Natalia laid back on Dana's chest playing with her huge Galaxy Note phone. Dana had put on a YouTube video of Doc McStuffins.

"Chris isn't that bad. Extra cocky and conceited. But, he's not that bad, maybe daddy wants to protect his little princess." Dana pressed her finger into Sydney's cheek. Sydney swatted her finger away.

"I mean, Chris is my baby but he does have some issues. I've never denied that."

Dana laughed. "No, you know who has issues is Vani and bitch ass Mark."

"What? What's goin' on?"

"Girlll, Mark is gone every night talking about he's grindin'. Nigga where? He and Vani fight, I mean throwin' bows, every other day. Remember last week Vani had on that all black shit and dark shades? He had gave her a black eye."

Sydney sat up looking into Dana's face making sure she heard everything correctly. Not Vani? Vani was always Sydney's backbone and rock, always ready to go zero to a hundred on anyone who came at her sideways. Sydney couldn't believe her bestie had been hurt, and what cut deeper is she couldn't come to her about it.

"Why didn't she tell me?"

"Girl, you know Vani always want to be tough for you. She couldn't bear to let you see a nigga get the best of her. He's cheating on her, I just know it. I've been telling her forever to leave his punk ass. But you know…"

"I'll beat that nigga's ass."

"Mark, got a little paper. I mean he ain't no Chris. Although, he walk around like he is. He's been robbing niggas for years. He tried to rob kingpin Preme, they say."

"What?" replied Sydney trying not to seem too eager to hear more.

"Yea. You know Preme is like Mayor of the fuckin' city. Preme is a fuckin' billionaire. They said that he planned a hit to get Preme at his annual back to school drive. He got cold feet because word got around that Preme had found out. I mean, I've never seen Preme face to face, but niggas said he is not to be fucked with." Sydney adjusted her top, as she flipped her hair over her shoulder. She decided not to tell Dana about their connection with Preme. Dana was her girl, but if she had learned anything from her past with Chris, was to keep certain family matters private.

"Well, Friday we are all going out! You know that Bundles and crew are having a concert. My girls are coming in from Connecticut Thursday, so I was thinking we could all hang out and give them a chance to experience S. Beach."

"I'm down. If Chris let's you." Dana looked at her phone, she had a text message she attempted to take the phone from Natalia, and she wasn't having it.

"Whateva, bitch. I will be linking up with you later this week, so we can make our plans for Friday night." Natalia began to cry as Dana took her phone away. Sydney took her out of Dana's arms attempting to settle her down.

"Oh, I'm sorry my little cutie cute. So, hit me up with details later."

"Bet."

"I'll ask Vani to go too. Shit, she need to go and find herself a new man. They both laughed out loud. Well, a'ight you two, get home safe. See you later." She reached over kissing Natalia's cheek. Dana got up adjusting her ripped denim shorts to cover the bottom of her round derriere. She was wearing a Bob Marley tank, with Jordan Concorde's on her feet. They embraced before leaving to their vehicles.

Sydney sped home meeting Chris in the driveway. He got out of the car, looking over at her. "You going inside?"

"No, I don't have to." Chris walked over to the Range picking up Natalia placing her in the backseat of the Benz. "Look, at my mami, she got a tan?"

"She has on sunscreen. Besides, nothing wrong with her being a sexy honey dip like her mama."

"Better not be calling Tubby a honey dip." He replied seriously. Sydney slid in the passenger seat, Chris got in the driver's seat and they were on their way. Once they were halfway there, Sydney turned down the music. "Baby, don't forget my girls are coming Thursday."

"I remember Syd. I don't know if I want to see your girls again."

"Why is that?"

"Your girls, always hatin' on the kid."

"Whatever. Tori is the only one who is not feeling you because you hit her in Boston." Chris became quiet as he thought about the day. He still didn't remember the blow by blow, he only remembered Sydney's words and afterwards he had blacked out.

"That was fucked up. I didn't have to hit shorty. But you know how my temper get, at that point all I see is fuckin' blood."

"Yea, you need to control that. What if when Tati is sixteen and she gets smart with you. You're not gonna beat her up."

"I'll never beat Tubby. That's my heart right there." Chris replied looking at her fighting her sleep in the rearview mirror. Sydney looked over at Chris hurt in her eyes.

"So, what are you sayin'? I wasn't your heart, when you beat me?"

"That was different. My mother and Natalia is at the same place here to me. He placed his hand over his heart. That's my blood for life. You here too, but in a different place. So, you shouldn't even go there." Chris looked over at her. He could see rage boiling up inside Sydney as she applied gloss to her lips. You know you my world ma. You know that I'll do anything for you."

"Mmmhmm" said Sydney as she threw the lip gloss in her purse, folding her arms across her chest as she looked out the window. Chris reached over kissing her cheek. "Gimme a kiss."

"No, drive."

"Come on."

"No. Pay attention to the road."

"A'ight. Chris merged into the far right lane, pulling onto the grassy shoulder. Sydney looked around at the cars whizzing by. Now, give me a kiss." Chris placed the car in park, removing his seat belt.

"Chris, what are you doing?" Chris was already out of his seat, kissing Sydney's neck and ear. She looked out the window trying to ignore him, as he worked his tongue down to her breasts. Her body becoming hot as she creamed in her panties. She gave in grabbing his chin kissing his lips passionately. She bit his chin gently as Chris began to lift the back of her shirt. "Baby… stop." She replied as she breathed deeply, wanting him badly at that moment. He unbuttoned her jeans as he slid his hand down into her perfectly waxed love below. She inhaled squirming in her seat. He kissed her ear again. He removed his hand, licking the remnants of Sydney from his fingers. She sucked his fingers, before buttoning back up her pants. Natalia coughed in the backseat. They both turned around looking at her. She was knocked out. "Look at you being nasty in front of the baby." Said Sydney.

"She's sleep. All my baby do is eat and sleep." They both laughed. Sydney looked over to Chris. "I'm gonna fuck the shit out of you tonight." She replied bluntly.

Chris looked over to her with a smile. "I know."

Chris put the car in gear as they got back on their way to the restaurant. Natalia had perked up soon as they walked into the restaurant. As if she immediately smelled the food and knew that was her cue. They were placed at a table, and ordered their food. Chris had went to the bathroom and as soon as he came back, their food had arrived. Natalia in her booster seat sipping lemonade in her sip cup.

"Oh yea, me and the girls are going to see Bundles at the club."

"When is this?"

"Friday."

"He gonna have his whole crew with him, or just him?"

"Babe, I don't know. I just found out today."

"So, you going just to go?"

"Pretty much, and be cute with my girls." Sydney smiled, as she dug into her salad.

"So… are you asking me or telling me?"

"Baby, however you want to take it."

"Oh, a'ight." Chris replied sarcastically. His face said everything, he was pissed. She knew he wanted to go, and a part of her enjoyed rubbing it in his face. Chris was a huge Bundles fan, he had every mixtape and was the next big artist to blow from New York. The rest of the dinner Chris kept conversation brief. Sydney began to think it had to be something deeper than the concert. On the drive home Chris turned off the music. "I have to go to Atlanta in a week." Sydney turned quickly towards him. "Why?"

"I have to meet with some distributors. Thinking of going into the liquor business, create a brand of Vodka."

"How long?"

"Maybe a week." She stared at him, not buying his story. She thought to herself, *he must think I'm fuckin' stupid.* Once they arrived home, Sydney got out of the car removing Natalia from the back seat. "You're tryin' to fuckin' play me! I know you are tryin' to get back in the game."

"Syd, I already told you, I'm done with that bullshit." She unlocked the doors, carrying Natalia inside holding her head as she stormed upstairs. "I'm tired of you fuckin' doubting me!" Chris slammed the glass front door, behind him as he walked over to the kitchen. Sydney halfway up their sprawling staircase turned around. "If I see or hear anything about you being back in that bullshit. I'm done!" She continued towards Natalia's room, placing her inside of her twin sized pillow top canopy. She removed her clothes placing her on a tank top and hello kitty thermal pants. She turned on the night light, kissing her forehead. She grabbed the baby monitor leaving quietly out of the room. Chris was approaching the top of the stairs.

"You always tryin' to threaten me with you fuckin' leaving. If you don't want to be with me, leave. Don't act like I'm fuckin' forcing you to be with me."

"You are definitely tryin' it. Don't front like I never said to you, I'm not bringing Natalia into that lifestyle. We are not going back down that road!"

"It wasn't bad, when you were spending my drug money on shoes and fuckin' clothes. Taking fuckin' trips, paid for your fuckin' classes."

"We have a daughter now. We have responsibilities to her!" They walked into their bedroom.

"You're the one to talk about responsibility." He replied sarcastically. He walked inside the closet removing his jewelry.

"Like I said, get back into that bullshit and *we* are gone!" Sydney walked over to her drawer grabbing a lace chemise slipping it over her clothes. She peeled her clothes off walking into the closet past Chris throwing her clothes in the hamper. Chris caught a glimpse of her bare ass in the lace chemise. She grabbed her favorite pillow leaving the room. She went over to one of the guest rooms. She turned on the television, walking downstairs to get a glass of water. Sydney heard Chris coming down the stairs she tried to hurry up. She whizzed past him, he grabbed her arm gently. "So, you're not sleeping with me tonight?"

Sydney looked at him, as in no you didn't. Attitude all over her face. "Did we not just argue? And you are gonna act like nothing happened?"

"I mean we argue every other fuckin' day. What's new?

"We have not settled anything or talked anything out. Nothing has been resolved."

"Yes, it was. I told you I'm done with that shit and you don't wanna believe me. You want to walk around with the stank face all night. So, there ain't shit else to say. "

"Good night, Chris." Sydney walked past him into the room. She grabbed her book bag and began studying over her notecards. Her phone rang interrupting her. It was Vani. "Hello."

"Hey girl. You busy?"

"Nah… well I'm studying. What's up?"

"I am soo fuckin' pissed with Mark. He's been out all fuckin' week, he comes in tonight telling me we need a break."

"What?! No, he didn't?"

"Yes, the fuck he did. I punched the shit out of his dumb ass tried to break his fucking nose." Sydney laughed.

"Girl, you should've."

"Yea, we got in a huge fuckin' fight. He hit me girl."

"What? Where? You need me to come by?"

"Bastard busted my lip and I got a black eye. I told him I'm done with his stupid ass. Just give me my keys and get the fuck out."

"Yass bitch!"

"I'm moving on. There are plenty other niggas out there. Fuck his tired ass. I blame myself for putting up with his shit this long. I knew he was cheating on me. I just kept thinking I'm gonna hold him down and get him back to where he needs to be, ya know."

"That's women everywhere girl. Always holding them down just to be shitted on. Are you okay?"

"Yea, I will be fine. I need to hit up a few stores tomorrow get something fly for this weekend. You want to go with me?"

"I have class tomorrow but, if you want to go after one, I'm down."

"That's cool. Just hit me up when you leave school, I should be done with my client then."

"Oh yea, you can come out with us to the concert Friday. My girls are coming down from Connecticut. Perfect time to get glam and stunt on these hoes."

Vani laughed. "Hell yea! You have definitely been down here too long with me. But, we stunt on these hoes every day we walk out the door. None of these basic bitches can touch us on our worst days." Sydney laughed laying back on the bed. She placed her notecards on the nightstand. The door crept open, she looked up to the doorway seeing Chris standing in his boxers. She turned over turning her back to him. "So when are you going to NY again?" said Sydney ignoring Chris' presence.

He walked over to the bed, gently caressing her bare ass. He climbed onto the bed towering over her body. He leaned in kissing her neck and ear. She shrugged him off, hoping he would go away. He continued biting on her neck and earlobe. Which sent goosebumps all over Sydney's body. Her sun kissed tan nipples were at attention. Chris worked his way down her chest kissing her C cup gems thru the chemise. "Mmhmm." Sydney replied to Vani on the phone. Chris went to the edge of the bed pulling Sydney's body down to him. He lifted her dress placing his face in between her legs. He gently played with her clit as he slid fingers inside her warm cocoon. A soft moan left her lips. "Chris..." she finally worked out. He continued to suck and play in her sugar walls."Mmmhm" she replied to Vani, this time which sounded more sensual than before. Chris climbed into bed he pulled Sydney's legs straddling his chest. She held the phone to her ear. He slid his body lower, to where she was sitting on his face. "Oh, shit... she finally worked out. She dropped the phone on the bed, grabbing on to the headboard. Sweet moans crept from her lips as she caressed her breasts. Chris went deeper as he poked her with his tongue. "I fuckin' hate you." Shouted Sydney. "I know..." Sydney slid off his face, working her way down to his dick. She removed his shaft, out of the pocket of the boxers. Already at attention, she let her tongue dance on the head, before devouring it in her mouth. Chris leaned forward sucking again on her leaking clit. She removed his boxers climbing on top of him. The initial feel of his girth sent a rush up her spine. She took in all of him as she slowly guided herself on to his nine inches. She moaned louder placing her hands in her hair. "mmm... I love you." She replied roughly.

"Hello." Replied Vani on the phone realizing they were having sex. She could hear Chris moaning as he slapped Sydney's ass.

"Fuck me baby! Oh shit!" moaned Sydney.

Vani listened in again. She couldn't help but get turned on a little herself as she heard the dirty deed going down on the line. She finally hung up the phone, imagining the deed in her mind.

The next morning Sydney woke up in the master bedroom. Chris was knocked out across her stomach. She gently peeled him away from her naked body. He moved over onto her pillow. Sydney looked down at his face kissing his lips softly. She reached for her phone on the nightstand seeing it was six-thirty, and headed to get Natalia for their morning shower routine. She went to her side of their walk in closet, which was lined in every designer one could think of. She fastened her La Perla brassiere as she pulled out a white tank and black knee length pencil skirt, Christian Louboutin studded flat sandals. Natalia in her robe, Sydney picked out a white tank for her and distressed jeans. She put her on a diaper changing her into her clothes, Sydney placed on her socks and Jordan 7 Retro sneakers on her feet. She sat in the plush recliner which was their reading time spot, to attack doing her hair, so Chris wouldn't have her in the headband. Sydney gave Natalia two French braids, with black bands on the end. As she rushed downstairs to fix a quick breakfast, she threw bacon on the griddle, placed Natalia in her high chair as she peeled a Halo Tangerine, she placed it on her high chair she went to town. Sydney quickly toasted her bagel and flipped Chris' waffle.

Chris soon came down stairs, smelling the aroma of breakfast. "Good morning."

"Good morning. She kissed him quickly as she scurried around the kitchen. Your breakfast is ready, waffles in maker, um shit forgot eggs. Make your own eggs."

"Syd, I told you we need to hire someone for that. So you not running around all crazy every morning."

"No, I cook for my family and number two I'm not having some random bitch in my house all day with my baby and my man." Chris shook his head at her comment. She kissed him again before walking over to Natalia kissing her face. Sydney grabbed her bag and was out the door. Chris took the waffle out and bacon, he sat at the table next to Natalia. He cut up pieces of his waffle placing it on a plate on top of Natalia's tray. As he watched her eat his phone dinged with a message from Nick saying that he got his car back. He sent him a message saying stay hungry, nigga. It's not over. Nick responded saying that he was coming thru the store to get a few new items. Chris carried Natalia upstairs so he could shower and dress. After hopping in the shower quickly he ran put on a Crooks & Castles Bomb First black tee, jeans and Givenchy sneakers and he was soon off to Reign.

On the way to Reign he decided to stop by convenience store to get a few drinks. He took Natalia out of the seat carrying her in his arms inside the store. Chris grabbed a bottle of smart water, a sprite, a pack of Starburst and a pack of gum. Natalia reached for a cinnamon roll he picked it up for her. He walked over to the register which was clear, the cashier was Puerto Rican and in her mid-twenties. She smiled making eye contact with Chris looking over his physique. "How are you doing today?' she finally worked out.

"I'm good." Chris reached into his pockets for his cash, he pulled out a twenty.

"Your daughter is beautiful."

"Thank you. Natalia lifted her head off Chris chest as if she knew she was being talked about. She smiled at the cashier blowing her a kiss. Chris chuckled. Yea, she's a ham."

"Yo, that was too cute." She gave him his total, she counted out his change placing it in his hand. She began to bag up his items as Chris struggled to put the change in his pocket. The cashier looked over the marks all over his neck, she smiled. She debated telling him about the passion marks that covered his neck, maybe he would be offended she thought. He had to pass a mirror right? She decided to let him be. Chris took his bag and left out the store. Once he arrived at Reign and walked in the back door. He stopped by his office leaving the bag inside and grabbing Natalia's walker he put her in it. Placing her in front of him as he walked up to the register. Jhené Aiko's "Lyin King" filled the store's speakers. John was in at the register cleaning the glass. "What's good boss?"

"Nice music. Definitely a change."

"Well, since we got the ladies in here now. Tati started this morning." She walked over from the front display with the clothes she had removed from the mannequin. "Good morning Chris." Chris couldn't help but look over Tati's body. She was wearing a tank and Herve bandage skirt that looked as though it was painted on her curvy physique. Black leather Louboutin pumps on her feet, she definitely had Chris' attention.

"Good morning. How are you doin' so far?"

"I'm good. I changed the display for this week. You like it?" Chris walked over to look at the display. "It's good. I like it."

"Thank you." She replied pulling her wand curled tresses out of her face.

"Yo, I'm going over to the store. Anybody need anything?"

"I'm good." Said Chris.

"Well, can you bring me back one of those Lipton Peach Tea drinks please."

"I got you." He replied as he walked out the backdoor. Chris walked back over to the counter where Natalia was in her walker. She had taken her toy and was banging it against the wall, hearing the noise, Tatiana walked over to the counter. "So, this is Miss Tati? She is adorable!"

"Yea, that's her. Miss trouble maker." They both chuckled.

"Can I pick her up?"

"Yea, go ahead, she will be here almost every day I'm here so might as well get used to her." Tatiana reached to pick her up out of the seat. Natalia opened her arms dropping the toy. "Hi, pretty girl. You're so cute, and look at your little Retro's. Natalia looked at her giving her side eye, as in *who the hell are you?* Chris looked over the mail that was laying on the back counter. Tati bent down placing Natalia back in her walker. John returned from the store. He handed Tati her drink, placing his own drink on the counter. He walked over to Chris, noticing the passion marks all over his neck. "What's up with this boss?" John walked over pointing to Chris' neck.

"What?"

"You didn't see your neck today?" John handed him the mirror. Chris smiled seeing the remnants Sydney had left of their evening. "Anyway, don't be worrying about me."

"I'm tryin' to help you out. N'ahmean, you the one looking like a leopard out here. They both laughed. But, you hear about Bundles' concert Friday?" Tatiana walked back over eavesdropping on their conversation. "Yea, I heard about it. You going thru?"

"Yea, I'm seeing if you want to go thru I know you fuck with the kid 'cause that's about all you play."

"Did y'all say Bundles had a concert Friday?" said Tatiana interrupting their conversation.

"Yea, what you know about Bundles?" said John.

"I did one of his videos a few months back. I have all of his mixtapes. Don't sleep on my aux cord."

"So you did a video huh?" said John with a smile.

"Not a flick, you perv. I'm not a thot." She replied with her hand on her hip and full attitude.

"Damn, it was a joke. I was just playing with you."

"Well, I'm letting you know. Don't get it twisted." Chris laughed out loud breaking the tension in the room.

"Damn, shorty went from zero to a hundred on ya ass. I guess Tati not as nice as we thought." Said Chris.

"I'm sweet as can be. Just don't try me and we'll be good." Tatiana smiled at them walking towards the bathroom in back, as customers piled into the store.

The store had a steady influx of customers coming in to get the latest sneakers. Tatiana and John sales were through the roof, Tatiana was a great addition to the store. Chris observed that she was attentive to customer's needs, kept a smile on her face and the male customers seemed to agree she was great eye candy. Around two, Chris had went to his office to check on Natalia who he had put down for a nap earlier. Tatiana was cleaning off the counter and glass. Sydney walked thru the door, John quickly panned over her body with his eyes, before realizing it was Sydney. "What's up Sydney? How are you?"

"Hey, John. I'm good. How are you?"

"Can't complain." Said John. Sydney looked over at Tatiana standing behind the counter, she immediately sized her up from head to toe. Chris walked out of his office with Natalia in tow. "Mama!" said Natalia as she saw her.

"Hi baby! Give mama some sugar." Chris handed Natalia to Sydney. Sydney kissed Natalia's lips. Chris leaned in kissing Sydney's lips.

"What's good ma? How was class today?"

"It was good. I got a B on my test. I need to study more, that's not acceptable."

"Don't beat yourself up. That's still a good grade."

"I wanted an A plus." They walked back to his office. Sydney changed Natalia's diaper, she handed the soiled one to Chris to discard. "Baby, I think it's time for us to put Tati in daycare."

Chris looked over at her as if he was offended. "Nah, I'm not cool with that. I mean you see these bastards on the news doing all types of crazy shit to people kids in daycare. Anyone touch my baby I will take a fuckin' case."

"I know. But, I think it's time she socialize with children. I mean I don't want her to be some sheltered weirdo."

Chris laughed. "My baby not going to be sheltered. I'm just saying I want to thoroughly inspect wherever we decide to take her." There was a knock at the door. "Yo." John peeked his head in, "Nick out here for you." "A'ight" Chris got up to step out of the office. Following behind John. Sydney soon followed behind them with Natalia. Three women came into the store scantily clad in their bikinis. They immediately got John's attention. "Hey Tati!" said one of the girls as they walked over to her at the shoe display. "Heyy girls. Y'all look cute?" John glanced at their bodies. One was Dominican, Black and Cuban. He was definitely enjoying the assortment each was curvy, and filled out their bottoms nicely. "How's it going?" said the Black friend.

"Good. I've had a good time."

"You missed the beach today. We met this director, and he wants us to be in the next Rick Ross video."

"Oh yeah. Bianca you check credentials." Said Tatiana with a smile.

"Girl, you know I did. I checked the Instagram and Twitter. He verified." Bianca was the Dominican friend, social media guru she always kept them up on what was going on the latest in everything.

"So are you going to do it with us?"

"I don't know. I've got a few modeling things coming up, plus being here."

"Well, let us know." They all walked towards the door, passing Chris and Nick.

"Oh, Chris these are my girls. Bianca, Gina and Erica. This is my boss, Chris."

Chris nodded. "What's good?" They smiled all replying hi in unison. Tatiana proceeded to walk them out the door. Nick's eyes followed Tatiana's body. "Who's the new girl?"

"That's Tatiana." Said John.

"Yo, she's fine. Who she fuckin' with?"

"I don't know yet." Said John as if he was on a mission himself to find out. Chris walked over to the counter where Natalia and Sydney were. Tatiana strolled back inside the store, heading for the break area. She glanced over at Sydney with the baby. She acknowledged her presence with a smile. "Oh Tati, my bad, this is my wifey Sydney. This is our new employee Tatiana." Sydney side eyed Tatiana again plastering a fake smile on her face. "Hi, nice to meet you."

"Likewise. Tati is so adorable."

"Thank you." Said Sydney dryly. Sydney looked over Tatiana's tight bandage skirt, D breasts, and contoured face, rolling her eyes. She looked away knowing herself and knew that attitude was probably beaming off of her, she definitely couldn't let this bitch think that she was bothered by her presence. Sydney smiled, flipping her hair over her shoulder, making sure the rock on her finger glistened in Tatiana's eyes. "Baby, we are going to leave." Said Sydney as she kissed Chris' lips. Tatiana continued down the hall. Sydney's work here was done. Chris said he would walk them out to the car, parked out front.

Sydney opened the passenger door, starting the car to let the window down as she strapped Natalia in her car seat. "How long has she been working here?"

"Today, is her first day."

"Hmmph." Sydney replied.

"How long you and Tubby gonna be out today?"

"Not sure. I need to stop by the library and get some dinner. Not long."

"A'ight, I'll call you."

"What are you doing after here?"

"Going with Nick for a minute."

"Okay, baby. I love you." She reached out to hug him. He placed his arms around her body cuffing her ass in his hands. "Why do you have to be so nasty?"

"What... it's mine." The store door opened. "Excuse me, Chris." Tatiana peeked her head out. "Telephone... he said it was important."

"A'ight." Sydney massaged his face, seeing her markings all over his neck. She smiled to herself, as she kissed his chin.

"We'll see you at home." She walked around to the driver's side and Chris waited until she drove off before he went inside. He walked back to his office taking the call.

"Hello."

"What's up? Who was that?" said Preme.

"New girl."

"I checked on situation. Everything good."

"A'ight. So, what's up Pop?"

"Come by, once you're done at store."

"A'ight." Chris hung up the phone, walking back out to the register. The crowd had wavered a bit. Tatiana stood arranging the glasses in the case. "So, that's Natalia's mother? She's beautiful. Your daughter looks just like her."

"What? Everyone says she's my twin." Said Chris as if he was offended she said Natalia wasn't his twin.

"No, she has your complexion and maybe smile. But, sorry Dad she looks like mommy."

Chris side eyed Tatiana. "That kinda hurt my feelings a little bit." Tatiana laughed. "Awww... it'll be ok." She caressed his back playfully before walking away. John looked on noticing the quick embrace.

Sydney had went by the library and grabbed the books she needed. She had arrived at Vani's salon. Sydney was exhausted, she placed Natalia on the ground to try to walk, she lifted her legs back refusing to place her feet on the ground. "Really, Tati... You're gonna do mommy like that?" She picked her up walking into the salon. Dana immediately saw them and rushed over to pick her up. She smiled seeing Dana, she kissed her on the cheek as Sydney made her way to a seat.

"Oh Sydney, I got some things for Natalia in the car remind me before you leave."

"Okay. Hello everyone." Said Sydney. "Well… what's up miss?" said Vani as she placed the finishing touches to her client's hair. Sydney looked over Vani's appearance. She was wearing a Moschino tank, skinny jeans and Gucci sandals on her feet. Oversized dark Chanel frames on her face, and bruises on her arms. Sydney got up from her seat. The client was done and walked over to the receptionist to pay. Sydney grabbed her arm. "He did this to you?"

"I'm good. You should see that bastard and his whip." Vani smiled.

"He shouldn't have put his hands on you."

"Yea, but we always fight. Nothing new here. This time I'm done with his lies, and bullshit. So, fuck him."

"Okay! Friday we are gonna have fun, pop some bottles, and get you a new man."

"Hell yea. But, is Chris letting you out?"

"Please, he doesn't *let* me do anything. I do what the hell I want."

"Right. Chris gonna be like, you not going nowhere."

"Whatever, bitch."

"You never told me if Chris liked your hair?"

"Oh, he loved it."

"I knew he would. You look sexy with it."

"I always look sexy." Said Sydney with a smile.

"This bitch. You ready to go?"

Dana got up to get the things from her car she handed Natalia to Vani. Sydney walked out opening her trunk. Dana came over with two huge gift bags. "Dana, what is this?" Sydney looked through the bags seeing designer clothes, shoes and toys. "You know when I see something I like for my little cutie, I can't help myself."

"Aww, thank you Dana. We appreciate it." Sydney hugged Dana. Vani came over handing Natalia to Sydney. "Give Auntie Dana a kiss, Tati." Natalia reached over kissing Dana on the cheek. She closed down the back as she strapped Natalia in her seat. Dana walked back inside, as a candy colored Chevy rode past them slowly. Vani looked over the car's rims and the riders inside. The car stopped. Sydney walked around to the driver's side of her car. "What up sexy?" Sydney turned around rolling her eyes when she realized it was Yogi. "Damn... she cold." Said the passenger.

"Chill, she good." Said Yogi as he licked his lips at Sydney's body. Vani walked around to see what was going on. The passenger sat up. "Damn... who that?"

"That's Mark ole girl. Said Yogi. What up wit' ya?"

"Sup Yogi." Said Vani. He motioned for her to come over to the window. She came a few steps closer.

"What's up?"

"Your girl. Why she acting all cold and shit."

"She's taken, boo."

"I know. I've met that pussy nigga. The passengers laughed. He looked over Vani's arms. What happened Van?"

"Don't worry about it." she replied placing her arm behind her back.

"Mark bitch ass did this? I can handle that for you, if you get mami to at least talk to me. Damn."

"Who says I didn't handle it already?" Vani replied folding her arms across her chest.

"A'ight Van. I'm still going to check that nigga 'cause I fuck wit' you."

"Whatever. Do what you do."

"Aye Van, tell her to come here real quick."

"Damn, you feelin' her, huh?" Yogi laughed, not even attempting to hide his infatuation with Sydney's exotic beauty. Vani went over to Sydney, asking her to come over real quick. Sydney sighed rolling down the window, to give Natalia some air. "What?" said Sydney standing feet away from the car.

"Hi, beautiful." Said Yogi with a smile displaying his gold teeth. Sydney rolled her eyes. Yogi's passengers immediately scanned over Sydney's body. "You still with ole boy?"

"Yes. I'm still very happily engaged." Yogi smiled at her brash response, which was actually becoming a turn on to him.

"So, when can I see you again?" said Yogi.

"Nev…" said Sydney.

"Well actually we are going to the concert Friday." Sydney shot Vani a unit that if looks could kill.

"Oh, word. I'll see you there sexy."

"No, you won't!" said Sydney.

"Yes, you will." Interjected Vani.

"A'ight see you Friday." Yogi pulled away he and his friends laughing as Sydney hit Vani.

"What the fuck was that?"

"I'm hooking you up with Yogi." Said Vani with a smile.

"Bitch, I don't want him. I'm happy with my man."

"Syd, Yogi is cool people. He can break you off with a little dough and its cute he really likes you. Normally, he's a straight ass in the streets, to see him all googly eyed over you, it's cute." They got in the car and Sydney started the engine.

"Vani, fuck him. I don't want him! Oh shit. I hope he doesn't know Chris or fucking Nick." Sydney's anger quickly turned into worry. This is just what she needed was for anyone to have seen this interaction and it got back to Chris there would be hell to pay. She thought back to the Walmart incident.

"He doesn't know Chris. They are in two different circles."

"Yea, a real nigga and a bum nigga. Said Sydney. I'm so pissed at you for doing that!"

"I'm sorry. It was a joke. I did it to piss Mark off he hates Yogi."

"You bitch. You used me?"

Vani laughed. "Okay, listen Friday just flirt with him and I will do your nails and hair for free. Just so he can fuck Mark up even more. After that, I'll tell him you're not interested. Please..."

Sydney looked over at Vani. "Whatever."

"Thank you Syd!"

"For the record, I hate you right now."

"I love you boo." Said Vani playfully.

"I don't know why you are trying to play match maker when I am happily engaged."

"Yea, today you are. You must have gotten some last night. Oh wait, I was there you did."

Sydney burst into laughter, forgetting that she had been on the phone with her when the deed went down. "Anyway, what I do with my husband…"

"He's not your husband. You're not married yet."

"Don't be a hater all your life Van." Said Sydney with a smile. They headed to the mall.

Back at Reign, Chris and Tatiana were cleaning up the store preparing for closing time. John had left early to tend to family business. "Do I work the same time tomorrow?" said Tatiana.

"Yea, that's fine." Chris closed the front fixtures.

"So, when are you going back to Boston?" said Tatiana trying to start friendly conversation to end the silence.

"Maybe in a few months."

"Oh okay. I may go this summer to visit my family."

"You have family still there?"

"Yea, my mom, dad and younger brother."

"So, what made you stay down here?"

"Because I can model and make good money. I've made a lot of networking connections since I've been here. Also, the weather here is everything."

"Yea, I don't blame you on that." Said Chris with a smile. Chris climbed down heading to the backroom. He emerged again, closing the register. "Once you're done sweeping. We're ready."

"I'm done." She grabbed the broom as Chris began to turn off the lights. Tatiana quickly hurried behind him as they headed down the hallway leading to the back door. Tatiana placed the broom in the storage room as Chris waited before turning off last light. He turned off the light the hallway was pitch black. Tatiana felt for his shirt, she bumped her leg up against the display which was close to door. "Ouch!" Chris turned on one of the lights. "My bad. You a'ight?" He turned around looking at her.

"Yea, I hit my knee."

"I thought you were right behind me."

She massaged her knee as she walked towards him. "Maybe next time, I'll hold on to you. I think you were trying to set me up on the low." She replied with a smile.

"Yea, maybe you need to hold on next time. I'm not paying for injuries, he replied with a smile. Besides, ladies want to be on me anyway. Ladies love the kid." Tatiana laughed out loud. Not believing how forward he was.

"You are a mess. Very conceited huh?"

"I mean, look at me. I'm a fly ass nigga." He replied with a certain cockiness and arrogance that was attractive. Tatiana couldn't deny his swag, he was definitely a force to be reckoned with. Something about his cocky bravado had become sexy to her. He opened the back door, the light hitting them on their faces. She walked over to her new edition Nissan Maxima. Chris walked over to his car. "See you tomorrow, Tati."

"Bye boss." She replied with a smile as she watched him get into his car.

Chris sped over to Preme's house anxious to hear what would be going on in coming weeks. His housekeeper met Chris at the door and brought him back to Preme who was in the living room. He walked into the room, Preme stood up hugging him. "Can I get you anything Mr. Garcia?"

"Yes, let me have some lemonade and club sandwich." She nodded her head walking away. Preme smiled.

"Why every time you come over you gotta be eating up my food?" They both laughed.

"So, what's going on?"

"Well, I'm leaving out Saturday. I have to go by mom's on Thursday."

"How long you staying?"

"I'll be there Thursday and Friday. I should be back in Miami Saturday morning."

"A'ight. You still want Tubby this weekend?"

"Yea, bring her by Thursday morning. I'll take her with me to see mom, and you can pick her up when you drop me off to the airport Saturday."

"You good with Tati for two days. You know it's been a while for you?" Said Chris with a smile. The housekeeper brought back his food and drink. He began to eat the sandwich. "Thank you."

"I'll be fine. You don't have to bring her clothes or anything. I'll get her new shit while out."

"Okay, and what else going on?"

"Darren will be here Saturday, to get with you on the details of everything. That Yukon that's parked out front drive that to Atlanta. You gonna have to meet up with local distributor name is Rock supposed to be meeting you in Buckhead. Now Darren will have to get you with a few new connects he set up. Make sure you have soldiers with you. Who are you going to take?"

"I'll take Nick. I think this time he's learned from his mistakes."

"Keep that nigga in check. I don't want any fuckin' slip ups! You hear me?"

"I got you, Pop. Did you look over those documents I gave you last time?"

"Yea, I studied everything. I'm good."

"Okay, I'm giving you the keys to everything. Keep in touch with Darren, and he'll keep you updated on next moves. Everything right now is on you. You officially runnin' New York, Connecticut, Jersey, Atlanta and Michigan. This is some heavy shit to carry, times with no sleep. Give these niggas no fucking chances. Whatever you earn and receive during this time it's yours. I need to clean some money anyway."

"Nah, Pop. I'm giving you your dough. I can't get down like that with you."

"Son, I'm good. Preme looked at Chris knowing he wasn't giving in. Fine, put it towards this new Vodka deal I'm about to work on. I know that will be a big investment for us, and you will be done with this shit for good." Chris smiled thinking of the empire they would build, the right way. Natalia would be set for life. Chris stayed over Preme's until after eight thirty. He sent a message to Sydney asking her what was for dinner? She responded "Pizza bring drinks." He stopped by the grocery store on his way home.

At the house Sydney was in the middle of giving Natalia a bubble bath. Vani was in the hall on her phone. She came into the bathroom. Sydney was on her knees sponging Natalia off. "Girl... Dana just told me Mark came up to the salon looking for me."

"Serious?"

"He better stop trying me before he gets his dumb ass merked out here." Sydney laughed at Vani's thug demeanor. Natalia was now pruning Sydney took her out the tub wrapping her in her robe. She placed a towel over her wet hair. "Let's go in Natalia's room." Said Sydney to Vani as she walked by with Natalia. Sydney went over to her closet going into drawers picking out her pajamas. It was a Minnie mouse thermal with matching pants. Sydney sat on her bed as she changed her. Sydney placed Johnson's lavender and chamomile lotion over her hands and feet. Sydney took a brush to her hair deciding to let it air dry. Vani looked around Natalia's room, which was suited for a teenage girl instead of a toddler. She looked over the collage of pictures Sydney had on the wall of their family. There was a picture on her nightstand of a selfie she and Chris kissing each other she was only three months. "Let's go downstairs. Get her some milk and she will be out for the night." Sydney placed her bedroom slippers on her feet as they headed downstairs. Chris came in the door with a few bags of drinks. Sydney placed Natalia in the playpen. "Hi baby!" "What's good ma?" Sydney came over kissing his lips. Vani sat down at one of the bar stools. "What's up Chris?"

Chris looked over at her. "Damn, shorty! What the fuck happened?" Vani gave him side eye until she realized she had taken her shades off. She was so embarrassed.

"She got into it with her friend." Said Sydney as she opened the refrigerator.

"Damn. You a'ight? You looking hit right now." Sydney hit Chris' arm.

"Yea, well you should see his fuckin' face." He looked inside the pizza boxes on the counter. "I got you your own pizza. It's in the oven."

"What you tryin' to say?"

"I'm not trying. I'm saying it, you're greedy." Chris smiled going into the oven pulling out the pizza taking three slices on a plate and a bottle of Gatorade upstairs. "Good seeing you Van. I'm out." Sydney walked over to the playpen handing Natalia her sip cup of milk she turned on the television. "My dress Friday is so fuckin' lit. It's going to be bomb as hell bitch. It's couture. No one will have it, and all I'm gonna say is I'm gonna be shining on these hoes!" Vani laughed out loud.

"Okay, bitch. I can't wait to see this shit!"

"I need you to wand curl my hair Friday morning and Dana do my nails."

"Yea. I'll do your hair if you talk to Yogi." Sydney put her finger up to her mouth shushing Vani. Hoping that Chris could not hear anything.

"I told you I'm not fuckin' doing it."

"Well, he is definitely coming out Friday. That is on you."

After finishing his food Chris pulled out the documents which Preme had gave him that he was to look over. He studied over them again, he stuffed the folder under the mattress, before dozing off to sleep. An hour later Sydney came up after she had placed Natalia in her bed. She took a shower, before climbing into bed with Chris. Sydney sat up in bed studying her note cards for Anatomy class, she was trying to memorize the systems. Around midnight, Chris' cell phone began to ring on the bed. Sydney looked at the screen, the number was a New York number. She looked over at Chris before answering, he was out. "Hello"

"Yo, is Chris there?" said the male caller.

"Who is this?" said Sydney angrily.

"This is Tarik. Who this Sydney?"

"Yea. What's up?" she replied not trying to go down memory lane with him.

"I was hitting up C, to see if he could meet up with me real quick."

"Oh, sorry boo. He's not going anywhere else tonight."

"Oh... a'ight." Said Tarik confused by Sydney's attitude.

"Good night." She replied ending the call. She looked over at Chris again turning his ringer off., as she turned off the light.

The next morning Tatiana had stopped by her bestie Gina's house, looking over her portfolio as she prepared to have lunch with a prospective client. "What time do you go to work?"

"Ten. Looking at your pics getting me a little jelly. I need to update my portfolio. These are amazing Gina."

"Thank you. So what's the deal on your boss?"

"Chris?" said Tatiana with a quirky smile and blush.

"Yes. Everyone is talking about him. What is the tea?"

"Oh... he's cool. I mean he is a'ight." Said Tatiana.

"Whateva Tati. Don't front. I saw the nigga, he's fine."

Tatiana laughed out loud. "Girl is he!" she fell back onto the couch as if the thought of him took her breath away. Gina laughed. "He definitely has paper, nice whip and he smells so fuckin' good!"

"Yea, when we came in, I was definitely checking his ass out. He single?"

"No. she said angrily. He's engaged or married one to this girl named Sydney. They have a daughter, who comes up to the store with him."

"Sydney? I don't know her."

"Yea, he told me that he wasn't from here. He's from Boston, I think he said came to Miami from NY though. I don't know where she's from."

"Have you seen her? What's her stats? He looking for a side chick?" said Gina laughing.

"I met her yesterday. She's pretty. She's a bad bitch." Said Tatiana as if she hated the words coming from her lips. Tatiana looked down at her phone. Gina looked over at her friend, she was definitely smitten by her boss.

"You want him don't you?"

Tatiana smiled. "I can't even front. I do. He's gorgeous. He's funny, cocky, and wait I'm not gonna do this. I am not a homewrecker."

"Anymore boo. You're not a homewrecker anymore."

"Shut up. I can't. He does seem cool, like a down ass dude. He's always got his baby, you have to see him with her. It's so cute. But he has this rough edge to him. You know he's gorgeous, but he's a thug. Not everyone pulls that shit off ya' know."

"So you want to fuck him?"

"Yes, Gina. Can I just taste it though and leave him alone? I just want a sample."

"Bitch, you know how I get down. If anyone can get it means that shit was never yours. Get your sample! And let me watch. Maybe let me join?" said Gina as she licked her lips. Tatiana laughed out loud.

"You are crazy bitch."

Chris arrived at Reign at noon, with Natalia in tow, he placed her in the walker. She was wearing an Aztec design romper which was tan, pink and green. Rayban's on her face, gladiator tan sandals and the faithful top knot and headband. She had in her diamond studs and Tubby nameplate pendant hanging from her gold necklace. Tatiana walked over. "Hi cutie." Natalia gave her stink eye as she moved herself away from her. "You don't like me today?" she reached down to pick her up. Natalia began to cry. Chris walked over. "What you doing to my baby?" he picked Natalia out of the walker, Natalia smiled happy she got her way. "Oh no she didn't. I see how you are." Said Tatiana playfully.

Chris smiled, looking over Tatiana's ensemble. She was dressed in black tank, jeans that fit her every curve and a pair of red Christian Louboutin pumps. She had a red Amaryllis flower over her ear. "Maybe it's that big ass flower?" said Chris.

"Are you saying it's ugly?" said Tatiana defensively.

"I ain't saying shit. But maybe that's the reason."

"And I thought I was fly today. I guess Tati told me" said Tatiana playfully. Chris told John he would be outside he took Natalia in his arms next door to the music store. The heat was unbearable today and the store had a crowd of randoms trying to soak in the air conditioning. Chris placed Natalia down as he looked over the selection of rap music. The bell chimed welcoming new customers as they piled in. A group of guys walked over to Chris' aisle, one of them distracted by his phone, almost bumped into Natalia. She clutched on to Chris' pants. He looked down picking her up. The guy looked up. "I apologize. My bad." He replied to Chris' piercing glare. His friend looked over at Chris eyeballing him as if they had met before. "There a problem?" said Chris bluntly.

"Nah, ain't no fuckin' problem." Said the friend his voice raised. Chris' phone vibrated in his pocket. He pulled out his phone, he put up his finger to the guys face. "I'll handle your fuck ass in one second. He answered the phone. Yo Syd, I'm gonna hit you right back."

"Let's take this shit outside pussy." Shouted the friend.

"Baby, where are you?"

"Next door." Chris hung up the phone picking up Natalia, heading to the door. "Nigga, what's good? I'll be outside." The store clerks had become quiet watching the spectacle about to ensue. Chris stepped outside, he placed Natalia down taking off his chain. Sydney came running out of Reign. "Baby, what is going on?" she grabbed his arm. He tossed his chain and phone in Sydney's hand. "Get Tati, while I 'roc this nigga."

"Baby, let it go. He's a non fuckin factor. Why even waste your time on a bum nigga." She picked up Natalia placing Chris' items in her purse. The man and his crew stepped outside. Sydney looked over at the guy, he looked as if he was a nickel and dime hustler. He was wearing a dingy white shirt and dirty faded jeans, dirty white chucks on his feet. "What's good pretty nigga?" said the guy as he stepped out the store taking off his shirt. The minute his shirt hit the ground Chris rushed him. Chris threw a haymaker knocking him to the ground. Chris immediately began kicking him in the face as he bent down pummeling him with blows. Sydney screamed trying to shield Natalia's face. She walked back in Reign. Natalia began to cry, thinking Chris was hurt. Hearing the commotion John ran out of the store. He saw Chris towering over the man, blood all over the pavement. John pulled Chris off of him. "Fix your fuckin' face nigga. You leaking! Next time you'll watch your fuckin' mouth in these streets, pussy!" Chris replied with a smile. On lookers stood in disbelief some filming the fiasco.

"Fuck you bitch." He replied as he spit blood out of his mouth. Chris jumped free from John's hold. He threw a right hook to the chin, which made a loud crack. The man fell to the ground, he was out cold. Chris continued to kick him, John grabbed him again finally getting him off the man's lifeless body. John pulled Chris into the shop. Sydney had placed Natalia in her playpen, she walked over to Chris. "What the fuck is wrong with you?"

"Syd, not now. Don't come at me with the bullshit." He took off his bloodied shirt.

"You let some pussy ass, bum nigga make you lose your cool and make a fool of yourself in front of everyone. You are better than this dumb shit! In front of your child, what were you thinking?!"

Chris walked away from her ignoring her complaints. He went to the bathroom wiping his face as he walked out he stumbled into Tatiana. "Are you okay?" she replied with a look of concern on her face.

"I'm fuckin' good." Sydney grabbed Natalia's bag and Natalia. "We are out of here. I can't believe you just did that."

"Why the fuck you dwelling on shit? I beat that pussy nigga's ass, now shut the fuck up about it."

"Chris, you know what. Fuck you. I'm out of here before you start talking to me like you don't have any fucking sense." Sydney stormed out of the store Natalia on her hip. She strapped Natalia in and sped off down the street. John walked over, "What happened man?"

"Pussy ass nigga walked in the store, first off almost walked over Tubby. Then nigga start talking reckless out his mouth, I had to school that nigga real quick."

John laughed. "Man, I saw people running over there and screaming. I was like what the fuck goin' on." John was a little shook he had never seen that side of Chris, as much as they joke around, John thought that Chris was going to kill that man. He definitely saw boss man in a new light. The store phone rang Chris already knew who it was. He walked back to the office. "What up Pop." He answered.

"What happened?"

"I'm good. I had to show this clown I'm not to be fucked with."

"You shouldn't even be concerning yourself with the opinion of fuckin' sheep. Mario is a small time, bitch ass clown. Why would you even be wasting your fucking energy on a bitch like that?

"I don't give a fuck who he is. You not gonna disrespect me."

"Yea... but..."

"Fuck that nigga. You come at me I'm gonna make sure you never forget that shit. I don't need you lecturing me and shit right now."

"Chris. Calm the fuck down! Listen, to what I'm saying?! You got bigger shit to be worrying about then some pussy nigga feelings. That pussy ass nigga talking about pressing charges and shit. Do you need that type of fuckin' heat on you? That nigga press charges and shit and what if you looking at a bid? You want to miss out on Tubby life over some fuck nigga?"

"Nah, of course not, pop. You right." Chris replied wiping his face. He thought over his actions, definitely wasn't the move he put Natalia in danger over some lame nigga. It had always been an issue for him to control his anger. He had to find a median. He had gotten lost in his own feelings that he forgot about Preme being on the phone. "I mean sometimes you have to fall back on this bullshit and petty shit. You feel me? Do you see me worrying about these petty ass niggas while I count my millions?"

Chris smiled. "I feel you pop."

"I'll see you tomorrow. Don't worry about this shit it's handled."

"A'ight." Chris hung up the phone. He stared at Natalia's picture on his desk. He was actually embarrassed fighting in front of her that was not the image he wanted her to have of him. He got up from his seat, he went into the closet placing on another shirt, walking to the storage room. Tatiana was in the back getting cleaning supplies. "You okay?"

"Yea, I'm just a little vexed I let that pussy take me there."

Tatiana leaned against the boxes, listening to him. "You know some niggas only understand getting touched. I heard people outside say he always ran his mouth, I bet next time he'll think twice." She replied with a smile. Chris picked up a bottle of Lysol.

"Yea, but my kid was out there. I could've took that shit different. That nigga could've pulled out on me and my kid." She nodded her head seeing his dilemma.

"I feel you. But, baby your always gonna have haters. You're young, you got paper, and you're sexy its always going to be some bottom nigga trying to get at you. May not have been the place... but shit happens. You are in control of your actions whether right, wrong and indifferent. The value in it all is the lessons we learn along the way." Chris nodded his head as they both left out of the room. Chris stopped by the mirror on the wall. "Yo, thank you for spitting a little knowledge to me."

"You're welcome. I mean when people going thru situations the last thing you want is to have someone adding more gas to the fire. Just making sure you were good." She patted him on the back.

"So... you think I'm sexy? He looked over at her. I knew it everybody love the kid." He gripped his chin admiring his reflection. He smiled showing his infectious bright smile and dimple. "You're a'ight." Said Tatiana dryly as she walked away she bit her lip.

At home Sydney had made Natalia a quick dinner and was watching television. She was still furious about Chris' actions today. Her phone binged alerting she had a text it was Tori telling her that their flight was coming in at nine am. Sydney told her that she would pick them up and she was excited to see them. Natalia was done with her dinner she was falling asleep in her high chair. Sydney cleaned up the kitchen, carrying Natalia upstairs for a quick wash up. Natalia woke up, Sydney decided to read her a book. She placed Natalia in their bed and changed into her own pajamas. Natalia laid in her arms looking at the pictures as she read her a book in Spanish.

"La princesa con la hermosa voz" she said out loud she heard Chris coming up the stairs. He approached the door, hearing Sydney from the stairs. "I never knew you speak Spanish fluently?"

"Really? I speak Spanish, Portuguese and French. And so will Tati." Natalia was now sleeping holding on to Sydney's shirt. Chris looked over at her, then to Sydney. "Syd..."

"Not now, Chris. Let me put her to bed and we can discuss this." Chris picked Natalia up out of Sydney's arms, she rested her head on his shoulder. He carried her to her room, tucking her in and kissing her face. She smiled in her sleep as he looked back at her before turning on the nightlight. Sydney was sitting up on their bed when he walked back in. "I don't want to talk about today. Because all you are going to do is get me upset again and we are going to argue. So let's drop it." Chris walked over to the bathroom stripping off his clothes. He took a quick shower, once done walking out to the bed in his boxers. "So, are you going to teach me Spanish?"

"You don't know any?"

"I know a little. I always wanted to learn, you know just in case ever have a situation go down."

"What do you mean?"

"When my mom was murdered, they contacted my family in Peru. They didn't know enough English, something got crossed up and I ended up in the boys home. That part of the story never made sense to me, but I can't blame them, what did they really know about me."

"But, why didn't they get a translator?"

"We were poor. I don't think they really wanted to help me out. They thought I was fucked up anyway after what I saw, I'd never be shit. So, they said fuck it let me rot away in that hell hole." Chris laid across the bed. Sydney looked over at him. "If you're willing to learn I will teach you. Are you watching Tati Friday?"

"Well, who else going to watch her?" Chris replied sarcastically.

"I'm only asking, before I get my plans set up for Friday. Are you taking Tati to work with you tomorrow?"

"Pops is taking Tubby tomorrow to visit her grandma."

"In Fort Lauderdale?"

"Yea. He's going to have her all day. I told you that."

"Well, have you packed a bag or anything for her?"

"Nah, he said that he will buy her all new shit and didn't need a bag. I'll bring the diaper bag and that's it."

"The girls are flying in tomorrow and I wanted them to see her."

"So, I guess you're not going to school tomorrow?"

"Nope. I'm playing hooky." She replied with a smile. Chris rolled over to her stomach. She massaged her fingers over his head, looking down into his face. "Why do I put up with your crazy ass?" said Sydney with a smile on her face.

"Because you love me, I'm your baby daddy and my pipe game crazy." She laughed out loud. She looked down at him kissing his forehead.

"I can't stand your cocky ass sometimes. Are you mad you can't go to the concert?"

"I mean I would have liked to go. But, I'm not vexed about having to spend the night with my baby. So, y'all have fun."

"That's very big of you. We need to start planning this wedding. At least have a date to work from."

"That's all up to you. You plan all that shit and just tell me where to be. I'm down for whatever you want to do."

"That's very sweet of you."

"I'm not an asshole all the time."

The next morning around seven am. Sydney woke up, pissed she had to be up this early. She put on Givenchy knit black biker leggings and black racer back tank which showed side boob, with Christian Louboutin Pigalle Ombre leather pumps she brushed her hair before quickly brushing her teeth. She heard Chris moving in the room he got up using the bathroom, before getting Natalia and taking her downstairs for breakfast. He made himself two microwavable sausage croissants and Natalia some French toast sticks which he also microwaved. He began cutting her food up when Sydney came down stairs. She looked over their food. "You didn't make any for me?"

"Nah, we had to fend for ourselves with the microwave jump-offs." Sydney laughed out loud.

"I'm sorry babe, I was going to make your breakfast. Chris looked over her outfit, realizing there was nothing covering her exposed side boob. Sydney walked over kissing Natalia's cheek as she sat in her high chair. She went over to the pantry grabbing a box of frosted flakes cereal. I don't need that anyway. I need to watch my weight."

"For what?" said Chris as he took a seat at the table.

"For Friday. I have this amazing dress and I need to make sure everything is where it needs to be."

"Oh yea." said Chris sarcastically. Chris dressed himself and Natalia, he received a text from Preme saying he was ready for Natalia to come by. Chris told him he would be by shortly. Sydney heard his conversation she went to Natalia kissing her and saying good bye. Her phone beeped saying that the girls had arrived she hurried out of the house, into the Range Rover on her way to the airport. Once Sydney arrived at their terminal, she pulled along the curb, seeing them huddled up with their luggage. She rolled down the passenger window. "What's good bitches?" "Syd!!" screamed Nadine. Sydney parked the car and popped the trunk getting out to greet them. Nadine was dressed in a beautiful floral print maxi dress, her hair was cut in a blond pixie cut. Which looked amazing on her bone structure. "Sydney, you look amazing! A baby where?" She hugged them all. Tori was in a RUN DMC shirt and denim shorts which barely covered her bottom, black Chuck's on her feet. They began to pile their things in the trunk as the security started to give them the side eye for their amount of time spent at the curb. Nadine looked inside the backseat. "Where is the baby?" "Oh, she is visiting grandpa today. But, I will make sure you guys meet her before you leave." As they were almost done loading their luggage in, Mercedes walked over. Sydney looked over at her still filled with rage after all this time.

"What the fuck is she doing here?"

"It's a'ight Syd. She's not going to try anything." Said Nadine.

"I told you, I didn't want her here." Sydney looked behind Mercedes seeing a woman peering behind her back. "Syd, this is Kiana."

"Hi, said Sydney dryly. She looked over the woman's physique she was brown skinned, five foot five, slender, Sydney guessed about a size four, her hair vixen sew in about twenty two inches and was dyed fire engine red. She was wearing a maxi dress and jeweled sandals on her feet. Look, I don't fuck with you! Said Sydney as she pointed at Mercedes. You are not going to be around my family or my house, and you're definitely not riding in my car."

"Really Syd? Whatever, I'll take a cab. It's not that serious."

"Let's go." Sydney walked around to the driver side. Everyone else piled in. Mercedes and Kiana walked back inside to get a rental car. Because if Sydney was going to be a bitch this whole trip they would definitely need their own ride. Tori hopped in the front seat and Nadine in the back. "This car is fly Sydney!"

"Thank you. I'm so glad you guys are here. It's been too long."

"I know. We need to get together more often."

"I can't believe Mercedes' bum ass is here. Did she really think I would let her be around my baby and my man? Bitch please."

Nadine laughed. "Syd, she's changed though. I'm not saying you should've welcomed her with open arms, I'm just saying that I don't think she would have tried anything with me here or with you."

"Nadine, I don't want to be cool with her. My new motto you burn me, fuck you I'm done. I'm done with that petty fake shit in my life."

"Well, excuse the hell out of me." said Nadine with a laugh?"

"What hotel are you guys staying at?"

"The Hilton Bentley S. Beach?" said Nadine as she looked up reservations in her phone.

"Yea, give me the address I think I know where that is. I need to type it in GPS." Nadine handed her phone to Tori who began to type it in the GPS. Once they arrived at the hotel, Sydney had valet to park her car. Once they were checked in and upstairs, unpacking their bags in their gorgeous two bedroom suite. She knew they had to spend a few coins on the room. It had an ocean view, and she immediately went over to the kitchen. "What would you guys like to do first?"

"Eat!" they both replied.

"Okay. Do you guys want to hit up a vendor or sit down and eat at restaurant?"

"It doesn't matter. I'm ready to hit the beach too."

"Oh, I have to go home and get my swimsuit on."

"Well, we are going to put ours on now." Sydney left their room and went out to the couch. Kiana and Mercedes had arrived and were checking out the suite. Mercedes took one glance at Sydney rolling her eyes, walking over to their room. Kiana walked over sitting beside Sydney. "Hi Sydney, I know you don't know me and all, but I understand you and Mercedes have some sort of unresolved beef."

"It's not unresolved. I just don't fuck with her."

"Well, I wanted to know if this week I would be welcome to go with you a few places."

"I mean, I don't have any beef or issues with you. I don't even know you. If you would like to come along you can come. But, I'm not taking Mercedes anywhere." Kiana nodded her head getting up going over to their room. Tori and Nadine walked out. "We're ready." Sydney stood up. "Let's go."

"You going?" Yelled out Tori to Kiana.

"No, I'm staying with 'Cedes."

They all walked out going down to valet to retrieve the car. Once in and on their way to Sydney's house. Nadine began to ask about the wedding proposal. "So, you never gave me the details on how Chris proposed to you?"

"Well, he took me out to this beautiful expensive restaurant. He had picked out my dress and shoes, and had a driver pick me up in Lambo. But after the dinner we went walking on the beach, and he said that he wanted to be with me and raise our daughter together forever. It was so sweet. He got down on one knee and proposed." Sydney stopped at the red light, placing her hand in the air so they could see her sparkling rock.

"It's beautiful Syd! You know he spent some coins on that!" Sydney laughed.

"I was speechless." They had reached the first gate leading into her community. There was an attendant at the gate he smiled seeing Sydney and opened the metal gate. As they proceeded down the winding road, Nadine and Tori gasped at all of the sprawling homes to the right and left of them. "These houses are like fuckin' mansions!" said Tori. Sydney pulled up to her house and quickly typed in the code, the metal gate opened. "Syd, this is your house? Shut up!" Sydney laughed. "This is our house" Nadine looked around at the beautiful columns which held up their beautiful palace. Tori looked around at the fleet of cars which sat in the driveway. The Mercedes G wagon, Lamborghini Aventador and Mercedes S class. Sydney parked the car going over to retrieve the mail from the mailbox. Tori and Nadine looked over the house. Sydney was definitely living the good life, she was set for life. Sydney opened the front doors and they proceeded into their immaculate home. "Sydney... this shit is gorgeous!"

"Thank you guys. I don't know if you guys wanted something to eat now, a snack or something. The kitchen is over there.

She pointed to her right. In the pantry should be any snack you can think of, thanks to my hubby. Make yourselves comfortable. I'm going upstairs to change." Tori and Nadine walked over to the kitchen. There was a group picture of them on the refrigerator door. Nadine took the picture down looking over their smiles. It was a selfie Sydney had snapped while they were in bed together one night watching a movie. Natalia in the middle, her wild curls everywhere. She had a smile on her face as she reached for the camera. Chris and Sydney smiled looking at her. Tori looked in thru the glass fridge door seeing the contents inside. "What the eff?" She reached in grabbing two Orange Gatorade drinks. She handed one to Nadine. They walked over to the pantry grabbing chips and cookies. They proceeded upstairs they walked over to Natalia's room. "Look at the baby's room? My shit wasn't this fly when I was growing up. I see why Syd ain't trying to come back anymore. "The baby has a walk in closet!" They walked into her closet which was the size of a bathroom. Her shoes lined the shelves, by designer. Nadine looked over the tags that were still on her designer clothes. Dolce & Gabbana, Versace Junior, DKNY, Kate Spade and Ralph Lauren to name a few. They left out of Natalia's room heading over to the double doors at the end of the hall. Nadine knocked softly. "Come in." Tori and Nadine walked in. "This house is everything Sydney. Natalia's room is bananas! Adopt me."

Sydney laughed from the bathroom. "Thank you." Tori sat on the ottoman at the edge of the bed. Nadine laid across their king bed. "Ah, this bed is so soft." Sydney walked out of the bathroom in a nude colored string bikini with pink trim and strings. They looked over her body. "Wait a minute bitch. You getting a little round back there?"

"Really?" Sydney looked back at her little apple bottom.

"Yea, you've got a little junk in your trunk now. Don't tell me you got some shots down here." said Tori.

"Girl, please. If I had got shots my ass would be bigger than this! This comes from eating and sexing my man on the regular."

Nadine burst into laughter. "I don't know if that was a little shade, but let me get off this regular sexing bed. But, you look good Syd. You've had a baby and you're still killing these hoes."

"I try to work out. But, I'm not gonna lie, since we've been here between classes and taking care of Natalia I don't have time. We are always on the go. Chris added a gym on to the house downstairs and do you think I step foot in there. Hell no." She grabbed a tunic out of closet. Which was pink and jeweled, she slid on Chanel sandals on her feet. Tori looked at the pictures of Sydney and Chris on her vanity mirror. She definitely felt some sort of way, she put her feelings on mute for the moment. Her phone rang on the bed in her purse, playing Beyoncé she smiled seeing Chris' face on her screen. "Hi baby."

"What's up? What y'all doing?"

"Getting ready to go to the beach and get something to eat."

"Oh okay. Tell them I said what's up."

"Chris says Hi." She said to them as she put the phone away from her ear. "Heyyy Hubby." Nadine replied. Tori replied hi as well.

"So, what are we having for dinner or are you bucking me tonight?" said Chris.

"I'm not bucking you, babe. We can have dinner what do you want to eat? When is Tati coming home?"

"He's gonna call me when they get back. Don't worry she's good. About dinner, I'm just messing with you. Have fun with your girls. I'll go over to the Jamaican spot and get some oxtails and rice. Maybe hit up Nick."

"Really Nick? Babe, you know I don't like Nick."

"Syd, I'll be on my best behavior. We won't get in any trouble." Said Chris being a smart ass.

"You tryin' to be funny Christian?"

"Why you always gotta call me by my full name?"

"That's your name isn't it? How late are you going to be out?"

"Not late. I'll call you. I love you."

"Love you too. Check on Tati."

She ended the call. They left out of the room downstairs and back into the Range. They decided on going to a Wingstop, everyone ordered lemon pepper wings, sweet tea and French fries. As they waited on their food to return. Sydney decided to get into their business and learn what has been going on with them. "So, what's going on with my girls? Any men in your lives?"

"Well, I'm taking a few classes trying to get medical assistant thing going. I currently work at the hospital as a registrar. I mean it pays the bills. I have a new boo I've been kicking it with."

"Oh okay. Is he cute?"

"Yea, he's cute. He's sincere. I mean he's been through some things but who hasn't. Yes, he in the streets on the grind. But, he's not taking that shit too deep you know. Some niggas be in that shit deep, he's trying to start a label and leave the streets alone." Said Nadine.

Sydney smiled looking at her friend. She reminded her of herself a year ago, defending her relationship to her parents on how Chris would change and he wasn't like everyone else. "You sound like me, talking about Chris." She finally replied.

"I love him Syd. We are going to do this I know it. He makes me laugh, he provides, I don't see myself with no one else."

"Wow. I'm happy for you. When can I meet him?"

"Soon… hopefully."

"And what about you miss silent. Said Sydney as she looked over to Tori. What's going on with you?" Their food came back and the waitress handed everyone their baskets.

"I'm just doing whatever. I'm not with one person in particular. I'm all about getting money these days, and I'm not going to work a nine to five to get it. So, I do fuck with a few dope boys and get money. It keeps my hair, nails and shoe game right so I can't complain."

"Really Tori? You hanging out with the hood niggas now what?!"

"Yea, what's wrong with it? You did it! Nadine is doing it."

"I'm not hating Tori, I'm just saying we are getting older and this fast life bullshit is not a game anymore. What is your plan for your future? What if they get cased up? What if they find out about each other?"

"Sydney, you are really taking this shit too deep. If anything goes down, I'll just move to a different nigga. I'm just sayin' if a nigga wants to spend checks on me why not?"

Sydney couldn't believe her friend. What happened to Tori her always opinionated, self-righteous bestie? She was shocked. She couldn't believe the things that were coming out of her mouth.

"Syd… don't stress over Tori she's stuck on this street life bullshit. I try to tell her, she's playing in a nasty game she don't want to caught up in. But, she's not hearing no one right now." Said Nadine as she bit into a wing.

"I don't appreciate you talking about me like I'm not sitting here. You two of all people have the audacity to judge me! Miss kingpin! This is my life and what I'm doing has gotten me an apartment, car and everything I want. I'm good. So enough about me. What is Chris doing?"

"He owns a high end clothing store. Which he is planning to expand. He saved up some money before he left the game and now we're set."

"So, he's completely out now?" said Nadine.

"Yes, he's done." Sydney sipped her tea. Tori rolled her eyes.

"Once a thug always a thug. It's still in him Syd. Believe me the first chance he gets, he'll be back. I can bet you a thousand dollars, he's not out yet."

"No, he's not. We have a daughter to raise. He knows better."

"Yea, knowing better and doing better are two different things. I'm telling you he is not out the game." Sydney rolled her eyes.

"What's good Tori? You seem like you have a problem with me or something?"

"I don't have a problem. I'm just talking with you, I'm just being real."

"I mean, I feel a lot of shade being thrown at me and I haven't done shit to you. I mean you don't hear me calling you a lazy ass bitch, because you'd rather lie on your back instead of making something out of yourself!"

"Really Bitch? We goin' there..." Nadine interjected. "Okay, guys stop. It's been a hectic morning, let's chill. We are best friends. Come on!" Tori rolled her eyes stuffing French fries into her mouth. Sydney looked over at Tori she had put on a few pounds, and was possibly a size ten. She couldn't believe the things Tori had said to her, they spoke on the phone all the time and everything was cool. What had changed? Sydney threw her napkin in over her half eaten food. "I will be in the car." "Sydney... wait." Said Nadine. Sydney threw up her hand exiting the building. Sydney's phone rang and it was Dana she told her to meet them on the beach. She said she was with Vani and they would be there shortly, they left outside heading to the beach. Once they arrived Sydney removed her tunic, spraying sunscreen all over her body. Nadine stepped out of the car looking over the sandy beach and palm trees. "It is beautiful here."

"I know! This was the first place Chris brought me when we arrived here. I was like I'm never leaving." Sydney pulled out the beach bag from the trunk with towels inside. They all walked over to the sand. Sydney found a good spot, handing them each a beach towel. Tori ripped off her tunic. "I'm going into the water." Sydney looked over at her muffin top which sat over her bikini bottom. Nadine looked over at Tori's body as well. She couldn't help but smile. "Bitch, you know you should've wore a one piece if you gonna be out here with your muffin top on display."

Tori laughed. "Bitch, I'm sexy. Don't hate." When she turned to run towards the water you could see the dimples and cellulite in her thighs jiggle as she ran. Nadine smiled taking off her top, grabbing Sydney sun screen and applying it to her arms. "What's up with Tori?" said Sydney.

"Girl, I don't know. Ever since you and Chris and that fight in Boston she's been bitter. I think she's mad because you chose Chris over her. She thinks that you moved here and forgot all about us."

"What?! But, I talk to her all the time. She's never said anything? I mean how fucked up is that you can talk to me on the phone but get here and want to act like a petty bitch?"

"That's what she told me. Maybe during this vacay y'all can get a resolution to this. I mean, because I would love for us all to be cool again. I mean, I'm a little in my feelings too. We are your best friends and we haven't seen you in almost two years."

Sydney looked at Nadine, had she been so consumed in her happy ever after that she neglected her squad who was there before everything. "I'm sorry Nadine. I mean I didn't mean anything malicious by it. When we moved here it was like we had to leave everything. I didn't mean to make you feel like I forgot about you. I'm sorry."

"Apology accepted. Now Tori on the other hand gonna take more finessing than that. You know that bitch can hold a grudge forever."

"Fuck her. It's too beautiful of a day to be stressing over her bullshit. I go thru bullshit every day with random hoes in the street do you think that I'm gonna waste my day entertaining hers. I'm going in the water. You coming?"

"What the hell." Sydney grabbed her iPhone snapping pictures of Nadine, and they took selfies together. Once near the water Sydney ran in getting completely wet. Nadine stood by dipping her foot cautiously into the water. Sydney ran over grabbing Nadine's arm. "Are you going to get in? or poke the water all day?" Sydney pulled her in throwing her into the water. Nadine screamed like a five year old as the cold water hit her body. "You bitch!" screamed Nadine as she got up chasing Sydney around the beach. Dana and Vani showed up. Vani was in a red string bikini which showed everything with its mesh material. Dana was in a black one piece, which had mesh material down the center and the back was completely out. Sydney and Nadine stopped chasing each other heading over to the towels where Tori had rested. "Hey Syd. We figured you were on this end." Sydney walked over hugging them. "So, my Miami girls meet my Connecticut besties. This is Tori and Nadine and this is my cousin Vani and Dana." They all waved at each other.

"So, where is my muffin?" said Dana.

"She is with her grandpa today."

"Awww... so how do you ladies like it here so far?"

"This weather is everything!" said Nadine.

"Yea, we have to show you guys all the spots and get you guys fucked up one good time while here. Gotta make it quick though Sydney may be on punishment after concert tomorrow." said Vani with a smile.

"Bitch, I hate you." She threw sand on her and they all began chasing each other in the water and on the sand. Tori had stayed on the towels and took a nap. Once it had gotten late and they were pruning they decided to call it a day. Sydney and the others had come over snapping pics of Tori sleeping. She woke up after the flash kept going off. "Really guys?"

Tori got up pulling her bikini bottom out of her ass. Vani looked over disgusted. Everyone put their cover ups back on and decided that they would meet up at the hotel room for pizza and drinks later. Sydney said she would drop them off and go home to shower. Dana and Vani said they would come over as well. After Sydney dropped them off she went home to take a shower. She met Chris in the driveway. Chris got out of the car looking at her ass as it peeked from under her tunic. "Where you coming from?"

"The beach. I told you earlier." She walked over to him kissing his lips. He wrapped his arms around her body, pulling up her tunic looking over her round derriere. He smacked her ass. "Ouch! What are you doing?" she replied as she tried to pull down her tunic.

"I needed to see what Miami saw today."

"I'm going to take a shower."

Chris opened the door. "You going to take one with me?"

"No, because I have somewhere to be in an hour."

"How you goin' to tell me no?" Chris picked her up throwing her over his shoulder. Sydney yelped. "Baby... you make me sick!" Chris carried her to the bathroom, he turned on the water. Sydney stripped off her bikini hanging it up on the shower door. Chris looked over her naked body, soon following her into the shower. Sydney was under the shower head scrubbing her body in soap. Chris came over kissing her neck and ear. "Baby... stop." Said Sydney softly.

"Why?"

"Because you're going to get me started and I'm going to have to leave."

Chris chuckled. "Well, come in at a decent hour. So, I can have you." He looked into her eyes kissing her lips.

"Aww... you want to be with me tonight?"

"I want to be with you every night. But for some reason you like getting me vexed."

"You're cute when you're mad" She placed the soapy sponge over his dick massaging it up his stomach and chest.

"Stop playing Syd. If you not trying to go there tonight". She moved her hand with a smile. "What time are you coming home?" she replied.

"I don't know. Call me." Once out of the shower they both got dressed in Balmain. Looking over each other's outfits to see if they approved, in ten minutes Sydney was out the door. She placed her hair up in a top knot and diamond hoop earrings in her ear. She called Nadine's phone once she was out of their community. "Did you guys get any drinks?"

"Yea, we um hit up this little store and got some soda, vodka and Myx moscato. So you can bring whatever."

"Okay, I'm gonna call Vani and see what they got."

"Okay. See you soon."

Sydney ended the call immediately dialing Vani. "Hey, what did you guys get?"

"We're at pizza hut. We got four large pizzas, some wings and cinnamon sticks."

"Damn, ya'll have gotten everything. What am I supposed to bring."

"Bring some cookies, chips and snacks."

"Okay, I'll stop by the store."

"Hey where are they staying?"

"Hilton Bentley, South Beach. I'll text you Nadine's number."

"Okay, I will call you when we get there. See you soon." Sydney headed towards local grocery store, Publix. She grabbed a shopping cart hurrying to the chips aisle. She picked up Doritos, Tostitos and Lay's chips with dip, she grabbed a few cases of soda. As she turned on to the cookies aisle, there was two women, early twenties talking loudly on the aisle. Sydney rolled her eyes, looking over the selection on the shelves. "So, have you seen Tatiana's new boss?"

"No bitch, when I went in there they were saying he was gone for the day."

"Listen... he is so fuckin' fine." Sydney glanced over at the girls, now listening in to their conversation.

"Is he black?"

"Girl, don't play with me you know I don't fuck with white boys. But, he mixed, I think."

"Oh okay. Everybody is always talking about Reign and him."

"He is fine. He got pretty ass eyes, tatted up and he a little muscular. He's sexy. I would definitely give him a taste and his lips…"

The friend laughed grabbing a pack of Oreo's. "So who is he with messing with?"

"He got a baby mama or whatever, they say. They said she's a basic bitch. She is not all that." Sydney looked over herself and then looked over at them. She couldn't hold it in any longer. One of the girls pointed to Sydney. "Is there a problem?" shouted the loudest girl.

"Actually, yes. Sydney walked over to them. The loudest folded her arms over her chest standing defensively. Sydney approached them with a smile on her face. "Hello, my name is Sydney. She slicked up her tresses with her left hand showing her rock on her finger. I overheard you talking about me and my man. Just for the record, I'm more than a baby mama, I am his one and only. Basic, I won't even address because you're wearing what I picked out honey. I can buy your life with my bag alone. So, for future reference you and all the other whore store groupies can know that Chris is mine, he's not checking for you thirsty bum ass hoes. This will be my last time addressing you hoes, don't come for me. She waved her finger from side to side. Now that I've given you a warning, carry on with your shopping and have a blessed day." Sydney picked up a package of Golden Oreo's walking off the aisle. The two women stood stunned that Sydney had come over to them.

"Fuck that bitch!" the loudest finally blurted out.

"See that's why you have to watch who the fuck you are talking about Erica. She's pretty though."

"I should've punched that bitch in her face."

Sydney left the store and was headed over to the hotel. She had valet to park the car and the doorman fetched help for the bags. Sydney tipped the man as she knocked on the door. Nadine came to help her bring the bags in. Tori had her Samsung Note attached to her Beats Pill playing her Pandora stations. Everyone was listening in to Vani's latest episode as she shouted into her phone. "You don't need to talk to me about shit! You wanted us to separate so it is, what it is. Stop fuckin' calling me with this bullshit!" Vani placed the phone on speaker. "A'ight Van. Let me hear you out with some nigga!" said Mark.

"And what? Me and Syd are going out with Yogi and his crew and ain't shit you can do about it."

"You going out with Yogi huh? Vanessa I will fuckin' body your dumb ass don't fuck with me."

"Bye, Mark." Vani hung up the phone. Nadine and Tori were speechless. Sydney smiled breaking the awkward silence. "I've already told your ass, I'm not talking to Yogi. I'm happy with my baby."

"Anyway, that's today. Let him be out with Nick tonight. You'll have a fit." Sydney hit her.

"Actually, he is out with Nick, and I'm fine." Sydney replied rolling her neck and snapping her finger.

"Wait, until he sees you at the club in your come fuck me dress."

"He's not going out tomorrow. He is watching Natalia. Besides, he'd start all types of shit if he saw my dress, which is why I'm getting ready at Dana's."

Everyone laughed. "Wait a minute Syd, don't have Chris crazy ass beating down my door." Mercedes and Kiana walked in. They waved at everyone before going back to their room.

"I can't wait for tomorrow night we are going to have so much fun!" said Sydney.

Mercedes listened from behind the door. "We are going out tomorrow night. I want to see if Syd can back up that mouth she's running." Said Mercedes with a mischievous smirk on her face.

Around two in the morning after they had finished off a bottle of vodka and wine, Sydney called Chris' phone it went to voicemail. Meanwhile, Chris and his boys were talking about the concert. Nick said he was going and that he wanted Chris to come. Chris had finally agreed and said that he was definitely going. Sydney looked down at her phone again, becoming furious that Chris wasn't answering her calls.

"What the fuck is he doing?" she called his number again. This time it didn't ring at all and went straight to voice mail, as if he declined the call.

"Uh oh, he bucking you Syd?" said Dana.

"Yea, and he's pissing me the fuck off." She got up from her seat walking over to the kitchen. Her phone rang she looked down at the screen seeing Chris' picture. "Hello?" she replied into the phone placing it on speaker.

"Yea. Where you at?"

"I'm still with the girls. What are you doing?"

"I'm over here chillin' with Nick. What up?"

"I just called you. Why didn't you answer?"

"I was doing something." Said Chris nonchalant.

"So, you ignored me?"

"Yo Syd I'm not about to get into this shit with you right now. What's good?"

"Whatever. Why couldn't you answer the phone?"

Chris sighed. "I didn't hear it."

"I thought you just said you were doing something. Which is it?"

"Syd, don't fuck with me."

"Are you on your way home?"

"Are you?"

"Don't be cute." Said Sydney snappily.

"Don't try to put on a show for your girls. 'cause we both know, what will be the end result of that. Only one of us gonna be hurt by it, and I'm advising you don't come at me with the bs tonight."

"Are you on your way home?!" said Sydney becoming annoyed with his attitude.

"Yea, I'm about to be heading home. I better see your ass there when I get there."

"Bye Chris." Sydney ended the call slamming the phone down on the counter. "He gets on my last fuckin' nerves sometimes!"

Vani sat up in the chair. "So, leave him." She replied half seriously.

"As much as he gets on my nerves. I love him. He's Natalia's father. I'd do anything for his punk ass." Nadine and Dana smiled. Tori got up from her seat. "Yea, you would do anything for that nigga."

"What are you saying Tori?"

"You know what the fuck I am saying. Don't act stupid!" Vani sat up, not liking the bass in Tori's voice. You could feel the tension rising in the room. The music stopped playing. "Tori... Chill." Interjected Nadine, grabbing her arm.

Tori shrugged her off. "No, fuck that. Let me tell them about how much she loves that nigga and just how far her fuckin' stupid ass is willing to go for him. Tori turned to the others. Syd moved to Boston to be with that bastard and his brother didn't like her, or the way he had been spending too much time with her. So, he tells Chris to stop fucking with her and he dropped her within the hour!" Dana and Vani looked stunned. Tori continued. "She had nothing! She called me to come pick her up after he hemmed her up or whatever. I drove all the way from Hartford to Boston, and they are arguing back and forth in the house. Chris tells Syd he doesn't give a fuck about her, calls her all types of bitches, hoes, and sluts." Sydney walked over tears forming in her eyes. "Why the fuck are you bringing this up?!"

"Because they need to know what you mean by, do anything for him! I get to the house, his homeboy is holding him from swinging on Sydney. We get all the bags to the car, Miss Sydney walks out the door…"

"Tori!" says Sydney.

Tori ignored continuing her story. "And shouts out fuck your mama! Well, everyone knows that the jack ass found his mother's dead body, so he has issues with that. He ran behind her grabbing her by the hair and sat on top of her pounding her. Me, being a good friend I tried to help her. This nigga hit me with a gun knocking me the fuck out. He had the gun pointed to the side of her head as he sat on top of her body!"

"Chris, pulled a gun on you?" said Dana, looking over at her friend.

"Yea and he left her with a busted lip and broken nose. Someone was too scared to go to the hospital or to police, so she hid at my house for weeks. This nigga has threatened to kill her, he's beat her and choked her. He didn't even claim Natalia at first! And she chose him over a person she's known over ten years, to some pussy she had only known a few months!"

Sydney couldn't hold back any longer, the tears began to stream down her face.

"You didn't have to bring this shit up! How dare you bring my child into this! Fuck you!"

"Bitch, shut up. You were dumb then and you're just as dumb now. He's not going to change! You're living some stupid ass fantasy."

Sydney walked over to Tori's face wanting to rip her eyes out. Dana grabbed Sydney. "Don't you ever talk about my family! You are just jealous because I'm fuckin' fabulous and you're a fat ass basic bitch! You have no man, no job you don't have shit!"

"Fuck you!" shouted Tori. Sydney reached over Dana slapping Tori across the face. Tori reached over grabbing Sydney's hair. Vani jumped up. "Now wait a fuckin' minute." Said Vani with her finger in the air.

"Fuck her. She's always going to be Chris' dumb ass punching bag! And we all know, he was cheating on you with Roxy. So how fuckin' special were you?" Sydney reached onto the table she picked up a wine glass throwing it at Tori it missed hitting the ground. Vani grabbed Sydney. "Cuz, let's go. Cause this bitch keep popping off at the mouth, I'm about to pop her in it."

"What's up? You can get it too? I'm not worried about your ass either!" shouted Tori.

Sydney wiped her face. "Fuck you Tori, You fat ass ugly bitch. You're mad because I'm happy and I have a family, living the good life."

"You don't have shit. You may fool these bitches but I know you. You crazy bitch was jealous of your own daughter. Yea, you tell them that you were mad because Chris was spending time with the baby than you. Psycho bitch!" Vani finally got Sydney out of the suite to the elevator.

"I hate her! I don't want her anywhere near my family." Valet went to get her car.

"Syd, don't trip over that stupid bitch. Mark pulled a gun on me and I chose to be with his stupid ass. That's your business not hers to be discussing in front of everybody. She lucky I didn't put my hands on her ass." Dana caressed Sydney's back she felt so bad for her all of her secrets revealed and put on display. Yes, she couldn't believe some of the things Tori revealed, but this definitely wasn't the place. "Are you good Sydney?" said Dana.

"I'm great. I couldn't feel better." Said Sydney as she wiped her face one last time applying lip gloss to her lips. Sydney got behind the wheel of her car. Vani walked over to her window.

"You want me to follow you home?"

"I'm fine." She smiled one last time before speeding off into the night. On the drive home she thought about when Chris jumped on her in Boston. She thought back to the time she came to New York while pregnant and he stripped her clothes off thinking she was wearing a wire. She began to cry. It hurt to think about all the things Chris had put her through. The women, the insults, and the fights all played in her mind like a montage. She sobbed the whole way home. Once home she pulled into the garage. She walked up the steps and into the house. She heard the television playing in their bedroom. Sydney walked over to one of the guest rooms downstairs falling asleep.

The next morning around noon, Sydney woke up confused to where she was. She looked around the room realizing she was home. She immediately thought about what Tori had said. She looked up at the door, seeing Chris standing inside the doorway. "You didn't want to sleep with me?"

"I'm going through something. Not today."

"What's going on? You don't want to talk about it with me?"

"No, I don't." she got out of bed in her clothes from yesterday walking past Chris in the doorway. She went up to their bathroom to take a shower. When she came out she put on a tan BCBG tunic dress and a pair of tan leather Christian Louboutin Wedge sandals. Sydney looked at her phone she had four missed calls. Dana, Vani and Nadine. She called Vani back.

"Good afternoon. How are you?" said Vani.

"I'm still pissed."

"Syd, fuck her. She's just a jealous bitch, because you have a man and family. If she had a man she'd know what it feels like to choose your nigga over some pussy!" Sydney laughed out loud.

"Leave it to you. To make me laugh today. I needed it."

"I mean, if you want me to beat that bitch ass for you. I'm down for it. You just have my bail money."

Sydney laughed again. "No, I'm good. Can you do my hair today?"

"Of course. Come thru around four-thirty. I'm booked all day. Everyone going to that concert."

"Well, I have to pick up my dress and I'll be by there."

"Okay, see you later girl."

Reign was packed everyone trying to get an outfit together for the concert. John was constantly bringing boxes out the back to restock items, Tatiana was swamped at the register. Chris came in through the back door, he walked up front to see the crowds. He immediately saw Tatiana at the register. She was wearing a sleeveless bodysuit, revealed side boob, tucked inside of a bandage skirt, Louboutin pumps on her feet. Her hair was slicked back in a ponytail which accentuated her face. Chris walked over to her. "What up Tati?"

"Hi Chris." She replied with a smile, glancing over to him as she quickly handed the customer their black gift bag. Chris looked over her outfit. "You look good today. I like that." He replied with a calm, which made Tatiana blush.

"Thank you." She finally replied. The register was clear she picked up the gift bags from the floor. Chris walked out to the floor to greet the customers. He walked over to John who was restocking shirts on a front table.

"What up Chris? You going to that concert tonight?"

"I don't know yet."

"We all going, from the store. You should come out. You haven't been out in months, nigga."

"I know." Said Chris as he helped John place the items on the table.

"Tatiana going to take my sister with her and her home girls."

"Oh, Tati going out tonight?" said Chris with a smile. Tatiana walked over to where they were, hearing her name being brought up. "What was that?" said Tatiana her hand placed firmly on her hip.

"I said, I didn't know you were going out tonight." Said Chris.

"Yea, I told you I like Bundles. Besides they came thru here this morning and gave me two backstage passes. They said they're looking for the best green in the city. So I told them I knew someone..." she smiled at him.

"Who says I have green?"

"Anyway... Here is the number for road manager, or you can come backstage with me and possibly deliver it?"

Chris smiled. "I don't do business like that shorty. You tell them to meet up with my man and can get that setup for them."

"So, are you going to come backstage with me?"

"I mean, yea, I'll go backstage with you. Just don't be all on me, I mean I know I'm fly and shit." he replied with a smile.

"Whatever, Chris!" She replied as she hit his arm walking away. Once she was out of view John walked over to Chris.

"So... um, what Syd gonna say about this shit?"

"Syd, don't know I'm going. If anything, she gonna be tryin' to buck me anyway. I'm not worried about Syd."

John laughed. "So you got this all figured out?"

"Nothing to figure out. I'm the fuckin' prince of the city, show these fuck niggas a day in the life. n'ahmean." Chris replied with a smile.

"Welcome back playboy." John saluted Chris as they looked out the front window of the store. Tonight was going to be epic.

At the hotel, Tori was in Mercedes' room talking about last night. Mercedes wanted all of the juicy details.

"So, you fought her last night?"

"Yea, we threw a few hands. I'm just sooo sick of her and Chris bullshit! She acts as if our lives are to be on hold for Chris. She hasn't sent us one picture, selfie nothing and the baby is damn near two!"

"Well, why didn't you tell her that?"

"I was drinking and the shit went completely left. My anger got the best of me and I wasn't able to say everything I wanted 'cause she got to talkin' reckless and I lost it."

"Are you going to be friends with the bitch?" said Mercedes.

"I don't know. Right now, if the bitch needed air I'd tell that hoe to die." Said Tori with a laugh.

"You know Syd is on this power trip because she think she's living this grand fuckin' fantasy and no one can tell her shit."

"I don't understand why y'all hate her though. She's pretty and she seems cool though." Said Kiana.

"Girl, you new. Fuck Syd! Wait, until you see her man, you won't be thinking her petty ass cute then." Said Mercedes. Tori looked over to Mercedes realizing they did not share the same beef. Tori could give two fucks about what Chris looked like. She hated him, and she hated him for what he made of Sydney. Mercedes on the other hand hated Sydney for having what she wanted, and that wasn't cool with Tori. Tori walked back over to her room, Nadine was picking up their clothes.

"I can't believe you exploded like that last night?"

"She pissed me off Nadine! She bucks me all the time and now she wants us to kiss her ass 'cause she is marrying that asshole. Fuck him! Fuck her!"

"First of all, how can you blame Chris? Maybe it's Sydney that didn't want to keep in touch with us. I mean we both know Sydney and when she wants to do something she is going to do it. If she wanted to keep up with us, she would've. Chris is not with her twenty four seven. Only takes a second to send a text. I mean if anyone should be mad it should be me. Sydney hasn't spoken to me in months! She speaks to you. I don't get shit! All I'm sayin' is on both ends its childish. To expose her dirty laundry like that was bullshit."

At the salon Vani was wrapping up her client when Sydney walked in. Sydney walked over to Dana's station since she was free. Dana got up walking over to hug her. Dana had felt horrible about how everything went down last night.

"Hey Syd. Where's my baby?"

"With her grandpa."

"Look, I just wanted to tell you, what your friend said last night, doesn't mean shit to me. I don't look at you any different and I've got your back boo."

"Thank you Dana. That means a lot to me, right now." Sydney hugged Dana.

"So, I know you gonna let me hook those nails up with real quick?"

"Yes. Are they free?"

"Don't be cheap boo. We know your man Mr. Cash don't do me like that."

"But, that's not me. That's him." Said Sydney with a smile.

"You know you tryin' it but for you, I will do it for fifteen. The only reason I play your little game 'cause you my girl." Sydney laughed out loud sitting down at her station.

Around seven that night Chris and Tatiana began to close up the store. Chris closed the shutters, locking the front door. "So where am I going to meet you?"

"I'll meet you out front. You won't be able to miss me."

"A'ight. I'll be up there around eleven. I guess I will see you then." She replied with a smile. They headed towards the back door. Tatiana grabbed on to his shirt as he prepared to turn the lights off. He looked back at her, clutching on to his shirt. "I know you're going to turn the lights off and I'm not hurting my knee again." Chris smiled flipping the switch. By the time they reached the back door, Tatiana's breasts were pressed into his back. The scent of his cologne sent a warm sensation through her body, he smelled so good. Chris opened the door the light hit their face, ending her fantasy. "A'ight Tati." Said Chris as he walked over to his car. "See you soon... Chris." Chris slid in behind the driver's side waiting on Tatiana to start up her car and drive away before he left. He called Preme to check on Natalia. He said that she was fine and that they would be back on Saturday. Chris headed to find him something to wear for tonight. As he headed to Bal Harbour shops his phone rang loudly. He looked down seeing Sydney picture on the screen. "Yo."

"Hi baby. What are you doing?'

"Stopped by Bal Harbour real quick. What's good?"

"Oh, I hadn't spoken to you all day. Just wanted to check on you see how you were."

"Well, earlier you had an attitude and said you didn't want to talk to me. So, I figured I'd let you do you today, instead of beefing with you."

"I'm good. I had got into a huge argument last night with Tori. She brought up things from the past... and things went left shortly after that."

"She brought up what?" Chris parked the car getting out walking inside.

"About me and you, Boston. She just aired our dirty laundry to everyone."

Chris stopped in his tracks. "What she say?"

"She was calling me stupid for staying with you. After you pounded and pulled a gun on me. She was talking about how you didn't claim Tati at first, and you don't care about me. I mean I can't lie I was in my feelings about it."

"Why she fuckin' worrying about what the fuck we do? Bitch, need to watch her fuckin' mouth."

"I don't know, where it came from."

"You tell that stupid bitch anything she got to say about me and mine, she know where the fuck I'm at. I don't appreciate her telling niggas our fuckin' business."

"Baby, she is just jealous. Don't worry about it. I'm over it now."

"She going out with you tonight?'

"Probably not with me. But, she'll be at the club."

"I don't like that disrespectful ass shit she tryin' to pull. I'll handle that bitch."

"Babe, it's okay, it's handled. I'm on my way home now. When are you coming home with Tati?"

"I'll be home in an hour."

"Okay, love you."

"Love you too."

Chris arrived home an hour and a half later. Sydney was downstairs in the kitchen eating a quesadilla. Chris came in taking his bags upstairs to the closet before coming over to her. He took a piece off her plate eating it. "What up?" He replied as he kissed her cheek.

"Hey, where's Tati?"

"Oh, they are on their way he said."

"Okay, is she good?"

"Yea, I just spoke to them. She's fine." Sydney looked at him as he took over her plate eating the remainder of her food. She looked at his lips as the cheese dripped off of them. She then thought about what Tori said last night. Sydney immediately thought of his lips kissing someone else, her blood began to boil thinking of sharing Chris with someone else.

"Christian... Chris looked over at her confused as if he was caught in the act. Were you cheating on me with Roxy?"

"What?!" said Chris defensively with an angry smirk on his face.

"Answer the question."

"Why you worrying about that old shit? The fuck this shit come from?"

"You cheated on me, didn't you? You fucked that nasty dirty bitch!" She pointed her finger in his face.

"Syd that shit was a long time ago. Before Tati and all that! Who told you that? That stupid bitch?"

"It doesn't fuckin' matter!" shouted Sydney angrily.

"I want to know why the fuck they spreading old shit about me."

"What fuckin' difference does it make? It's the truth! Who's to say you're not fuckin' one of your whore store groupies!"

"And if I am? What the fuck you gon' say you leaving? That's all I hear, you leaving, you done." Said Chris mocking her.

"Fuck you! You lyin' cheating ass bastard!" she got up from the barstool, throwing the plate at the ground. It shattered on the floor. She stormed upstairs to their room slamming the door.

"That's what the fuck we gon' do is break shit. Huh?" Chris grabbed the cup off the counter throwing it to the ground, he grabbed an expensive dish off the counter throwing it to the ground. "Ain't this what you wanted Syd? For me to get vexed and act a fuckin' fool? Huh?" he walked upstairs to their bedroom. Sydney was in the closet packing her bag, Chris came into the closet. "I have not cheated on you since we've been engaged Syd!"

Sydney clapped her hands together sarcastically. "Bravo! So that means before then you were fuckin' any and everything else?"

"You know what Syd, fuck you. I'm not arguing with you over this shit! You want to act like a bitch, fuck you!"

"Don't argue." She closed up her Louis Vuitton duffel, walking past him. She headed down the stairs. Chris walked over to the top of the stairs.

"Where the fuck you going?" said Chris.

"Out. To show my tits and ass. Maybe someone else will appreciate it!"

"Oh word. Chris smiled. Show ya' fuckin' ass Syd."

"I will. Fuckin' bastard!" she shouted as she left out the front doors. Chris walked back into their room furious he threw the pictures down from their closet island. He walked down to the pantry pulling out bottles of alcohol. D'usse, Grey Goose and Remy Martin. He took a sip of each before heading upstairs to the shower, once out he stood in the closet in a pair of boxer briefs and wife beater. He looked over his clothing selection, feeling a buzz from his cocktail. He took another sip from the Grey Goose bottle. He settled on a black Givenchy black star shirt, Givenchy black pants and the Tyson Black Givenchy sneakers. He placed a dark pair of matching aviator frames over his now red eyes. Chris walked over to his jewelry drawer. He picked out two diamond necklaces and bracelet, switched out his watch. He glanced over at his reflection in the mirror. "Damn, I make this shit look good."

At Dana's condo, everyone was drinking as they got ready, applying makeup and accessories. Sydney had hogged Dana's bedroom and locked the door, so she could get dressed alone. Dana was wearing a black satin romper with wing shaped arms and v neck opening in front which exposed her breasts which sat up high with help of her push up bra. She pulled the short bottom from her thighs placing her wedge shoes on her feet. Vani was wearing a tan thin strapped dress which exposed side boob and barely stopped past her ass. The dress material was thin and her areolas and tattooed love below could be seen through the dress in the right lighting, Christian Louboutin crystal pumps on her feet. Nadine was dressed in a white crop top and bandage skirt, Jimmy Choo pumps on her feet. "Syd, everyone is ready let's go!" Sydney opened the room door a smile on her face as she modeled her ensemble as if she was on a catwalk. Everyone's mouth dropped, they were speechless. Her dress was made of a nude mesh material and crystals covered her over her breasts and the crystals gathered covering her vagina. The back was completely exposed with a small piece of crystal mesh covering her ass. Sydney had one of Chris' diamond chains with diamond cross pendant on her neck, her engagement ring was gone. "Check you out. This is the outfit it's cute, hoochie!"

"Thanks boo."

"You got a little dunk back there. You are definitely going to start some shit tonight!" said Vani with a smile.

"Whatever, I've always had a little something back there."

"That comes from Natalia and Chris." Said Dana.

"Fuck Chris!" said Sydney with a smirk of disgust on her face. She picked up her phone, and lipstick. "Let's go."

Everyone followed behind her piling into the Range Rover, not asking any further questions.

Chris was headed on his way to the club in his Lamborghini Aventador, black on black. He rolled up a blunt and smoked the entire way to the club. Sydney and her girls were already in the club and had a table downstairs. When they walked thru the club all eyes went to them, and Sydney's dress. Sydney ordered two gold bottles of Cristal. The bottle girl gave them each a glass, as she popped the cork pouring it into each of their glasses. Once everyone had theirs, they each put it in the air. "Here's a toast to my girls. The baddest motherfuckas in this bitch tonight! Love y'all. Salute!" everyone clinked their glasses before drinking.

Chris arrived out front around eleven forty-five. He parked up front diagonally, his car set up front as a display. He lifted up the door stepping out of the car. "Is that a Lambo?" girls replied immediately taking out their phones snapping pictures. Nick and Damien were parked up front in a Mercedes. Nick walked over to him after he closed down the door. "That's how you come thru, nigga! What's good?" They gave pound. Chris smiled he was definitely faded at this point. He smiled. "I always do it big right." Damien examined the tires.

"Yo, this shit clean nigga." Chris went around to the front of the car and got the bottle he had stored inside. They walked over to the line, all eyes on Chris with his bottle of Remy in hand. Almost ten people back in the line he saw Tatiana and John. He walked over. "What's good nigga?" said Chris as he dapped up John.

"I'm good. I see you doing it big tonight boss. I like." He nodded for him and his crew to come with him. He looked over Tatiana's outfit. She was wearing a pair of leather shorts which barely covered her ass with a Versace corset tank, Giuseppe Zanotti cut out over the knee boots, her hair up in a sleek ponytail. Chris smiled at her. "Check you out. You ready to go in?"

"I was waiting on my girls."

"A'ight. I don't have time for no lines ma. We can wait in my car until they come."

"Okay." Chris took her hand escorting her out of the line. He glanced a peek at her apple bottom as she swayed in front of him. She definitely had his full attention. Inside the club the dj continued to give shot outs over the music on the microphone. "We got the rich niggas in the building tonight. Bundles in the motherfuckin' building! We the best in this bitch tonight! We got the prince of fuckin' 305, Cash pulling up in a fuckin' Aventador tonight! Make some fuckin' noise for the kid!" He scratched in Drake's "Energy" as the crowd went crazy. Sydney sat drinking ignoring the dj and his shot outs.

Chris and Tatiana sat inside of his car. He took off his shades placing them on top of the buttons in his center console. "Damn, Tati you looking sexy tonight."

"Thank you. She replied with a blushing smile. You look sexy yourself."

"I do?" said Chris sarcastically with a smile.

"You know you do." She replied looking over his body. Chris began to fire up another blunt he had in the center stash. "You mind if I smoke?"

"No, you're good." He began to smoke his eyes low as he vibed to music on the radio. "You have very sexy lips." Said Tatiana as she looked into his face. Chris smiled at her, biting his lip. Tatiana didn't know if she had caught a contact, but it was taking everything in her not to rip off Chris' clothes and fuck him right there in the parking lot. She looked out the window her phone beeped. She answered the call. "Hey where y'all at?"

"I'm outside with Chris waiting on y'all. Well, meet us inside VIP. Bye." Chris put the blunt out, taking another sip of the Remy.

"What's good?"

"They'll meet us inside."

"We'll let's go. He placed his shades back over his eyes. He handed the bottle over to Tatiana. I know it's a little ratchet and shit, but you want a sip. I don't have a cup but I thought it'd be rude to drink in front of you."

She smiled taking the bottle up to her lips. Chris looked over at her smiling. Tatiana didn't want the drink, she only wanted to have her lips close to where his had previously been. Chris placed the bottle on the passenger floor after she finished. Chris stepped out of the car letting the door down, he waited on Tatiana to come around. She definitely felt a buzz. Chris smiled. "Come on over here, I'm not gonna bite." Tatiana walked close to him. Chris walked over to security. "How many Chris?" John came over to him. "These two for now." The bouncer allowed them in VIP, Chris let Tatiana walk in front of him. Chris walked upstairs seeing his crew already had a section. They began playing Future's Trap Niggas. Chris walked over to the table giving everyone pound again. "What's good nigga? You look lit."

"Nigga, I'm good. This is my home girl Tatiana." She waved hi nervously, feeling awkward being the only woman at the table of men. Tatiana sat down beside Chris. Nick looked over at her remembering her from Reign. "What you drinking on? Said Chris as he turned to her. The bottle girl came over, to take her order. Look Tati, you know money ain't shit to me. Get a bottle of whatever you want, a'ight?"

"Okay. Can I have a bottle of pineapple Cîroc please? With simply lemonade please. Thank you." Chris turned to Nick. "I didn't think you were coming out nigga." Said Nick.

"Well you know with me... always expect the unexpected." She came back with Tatiana's bottle. She mixed her drink, looking around at the room. When the dj switched the song to Meek Mill's "Check" She hopped out of her seat, she moved away from the guys she began to twerk her ass to the beat. She soon had everyone's attention. She walked over to the guys grabbing Chris hand to get up from his seat. As soon as she got him up she took him over to a wall and began grinding her body all over his dick. She placed his hands on her thighs as she bent her ass over. Downstairs, Sydney was on the dancefloor, dancing with Vani, when she felt a hand up her back. She cringed her neck turning around, seeing Yogi. She immediately checked her surroundings, startled.

"What up sexy?" said Yogi with a smile.

"Hi." She replied, which was more inviting than their previous encounters. He looked over her body, biting his lip.

"You look sexy as fuck tonight. Let me get another look at you. He placed her hand in his as he twirled her around. He immediately looked over to her empty finger. I see you not wearing the ring." He smiled as if in that moment he had won a first place prize.

Sydney smiled back at him. "Nope, I'm not." Vani looked over at them, sitting down on the seat taking in every moment of the conversation.

"You want another drink?"

"No, we'd like another bottle." Said Sydney with a smile.

"A'ight, come talk to me" Yogi led Sydney over to his section which was located closer to the speakers in the cut, it wasn't as nice as her area up front. As they made their way through the crowds, men attempted to grab Sydney's ass and arm, but Yogi wasn't having it, he quickly dismissed their advances. Once over to his section, Sydney looked over at his crew they all looked like grimey, cornballs she quickly changed her mind. "How about we go over to the bar, for my bottle? I will talk to you there. This is not my scene." Sydney knew she had Yogi wrapped around her finger, he would do anything she asked right now. He agreed walking her over to the bar. He made a spot for them in the crowd and he ordered her another gold bottle. Definitely wasn't in his budget, but if that was what it would take to get Sydney on his team he was down for it. As the bartender went to get the bottle, the dj switched the song over to Rico Love feat Plies "Drunk in love" remix to get the ladies to the floor. Sydney smiled throwing her hands in the air. She began to whine her body to the music. Yogi looked back at her giving her his full attention. "What?" she replied seductively. Yogi smiled. "Nothin' just watching you move." She smiled at him flirting, flipping her hair over her shoulders. "Watch this…" She placed her arms around his neck, placing her lips inches from his ear. She began to grind her chest against his before turning around poking her ass onto him as she grinded to the beat. Sydney touched her toes, while throwing her ass in a circle. Yogi couldn't help but grab her hips, she had every part of him at attention, and he had to have her tonight.

Meanwhile, upstairs Chris had Tatiana sitting on his lap. Her friends had come up and were mingling with Chris' crew, she grabbed his watch looking at the time. "I guess we can go backstage now."

"Let's go."

They walked backstage and they were greeted by a bouncer. Tatiana threw up their badges, he opened the door allowing them into Bundles' room. They were immediately greeted by the aroma of marijuana. The smoke filled the air. Bundles walked over to them, embracing them with a handshake. Chris smiled. "I see you got my delivery."

"Yea, good looking out my dude."

"This the best bud ever, n'ahmean! I heard you the prince of the city."

"Something like that." Said Chris nonchalant.

One of Bundles tour members walked over. "This the nigga that was out front in the Lambo."

"Word, that you?"

"Yea, but that's nothing. Just wanted to let you know I fuck with your music and shit. Take that delivery as a one-time welcome to my city gesture."

"Appreciate it. Yo, you have to come on stage with us son."

"A'ight, I'll come up for a second. But, that's not really my scene. Feel me?"

Tatiana nudged him to go on stage. "A'ight come up with us for one track." Said Bundles. Tatiana smiled, finally interjecting "Can we get some pictures with you?"

"Of course." Chris took a few with Bundles and then the three of them took a few for the club website. Chris was nonchalant the whole time as if he was unbothered by the whole meeting. But Tatiana knew he was gassed to be with one of his favorite emcees. They came bringing Bundles a microphone he began shouting into the microphone. "Is New York in the fuckin' house?! Miami what's good my g's! You could hear the crowd screaming hearing his voice. The music cued in as he stepped on the stage with his crew behind him. Women flooded to the stage, immediately placing phones and cameras in the air. Chris stood at the back of the stage a bottle of Remy in his hand. After three songs Chris was in a zone vibing with Tatiana. Sydney and her crew were at the front of the stage, Yogi not leaving her side stood behind her with his arms wrapped around her stomach caressing her as if letting everyone know she was his. "Ayo, before we go any further we got a special guest to show some love for! The dj stopped the music. Give it up for y'all mothafuckin' prince of Miami, showed us madd love tonight! We 'gon dedicate this next track to him. 'Cause no nigga in 305 fuckin' with him right now! Come up Cash. Help me out with this one my g." Tatiana smiled, as Chris walked up to the front of the stage the spotlight on him as the lights hit his face. He and Bundles gave pound, as Bundles handed him the microphone. The crowd went crazy as women snapped pictures of him, grabbing at his pants. Chris smiled.

"Listen… all you fuckin' crab ass niggas not seeing me. I does this shit! Get your fuckin' weight up niggas!" Bundles crew began laughing as Chris handed him back the mic as if stating he was done. Sydney in a zone realized she heard Chris' voice. She looked to the stage realizing Chris was standing center stage, bottle in hand, he was looking in the opposite direction. She immediately froze up. Vani who was standing a few feet away from her, leaned over. "What the fuck is Chris doing on stage with Bundles?"

"I don't know." Replied Sydney looking like a deer in headlights. Panicked and nervous she didn't know what to do. The beat cued in for Jim Jones "We Fly High" Chris placed his shades over his eyes. Bundles crew gathered around Chris as he went into his waist, he popped the band on his stack making it rain over the front row. The crowd began to scramble for the money. Chris smiled looking over the crowd. He immediately saw Vani in the front row, he scanned his eyes over who was standing beside her. His eyes immediately went to the mesh, jeweled revealing dress Sydney was dressed in. She and Yogi had moved back from the stage to blend in with the crowd. Yogi had Sydney wrapped in his arms as she grinded to the beat. Chris' eyes were glued to them, blood in his eyes, his high was gone. He turned around to leave the stage, Bundles' crew grabbed him to bring him back to the stage. Chris was furious. Sydney stopped dancing, when she realized Chris was no longer on the stage. She looked around the room, removing Yogi's hands off her body. "I have to go."

"Why? Because your pussy nigga in here?"

"Look, it was fun, but I don't want any shit tonight. He will definitely blow this bitch up."

"Fuck him. If you was fuckin' with ole boy you would've had your ring on tonight."

"Listen... I have to go, this is over!" Sydney quickly rounded up the girls leaving Yogi behind. They scurried out of the club. "Mercedes and Tori in here. What about Chris ass on the stage bitch?!"

"I don't even want to talk about that shit." Sydney walked through the crowd, guys grabbing at her arm. She brushed them off, trying to walk as fast as she could to the car. Yogi appeared again, he put his arms around her pulling her over towards his car. "Let me talk to you." She looked around seeing Vani on the other side of the car talking to his friend. Sydney walked with him to his car. He sat down in the driver's seat, sitting Sydney on his lap. "So, you never gave me, your number so I can get at you."

"Um..." said Sydney.

"How about Tuesday all of us go out to dinner? I'm trying to show you I'm not about games. Ever since I saw you in Walmart, I've been thinking about you. You fuckin' beautiful."

Sydney smiled at his compliment. He massaged his hand over her thighs. "We'll see..." said Sydney seductively.

"I want you Sydney." He rested his face on her arm kissing it. Sydney looked past him seeing that more people were coming out of the club, she got up from his lap. "I have to go." Yogi tried to pull her back to his lap. She resisted. "Vani, let's go!" Sydney panned the new crowd of patrons flooding the parking lot she saw Tatiana from Reign, she looked over her outfit, she had a smile on her face. "Me and Chris had soo much fun!" Nadine and Dana who had been chatting together, saw Sydney's facial expression as she looked at Tatiana, Dana came grabbing Sydney by the arm. "I'm so tired of these fuckin' hoes! Fuck you bitch!" Sydney yelled out her middle finger in the air. They had finally got Sydney over to the car, Dana realized Sydney was too intoxicated to drive she decided to drive them back to her home. Once at Dana's everyone piled in and began talking about what happened tonight. Everyone began to talk about Chris on the stage, Sydney was speechless.

She went into Dana's bedroom to change out of her clothes her cell phone rang loudly. She looked on the bed where her iPhone was, seeing Chris' picture on the screen. She answered the phone holding up her dress over her breasts. Before she could say anything, he interjected.

"Bring your ass outside." said Chris, his tone calm.

"What?"

"You heard what the fuck I said. Bring your ass outside." He repeated.

"I'm changing my clothes. No."

"Bring your ass out the fuckin' house or I shoot this bitch up."

"Okay, I'm coming." She pulled her dress back up over her body, she slid back on her shoes, walking out to the others who were in their pajamas.

"Where are you going?" said Dana.

"I'm going outside. Sydney replied nervously her voice shaking. Chris is here. Just listen out by the window please. Sydney walked out the front door the street was dimly lit. She walked over to the driver's side of the car, standing inches away from the window. She bent down at the window trying to see inside the dark tinted windows. The window rolled down halfway, exposing his red eyes. "Get in." Sydney sighed not wanting to cause a scene she looked over at Dana's front window and then back at the car. Chris had rolled the window up. She walked around to the passenger side of the Lamborghini. She opened the door sliding in, she glanced over at his eyes. "Close the door." She closed the door. Chris looked over at her, seeing her nipples showing through her dress. "What the fuck is wrong with you?!" He shouted. Sydney tried to look away not wanting eye contact with him, saying nothing. The doors locked, as Chris began to rev on the gas. Sydney was petrified. "Chris please unlock the door." She reached her hand around the panel in the dark trying to unlock the door. "Let's go for a fuckin' ride."

"Chris... no!" Chris backed out of the driveway. Sydney continued trying to open the door, which was unsuccessful. She became panicked.

"Why the fuck you trying to run away from me?"

"Chris, please let me out of this car." He looked over at her placing the car in gear and speeding off down the road. Chris went barreling through the city streets at sixty miles per hour. Sydney placed on her seat belt clutching on to the seat with everything. He headed towards I-95 North, once on the highway he began going over one hundred miles an hour. "Chris where are we going?" her voice trembling.

"I'm going to talk to you. We can't talk anywhere else." Chris began to switch lanes erratically, cars quickly moved out of his path.

"Chris, you are scaring me? Are you drunk?"

"Oh, I'm scaring you huh? Why must you always piss me the fuck off?! Why you always trying to have me be this angry ass nigga all the time?" He shouted his words almost slurring.

"Chris... don't do anything crazy." She replied looking over at his face. He swerved across two lanes sliding over to the shoulder. He turned the car off.

"I gave you everything! A fuckin' house, cars, buy you whatever you fuckin' want! You don't appreciate shit I do for you." Sydney sat silent, looking out the front window trying not to have eye contact with him at all. She could feel his eyes piercing her body as he stared at her in silence. He balled up his fist pounding it on the center console. "I catch you at the club, cuddled up with some bum ass nigga. Is there something wrong with me? He said to himself sarcastically. He pointed his finger in her face. You take me for a joke?" said Chris.

"Chris… please don't hit me." said Sydney calmly.

"I've got to be a fuckin' joke! My woman go to a club dressed like a fuckin' hoe and dancing on some broke ass nigga, in front of my face. He scratched his head, trying to erase the visual of Sydney with Yogi out of his mind. I gotta be fuckin' crazy!" He punched the steering wheel, he stared at Sydney, thinking about Yogi's hands all over her body. He pulled his gun from his waist. He cocked the gun resting it on his lap. "Why do you always get me like this? Did you ever truly feel this way about me?" Sydney began to tap her fingers nervously on her legs. Chris pointed the gun at her left hand. "Where is your ring?" said Chris calmly.

Sydney quickly covered her hand. "Um…"

"You don't give a fuck about me! I wear this bullshit you gave me every fuckin' day, when hoes trying to get at me, I'm blocking these bitches telling them I'm rocking with you! Fuck you! Chris shouted. I can't even…" He replied as if he was talking to himself. He got out of the car walking down the side of the road. Sydney didn't know what to do, she had never seen him act like this. She was literally shaking with fear. "Christian…" she called out to him getting out of the car walking a few feet towards him.

"Don't fuckin' talk to me! I feel like beating the shit out of your fuck ass, so don't say shit to me! Stay the fuck away from me!" Sydney quickly retreated not wanting to escalate the situation any further she decided to call Vani. Chris came back over to the car sitting on the front smoking a blunt. The phone rang twice.

"Hello?" said Vani sleepily.

"Vani… Chris has taken me to 95 north. He's acting suicidal and I don't know if he's…" The call ended. Sydney looked at her phone the battery was dead. The phone powered down. "Shit!" she yelled. Chris opened the door sliding back into the driver's seat. He looked over at Sydney again.

"Fuck you!" He barked as he started the car, the tires squealed as he pulled back into traffic. He got off at the first exit. "You love those bitches more than you do me, so go live with them hoes and that pussy ass nigga." Chris accelerated to over seventy five miles per hour in a residential area. They had approached Dana's street, once her home came into view Chris slammed on brakes, the force sent Sydney forward she hit her face on the dashboard. She felt as if she could've flew thru the windshield. "Get the fuck out!" Sydney quickly found the handle getting out of the car. She looked back over at Chris, the gun rested on his lap. "Chris…"

"Don't say shit to me! Get the fuck out! I'm done with you! Shiesty ass grimey bitch! I swear on my mother I hate your dumb ass." The tears finally streamed from her face as she walked towards the front door. Chris took off down the street, Sydney rang the doorbell falling to her knees on the porch.

Dana opened the door hearing her rapid knocks and hearing the tires squealing down the street. She bent down picking up her fallen friend. "Are you okay?" Sydney lifted her head placing her head in her hands, crying hysterically. She finally got to her feet as Dana helped her inside. "I was soo scared Dana. I knew he was going to kill me. I could see it in his eyes Dana." Vani came over hugging Sydney.

"Oh my god, Syd." Said Vani. Sydney walked back to the bedroom, her body still trembling as she placed on her pajamas. Nadine was knocked out on the couch. Sydney took a seat on the bed, next to Dana and Vani. "I have never seen him like this. He was on some psycho shit. His mind was gone." Sydney caressed her neck softly, trying to grasp everything that happened.

"Did he touch you?" said Vani.

"No. But, what about my baby? I mean he is in no condition right now to be around a child."

"I don't think right now is the time for you to go over there. I mean it's late, and I don't think you going over there would be a good idea." Said Dana calmly. Sydney placed the blanket over head. "I just want this night to be over. I can't believe this happened tonight."

The next morning everyone slept in late. Sydney was the last to wake up at one in the afternoon. Nadine and Dana were first up and Dana had made pancakes, everyone was dressed sitting around the table discussing last night and filling Nadine in on what happened after she dozed off. Sydney walked out to the kitchen in her Victoria Secret Pink V-neck tee and matching sleep shorts. She looked horrible. Her eyes were red, with raccoon circles around them. "Good morning Syd? How are you feeling?" said Vani.

"Hi guys. I'm fine. I just want my baby." Sydney walked over to the stove grabbing a piece of bacon and made herself a cup of mint tea. Everyone looked at Sydney as if watching an accident, wanting to see what her next move would be. Everyone knew she wasn't okay, you could see it on her face. Sydney took a seat at the table, twirling her engagement ring on her finger. She took it off staring at it. The tears began to fall down her face, as she tried to hold back. "Aww... come here Syd." Said Dana as she got up to hug her.

"I'm okay. I just want my baby!" she replied as she wiped the tears from her eyes.

"Well, let's go get my fuckin' cousin. Let's go!" said Vani as if she was ready to fight.

"I can't, not just yet. Chris is going to go berserk and I don't want to do that shit in front of Natalia, you know what I mean."

"Fuck him! If you want your baby let's go do this!" Nadine looked out the front window looking for Sydney's car. "Syd... where is your car?"

"What? It's not out there?" Sydney got up going over to the window, it was gone. "Shit! Chris took it with the spare keys. He's done with me for sure now."

"How he gonna do you like this?!" said Nadine angrily.

"What the fuck am I gonna do? He kicked me out."

"You can stay with me until you get yourself together. I have a spare bedroom it's yours if you need it."

"My clothes and everything are at the house! I'm not going to take this shit! That's my house and my baby!"

"Sydney what are you about to do?" said Dana trying to be the voice of reason.

"I'm going home." She went into the bedroom packing up her bag and changing into her spare clothes distressed jeans and tan shirt. She washed her face, and applied moisturizer, placing her hair up in a top knot, Christian Louboutin sandals on her feet.

Meanwhile, Chris had been up since dawn when he had the car towed home. He was on his way to Preme's house to take him to the airport. He had stopped by McDonald's to get food for Natalia and get himself a coffee. Once at Preme's he parked in the driveway, still feeling a bit of nausea from his hangover. He placed his shades over his eyes. Preme greeted him at the door, with Natalia in his arms. He picked up Natalia. "Ay daddy's princess! You miss me?" she smiled as he kissed her cheek, she hugged his neck tightly. "Dada!" Preme reached over hugging Chris. He followed Preme over to the living room. Chris looked on Natalia's neck she was wearing a new rose gold necklace, pink diamond studs in her ear and a diamond bracelet on her wrist. He shook his head, every time Preme kept her she came back with an abundance of jewelry. "So I see once again Pop has iced Tubby down."

"Well, it wasn't just me this time. Everyone was happy to see her, everyone brought her something. She got more shit than me." Preme laughed. "So, you went out last night?"

Chris sighed. "I wish I hadn't."

"Why? What happened?"

"Me and Syd pop... I can't explain how vexed I get with that girl."

"Ah shit, what she do?"

"Pop, she came to the concert basically fuckin' naked. Showing everything, tits and ass, in this see through shit. I look out catch this bitch on the front row hugged up with some bum ass nigga. Like its nothing." Chris threw his hands up.

"WHAT?" said Preme angrily. The bass in his voice scared Natalia, she latched on to Chris' arm.

"Pop, I get so fuckin' vexed with that bitch. Last night I contemplated bodying her ass, n'ahmean. I think she does this shit to see me get to this point. For her to do this disrespectful shit, she had to know it was a wrap." Preme looked over at his son. He could see the hurt in his eyes, the stress was all over his face, yet he knew it hurt him more that he hadn't handled her. "I don't know what the fuck to do Pop. I can't do what the fuck I want to her, because of Tubby. Yo, she testing my fuckin' patience. I just can't see letting this shit ride."

"Son, look calm down. Don't do anything drastic. I noticed ever since y'all had the baby there has been something different with her. I've noticed different shit in her demeanor. What you need to do, is stay the fuck away from her. You don't need to bring any heat on yourself right now. I thought when you got engaged y'all wasn't ready for marriage. Don't give her any reaction that's what she wants to tear down everything you've built. The best thing to do is for y'all to go y'all separate ways."

"I got you Pop. The fucked up shit about it is, I love that girl man. I would do anything for her. That's what fucks with me more than anything. I have no control over my anger when it comes to her. Damn."

"That's what love does to you son. I can't tell you how to live your life, all I can say is do whatever is best for you and Tubby. But, in my opinion these strong urges and shit you having about her is a liability and with the moves you trying to make, she a fuckin' casualty. Trust me y'all situation fuckin' toxic."

Chris looked at Preme. He took in the words he was saying. Were they toxic? How could something that was toxic create the best thing that ever happened to him? He looked down at Natalia as she sipped from her cup. In that moment he knew one thing for sure that he and Sydney were done for good. He looked over at Preme. "Enough about her. Are you ready for your trip?"

"Yea. I guess." Chris looked over seeing two small Louis Vuitton suitcases. "That's all you taking?"

"I only need the essential shit. Whatever I need I'll buy there." Chris got up handing Natalia over to Preme. He walked over picking up Preme's bags. His housekeeper walked over to get the bags. "I've got it. You take a break. Preme got up with Natalia heading towards the door. Once everything was in the car and Preme gave his staff last requests, he handed spare keys to Chris. Chris strapped Natalia in her car seat and in minutes they were off to the airport. On the way to the airport Chris began to think about how everything was now in his hands. He immediately thought of the promise he made to Sydney. Fuck her. His thoughts were interrupted as Preme began to speak. "Everything is in place. You're leaving for ATL Tuesday, stop by Orlando, Darren wants to get up with you to go over details. I'm gonna call you tomorrow about the conference call. Everything you need is in basement, you just go and handle the collections with distributors should be no problems. These are niggas who I have long histories with and they keep shit moving. Chris looked in the rear view mirror seeing Natalia playing with a doll. Keep your eyes open and stay ready feel me."

"I got you Pop." They arrived at the airport. Preme's jet was waiting, Loco was standing beside the aircraft waiting on his arrival. Chris parked the car hugging Preme. "I'm going to miss you son. I know you will do just fine I have no worries of you taking over. You built for this." He kissed Chris forehead, patting him on the back. He got out reaching in to the backseat to kiss Natalia. She smiled kissing his cheek. "Damn, she looks just like you." Said Preme as he looked over his granddaughter.

"You say that like it's a bad thing." Replied Chris with a chuckle. Preme laughed walking over to Loco. After embracing Loco and the pilot he began to walk on to the jet. He looked back at Chris one last time waving at him. Chris got back in the car. He took in a deep breath, thinking he definitely had big shoes to fill. He wouldn't let him down.

Sydney and Dana had used Sydney's card to get in the first gate to her community. They were now at the second outside her house trying to type the code in, it kept beeping displaying invalid code. Sydney was furious. She stood outside in the beaming sun trying over and over again. Her neighbors across the street who she rarely spoke to were going out for an afternoon stroll with their two Havanese dogs. They looked over at her thinking why would someone be standing at the gate. Embarrassed, she stomped over to the passenger side. "Take me back to the main gate." At the main security gate the Security guard was inside the booth cleaning the glass window when they pulled up he immediately smiled as if he was in an infomercial. Sydney got out the car walking to the booth. "Hello Ma'am how may I help you?"

"I live in 2319 and I wanted to know, what's going on with my security gate? It's not taking my code."

"Oh no. he replied dramatically. May I have your name?"

"Sydney Cruz."

"Do you have identification Miss Cruz?" Sydney handed him her driver's license. He typed her name in his computer. He handed her back her identification. "I'm sorry Miss Cruz. Mr. Garcia had the gate changed this morning."

Sydney's mouth dropped. "Really?! That fuckin' bastard!"

The guard smiled at her. "I'm sorry. Did you want me to leave a message for him?"

"No, thank you." Sydney walked back to the car getting in. She was fuming. She slammed the car door as she searched for her phone in her purse. "That fucker changed the codes!"

"You're kidding?"

"I'm so fuckin' serious. I'm going to call his ass right now." She began dialing his number. Chris had pulled in to Preme's to take the SUV he would be using for the trip. He heard his phone ring in his pocket. He looked down at the screen seeing Sydney's face. "What the fuck you want?" said Chris as he answered the phone.

"Where the fuck is my child?"

"She good. What the fuck you want? Why you on my line? I told you lose my fucking number and shit, I meant that."

"You changed the codes on the gate. How am I supposed to get my things? I need my clothes."

"I don't give a fuck about what you need! Stop calling my phone with the bullshit. Ask that pussy ass nigga you was hugged up wit' to get you something to wear."

"FUCK YOU!" shouted Sydney into the receiver.

"Bitch, fuck you! Lose my fuckin' number." Chris ended the call. Sydney looked down at the phone seeing call ended. She was furious she tossed the phone into her purse. "So what are you going to do?"

"I don't know. He's not letting me back in the house."

"But, he can't do that, your baby is there!"

"I know." Sydney scratched her head nervously, thinking of what her next plan of action should be.

"What are you going to do about clothes?"

"I have about five grand left from last night. I didn't bring my credit cards or anything."

"But, that's enough to get you some clothes and things to get you by for a while." Sydney thought of just a day ago five grand was nothing to her, pocket change now today it was all that she had. She had no house, no car, no man, and no baby.

"I don't have a car. How am I supposed to get to my classes? I mean I'm supposed to start my life all over? I have nothing."

"Syd, listen. You can stay with me until you decide what you want to do. Or as long as you want for that matter. What's mines is yours. You can use my car for school if you need and drop me off to the salon."

"Thank you Dana. I really appreciate you having my back. I will stay with you. I think what I'm going to do since this week is finals, my last one is on Wednesday. Thursday, I'm going to leave to California to visit my dad for a little while. Get my plans together. I guess in the mean time I'll get money from Yogi to hold me over until I leave." Dana looked at her friend, she felt bad that everything Sydney had was taken from her overnight. She didn't know what to think of Sydney's idea that talking to Yogi would make things better. She put her negative thoughts away in the back of her mind. The best thing now was to be there for her best friend.

Chris arrived at Reign, the store was empty. John and Nathan were sitting on the bench in the shoe section, Tatiana was arranging bags behind the counter. Chris walked over to her, Natalia in his arms. "Hi, how are you?" said Tatiana happy to see him.

"I'm good. You?"

"I'm good. I had an amazing time with you last night. I have the pictures we took last night, I want to show you." Tatiana walked back to her purse in the locker. She came back with a handful of pictures. Chris put Natalia down in her playpen. She handed the pictures to Chris. The first one was of Tatiana by herself.

"These came out good." Said Chris as he flipped through the pictures. The next few were pictures of himself, sitting in VIP, with Bundles and one with him and Bundles' crew. Chris smiled. "I look pretty damn good to have been faded." Tatiana laughed. He then saw the last three pictures he didn't remember taking. One was of he and Tatiana hugged up him grabbing her ass, the next was of her sitting on his lap, the last was of him and his crew. "When did I take these?"

"After the show. We went back to VIP. You don't remember?'

"Nah."

"You were fuming! I was trying to calm you down. I figured we could get you back to your boys and maybe they can calm you down. I mean, it worked for a moment. It was crazy, you were so angry."

"Yea, I had a situation to deal with last night." He handed the pictures back to Tatiana.

"Oh, you can keep those. Those are your copies. I got my own already."

"Thank you. Chris took the pictures sliding them in his back pocket. I had a good time vibin' with you last night Tati, we got to do that again."

"Same here." She replied with a flirtatious blush. John walked over to Chris interrupting their conversation. "What's good?" said John as he dapped Chris. They walked over towards the front of the store. "You good today, 'cause last night you was gone my nigga."

"Yea. I'm good. I'm glad I was faded because if I was myself, I might've killed Syd last night." John laughed thinking Chris was joking, although a part of him was being one hundred percent honest.

"Yea, I heard you saying that you was going to kill her. What happened? I heard Damien say somethin' about she was in the club with another nigga?"

"Yea. I lost it."

"So, what you gonna do son? That's some grimey shit."

"It's a wrap. We done. Finished."

"Damn. Although, shit was grimey I think y'all gonna get back together. I've been around y'all there is fuckin' love there. Y'all got Tati and shit."

"The way I feel right now. I'm probably going to hurt Sydney. So, to keep myself from doing some crazy shit. She has to go."

"So, what y'all gonna do about the baby?"

"I'm going to keep her for now. I can't deal with Syd right now. I know me."

"Damn, man. I wanted to see y'all make it and do that shit."

"Well, shit change." Said Chris. He looked out the store window watching the cars pass by on the street. Tatiana was eavesdropping, she smiled brightly hearing Chris confirm he was done with Sydney. She walked to the back feeling like she was on cloud nine.

"So, its official my nigga back on the market?" said John with a smile.

"Yea, its official my nigga, I'm back. Don't get too happy, mean it's a wrap for you. Cash season has returned." John laughed out loud, dapping up his man.

Sydney and Dana had arrived back at her house. Everyone was packing up their things, Vani came out seeing Sydney in the outfit she had on earlier, no baby. "What happened?"

"Girl, that bastard changed the codes on the gate. When I called his punk ass he basically said fuck you."

"No, he didn't?!"

"He's going to give me my baby."

"You know he lost his fuckin' mind! I knew I should have went with you to the house. Shit, let's go up to Reign. He can't do this to you Syd!" Vani shouted her adrenaline pumping.

"I can't. I can't believe he kicked me out." said Sydney. Vani became annoyed by Sydney's woe is me act. Vani looked over at her cousin, she was weak she thought. She would have never allowed Mark to kick her out and not do anything about it. She decided to wash her hands with suggestions. Vani sat down on the couch.

"So, what are you going to do about it?" said Vani.

"I'm going to give him a few days, then we can come to an agreement."

"A few days! Syd, he cannot keep your daughter from you!" said Vani trying to calm herself.

"Vani, I know what I am doing. If I go there now, he is going to flip and probably try to kill me. You were not in that car last night. You didn't see the look of rage on his face."

"No, I wasn't. But, maybe you should've seen him last night! Trina just messaged me and said she saw Chris in VIP booed up with some bitch last night." Said Vani.

"WHAT?"

"Yea, said she was up there with Kevin and she said he bought the bitch bottles and they wasn't even trying to be low key with it. She was on his lap and shit!"

Sydney smiled. "Oh, really... so he's going to sit here and act like I was the only one in the wrong!"

"That's what I'm saying, go to Reign and ask him about that bitch." Said Vani trying to gas Sydney up. Sydney thought about the fact of another woman openly on Chris last night in front of everyone. She was beyond pissed, but who was she to get mad. Karma is a bitch.

"I'm going to go lay down for a minute."

"You okay?"

"Yea, I just need a moment." She replied walking back to the bedroom.

Meanwhile, at Reign it was closing time. Tatiana was helping Chris pack Natalia up. She went to the front locking the door, she had Natalia's baby bag over her shoulder, and Chris was breaking down her playpen placing it in his office. Tatiana walked over to his office, he had Natalia in his arms. "We had a good time last night huh? How much money did you lose?" she replied with a smile.

Chris chuckled. "Yea, I needed that. It's been a minute. I lost about fifteen g's I think?"

"Shit! You could've given it to me if you were gonna toss it. I'm trying to decorate my new place." Said Tatiana.

"Oh, you have your own place?"

"Yes. I live in a townhouse in Miramar."

"That's what's up. Independent shorty." Replied Chris with a smile. An awkward silence filled the room. Tatiana couldn't help gazing into his eyes. Natalia coughed, interrupting their silence Chris walked to the back door to leave. Tatiana soon followed behind him. Once outside he locked the door and headed to the backseat to strap Natalia in. Tatiana came over to hand him the baby bag. "Thank you, Tati." "Anytime... Chris." She replied as she licked her lips. She walked over to her car. Chris watched her walk away before heading over to the driver's side. Tatiana started up her car, glancing once more at Chris. Their eyes met, she smiled again, thinking in that moment she had to have him. She would have him in her bed.

Two days later, it was Monday night. Chris hadn't spoken to Sydney since the gate issue. Sydney had been living with Dana and had drove her car to school that morning. She spent the last days at the salon with the girls trying to wrap her head around her new life. She hadn't went out with Yogi or called him for that matter, but she had told Vani she was considering his Tuesday dinner offer. Sydney had went to the mall Sunday and bought a few items from H & M, it wasn't her usual expensive taste, but she figured it could get her by until she went out to California. She was studying for her exam on Dana's laptop when her phone rang. It was Chris. She panicked, taking a deep breath answering the phone. "Hello?"

"Yea. Meet me at the store in about twenty minutes."

"Why? What's going on?"

"Don't ask me no questions. Just meet me there." He hung up the phone. Sydney got up from the desk, she went into the room grabbing a Victoria Secret pink hoody from off the bed. She walked back out to Dana. "Dana, can I borrow your car?"

"Yea. Where are you going?'

"To meet Chris at the store."

"You want me to go with you?"

"No, I'll be okay." Dana got up handing her the keys. "Call me if you need me." She rushed out the door to the car. Once inside she checked her makeup in the mirror. She ran her fingers through her hair, not wanting Chris to see her looking miserable. She looked over her outfit. She was wearing skinny jeans which looked painted on her curvy figure, and a sleeveless lace and crochet blouse, Christian Louboutin sandals on her feet. She applied MAC Bombshell lipstick to her lips, and was on her way. She arrived to the back of the store around eight thirty. There was a Black Yukon parked at the back of store. She parked the car getting out. The driver side of the Yukon opened, out stepped Chris. He was wearing a white tee and Givenchy cross joggers, Jordan sneakers on his feet. Sydney looked over his body, she couldn't help but look at his arms. She quickly shifted her eyes up to his face, he looked stressed as if he hadn't been sleeping. They stood face to face. Chris wiped his face. "I'm going away for a minute. I need you to keep Tati for me." He replied dryly.

"Where is she?"

"She's in there." Sydney walked over to the back door of the SUV. She opened the door, Natalia was in her car seat sleeping. She reached into the car hugging and kissing her face. Natalia smacked in her sleep, refusing to wake up. "Wake up mama." Said Sydney. Chris walked over to the car beside

Sydney. "I'm going to let you come back to the house, because all of her shit is there. But, I'm telling you now. Don't try nothing stupid! You try to take Tati away from me I promise on everything, I'm gonna fuck you up!" Sydney turned around after hearing his threat. "You don't control me."

Chris smirked at her pointing his finger in her face. "Don't piss me off Syd! I will take Tati with me and let you stay bumming on your girl couch." Sydney rolled her eyes. She closed the door. "When are you leaving?"

"You just be there tonight." Said Chris bluntly.

"How am I going to get in the gate?'

"I changed the codes back. I don't want my daughter out all night. And you better not have her around that bitch ass nigga either. I have to make a stop. I'll see you at the house by ten thirty."

"Okay." Chris turned away walking back to the driver's side without saying goodbye. She ignored his attitude as she slid back in the car. She was excited to be going back home to their palace, with their King sized bed and all of her things. Once she arrived at Dana's she rushed into the house, throwing her things together. "So, what happened?" said Dana.

"He's leaving for a while he said and he wants me to come home with the baby."

"Really? How do you feel about that? Sounds a little crazy to me?"

"I mean it does seem a little off. But, he seems like he's calmed down. I'll be fine. I have to hurry up and get my things together. I have to be there by ten thirty."

"He gave you a curfew?" said Dana with a laugh

"Yea, I know. I'm just going along with it for Tati. Can you drive me over there?"

"Of course." About thirty minutes later they were outside of the gate to the house. Sydney went around to the keypad and typed the old code in and the gate opened. The Yukon was parked in the driveway, Dana pulled up behind it. She got out the car grabbing her bag of clothes. The front door opened, Chris stood at the door with Natalia in his arms. Dana waved at him, trying to be cordial. He gave her a head nod before leaving the door. Sydney turned around looking at her bestie. "Thank you Dana for everything. From the bottom of my heart. I love you girl. Call me."

"Girl you know I am. I got your back 'til the end boo." She hugged Sydney. Sydney carried her bags walking towards the door. Dana sat and watched her friend as she walked inside the door closing behind her. Sydney looked around it was spotless. The house smelled of Lysol Mango and Febreze. Chris had left upstairs to put Natalia in her pajamas in her room. Sydney walked upstairs to their bedroom, she dropped her bags in the closet. She looked over at their California King bed, the memories they had in it played in her mind. She thought of them lying in it telling old stories while eating cookies and cream ice cream. Chris walked into their bedroom, Sydney quickly moved over to her drawer pulling out her pajamas. He walked past her going into the bathroom. She slid her clothes off, revealing her naked body. Chris walked out of the bathroom, glancing over her body. He had a quick thought of all the things he used to do to her body, when it was his playground and anything was a go, he sighed walking out of the room. Sydney slid a lace chemise over her body, throwing her clothes in the basket. She laid across the bed, turning on the television. She immediately felt as if she was in heaven, the feel of the duvet on her body in her soft comfortable bed.

Chris walked back upstairs to the room. He closed the room door behind him. Sydney immediately jumped up, getting out of bed. Chris came over towards her. "Why the fuck did you do that to me?" said Chris his voice loud and demanding.

"Why the fuck did you cheat on me? You fucked Roxy! All I did was dance with a nigga!"

Chris eyes were low and he reeked of weed. "That wasn't when we were fuckin' engaged! You took your fuckin' ring off! Chris began to get angry. You thought I wasn't going to be there, and figured you'd chill with that punk didn't you?" Chris pointed his finger in her face.

"Chris... listen." Said Sydney dryly. He interjected. "Do you know how much I did love you? I would've done anything for you! He sat down on the bed trying to calm the rage he had inside to hurt Sydney. Sydney looked over at him seeing that he was truly hurt by what she had done. She wasn't convinced he was completely innocent himself that night, but a piece of her felt horrible for the way she had hurt him. She shook the feeling out of her mind thinking about the car ride. Don't be stupid Syd, she thought to herself. She crossed her arms over her body defensively.

"And you don't give a fuck how I feel. You were just using me, huh?!"

"Chris... you have a lot of issues you need to deal with." Chris jumped up from the bed, standing to her face.

"What about the shit you need to deal with? I'm not the only crazy motherfucker in this room. So stop coming at me like that! You always bringing up old shit thinking I'm fuckin' this or that bitch. When I was always one hundred with you! Insecure ass!"

"Really? I'm insecure? You gave me a fuckin' reason to be insecure!"

"What fuckin' reason?"

"You always flirting with the next bitch or hoe that comes in your presence." Shouted Sydney.

"Flirting and fucking two different things. All I want to know is what in your crazy ass head said to go to a club and be hugged up with some bum ass nigga? You couldn't do better than that? I mean, if you gonna go and do some fuck shit like that at least get a nigga who got something."

"Who says I wanted him?"

"You stood at a concert in front of every fuckin' body with that pussy!" Sydney could see the veins forming in his face and hands. She decided it was best she leave the room. Chris grabbed her by the throat before she could move, she yelped as he pinned her to the wall. "If you have my baby around that nigga or I hear anything crazy, I'll make sure you never see Natalia again. Fuck with me." He hit her head against the wall tightening the grip on her neck. Sydney looked into his face. "See this is why we can't ever get anywhere because of your crazy ass temper."

"Oh yea, and what causes me to be angry." Sydney looked into his face with helpless eyes. His grip was taking the life out of her. Chrs' face showed pure hate for her, and in that moment she went with the voice in the back of her head telling her she was wrong for what she did. "Christian... I'm sorry. I'm sorry I hurt you." She replied softly with every breath she had. He looked at her, hitting her head again against the wall before releasing his grip. "Whatever." Sydney caressed her neck as Chris turned away to leave the room. She grabbed his arm, taking a deep breath. He looked back at her with disgust.

"I honestly didn't know that you were going to be at the club that night. I had no intentions of meeting Yogi there. I was in my feelings, of what happened the day before and he was there. I'm sorry."

"You sorry, why the fuck you do it? We were engaged do you know what the fuck that means?"

"Do you know what it means?" she barked back.

"What the fuck you trying to say?" said Chris.

"You know exactly, what I'm saying!" Said Sydney.

"Yo, I can't even be in the same room with you. Just thinking you let that nigga be all over you." He looked at her shaking his head disgusted. He left out of the room. Sydney watched him out of the door. She went over to the mirror to look at her neck, contemplating if her coming back home was a good move. She and Chris would argue every day and would only be a matter of time before it escalated to Boston again. Natalia began to cry from her room. Sydney heard her over the baby monitor. She walked out of the room to get her. Natalia was wet, she changed her diaper giving her a new sip cup of milk. As she looked down at Natalia she realized she had made the right decision, nothing was more important to her than being there for her baby. She cradled her inside of her arms rocking her back to sleep. In minutes, they both were sleep. Chris came upstairs to bring his last bag down. He saw Natalia and Sydney sleeping. Natalia lay on top of Sydney's chest her arms cupped around her body. Sydney's arm around her body. He looked over them, before grabbing the bag heading downstairs and out the door, heading to pick up Nick.

When he arrived at Nick's house he met him in the driveway. His bags outside. He unlocked the doors, so Nick could get in. "What up nigga?" said Nick.

"What's good? You ready?"

"Yea. He threw his bags in the trunk, walking around to get in the passenger seat. Once he was in Chris backed out of the driveway. Where the baby?"

"At the house with Syd."

"Oh, y'all made up?"

"Nah, I just don't want her sleeping at someone else house when my baby have her own bed at home."

"I feel you. What was up with you and the girl at the concert?"

"Tatiana? She's my home girl from Reign. She cool." Said Chris.

"At the concert y'all seemed a little more than cool my nigga. You was acting as if you was gonna fuck her right there." They both laughed.

"Nah. Don't get me wrong shorty sexy as fuck. But, after this shit I'm not trying to get tied down with anyone right now."

"So, you and Syd engagement off for good?"

"Yea. As of right now, Syd is just my baby mama." Nick shook his head as they cruised down the highway heading to Orlando.

The next morning Sydney woke up panicked. She had forgot she had class, who would watch Natalia. She quickly called up Dana and she happily said she would. Sydney quickly rushed over to the bathroom hopped in the shower. She threw on a black tunic dress, and fedora over her head, she threw on a pair of Giuseppe Zanotti boots. She woke Natalia up giving her a quick wash up, she placed her in a pair of black skinny jeans and a pink DKNY top with custom Black and pink Air Jordan 4 Retro shoes. She hurried downstairs throwing diapers, snacks and juice into her bag and in minutes were in the Mercedes heading to Dana's.

In Orlando, Chris and Nick had checked into a hotel room for a few hours on International Drive. It was the Westin, Chris just needed a few hours of sleep after the drive. Now that he was up he was on his phone setting up meetings with local distributors so he could collect payments. He had spoken to Darren first and he was to meet him at his house, to go over plans, he had messaged him the directions and he planned on placing them in the navigation. He then remembered Sydney had class today he wondered where she had took Natalia. He pulled out his phone calling her. "Hello."

"Yea, where's Natalia?"

"I'm in class she whispered. She's with Dana."

"When are you going to pick her up?"

"I'm almost done. I will pick her up when I leave."

"A'ight." The phone beeped saying that the call was ended. Sydney looked at the phone, pissed that he ended the call so abruptly. Chris and Nick headed over to Darren's house. He said that he lived in Windermere. As they followed the navigation to his home he realized that he lived in a gated community as well. Chris looked around at the houses which looked almost like the community Preme lived in. Darren's house sat at the end of a cul de sac with a beautiful lake view in the back. They approached the gate buzzing in, Darren came over the screen. "Come on in." The gate opened showing his beautiful nine thousand plus acres home. There was palm trees and plush greenery inviting you as he stepped out of the car in his circular driveway. There was a Bentley Continental in the driveway and a Porsche Cayenne. Chris and Nick both walked towards the double doors as Darren emerged outside. He was dressed in a linen shirt and pants, his skin tone hazelnut with piercing brown eyes. He and Preme had similar features, but Darren looked more corporate and more approachable. "What's good nephew?" said Darren as he reached out to embrace him. He hugged Chris quickly before shaking Nick's hand. They walked inside. "How was the drive?" said Darren as he led him into his immaculate foyer. Columns sat in the middle of the floor holding up this ivory masterpiece, everything was neatly in place and looked like a model home. "It was good. Can't complain." Said Chris. Darren led them over to the kitchen. "You know we have a lot to handle in these next weeks while Rich is away."

"I know. I'm ready." Darren walked over to the fridge. "Want a drink?" they both declined. Darren looked over at Nick. "We're not going to have any slip ups with my nephew involved." Nick shook his head feeling the heat being shifted in his direction. Chris laughed at Nick being placed on the spot. They followed Darren back to his office. Three women walked down the stairs had to be in the early twenties. The one in the front was tall, brown skinned, thick with almond shaped eyes, immediately smiled seeing they had company. "Hi Dad. Who's this?"

"Oh, Chris you didn't get to meet your cousin at the party. This is my daughter Alexis we call her Lexi. This is Preme's boy Chris."

"Oh my god! Hi!" She replied as she walked over to hug him. "What up cuz." He replied with a smile. "She's about the same age as you."

"Nice meeting you. You're so handsome." She replied.

Chris smiled again to her and her friends as they headed into this office. No time for games he was going to keep this strictly professional on this trip. You could hear her and her friends chattering about Chris' looks as they left the room. "Oh my god he is fine! Where is he from?" said one of them.

"Miami." Said Alexis.

"Well, he and his homeboy are cute. Alex hook us up."

"Uh uh. Lauren I'm trying to get Chris for me. You can have the friend boo." Alexis laughed at her friends about to fight over Chris. "We'll see. We don't know his situation yet. I think he has a baby."

"Don't do that, Lexi. Don't block." They all laughed walking to the kitchen. Inside the office Chris sat down at the chair as Darren sat behind the desk "I own a crib in Georgia, y'all will be staying there. You going to need to call Rock and see what's going on. We had our people send the shipment thru, he knows he owes you…"

"A quarter mil." Said Chris chiming in. He remembered from the folder he had received from Preme with all the information he needed to study. He had burned it outside last night.

"You studied. Said Darren proudly. It's a few agents we need you to do a few drop offs to and a judge. Go check on the stash houses in Decatur, Bankhead and Macon. A few soldiers out there. Time to do a creep up on this niggas. We got a BBQ joint down there named Joe's we pass some cash thru, they owe you one hundred grand."

"Damn pops, got paper coming out of everywhere." Said Chris. Darren's house phone rang, he answered, and it was Preme. "What up, let me put you on speaker. Darren pressed the button. What's good son?"

"I'm good Pop."

"I handled shit with the agents and judge before I left so don't worry about that stop. Just get up with Rock, check the houses and BBQ joint. Also, check on the dealership in Buckhead, he can give you that information. I don't want any slip ups, you hear me?"

"I got you." Said Nick, figuring it was directed at him.

"A'ight son. We may have this liquor venture popping off sooner than later. When I come back we may start the launch, been getting a lot of shit done while here."

"Yo that's what's up Pop."

"A'ight, I'm getting off here. Be safe."

"One." Said Chris. Darren hung up the phone. "Yo, Unc where the bathroom?"

"Second door on the left."

"A'ight." Chris left the room as he walked down the hall, one of the girls Chloe was walking back to Alexis' room. She quickly rushed back into the room. "Lex, I just saw your cousin going to the bathroom. Hook me up!"

"Really Chlo! Y'all acting real bananas over Chris." Alexis walked out of her room into the hall. When she heard the toilet flush she signaled for Chloe to come by the door. "Hey Chris." Said Alexis as she walked towards him. He turned around. "What up?"

"My home girl is feelin' you. You with someone?"

"Nah, not right now." Alexis cleared her throat and Chloe came out of the room. Chris looked her over she had caramel skin, long platinum blonde hair, medium build. You could tell she had a boob job and a round derriere. She was wearing a crop top and leggings which showed her every curve. She was attractive, Chris figured he would play along.

"What's your name ma?"

"Chloe." He shook her hand. "So how long are you here?"

"'til tomorrow." Said Chris

"Maybe we can all go out tonight, so I can get to know you a little better." Said Chloe.

"What's good in Orlando?"

"There's a lot to do. I mean, whatever you want to do, I'm pretty sure it could be made possible for you." She replied with a seductive smile.

"Well, me and my nigga probably gonna hit up some stores and handle some business before we head out. Maybe we can chill over dinner."

"That's cool. What mall are you trying to go to?"

"Wherever the good shit. Givenchy, Gucci…"

"You probably want the Millenia mall. They have all that."

"A'ight, how about we meet y'all there after we finish some business. I'll give you my number so you can let me know when you get there." She pulled her iPhone out of her pocket typing in his phone number. "Call me later ma." Said Chris. He touched her face walking back towards the office. Chloe nearly fainted. Once he was out of sight she ran back in the room. "Bitch, I gotta go home and change clothes." Alexis laughed looking at her friend. Chris was to go to get a pick up from the Florida mall. He decided to he would do that quickly before heading over to meet with Alexis friends. The pickup went smooth and quickly he told the guy where to meet him and how to have the money. They did the exchange no problems, although he had Nick positioned and ready just in case anything popped off. Chris placed the duffel in the trunk under the floorboard while they were in the parking lot. Chris typed in the location, Chloe had called and said she they were on their way, to meet them upstairs outside of the Versace store. Chris had filled Nick in, on the mall date. "My cousin home girls want to get at us. I told them we would meet them at this mall and chill for a minute."

"A'ight, when we eating?"

"After here we can grab something to eat." Chris and Nick had arrived at the mall first. Once they went upstairs looking for Versace they had to go inside and see what they had. Chris ended up buying some shoes as they were walking out the store they bumped into the girls. "What's good ladies?" said Chris with a smile. "Hi" They all replied. The girls had all changed into tight fitting dresses and skirts, they also had brought an extra friend. "Hi guys, this is our other friend Ayanna who was gonna hang." Chris greeted her, his mind began to think what had he gotten himself into. Chloe came to his side. "So, Chloe you hanging with Chris and Tiana going with Nick, and Lauren is going to hang with me. We'll meet y'all back for dinner?"

"A'ight" said Chris. He and Chloe went in their own direction. An hour later Chris and Chloe were outside of Bloomingdales and she began to second guess herself being with someone like Chris. The whole time they were in the mall together girls kept flirting and throwing themselves at him as if she wasn't even there. She was jealous and he wasn't even her man. Nick had messaged Chris and said where was he? Because he was ready to go. Chris replied back the location with lol. Soon as they left out the store they saw Nick and Tiana. "Yo, C, we gotta go. Received this text from pop said we need to hit the road."

"Damn, said Chris. We're gonna have to get a raincheck on dinner."

"Oh man. Said Chloe. Damn, well it was good meeting you. If you ever here again hit me up?"

Chris hugged her. "No doubt shorty." Everyone exchanged hugs. Once the girls were out of sight. Chris burst out laughing. "Good move son, that broad was boring as hell. I couldn't get her to say shit."

"Did you see the bitch I was with? She got some knobby ass knees and kept touching on my face and shit, I was about to smack shorty. Don't put your nasty ass hands in my face, and she had fuckin' rough ass fingers. Like she a mechanic some shit." Chris laughed out loud. "Now what the fuck we gonna eat?"

"There's a food court in here. Let's get that shit and be out before we see them hoes again."

"Hell yea." They both laughed heading towards the food court.

It was Thursday, and the girls had went back to Connecticut, the day before. It wasn't on a good note. Tori was still angry with Sydney and Mercedes and Kiana left on Tuesday after it became awkward being in same space with Sydney. Out of Sydney's Hartford crew Nadine was the only friend she had left and Sydney made sure she met Natalia before leaving. It was ten am and Sydney had already had her tickets and was packed to go. She sat downstairs awaiting Vani's arrival to take her to the airport. She heard a buzz at the gate she grabbed her Louis Vuitton rolling bags in her hand. She let Vani inside, and she came in helping her with the bags, within an hour they were at the airport. Vani pulled up to the Delta terminal. Sydney got out of the car getting Natalia out. She checked their bags with curbside. She walked back over to Vani hugging her. "Syd, what is Chris going to say?"

"Fuck his feelings. Look at this!" Sydney handed Vani a picture of Tatiana sitting on his lap straddling him. "She works at his whore store!"

"Wow, replied Vani as she looked over the picture it was risqué, it looked as if it could be the foreplay to a porno flick, the look they had in their eyes. Vani handed her the picture back. "I can't believe this Syd. How long are you going to stay in Cali?"

"I don't know. I just need a break from him and all this bullshit here. I'm at the end of my rope right now. I can't take this shit, so to save my sanity, I'm out."

"Aww... I'm gonna miss you two. Have fun." They hugged each other. Vani reached over kissing Natalia on the cheek. Natalia waved bye to her, as Sydney adjusted her on her hip.

"Well, we've got to go. Remember you don't know where I am. You haven't seen me."

"I know. I got you boo, I'm not telling shit!"

"Thank you. Love you girl. Speak to you soon." Sydney turned to walk in the airport. She soon walked through TSA and in moments was boarding a plane to Los Angeles. Meanwhile, Chris was in Atlanta fuming because he hadn't spoken to Sydney in two days. He called her number again, this time it went straight to voicemail. Sydney took her seat in first class placing Natalia on her lap. She looked down at the picture of Chris and Tatiana one last time. *You asked for this shit! Fuck you!* She thought to herself, as she pulled out a little fleece for her and Natalia to cover up in. In moments she drifted off to sleep.

When she awoke, she looked down at Natalia who was snoring on her chest. She looked out the window to see where they were. The pilot announced over the intercom to prepare for landing. Sydney couldn't believe she had slept for five hours. She looked down at her phone to see if it had switched to Pacific Time, she called her father. "Hey baby. I'm on my way I should be there any minute."

"Okay. We will be waiting outside" Once they landed Sydney was ecstatic to finally be free. She felt the move would be a push in the right direction to a new life for her and Natalia. She retrieved her bags, and waited outside at the terminal. Natalia woke up looking around at their new surroundings confused. "Da da. Said Natalia with a smile. Sydney's phone rang it was Chris again. She ignored the call. Within ten minutes Gavin pulled up to the curb, in a Mercedes, in an Armani suit. He parked the car getting out to greet them. "Look at my princess!"

"Hi Daddy!" said Sydney as she hugged him. She had never been so happy to see him in her life. "And who is this my little bella?"

"Yes this is Natalia Maria Garcia. Your granddaughter." She handed her over to her father so he could hold her.

"Oh look at those eyes. She is beautiful, Syd. Hi, mama!" said Gavin as he tickled her. Natalia looked at him with a smirk that said *who the hell are you?* Sydney laughed at Natalia's rude expression. He patted Sydney on the back, Sydney grabbed the car seat placing it in the car. She strapped Natalia in back, hopping in the front seat. Gavin placed their bags in the trunk before getting behind the wheel. "So, how are you doing Syd?" said Gavin as he pulled away from the curb.

"I'm good. Just finished another semester of classes and taking care of Tati, has been my days lately."

"I'm glad you're still in school. What about that asshole? Are you still with him?"

"It's complicated. But, we are separated."

"Separated? Is he at least taking care of his child?"

"Somewhat…" Sydney replied as she looked out the window at the passing cars. Gavin grimaced. "I knew you should have never gotten dealt up with that thug! How does he treat the baby? Is he good to her?"

"He's a good father, I guess."

"You guess? What does he not take responsibility? I knew he was all talk when I met that asshole. You know we can take him to court and get full custody of the baby. If he's not going to handle his responsibility like a man willingly, the law will handle it forcefully. Natalia doesn't need a half ass father."

"I don't know about legal action yet, Dad. We'll see give it a little time." They headed towards Gavin's place in Calabasas. Sydney became anxious wondering what California would have in store for her. After stopping to pick up groceries, they finally pulled up to Gavin's beautiful home, it was in a gated community, two story home with immaculate greenery and shrubbery covering the front window. The community was beautiful every house looked like it was out of a made for television movie. Sydney got Natalia out the back seat following Gavin into the house. Once inside the house was gorgeous, granite countertops, a lanai with fireplace and was cozy. Sydney could admit it wasn't as extravagant as her and Chris' Miami home. But, it definitely gave an aura of a cozy family home. Gavin brought the bags in Sydney sat down on the stool holding Natalia in her arms.

"Make yourself comfortable Syd. Your room will be downstairs first down on the right down this hall. I would give you a tour, but I'm running late. Happy to have you here. Call me if you need anything." He kissed her cheek, heading back out the door. Sydney walked down the hall, looking at the room. It had a queen sized bed in it and a dresser, forty inch television on the wall. Sydney frowned as she looked inside the small walk in closet. She sat down on the bed, placing Natalia down. She turned on the television to Nick Jr. to keep Natalia occupied. Her phone rang again, it was Chris. She decided to answer. "Hello."

"What the fuck is wrong with you?! I've been calling you for two days! What the fuck are you doing?"

"I've been busy. What did you want?" said Sydney bluntly.

"What did I want? Who the fuck you talking to Syd? I've been calling your dumb ass to check on Natalia."

"She's fine." Chris sat back in his chair taking in Sydney's responses.

"I don't know what the fuck got into you. Or what the fuck your problem is. But, when I call and you have our fuckin' daughter you answer the phone!"

"Anyway... I found your pictures."

"What, fucking pictures?"

"You know the ones of you and the bitch from your whore store sitting on top of your lap. In the little ass shorts, kissing all on your face. What the fuck were you thinking we were engaged?" She said mocking him.

"Yea. What the fuck you trying to do throw that shit up in my face? I was wrong to have her on my lap. But you, the shit you pulled was just grimey. You was willing to throw our shit away over some pussy nigga."

"Really Chris? You sound crazy as fuck. If I'm grimey for dancing with him, you did the same shit letting some basic ass, employee of yours straddle your fuckin' lap in front of the whole club!"

Chris became quiet thinking she may have got him on that one. He decided to retreat. "I don't fuck with Tati like that. She had hit me up on some business shit at the club that night. We had some drinks, I was fucked up. I didn't remember half of that shit. Point is she knows me and her just cool."

"So, it's okay for you to be cool with a bitch that clearly wants to fuck you. You know you put me thru hell that night all to find out you were doing the same shit! I'm over it. We argue all the time, and you clearly need anger management."

"Why you always bringing up what the fuck I need?"

"Because you do need help."

"Anyway, Tell Tubby I love her. I'm gonna call later on the home phone I need you to give me this number in the office I forgot."

"Whatever." Said Sydney as she ended the call. Sydney gave Natalia a bath, afterwards making a sandwich before taking a nap to get over the jet lag.

Chris had stopped thru Macon and was to check on the stash houses. After he went to two different houses word quickly got around and the next stops were ready, everyone in place with no issues. They continued on to Atlanta, Chris called Sydney for the number no response. He and Nick had decided to stop by Gladys Knight Chicken and Waffles because Nick had told him he had to try the food, so that was there next stop. Chris called Sydney three more times. No response. He became angry thinking about what she was doing and why she wasn't answering the phone. He tried to calm himself, maybe she was busy or she had took a nap with Natalia. Once they arrived at the restaurant and were seated Chris couldn't help but wonder what was going on home. He called one last time. No response.

He looked thru the photos in his phone of Natalia. He was missing his baby, he had to get home soon.

It was now Tuesday and Sydney had not told Chris she was in California. It was two pm, Pacific Time and she had decided she had spent enough time in the house already. She was ready to hit up the malls and get her feet wet in her new city. Gavin had told her he left the Lexus ES in the garage for her to use if she needed to get around. She got dressed placing Natalia on a Dolce & Gabbana printed dress with matching bloomers and ballerina flats. She placed a flower head band around her head and let her flow freely today which fell down her shoulders. Sydney loved her curls. Sydney got dressed in a bodysuit over a Herve Leger black skirt, her curls fell in a loose pattern she used a few pins to pull it all to one side. She slid in a pair of Christian Louboutin mesh and suede four inch heels and was ready to head out the door. Once in the car she typed in Saks and Celine in the navigation system. She soon was directed to Wilshire Blvd in Beverly Hills. She connected her iPhone to the car Bluetooth, as she drove down the road. Vani called. "Hello." Said Sydney.

"Hey girl. How is your vacation going?" said Vani her voice booming through the cars speakers.

"It's going good so far. Besides, you know it was only a matter of time before my dad got on my nerves." Sydney laughed out loud.

"I figured that, would happen soon enough. What happened?"

"He's been asking about Chris. What am I going to do? I need to leave him and get my life together for good."

"Did you tell him why you guys separated? About the club?"

"Girl, hell no. You know he hates Chris and calls him a thug every five seconds."

"Wow. Said Vani laughing. So, have you told Chris you're out there yet? I know he's been blowing you up by now."

"Yea, he calls at least twice a day. But, he doesn't know I'm out here. I answer if I feel like it."

"Okay... diva. He's gonna be so fuckin' pissed with your ass."

"I know. He's always pissed. Fuck him." they both laughed.

"Well, Dana told me to tell you bring her muffin back. When are you guys coming back?"

"Tell her that we will be back Friday or Saturday. I haven't decided yet."

"Oh, okay. I will let her know. Yogi been asking about you. Asking when he can see you again, you have that nigga wrapped around your finger bitch."

"Girl, I am soo not interested in him. I don't know what came over me that night to even entertain him at all. Maybe me being pissed with Chris and drunk, I don't know."

"So, you getting back together with Chris?"

"I don't know yet. I mean I do love him. I know we argue and fight like no other, but I always have a sweet spot for his crazy ass. I just want him to control his anger."

"Okay. I know y'all clearly got history. But, y'all have a baby. Y'all can't be out here acting reckless, I mean pulling guns and shit."

"I know. I know. He would never do anything to hurt Natalia I know that. And I don't think he would ever pull out a gun on me around Natalia."

"All I'm saying is for you to think before you come back home to this bullshit. Chris has already shown you, who he is, and what he's gonna be. Just be smart."

"I hear you. But Chris isn't bad all the time. It's when he's angry, that's the side I want to change. But he is a good father, he would do anything for Tati, I know that. He's also good to me. But there is no middle with us we are either good or a disaster. I want a happy middle."

"So what if Chris is back in the game? What are you gonna do?"

"You know I don't really care about him and the game right now. Right now, I'm focused on my future and how I can be a better me to be a better mother and provider for Natalia. I also have to stop being selfish, with Natalia's relationship with her father. That is a beautiful thing for a daughter to have that bond with her father the way they do. Maybe I was wrong to break that up and come all the way out here. You should hear how many times she's call out daddy since we've been here. Maybe I made the wrong decision."

"Don't do that shit! You always get hard on yourself. He was out with some bitch at the club, that same night! So, if you're wrong what the fuck does that make him? You're letting him get over, and it's not cool Syd."

"I understand, what you're saying Vani. But, I have a lot to lose. I know I've physically moved away, but I can't just say fuck you to him and go on my way. We have a family."

"Syd, I'm just saying don't be Chris' punching bag." Sydney looked at the car display screen, thinking to herself *did she really just say that shit to me. Mrs. Mark's punching bag!*

"I hear you girl." Said Sydney she was now approaching the Saks parking lot.

"I'm just saying next time he puts his hands on you, I'm gonna fuck him up myself. But, I love you girl. Be safe. I can't wait to see you soon."

"I love you too girl. See you soon."

Sydney parked the car, checking her surroundings she looked at Natalia in the back seat. Natalia smiled banging her cup against the car door. Sydney went to the trunk to get her stroller out. Gavin had a few legal boxes in the trunk Sydney began to sift through the items to locate the stroller. She got the stroller out it was hot and she had begun to perspire after fighting to get the stroller out. She opened the back door to get Natalia out of the car. She placed her on her hip as she tried to flip the stroller open. No luck. She became frustrated, she placed Natalia beside her leg. Sydney looked up seeing a group of men, walking into the mall, she turned away not wanting to embarrass herself any further with the stroller.

"Let me help you mama." Said a male voice. Sydney grabbed Natalia's hand, pulling her closer as she turned around to see who the face behind the mystery voice was. He was gorgeous, six feet tall, possibly mixed, dark brown eyes, long lashes and tattoo sleeves on both arms. His wide warm smile made Sydney let down her guard to converse with him. He picked up the stroller and opened it one pull of his pulsating biceps. He placed the stroller down in front of Sydney, giving her enough space so she didn't feel uncomfortable of his presence.

"Here you go."

"Thank you." She replied with a smile as she placed Natalia down in the stroller, lifting the shade. The guy looked over Sydney's body and stopped at her face, her exotic beauty was definitely mesmerizing.

"Damn… you're beautiful. If you don't mind me saying." He replied with an awkward smile, trying not to seem too forward.

"Thank you." She replied trying to contain the blush on her face.

"Dominic."

"Sydney." He shook her hand. "Who is the little one? She's adorable too." "This is Natalia." said Sydney. "Pleasure to meet you both." He replied with a smile. His demeanor was respectful, yet his tattoos screamed he had a street side to him. She did a mental checkpoint of his outfit. He was wearing a Crooks & Castles shirt, which fit nicely to his muscular frame, dark jeans and Retro Jordan sneakers on his feet. No jewelry on his neck only a watch, which was Cartier, and diamond studs in his ear.

"So, Sydney are you with someone?"

"No, I'm single." She replied. The words almost jumping off her tongue.

"A'ight. Can I take you out sometime? I mean I'd like to see you again."

"That will be fine. Where's your phone?" He pulled out his Samsung Note phone, he handed it to her with the screen already unlocked for her to type in her number. "It's an out of state number. I'm not a Cali girl."

"I just knew you were to pretty to be one of these fake LA broads. Where you from?"

"Originally, Connecticut. But, I live in Miami."

"Okay, east coast shorty. I'm from Jersey."

"Really? What are you doing here?" Sydney looked over and realized they had an audience. Dominic's friends had waited across the street and now that their conversation had gotten deep, they told him they would see him later. He waved at them saying go on. "Oh, I'm sorry to hold you up from your friends." Said Sydney sympathetically.

"It's a'ight. I can see them niggas every day. I may not be able to see you again. He smiled. But, on your question earlier I'm out here because I am a music producer and DJ."

"Really? That's cool. How long have you been doing it?"

"About six years."

"And may I ask how old are you?"

"I'm twenty-three. You? I know you never ask a lady her age but…"

She laughed. "I'm not mad about it yet so I will tell you. I'm twenty-one. I don't want to sound like a groupie but have you worked with anyone big?"

"I don't mind you checking my receipts. He said with a smile. I've worked with Mos' Def, Remy Ma, Snoop, Meek Mill, Mobb Deep and Dipset to name a few. I try to stay low key and keep it only about the music. I'm not in it for the money, but the love for the music. Try to stay grounded and humble, not on no fake celebrity shit."

Sydney smiled. She found it attractive how he spoke of his love of music and that he was humble. There was definitely something different about him than any guy she had ever talked to before. She was intrigued, she had to know more. "Do you have any kids?"

"Not yet. One day hopefully. What about you, what brought you out to Cali?"

"I'm visiting my dad, checking things out before I make this a possible permanent move."

"That's what's up. Have you been out in LA yet?"

"No, I don't really know anyone out here."

"Well, I'm doing a party tonight. I'd like you to come through."

"Um… I'd like to, but I don't know my way around yet."

"We'll make this happen. I'll have a car service to pick you up. I have your number. I will have them scoop you up and bring you out tonight."

She looked into his eyes. There was something sincere about him. "Okay. We can do that."

"A'ight, so I will see you tonight?" He said as if he couldn't believe she said yes.

"You will see me tonight,"

"Damn, just to think I wasn't going to come out here today. I would've missed you."

Sydney smiled. "So you should be happy you came? And thank my crazy ass stroller." He laughed out loud.

"Right, I'm happy, I'm just trying to not be all corny and smiling ear to ear. You're beautiful."

"Thank you again, Dominic. She replied. So, call my phone so I can have your number." He dialed her phone and it began to ring in her purse. I will lock you in once I get into the shade." He smiled reaching out to give her a hug.

"A'ight, see you later." He waved goodbye to her hurrying off across the street. Sydney watched him walk away. Dominic was definitely eye candy, but she was already smitten by his boyish charm and smile. She had to find something new for tonight, and a babysitter.

Back in Atlanta, Chris was downtown. He and Nick had just left the meeting with Rock, Everything went smoothly without any problems. Chris got the money and Rock had informed business was well, that they couldn't get enough of Preme's product. Nick had been doing well that week, following all orders. Chris felt that he had gained a bit of room, and that maybe he could let him handle the next stop on the trip. Chris figured if he gave him a little responsibility he could go back and tell Preme and Mart how good he did, they would trust him again. They stopped by the Lenox mall for a little retail therapy.

They walked inside a jewelry store. Chris immediately saw a small diamond Hello Kitty necklace which caught his eye. He immediately thought he had to get it for his Tubby. He soon ventured to the women's section surprising himself as he saw a beautiful pair of diamond hoop earrings. They stopped by a few stores, the last store was Neiman Marcus, Chris had a few bags in his hand from all of the other stores but he wasn't finding anything in Neiman's he wanted. He went over to the men's shoes, nearly stopping dead in his tracks as he saw a familiar face standing at the jewelry counter. It was Sarah yelling into her phone. Chris walked closer to hear her conversation better. "No, I told Eric to do what he needed to do. I told you! I could get up with the guy down here if you listen… I understand that… but he's over everything. I'm not doing that shit with no money. What about the attempt? Chris was circling the jewelry counter acting as if he was looking inside of it, across from Sarah. Did you get a location on the bastard? How the fuck did you lose him? Ben sometimes…I wonder what the hell would you do without me! I have to do everything. I'll get a location from my source. What about that bitch in Boston? WHAT?! Why won't they let that bitch be…? Your fuck ups, I tell you. I'm going to get my nails done. Tell Eric if you see him to call me." Chris had heard everything. He wanted to hem her up right there in the store.

He wanted more details, he decided to follow her out of the store. Just as he eased closer to her his phone rang loudly. People looked around, he picked up the phone. Answering it. Sarah looked directly in his direction. She looked at him as if she saw a ghost. Sarah followed him with her eyes, not daring to move her planted feet. Chris walked away talking on his phone. Sarah immediately pulled out her phone. "I found him! He's alive." She watched him until he disappeared within the rack of clothes. Just as she looked around again to see where he was located, Chris walked directly in front of her lifting his shirt showing his gun on his waist. Sarah became startled, she backed into the counter ending the phone call.

That night, in Los Angeles, Sydney was getting dressed to meet Dominic at the club. Gavin was to watch Natalia. Sydney looked at her reflection as she slid the form fitting Herve Leger bandage dress over her body. She looked at her breasts in the mirror, adjusting them in her La Perla bra. She placed pins in her hair as she brushed her hair over to one side. Sydney turned on Pandora on her iPad as she applied her makeup, and placed her Christian Louboutin pumps on her feet. "Where are you going?" said Gavin looking over his daughter's provocative attire. "I'm going to meet a friend at the club."

"Be careful, Sydney. Call me when you're on your way back." Said Gavin, being an overprotective father.

"Daddy, I will be fine. Don't worry." She walked over kissing his cheek. She looked down at Natalia who was in his arms, she kissed her lips. "I'm always going to worry about you Sydney. You're my daughter." "Okay, dad. Take care of my baby. Call me if you need me." The car service had pulled up outside and she walked out to meet the driver. Gavin watched from the window as Sydney slid into the backseat, the driver closed the door walking around to the driver's side of the SUV. They arrived in West Hollywood, her phone rang. "Hello."

"Hey beauty, are you here?"

"Not yet. We just got on Sunset?"

"When you get to the door, tell them you are with DJ Skillz. Your name is on the list, as Beauty."

"How do you know that's my name." said Sydney being flirtatious.

"I looked at you." Sydney blushed, his game was cute. She loved that he was so genuine, that his game wasn't an act.

"We are pulling up now. Where will I find you inside? I mean I guess follow the music eh?" she replied.

"No worries. They will bring you to me."

"Okay, see you inside." The driver came around to open her door. Sydney handed him a tip, although he declined saying that he had already been compensated by Dominic. She placed the twenty in his pocket anyway. She looked at the crowd waiting in line. She put her head up walking up past the lines to the rope. "Hi, I'm on the list with DJ Skillz." She looked up at the bouncer who looked as if could break her body in two. "Name?"

"Beauty." Said Sydney confidently. The bouncer looked up from the iPad he had in hand into her eyes. He softened a bit smiling at her. "Yes, you are. How many?"

"Just me." He pulled back the rope letting Sydney in. There was a man behind the rope dressed in all black Armani dress attire, with in earpiece in his ear. He signaled for Sydney to follow him. Once inside of the club Sydney immediately looked up in the air at the rows of chandeliers and gold everywhere. The club was very chic, modern and New York inspired. She immediately thought of Leonardo DiCaprio in The Great Gatsby. As they walked up stairs to the DJ booth, Sydney began to dance to the music. Nicki Minaj's "Truffle Butter" came thru the speakers. The guy led her to the back of the booth where he had a private table. Sydney looked at Dominic behind his MacBook Pro with his Beats by Dre gold headphones on his ears. He was wearing a black flannel shirt, dark jeans and Jordan Concord's on his feet. His black Yankee fitted turned backwards. Sydney inched closer tapping him on his shoulder. He turned around looking at Sydney, with a smile. He took the headphones off. "Yo, you made it. Look at you." He hugged her body, she immediately smelled the Dolce & Gabbana The One cologne he was wearing. "How are you?" said Sydney. "I'm good... now. Hold that thought. He leaned over to the mic. Where all my sexy ladies? Make some noise! He began to hit the horn sound effect, as the women screamed.

He began to scratch and mix Rihanna's "Work" The crowd went crazy. Let's go! As he cued up the next songs he took off the headphones, looking back to Sydney. She was dancing to the music, she began to rock her hips seductively. Dominic watched. "You want a bottle or a drink?"

"I'll take a drink." Dominic signaled for the waitress to come over. "Get her whatever she wants all night."

"I'll take a sex on the beach." The waitress left. Dominic led Sydney over to his table, they sat beside each other on the sectional. "What else can I get to know about you?" said Dominic.

"Don't you have to play the music?"

"No, I'm on break." The waitress came back with Sydney's drink with a pineapple on the side. Sydney sipped before placing the drink in front of her. "So mama, tell me what I should know about you? What are you into?"

"I mean, I love to shop. I'm high maintenance, love having a good time, and college student."

"Oh okay. What are you majoring in?"

"Nursing"

"Oh, so you can take care of me. I like that already."

"I like to help people."

"That's good. Means you have a good heart. How old is your daughter, Natalia?"

Sydney smiled, impressed he remembered her name. "She's almost two."

"Okay. What about her father?"

"What about him?" said Sydney almost defensively thinking about Chris. He was the furthest thing from her mind.

"Are you still involved? Friends with benefits. Does he take care of his daughter?"

"Um... no. We are not together. But, he is a good father to Natalia."

"That's good. We need more men like that."

"Yea. But, then what are we women going to complain about?" Sydney took her drink taking a few more sips.

"See, you women love drama."

"Oh, whatever. Some of you niggas are just as petty as females." Said Sydney with a laugh.

"Yea, you right."

"So, are you in LA permanently? I remember earlier you said you were from Jersey."

"Well, I've been out here awhile now, I'll be going back to Jersey soon. I have this radio gig that may happen. I've been working on a few songs with a few different artists that should be hitting radio soon."

"That's amazing. Congratulations!"

"Thank you."

"You're welcome. So, tell me about you, Mr. DJ?"

"Like I said, nothing much to me, I'm real humble and chill. Stay working and busy, when not working home body actually. I'm only out on scene when working. I have a sister in Baltimore. Do you have any siblings?"

"No, I'm the only child."

"Oh, so you're spoiled rotten huh?"

"Well, I do get my way… sometimes." Said Sydney with a mischievous grin.

"You probably get your way all the time."

"I don't. I'm not a brat." Sydney hit him playfully.

"Look at your smile. Yo, you're too much."

"I know. But, you're not that bad yourself sexy. So, are you going to show me how to DJ?" replied Sydney as she looked into his face. "Yea, I'll show you." He held his hand out to help her off the chair. Sydney placed her hand in his as they walked over to the booth. As the night went on Sydney had a blast. Dominic was the perfect gentlemen, although he was preoccupied with his duties of the night he still managed to give Sydney all of his attention. After closing time, Dominic asked Sydney if she wanted him to call the car service back to take her home. She said no, that she would let him drive her home. They walked out back to his car he had a BMW six series Gran Coupe which was Black, with dark tinted windows. He walked around opening the passenger door, for Sydney. "Thank you."

"You're welcome. He closed the door walking around to the driver's side. Are you hungry?"

"No, I'm good."

"A'ight. So where are we headed?"

"To Calabasas. I have it already plugged in my phone if you need the directions."

"Yea, you can go ahead and play that." Sydney connected her phone to the car audio so he could hear the directions. As they rode thru the city, laughing and talking as if they had known each other for years. They both were intrigued, their chemistry was magnetic and both wanted more. Once they pulled up to her house, Dominic put the car in park walking around to the passenger side to open the door for her. Sydney blushed, thinking when was the last time Chris or any man she dated had opened her car door. "I had a good time with you tonight Sydney. I'd like to see you again."

"I'd like to see you too." Sydney replied seductively. Her sex appeal effortless, made Dominic smile.

"So, I will call you later on today. Maybe you can bring your shorty up to the studio or we hang out at the beach."

"We may can do that." He reached out to hug her, as he reached in enveloping her within his strong arms, he kissed her cheek. "See you later beauty." He pulled away looking into her eyes as she smiled turning to walk to her front door. Dominic waited until she was safely inside, before driving off into the night.

Back in Atlanta, it was early morning and Chris and Nick had got up early to get breakfast as the Waffle House before he checked on business at the stash houses. Once they were done they headed to the location for the pop up, to see how things were. As they rode thru the streets, he saw a few niggas hanging out on the corner. All trying to get a glimpse inside of their SUV, not recognizing the car. Nick stopped the car at a brick house with a metal fence around the yard. The house, the third on the block, looked abandoned and vacant. Chris looked at a few men hanging out at the house next door. Chris adjusted the gun on his waist, getting out of the car. A group of girls emerged in their direction all scantily dressed, Chris ignored them resuming his walk to the house. Nick quickly stopped one of the ladies who was wearing a white tank and denim shorts that barely covered her ass. Chris remembered from the paper work, the front door had no entry, so he walked towards the side of the house. As he got to the corner of the house he realized there was an open shed, he looked at it, diverting his attention. As he looked back forward there was a figure in front of him in a skimask, dark hoody and jeans. Chris reached for his gun in that moment the assailant stabbed him quickly in the stomach. "Fuck!" shouted Chris in agony. Before the assailant could get another stab in, Chris punched him in the jaw. The force of the blow made a sound as if his jaw had broken. The assailant reached for Chris' gun, a scuffle ensued. The assailant grabbed the chain from Chris' neck before punching him in the face. Chris fell back against the house as the assailant took off towards the street. Chris finally retrieved his gun, blood seeping from his shirt, and fired one shot in his direction. It hit the assailant in the shoulder he grimaced in pain. Nick heard the gunshot he ended conversation with the ladies heading over to the house. He saw Chris' chain in the assailant's hand as he lay on the concrete. He immediately shot him in the chest, grabbing Chris' chain from his hands. "Fuckin' pussy." Chris emerged from around the house limping holding his stomach. "What the fuck were you doing?!" shouted Chris.

"Yo, my bad."

"Really nigga? Your fuckin' bad? You're fuckin' worthless! I'm getting hemmed up and your fuck ass out here fuckin' around." Once he was in arms reach of Nick he punched him in the face. Nick grabbed his face, furious. "You mad pussy nigga? I wanna see you fuckin' touch me!" Nick stood furious, not uttering one word. Chris walked over to the man lying in the driveway, wheezing for breath, clinging to his last moments of life. Chris reached down grabbing the mask off his face. He was a young nigga, about seventeen years old with gold teeth and a tattoo on his face. He was about two hundred pounds. "Who sent you here?" said Chris.

"Layo" said the kid weakly.

"Who?!"

"They call him Leo." He said weakly as he began choking on his own blood. Chris began to feel light headed, he stood up looking over the kid. "Get his fuckin' phones off him. Nick bent down grabbing the phone out of his pocket. Once he had the phone, Chris looked over the kid again, he shot him again. "Get me to the nearest fuckin' ER." They drove out of the city limits and Chris was stitched up. He stayed in the hospital for two days. Police had come asking questions, Chris gave no information saying that he was robbed at a gas station. Chris had no words for Nick, every time he saw his face he'd build up with rage. Chris pulled out his phone to check on Natalia. It was eight thirty at night in Atlanta and around five thirty in California. She and Dominic were at a movie, Sydney stepped outside telling Dominic it was her mother. "Hello."

"Yo... I've called you five fuckin' times already. Why can't you answer the fuckin' phone?"

"I was busy. What do you want?" she replied bluntly.

Chris attempted to sit up in bed. "Where the fuck is Natalia?"

"She's good. Is that what you called me for?"

"What you doing? Why are you trying to rush me off the phone?" said Chris angrily.

"Because I was in the middle of doing something and you interrupted me." Chris became angry ending the call. He sat up in bed pondering Sydney's behavior and attitude. Chris had this feeling that began to sizzle in the back of his mind, something was up. He decided he was going home. Chris sat up on the side of the bed removing the bandages from his arms. Nick walked into his room, with a phone he had stolen in the waiting room. "I called the number from that kid's phone. A woman kept answering the phone."

"Give me the fuckin' number!" Nick walked over handing him the phone. "I also want to let you know expect a fuckin' beat down, when I get out of this bitch and I'm one hundred. When we get back, I'm done with yo' bitch ass. I do better by myself. You just a punk ass nigga like pops said."

"Yo, C. You didn't have to say that shit!"

"What the fuck you gon' do, nigga? Shut the fuck up." Chris called the number. The phone rang a few times, and a woman answered the phone. "Yo... Leo." Said Chris.

"What did you need?'

"I handled that for you."

"Hadn't heard from you. Thought rumors were true. Money is where I said before."

"Look I need to lay low. Cops been on me. Can you bring it by downtown Peachtree?"

"I'll see what I can do." The woman hung up the phone. Chris handed Nick the phone. "Get a trace on that number and toss that phone, somewhere."

Meanwhile, in California, Sydney had left the movie with Dominic and was now at home watching television with Natalia. She decided to call Dana, and get the tea on Miami. "Hello," said Sydney cheerfully.

"Well, hello! How the fuck are you?" they both laughed.

"I'm good. We're good."

"You sound happy. You know I need more details than that generic answer. How's my muffin?"

"She's good. Making a mess all over the floor, doesn't listen. Wonder where she gets that from?"

Dana laughed again. "You know where she gets that from. You and her daddy. How's LA?"

"Weather is amazing. So, much to do here you have to come and I met a new guy."

"So, that's where happy is coming from. What's he like and what's his name?" said Dana.

"His name is Dominic. He is super gorgeous and polite. I mean he is very well mannered and a gentlemen. He is so genuine and funny. I mean when I'm with him we laugh all the time. He's a DJ and Producer. Dana, he treats me like I'm a queen."

"What?! He sounds like he is everything, honey. Does he have a brother? Just kidding. I'm soo happy for you. So, now that you've met Mr. Perfect are you coming home?"

"I don't know yet. I'm really happy here right now."

"I can tell I hear it all in your voice. But, what about Chris?"

"Dana, I'm soo tired of Chris and his bullshit this last time was the end for me. He has taken my love for granted, so I'm going to see what else is out there. Right now that is Dominic."

"I got you. But, you and Chris together was everything. I know right now a part of you is still hurt from the pictures but you loved him Sydney. Are you seriously saying all that love is gone forever?"

"No, I love him no matter what. But, I'm over his shit Dana. Somewhere our love has left us, I'm not trying to go back down that road again. I'm ready to love someone who loves all of me, genuinely."

"I got you. I just don't want you to move. When will I see muffin? But, go where your heart tells you boo. I'll have your back no matter what."

"Thank you. But, I haven't decided where my permanent situation will be. It will only be so long before my dad works my nerves. I have been thinking of moving back to Connecticut with my mom. But, I will definitely keep you informed."

"You better. But, nothing going on down here. I've been to Reign they have those pictures up of Chris and Bundles at the club. I've just been shopping and working. You know how I do."

"Yes, I know you. How's Vani?"

"Girl, still Vani. She and Mark are officially over now she called the police and put a restraining order on his ass. He kept showing up everywhere, girl he tried to jump her outside of the salon. I told her I've been telling you for years to let that crazy ass abusive nigga go. I'm happy she finally listened."

"I can't speak on her for being stupid to stay, cause of my situation over the years with Chris. However, although I'm happy in my life and enjoying the company of this great guy. I'm always going to think about Chris. I feel at this point, I just want him to have closure and be happy. If Chris can find happiness and peace that will be all I ever wanted for him."

"Takes a real one to want that for an ex nigga."

"I know. Dominic has shown me that. Don't sweat the fuck shit. I've moved on, I just want Chris to do the same."

"Well, I have to go get my food out of the oven. It was good speaking with you. Bring back my muffin, and I'm so happy for you girl."

"Bye girl."

That night Chris and Nick were to leave Atlanta that next morning, because Chris was still weak. He received a call on his phone from an unknown number. Chris answered, thinking maybe it was Preme. "Hello."

"Yo, Chris this Tarik."

"What up?" said Chris bluntly looking at the time it was after midnight.

"I've been trying to get up with you. I called you before and spoke to Syd. She never told you I called?'

"Nah. What's good?" said Chris impatiently.

"They're exhuming your mother's body in Boston. They had it on the news."

"What?" said Chris, as he sat up in bed wanting to hear where Tarik was going with this news. He wanted to see if it added up with Preme's news previously given in Miami.

"Yea. They found some new clues or some shit. Said something about tampered evidence before. I figured you didn't know because I haven't seen you on the news. They've been looking for family members."

"How long this been going on?"

"A few weeks now."

"A'ight. Good looking out." said Chris.

"Oh, before you go. About that Maino shit…"

"Who?" said Chris bluntly.

"Maino"

"Who the fuck is that? But, you remember New York right. Be safe, my nigga." Chris ended the call sliding off the bed. He walked over to Nick who was sleeping on the chair. "Let's go nigga. Get the fuck outta this bitch." Chris turned the phone off throwing it in his bag. Nick got up gathering their things. Chris placed on his clothes tucking his gun in his waist. Nick went to guard the door. The nurses at the station were all talking over coffee, Chris and Nick walked in the opposite direction heading for the elevators. They hopped into the SUV speeding off into the night. Once they were safely on the highway, Chris pulled out his phone calling Preme. "Hello"

"Pop… I need to talk to you." Said Chris trying to calm his nerves of everything that happened tonight.

"You a'ight? What's up?"

"Pop, I got some issues I can't deal with right now or fuckin' build on right now. Call me on the house phone tomorrow."

"A'ight, son. I'll hit you tomorrow. You good?"

"Yea, I'm good Pop."

"A'ight talk to you later." It was the middle of the night Preme, turned on his light making a few calls. Chris tossed his phone out the window, it shattered on the highway as he sped towards Miami. They arrived back in Miami around eight a.m. Chris was exhausted, all he could think of was his bed. He dropped Nick off and when he arrived home it was close to nine a.m. He walked into his palace, throwing his bags on the floor. Chris headed towards the stairs, he looked over at Natalia's picture on the wall, and he walked straight to his room falling out onto the bed. He didn't wake up until after six that night. He awoke confused and sore, he looked around the bed realizing he was at home. He leaned over turning on the light beside his bed.

He got up from the bed walking over to the closet, as he looked over their closet. He realized Sydney's shoes which usually lined the shelves by color were missing. He looked over her rows of clothes and realized they were bare. Chris walked over to the bathroom. When Sydney took a shower she always left her towel on top of the counter. Today it was placed neatly in the basket. Chris could feel his blood beginning to boil, he walked over to Natalia's room. Her closet was bare, and a few of her baby bags were missing. Chris scratched his head, walking over to the room grabbing the cordless phone, dialing Sydney's number.

"Hello?"

"Yea…Where you at?" said Chris.

"I'm out with Dana." Replied Sydney defensively.

"Oh yea, where's Tati?"

"She's here. She's fine."

"Bring her home. I want to see her."

"You're home?" said Sydney nervously.

"Yea, that's what I said. So, enough of the questions, bring my child home."

"We're in Orlando."

"Why the fuck are you in Orlando?"

"Don't talk to me like that! I'm here with Dana visiting her family."

"A'ight Syd. I'm gonna try not to blow up. I will call back later and I expect y'all to be on 95 then." Chris hung up the phone. Sydney laid back on the bed, next to Natalia who had just woke up from her nap. She was unbothered by Chris' threat, she decided to call Dominic. "Hello."

"Hi. It's Sydney. How are you?"

"What up Beauty. I'm good. How are you?"

"I'm good. I wanted to see you. What are you up to?"

"Well, I was leaving the studio about to get something to eat. I can come get you and we get a bite together?"

"That's fine. See you soon." Sydney slid off the bed throwing on a LA tank and a pair of distressed skinny jeans which were low and showed off her amazing figure, Christian Louboutin sandals on her feet. She quickly changed Natalia. Gavin came over to her door. He knocked twice. "Come in."

"I wanna take the baby to mama's."

"When?"

"Now. Mama has been asking about her. I've been saying I was going to bring her by."

Sydney smiled thinking how perfect was her father's timing. "Okay dad. Do you need her bag or anything?"

"Yea, I'll grab it from the living room. Where are you headed?"

"Out with Dominic."

"Oh, you're getting pretty close with him eh?"

"Yea. He's sweet." Gavin looked over outfit, which exposed side boob, stomach and back was exposed. "Are you wearing that?"

"Um…yes." Gavin shook his head. "Alright, lock up. See you later." He kissed her cheek picking up Natalia heading out the door. Moments after they left Dominic pulled up outside. Sydney met him in the driveway, he walked over to her hugging her body. "Look at you, I like those jeans on you. It shows one of your best assets."

"What's that?"

"This…" He caressed his hand over her ass. She laughed. "Thank you." He walked over to the passenger door opening it for her. Sydney slid in to the passenger seat, placing on her seat belt. Dominic got in behind the wheel. Sydney looked over to him. "When can I get to see your place?" said Sydney.

"Whenever, you want. You want to see it today?"

"Yes, I want to see it."

"After we eat, we can stop by. You want Mastro's?"

"No, it's okay. I want something light like The Cheesecake Factory."

"It's whatever you want, beauty."

They went to The Cheesecake Factory in Beverly Hills, once done Dominic paid the tab and Sydney made sure to order a Snicker bar chunks cheesecake. Stuffed Sydney and Dominic walked down Beverly Drive, to check out a few stores. They walked hand in hand, Dominic stopped looking into Sydney's face. "Yo beauty... I'm really feeling you. Ya know, I like being around you."

"Aww... I've been really enjoying being around you as well."

"I know it's early... but I can see myself getting serious with you. Only thing about that, I need to be forward with you. I'm gonna need you to be honest and one hundred with me. I can't deal with a shiesty female. I'm an open book."

"I understand. I feel the same way about you." She looked up into his eyes. She placed her arms around him kissing his lips.

"All I ask is that if you have any problems come to me. Honesty and communication, beauty." Sydney nodded her head in agreement. She loved his direct approach, she thought in her mind. Here is a real man, who wants to know me for me. She immediately thought those were the two things missing in her and Chris' relationship. Here is a gorgeous man, with a successful career and wanted to start a relationship with her with a solid foundation. She smiled at him again. "I will." He kissed her lips. He placed his hand back in hers as they walked on. After shopping over an hour, Dominic was to show her his West Hollywood Condo.

Back in Miami, Chris had left to store for medicine for pain relief and food. As he walked through Publix, he quickly picked up a bottle of Tylenol. He walked back to the deli ordering a sub, before walking towards the front. He looked up ahead seeing a woman standing at the end of the aisle looking over the soft drinks. She was wearing a pair of leggings, Jordan shirt and Jordan sneakers on her feet, and blonde hair. Chris looked over her body before walking past her. She turned looking into his face. "Chris?" He turned around stopping in his tracks looking into Vani's face. "What up." Vani looked at his posture, he was bent over as if he was in pain and was walking with a limp.

"What's wrong with you?"

"I'm good. How you?"

"I'm okay. How's the baby?" said Vani with a smile.

"I don't know yet. I'm supposed to see her later today."

"Oh, you're going to see them?"

"Yea."

"Aww… so you two getting back together?"

"Maybe. I don't know yet."

Vani placed her hand on her hip. "You sure you well enough to go to Cali?"

"California?! Who goin' to Cali?" shouted Chris, his demeanor quickly shifted. Vani could see the rage in his eyes.

"Um… I meant..." replied Vani stumbling over her words.

"Who in Cali? You didn't say that shit for nothin'?! Sydney in fuckin' Cali with my fuckin' baby?"

"Um… no." Shoppers began to look over at them, listening in on the conversation.

"Don't fuckin' lie to me!" shouted Chris as he pointed in her face. Vani was lost for words. She looked at the hurt in Chris' face, he looked so good. She took a deep breath.

"Sydney is in Cali. I told her not to go, she wouldn't listen to me. I'm sorry Chris."

Chris smirked, taking in the information she had given him. He walked calmly towards the register, not uttering another word to Vani. Vani stood in awe wondering what he was going to do next. She watched his back as he walked outside to his car.

Sydney and Dominic had arrived at his home. It was a two story, modern condo, high ceilings and Italian cabinetry. The living room area was all black and white, black leather couches, seventy inch television, with a filled book shelf. An avid reader, Sydney was impressed. "This is nice."

"Thank you" Dominic replied as he continued the tour of his three bedroom home. Which included a studio, guest room and the last room was his bedroom at the end of hall with balcony. Sydney walked in immediately walking into his walk in closet which was the size of a decent size bathroom. She looked over his shelves of sneakers. He had over three hundred pairs. Sydney smiled picking up a pair of Lebron James nine South Beach Nike's. "Do you have enough shoes?" she replied sarcastically.

"Yea, one thing I gotta stay fresh. Keep my shoe game one hundred."

"I guess." She placed the shoe back down, walking out of the closet. Sydney climbed on top of his King bed. "Can you get me something to drink?" said Sydney sweetly.

"Sure. What would you like to drink?"

"Surprise me." replied Sydney seductively. Dominic smiled leaving out of the room to the kitchen. Sydney heard him getting ice from the ice maker on the refrigerator. Once she heard him coming back to the room she ran her fingers through her hair. Dominic stepped back in the room, seeing Sydney laying on top of his bed topless in a black La Perla lace thong. Dominic's mouth dropped as he took in Sydney's naked torso. He placed the drink on the nightstand. Sydney climbed on all fours, as she tugged at his shirt. "Come here..." said Sydney seductively. Dominic climbed into bed kicking off his shoes. Sydney pinned his body underneath hers as she climbed on top of him. She lifted his shirt, kissing his chest and ear sensually before removing his shirt completely. As she began to feel him rise underneath her, she smiled. Sydney leaned over to his ear. "I feel you papi... come take me." She bit his ear lobe. Dominic grabbed her body, smacking her ass. He flipped her over on her stomach, removing his pants. "I'm gonna fuck the shit out of you baby." Whispered Dominic as he pulled her hair from behind.

Hours later, they lay in bed together, completely naked. They had went three times, both sweaty and stuck to one another. Dominic removed the condom, tossing it in the garbage bin beside his bed. "Damn, ma. He caressed her ass. Now, I'm never letting you go." He kissed her forehead.

Sydney smiled. "You were amazing yourself. That swing was everything." She caressed his chest, taking in his scent. Her phone rang and she reached over to the nightstand to look at the screen. It was Chris. She declined the call, turning off the phone. Dominic reached over kissing her back, she turned over kissing his lips gently as they drifted to sleep.

In Miami, Chris was fuming that Sydney was not answering his calls. His anger began to boil over and he went into the safe grabbing his gun, heading out the door. He drove over to Dana's house, his gun on his waist. He began banging on the door. Dana soon came to the door startled. "Who is it?"

"Chris."

Dana opened the door seeing Chris' pissed expression. "Hi Chris."

"What up. Syd here?"

"Um... no."

"Where is she? She's supposed to be with you?"

"Um... yea we were."

"You went to Orlando today?"

"Yea." said Dana going with the story he was giving.

"What time you got back?"

"Um… a little while ago."

"Don't fuckin' lie to me, about my fuckin' child!" Chris' voice rose and she could tell he was angry. After the stories revealed at the party she wasn't about to rub him the wrong way, but she wasn't going to snitch on Sydney.

"Chris… that's all I know."

"Why the fuck you tryin' to play me right now? Syd in Cali?"

Dana was shook. *Fuck!* She thought in her mind. She tried to regain her composure so he wouldn't see the lie written all over her face. "Look, Chris. I haven't spoken to Sydney in a while. I don't know anything."

"A'ight, we'll see who knows what when I start fuckin' niggas up. I've already told y'all before. I'm nothing to be fucked with. You heard?!" "Chris… please…"

"Nah, fuck you. I tried to be nice. Y'all wanna play games! We'll see who have the last fuckin' laugh." Chris hopped back in his car, feeling satisfied he had the clarification he needed that Sydney was in California. Once home, he got on the laptop buying the next flight out of Miami to Cali. The tickets were all sold out for today, the next was tomorrow and he made sure it was first class.

Dana went inside her house frantically calling Sydney's phone. The phone was off, went straight to voicemail. "Shit! Sydney turn on your fuckin' phone!" shouted Dana. The next morning Sydney woke up underneath Dominic's arm. She gently moved his arm, climbing out of bed. She picked up her phone from the nightstand going over to the bathroom. When she powered her phone on she had over ten text messages from Dana. They all said to call her, she placed the phone on the counter deciding to call her once she got home. Sydney hopped into the shower, wrapping a towel around her body as she grabbed one of Dominic white tees out of his closet, she slid on her jeans over her naked body. Sydney walked out to the kitchen, going to the fridge making eggs and sausage. She sat down at the bar eating. Dominic came up behind her, he kissed her neck. "Good morning." Said Sydney.

"Good morning beauty. Aw, you made breakfast. Thank you."

"You're welcome. But, I'm going to need to go home soon. I know my dad is getting ready for work and I need to get Natalia."

"Okay, no problem. Let me take a shower real quick. I'll get you home. I'll head to the studio once I drop you off."

"Oh, are you working with someone today?"

"I'm working with Tinashe. Well, I have worked with her before."

"Oh, that's cool. Good luck. May your creative juices be great today." Said Sydney with a smile.

"Thank you. Can you wrap up the breakfast for me in a container in pantry?" He leaned over kissing her lips. Once he was out of shower and dressed they were on their way. Dominic's phone rang, he looked at the screen answering. The phone went to the car system in his car. "Hello."

"What up Dom? What you up to?"

"Good my nigga. Chillin' with my girl, Sydney. What you up to?"

"Seeing if you wanted to go to this day party in Malibu later. Good networking joint, execs gonna be in the building."

"Yea, that's cool. Let me see what Syd is doing and I'll hit you back a'ight."

"A'ight. Hit me back." Dominic ended the call looking over to Sydney. Sydney had a smile on her face. Chris would never put his phone call on speaker while she was in the car and she thought it was sweet he considered her feelings first, definitely was a change. "That was my homeboy Brandon. As you heard they having a day party I think Def Jam and different artists."

"Sounds fun. You should go, I'll stay home and spend time with Natalia. Have fun with your friends." She leaned in kissing his cheek.

"A'ight, I didn't know if you had plans or not. But, I will see you after?"

"Of course." They arrived at her house. Dominic got out of the car to open her door. He hugged her tightly, kissing on her neck. Sydney blushed, as she grabbed his chin kissing his lips. "See you later."

"Bye." She walked over to the front door, using her key. She was greeted at the door by Gavin holding Natalia in his arms. "Have fun last night?"

"Huh?" replied Sydney as she took Natalia from his arms.

"You were out all night. Doing God knows what, I was worried about you."

"I got... tied up. I forgot to call."

"You forgot?! You need to be more responsible Sydney!"

"Dad, not now."

"Not now?! You don't tell me when the hell I can talk to you. All I am asking is for you to have just a little decency to call when you decide to be out all fucking night." "Okay, dad. I'm sorry." Sydney took Natalia with her into her bedroom. Gavin came behind her. "I'm going to the office." "Bye." Shouted Sydney from behind the door.

It was almost eleven, in Miami, Chris was up and dressed. He had a Louis Vuitton book bag with a few of Natalia's items in it, and two stacks of cash. The home phone rang on the counter, he picked it up seeing Preme's number on the screen. "What's good son?"

"What up pop. It's a lot of shit going on. Syd left with the baby."

"What?!"

"Yea, I came home and she went to fuckin' California with Natalia. I'll be leaving out in a few hours to go get her. Then, I got fuckin' hemmed up in Atl, one in my stomach."

"Where the fuck was Nick?"

"Looking pop. Running his fuckin' mouth with some bitches."

"Oh word. I'll teach that pussy a little lesson. Don't worry about it, it's a wrap. You a'ight?"

"I left the hospital early, after Tarik called on some fuck shit. And I saw Sarah, Ben's wife at the mall. I need some fuckin' meds. I'm sore as shit."

"A'ight, I'll text you a doctor who can get meds for you. Dr. Malack in Lauderdale, look him up. He's got a few offices in Miami as well, I'll have him fill you a prescription and check you out make sure you good."

"That's a'ight, pop. I'm good. I'm more concerned with getting my baby. I can't sleep not knowing what the fuck is up with her, n'ahmean. She could have my child around any fuckin' body."

"Go get the baby. You need to stop by the doctor. I'll have Darren take over in the meantime. You need to rest."

"A'ight pop. I'll go by the doctor. Text it to me, I got my old Blackberry for now. Send me the address. I will still go to Connecticut for you. Just give me a week."

"It's no problem. Your health and my granddaughter is more important than this game. I'll check back with you later. What happened to your phone?"

"I trashed that shit. I'll get a new one on my way to airport."

"A'ight son."

Chris hung up the phone, and he received a message to the Blackberry. He headed outside to the car, speeding off down the road to Dr. Malack's office. Once there Dr. Malack took him back immediately, he checked his wound and gave him some Lortab's. He wrote out another prescription for him for later. Dr. Malack informed Chris that he was fine and the doctors did a good job with patching him up. He recommended Chris get some rest. Once they were done Chris asked about the check, Dr. Malack simply replied, "Your father covered it. Anytime you need my services you call me okay." He gave him his personal cell phone number. Chris left heading to ATT for a new phone. Once there he immediately walked over to the latest iPhone which caught his attention, it was gold. Chris picked up the phone and began to play with it. The sales representative walked over. "Hi, may I help you?"

"Yea, I lost my phone. I want to buy this one. Also, I wanted to know if I could track the other phone on my account."

"Sure, step over here and I can take care of all of that for you. She led him over to her computer at the desk. May I have your name and phone number on account?" Chris gave her the information, showing his Driver's license. She pulled up the account, she looked over the secondary phone on account. "It seems the other phone is in the California market. Looks like Los Angeles area, to be exact."

"That's all it shows."

"Unfortunately, that's all I can see at this time."

"Well, let me get the phone. Once getting iPhone with highest storage a few accessories and charging dock. His order came up to close to a grand. He handed her cash, she handed him the change and activated his phone for him. After everything was complete he headed to the airport. Once he arrived at the airport he checked his bags to make sure that he had everything. Once confirmed he walked into the airport and in minutes was boarding the plane. He took one of the pills before drifting off to sleep on his five hour flight. When he awoke they were preparing for landing. Chris looked out the window, admiring the view.

Sydney and Natalia were at home enjoying Nick Jr. Sydney had just finished dinner. Beef, Broccoli and rice. She came back into her bedroom with a sip cup of Juicy Juice for Natalia. "Da Da." said Natalia as she looked at Sydney. Sydney smiled back at her. "You miss your daddy mama?" Sydney sat on the bed pulling out her phone. She placed Natalia on her lap, showing Natalia a picture of Chris in her phone. "Daddy." said Sydney as she pointed to the picture. Natalia smiled looking at the picture. "Da da." "Aww, your daddy loves you tati. You miss him huh? I miss your daddy a little bit too." She reached down kissing Natalia's cheek. Her phone rang interrupting, Dana's picture appeared on the screen.

"Hello."

"Damn, bitch! I've been calling you all night!"

"I'm sorry. I was with Dominic last night."

"Oh, you two are serious now?"

"Well, I really like him. We slept together last night. I'm definitely enjoying his company."

"Obviously, he laid the pipe down strong your ass turned your phone off and couldn't respond to me. So, are you moving there for good?"

"Right now, I don't know. I was thinking of maybe Connecticut. I haven't decided yet."

"What about school?"

"I'm still going once I get stabile. I just don't see me in Miami anywhere around Chris right now."

"Well, you definitely need to get in school. If you are going to support Natalia by yourself and not be with Chris." Sydney looked down at her bare ring finger. "I can't believe, me and Chris are over. I mean, at one point, Chris was my everything."

"He could still be that. But, you know sleeping with Dominic ended that."

"Don't get me wrong Dominic is amazing. It just hurts a little after all we have been thru, that we ended like this. I guess we've grown apart."

"Oh, now I know what I called for. Chris came over last night, mad as hell! He knows you're in Cali!"

"WHAT?!"

"He knows girl! I didn't tell him shit, it was as if he already knew. He came out point blank and asked me are you in Cali? I was like I don't know shit."

"Oh, my god. He is going to flip the fuck out." Sydney got off the bed and began pacing around the room.

"Yea. He asked me had I spoke to you? Did we go to Orlando? I just started going along with whatever he was saying."

"Oh, shit. I meant to call you, he called me and I told him that we were in Orlando. To buy me some time."

"Yea, you should've given me a heads up! But, it's okay I had your back I didn't say anything."

"I want to know how the fuck does he know I'm here. I only told you and Vani."

"I'm telling you right now, I didn't tell him shit. Vani has been at the salon all day. I don't know if she was running her mouth there. But, I don't think she would've told. What are you going to do?"

"I don't know. I don't think Chris is going to come all the way to California. Besides he doesn't know my dad's address. So, whatever, I'm not worried."

Chris sat on a bench at the airport. He pulled the laptop from his bag. He logged on to the internet onto a people seekers website. He typed in Gavin Cruz in the search bar. It gave a few hundred listings he narrowed it down quickly by area. He took out a credit card to pay for the service. He wrote down the address. He signaled the first cab he saw along the curb. The driver was a middle aged, White male with a balding head and beard. "Where to?" "Calabasas." Chris replied. He handed the driver the piece of paper with the address on it. "I can get you here. So, is this your first time to LA?"

"I'm not in a talking mood. I'm going to need you to wait when I get there. Keep the meter running."

"Okay." An hour later after the driver decided to take the scenic route they pulled along the curb of Gavin's home. Chris placed the backpack on his back. He left the computer on the backseat. He walked over to the front door, and knocked twice. "Who is it?" said Sydney. "Chris." He replied calmly. Sydney approached the door, not hearing his response. She attempted to look through the peep hole. She opened the door, seeing Chris in front of her face. Her mouth dropped, her immediate reaction was to close the door. She tried to slam the door, Chris stopped the door with his foot as he proceeded inside. Sydney ran away from the door, running back to her bedroom to get Natalia. Chris came behind her with speed pulling her by the hair, throwing her to the ground. She screamed in agony. "What the fuck were you thinking? Shouted Chris as he stood over her. I've told you, I'm nothing to fuck with. You of all people should know that shit by now!"

"You are not taking Natalia from me! Fuck you!" She lifted her leg kicking him with all her might in the stomach. Chris held on to his stomach. Sydney tried to get to her feet. Chris kicked her in the stomach. He walked towards the bedroom. Natalia was sitting up on the bed. "Da Da!" she replied happily.

"Come on mami. Let's go home." Chris picked her up in his arms kissing her face. He proceeded to walk out the room. Sydney was standing in the hall. "You can't take her away from me! I am her mother!"

"I'm not fuckin' arguing with your dumb ass. Get the fuck out of the way."

"NO!" Sydney stood blocking his path resiliently. Chris walked past her unbothered. As he past, Sydney grabbed on to Natalia's leg. Natalia began to scream, frightened. Chris turned around punching Sydney in the face, the impact sent Sydney falling backwards onto the wall. She held her face running over to the kitchen, grabbing a carving knife wielding it in his face. "If you walk out of this house with Natalia, I will fuckin' cut you."

"You're not fucking stupid Syd." Natalia began to cry as Sydney pointed the knife at Chris. Chris grabbed Sydney's arm pulling it behind her back as if he was to break it. "Oww…" she screamed as she dropped the knife. "Stop fuckin' playing with me!" Chris shouted as he threw her to the side. She fell into the end table hitting her eye. "I HATE YOU!" she began to scream through tears as blood trickled down her cheek. Chris walked out to the cab placing Natalia inside. Once safely inside, Sydney came charging out of the house she began punching him repeatedly in the back. Chris closed the cab door, turning around grabbing Sydney by the neck. He tightened his grip, as Sydney's legs dangled in the air. "I told you don't fuck with me! You was gonna take my child clear across the country and not tell me shit! Did you think I wasn't going to find out?! I'm done with your stupid ass. Forget you fuckin' knew me, lose my fuckin' numbers and all that. Stupid ass bitch!" Sydney's face became pale, Chris released his grip from her neck. Dropping her body to the ground. Chris took off his ring throwing at her face. He climbed into the back of the cab, the cab driver sped off. Sydney lay on the sidewalk. A neighbor who was watching from their driveway, came over to help her. "Are you okay? I have called the police."

"I'm fine. Leave me alone." Sydney pulled herself off the pavement rushing into her house. She ran towards the bathroom to look at herself. Her eye had swollen up to the size of a golf ball, blood all over her shirt. Her neck was covered in bruises. She heard the front door open, she frantically tried to cover her neck with foundation. "Sydney?! Sydney, where are you?"

"In here." said Sydney.

Gavin walked over to the bathroom door. "Why is there police outside?"

"I don't know."

"Sydney, come out here right now!"

"In a minute."

Meanwhile, Chris and Natalia had boarded a flight back to Miami. Chris sat her on his lap, he smiled kissing her face. Sydney finally came out of the bathroom. "Where's Natalia?"

"She's gone." said Sydney holding back from tears.

"Gone where? What happened to you?" said Gavin as he looked into her face in the light.

"Chris took her."

"He put his hands on you. I'll kill him!"

"Daddy, I'm okay."

"Fuck this! We are taking you to the hospital. You are pressing charges against that ass hole! I don't know what the fuck is wrong with you defending that asshole. Let's go." At the hospital, Sydney's eye was checked out she would need two stitches, the doctor confirmed the bruises and abrasions on her neck. As she was resting, Gavin came in with a police officer. Sydney looked over at the officer. "Dad... I told you..."

"Sydney, don't be stupid. This bastard beat up my daughter and kidnapped their child."

"Does she have custody?"

"No, but we want to press charges!" said Gavin assertively.

The officer looked over to Sydney. "Ma'am, do you wish to press charges?"

"Yes, I want to press charges. His name is Christian Garcia." The officer began writing down his information in his notepad.

The next day Chris and Natalia were home he had given Natalia a bath. Chris was in pain, he had took a pill to relieve some of the pain. He was so furious with Sydney he took all of her clothes from the closet throwing them in garbage bags and placing them at the curb. His cell phone rang, he knew it was Preme he was the only person he had given the number to. "What up Pop?"

"Hey, how are you?"

"I'm a'ight. Taking these meds, I'll be good. What's up?"

"I got word about you and Syd's break up and situation. She's pressing charges."

"What?" said Chris pissed.

"Yea. She's saying she's got information on other shit as well."

"I'm so sick of her fuckin' ass pop."

"Either you go away for a while to get away from this bitch. Or I handle shit my way, and no one gonna be happy."

"Pop, she's not stupid. I'll handle this shit."

"A'ight, I'll let you handle that. Keep your eyes open stay clean, you feel me. I'll get back in touch with you in a few weeks. Get rest."

"A'ight." Chris fixed Natalia a hot dog, cutting it up in little pieces on one of her trays. He sat her beside him on the bed, as he laid back for another nap. When he woke again it was after five-thirty. Natalia had her back laying against his chest, watching television. He woke up changed her diaper and decided to get dressed and get out of the house. As he walked around their room he took every picture of Sydney out of their bedroom and placed them in Natalia's room. Once dressed he headed in the G wagon over to Reign. He met John as he walked in the back door, they hugged, John touched Natalia's cheeks. "What's good boss? Haven't heard from you in a minute?"

"Yea, I had a lot going on. I'm single now. Gotta make sure Tubby straight."

"Yo, you and Sydney done for good?" said John in disbelief.

"We weren't going to work. I tried to make that shit work, but, fuck it!" said Chris solemnly.

"Damn. Well, sometimes you gotta do what you gotta do. Glad you back. We've been busy in here, a lot of new shit that I think is going to do well. We have this rap group wanted to shoot a music video in here next week. I'll get to you on the details. Tatiana been pulling her weight, big help." John and Chris walked out to the floor. Tatiana was wearing bebe Peekaboo crop top and skirt set which was in green, Manolo Blahnik pumps on her feet. Her breasts were spilling out of the cut out in the front of her top. "Hi, Chris. How are you?" She replied with a smile as she opened her arms for a hug. Chris hugged her, glancing quickly over her derriere in the skirt.

"I'm good. How you?"

"I'm good. I've missed you. I mean, seeing your face." She blushed, pulling her wand curled tresses out of her face.

"Oh yea. Well, I missed... my store. I was praying it would still be standing when I came back." They all laughed. Natalia yawned listening to their conversation. Tatiana reached over playing with her hand. "Hi, cutie." Natalia smiled at her, immediately wanting to touch her hair. "Let's go take a look at the books." Said Chris. They walked back to Chris' office. He walked around his desk, taking a seat. As John went and got the books from the safe. He stood beside Chris opening them. Chris looked up seeing Sydney's picture in a frame on his desk. He quickly grabbed the picture from his desk tossing it and the hundred dollar frame in the garbage. John looked over at him, realizing he was serious about ending it for good with Sydney.

A week later. Sydney was at home and Gavin was at work. Dominic called and said he would come by, so they could talk. She hadn't told him about Natalia or Chris for that matter. Today, she felt she should tell him all that transpired. If she wanted to keep a healthy, open relationship. Ingrid had called and told Sydney to come home. She hadn't made a decision yet, but Hartford was looking like her best option.

Dominic arrived after four pm. He was wearing a Jordan Hoody and a pair of jeans, Timbs on his feet. She could tell from his face he was exhausted. He had been in the studio all night. Sydney had threw on a pair of grey leggings and a Fine Ass Girl black tank. As soon as she opened the door, Dominic smiled happy to see her. "Hi sexy." He hugged her kissing her cheek. "Hi." She replied solemnly. He walked past her taking a seat on the couch, he realized her demeanor was serious.

"I need to talk to you." She sat on the recliner which was across from him.

"A'ight. What's up?"

"Well, it's about Natalia's father... I wanted to tell you, because I feel we have gotten closer and there is definitely something going on between me and you."

"What about him?"

"We had a very stressful relationship. He was very aggressive, possessive, and crazy and at times we physically fought each other. We had been through a lot together, we were engaged. When I initially came here I was running away from him. I wanted to make him hurt, the way he hurt me, so I took Natalia and moved here without him knowing. I knew, in doing that would be the sweetest revenge to the pain he caused me."

"Okay..." said Dominc not wanting to give his opinion yet, but be a listening ear. He knew this had to be hard for her.

"Well, last week while you were out at the day party. He showed up here, we fought and he took Natalia with him. I did fight back with everything I had. He punched me, and I had to get stitches on my eye." She lifted her hair so he could see her scar.

"Why didn't you call me? How dare that coward put his hands on you?!" replied Dominic.

"I panicked. I didn't know what to do. But, I'm going to take legal action to get custody of my baby. It's a lot of mixed emotions right now, but I wanted to be completely honest with you. I didn't want you to think I was holding anything from you."

"I'm glad you told me. What are you going to do for money to show the court you have income, a house you know?"

"Yea, I'm trying to find a job here or my plan is to move back to Hartford with my mom. I don't know yet. I just wanted you to know what was going on."

"I'm glad you came to me. I have your back one hundred percent Syd. If Connecticut is a better choice for you, to get your daughter I won't stand in your way. I'll miss you though."

"Aww… I would love to stay here if the situation was better with a job and my dad didn't get on my damn nerves. Besides, I didn't want to even ask you to leave everything you have going here, you know."

"Well… actually, I do have something to tell you as well. I'm going to New York in a couple weeks for promo. I will be on the east coast for a few months."

"Wow, you should be excited. That's good news right?"

"Yea. I'd be happier if I could bring you with me. It's hectic and stressful. I don't want you to be bored with it. The offer stands if you would like to come out."

"No, do your thing. I'm happy for you. If I move to Connecticut we can definitely spend time together. Have fun!" She got up from the recliner sitting on his lap. She kissed his lips.

"A'ight, but enough about that. Let's work on getting your baby back." He kissed her cheek and eye where her scar was. "How did I get so lucky, to get an amazing guy like you?" She looked into his eyes, kissing his lips again.

A week later, Chris had recovered and was in the process of redecorating the house. He had taken everything that was of Sydney's or of her liking and threw it in the garbage. He was downstairs cleaning up, Natalia was walking around the coffee table. Darren called and asked Chris if he was still going to Connecticut and if he would need someone to go along. Chris decided that he would go alone. He was not about to have another Nick situation. Darren had also informed him that Preme needed him to check on his strip club. He picked Natalia up heading out the door. On the way Chris looked back at Natalia in the rear view mirror she was clapping her hand and saying something Chris couldn't make out. He lowered the volume on the stereo so he could hear her. She was saying I love you in Spanish. She kept repeating "amo da da... amo ma...ma" He smiled listening to her the rest of their drive. He stopped by the strip club to check with staff made sure everything was good. John called and stated that the staff was coming over his place tonight to watch a boxing match. Chris said he would stop thru, and that he didn't need nothing crazy going down since he would bring Natalia. John told him to bring her and everything would be fine. He suggested for Chris to bring drinks and ice. Chris stopped by a store grabbed a cart, planning to get a few items and be done. Soon as he walked through the store's double doors, he ran into Vani.

She was wearing a black, long sleeved crop top which laced up in front. Her breasts barely contained by the laces. Bare midriff over a camo mid length skirt which looked as if was painted on her body. Chuck's on her feet. Chris sighed, he was not in the mood for conversation. "Hi, Chris! How are you?" said Vani as she walked over to him.

"I'm good. How are you?"

"I'm great. Still working at my salon, doing what I do. She looked over seeing Natalia who was looking at her. Oh, look at my cutie pie!" She pinched Natalia's face touching over her hair. She could tell that Chris had done it. "So, what are you and Sydney going to do?"

"It's been done. Were through."

"Damn. I told Sydney not to go to Cali. That was a bad move." She replied shaking her head empathetically.

"Well, she made her own decisions." Women walked by eyeing Vani as she spoke to Chris. She flipped her hair over her shoulder, placing her hand on her hip.

"Yea... so... you're back on the market?" She replied with a smile.

"Yea, I guess you can say that. Why?"

"Because, I know a few women that's trying to get at you." She replied with a smile.

"Well, I'm not looking for anyone right now. Focusing on Natalia right now. You feel me?"

"Aww... that's so sweet. She's a daddy's girl. Well, if you need a sitter or a hand, hit me up."

"We'll see." Said Chris.

"Well, it was good seeing you Chris. You look good. Keep in contact." She ran her fingers across Chris' chest before walking away. Chris looked at her shaking his head. He couldn't believe she had come on to him like that. Vani was always flirtatious, but today he definitely felt she was doing too much. He wasn't in the slightest interested. Chris quickly picked up the items and in about fifteen minutes was heading up to the register. As soon as he got in line a group of men with a cart stood behind him. Chris moved the cart up and looked back at them. It was Yogi and the man who Chris had fought at the store. He looked at Chris as if he was going to say something. Chris began to take his items out of the cart. "That's him.... from the store."

"Oh, that's the nigga you fought."

"Bitch ass..." He mumbled under his breath. Chris turned around to face them.

"You got somethin' to say nigga?" Mario said nothing. He looked away. Yogi came forward, "What you gon' do about it?"

"He already know what's up. You don't want them problems wit' me fuck boy."

"Yea, you know what's up. That's why I fucked your bitch!" said Yogi.

Chris smiled. The cashier began to scan his items. Chris focused back on Yogi. "You fucked my bitch, little nigga? What my dick taste like, pussy?" The cashier gave Chris his total. He went into his pocket pulling out a stack of his cash. He peeled off a few bills handing it to the cashier. Placing the bags back in his cart. "Chris!" He heard a voice shout. He looked up seeing Martin walking in his direction with his man. "What up?!" said Chris as hugged him. "How are you?" said Martin.

"Healing. Shit, I'll be a'ight."

"Yea, I'm sorry about that. Preme told me about Nick's slip ups. Which has been handled."

"Yea, I can't fuck with Nick no more. It's a wrap after that shit."

"No, I get it. Nothing personal. It's business. He's bad business." The cashier handed Chris his change he headed out continuing his conversation with Martin. Yogi and Mario were stunned, everyone knew Mart just as much as Preme. Hood legends. They were eavesdropping trying to hear what they were talking about. "He know Preme?" said Yogi.

"That what it sounds like."

"How does he know Preme? Is what I need to know? He gotta know him good he in here talking to Chaz."

"Everyone know Chaz and Preme."

"Exactly. I'm gonna find out."

Chris had finished talking with Martin and was loading his items in the trunk. He strapped Natalia in and got behind the wheel, heading home. He brought in his groceries, gave Natalia a bath and took a shower. He fed Natalia before heading over to John's.

John greeted him and Natalia at the door. Natalia was sleeping on Chris' shoulder, everyone greeted him, as John led Chris back to the guest bedroom to lay Natalia down. It was a queen sized bed. "Do I need to ask who has been laying in this bed?" John laughed. "I just put clean everything on here." Chris looked over the bed not buying John's response. He went inside Natalia's bag pulling out her Hello Kitty fleece blanket spreading it over the bed. "Just in case. No shade. But, I know you nigga." He laid Natalia down on the bed placing a sheet over her body. He placed pillows around her and on the floor, just in case she rolled. She was at times a wild sleeper. They walked out of the room leaving the door cracked open. "Hi Chris." Said Tati, from the kitchen. "What's good Tati?" She walked over hugging him tightly.

"What is this a store meeting?" said Nathan from the couch. Everyone laughed. Chris looked over the food that was spread out. "Why don't you go get the ice and drinks out my trunk." He tossed Nathan the keys. John followed him outside to help. Tatiana walked over to Chris placing her hand on his back. "You want a drink Chris?" Before he could reply she had opened a Heineken and handed it over to him. "Thank you."

John and Nathan, handed the items over to the other girls in the kitchen as the men made themselves comfortable on the couches. As the Showtime commentators came across the screen. John began to school everyone on the undercard fighters. Nina, Tati and one of John's groupies and her friends placed the drinks and ice in the cooler. Tati pulled out her Mac lipglass to reapply to her lips. "So, when are you going to make your move?" said Nina.

"When it's right. I know Chris. He's not going to be checking for me until this bullshit clears with his baby mama."

"I mean... but how long is that gonna take. He is fine, Tati. You don't want to wait too long."

"I know. He's sexy. But, it's not just that... I like being around him. He makes me laugh. I got this."

"Damn... stick his ass!" shouted Chris from the living room. All of the women looked at each other. Tatiana heard Natalia moving in the bedroom. She went down the hall to check on her. She was sitting up on the bed, a second from tears. Tati picked her up, cradling her in her arms as she rocked her gently. Natalia placed her hand on Tati's back caressing it as she dozed back off to sleep. Chris came back to the room on his way to the bathroom. He saw Tati rocking her. "Oh, she woke up?" Chris reached out to take her. "Yes, she's going back to sleep. Tati turned so he could see her face, sleeping on her shoulder. She's fine. Go back and watch the fight. I got her."

"You sure?"

"Yes. She's fine. Go enjoy yourself." Chris kissed Natalia's forehead, before going back out to the guys who were shouting about the knockout about to go down. Halfway through the main event, Chris didn't want to leave but the fight was dry. Besides he had a few shots. He decided it was getting late and he needed to get Natalia home and in her bed. He packed up Natalia's bag, placing her over his shoulder with her fleece over her face. Tati followed Chris outside to assist him with Natalia. Chris strapped Natalia in the backseat. Tati grabbed the baby bag off his arm sliding it on the front seat floor. "Yo, thank you for helping me with Natalia tonight. I appreciate it." He walked over hugging her. "Anytime." She replied as she nuzzled her face in his neck, taking in the scent of his cologne. "See you tomorrow." Chris slid in behind the wheel, Tati smiled watching him back out of the driveway. She felt on top of the world.

A Month Later

It was mid-May, Preme had come home two days ago. Preme had made good connections for the Vodka deal and had sent Chris a few drafts on design for bottle. Things were coming along. Chris hadn't heard from Sydney since the day he went out to California to retrieve Natalia. He had been thinking about her, as in thinking of her for Natalia, but as far as rekindling anything that was not an option in his mind. Chris and Tatiana had become close, at times inseparable. There was definitely chemistry between them two, but they both were hesitant to put a label to their new found friendship.

Back in California, Sydney was driving to a store, to pick up a few items for dinner. She had spoken to her mom and decided that it would be best for her to move back to Connecticut. Against Gavin's will, Sydney had decided to drop the charges against Chris. She felt right now she wasn't financially able or in the best living situation to take care of Natalia the way she was accustomed to. Being with Chris was the best decision in her eyes, until she figured out her situation. Dominic had left to New York, a week ago, and she was missing him like crazy. They talked every day for hours, she hadn't been feeling well, dealing with Natalia's absence and Chris situation. She missed Dominic giving her his undivided attention and affection, which she grew to love. As she pulled into the parking lot her phone rang. Dominic's picture flashed on the screen for FaceTime. She answered. "Hi, baby! She replied holding the phone up so he could see her makeup free face.

"Hi beautiful. How are you?"

"I'm okay. I haven't been feeling well. But, how are you?"

"I'm good. But, what's wrong? Are you okay?" She looked at the screen at his concerned face.

"Yea, I'll be fine. I've been stressed you know since Natalia left. Not being able to see her. Then dropping the charges against Christian and now moving. It's a lot." She ran her fingers thru her hair placing the phone on the center console.

"I'm sorry baby. I wish I was there with you. I'm here for whatever you need baby. Just think soon you will be here on the east coast, and you'll be closer to getting Natalia back."

"You're right. It's hard. This is the longest I have ever been away from her since she was born. But, I can't wait to be home again and to see you."

"I can't wait to see you too. You've grown on me. I've fallen for you." He smiled into the phone, which made Sydney blush. He was such a gentleman and sweet, his positivity at times was magnetic. She blew him a kiss. Her phone beeped saying Dana was calling. She looked up at the screen. "Hey babe, that's my home girl in Miami. I'm going to call you back."

"A'ight." She ended the call, answering Dana as she got out of the car walking into the store.

"Well, how have you been stranger?" said Dana.

"I know, it's been a minute. After Chris came here and took Natalia, my life has been hell. I got stitches on my eye. I was going to press charges, but I decided its best for Natalia to be home with Chris. Where she is stable. I'll be moving back to Connecticut soon."

"What?? Bitch, you should've been calling me! I thought you and Chris had settled that shit which is why when Vani told me she had seen the baby, I didn't ask any other questions. Since you never answer either. Vani said that she is getting so big. Chris had her in diamond hoops, she had her hair out Vani said it's damn near down her back now. Mouth full of teeth."

Sydney almost wanted to cry thinking of her baby and how embarrassed she felt for someone else to be giving her updates on her baby. "I miss her soo much." Sydney walked down the feminine products section.

"When are you moving to Connecticut? You're moving in with your mom right?"

"Yea. I'll be moving next week."

"When are you coming back to Miami?"

"Dana, you know I can't be around Chris. This last incident, I don't want Natalia to be around that type of energy."

"Well, I think Chris has moved on from that."

"What do you mean? He's fucking one of his whore store groupies?"

Dana laughed. "Vani said that he is single. He hasn't been linked or messing with anyone since you two split."

"Well, that's good. Maybe he can work on himself." Sydney picked up two pregnancy tests. Placing them inside of her basket.

"I wanna see you girl!" said Dana.

"Well, come up to Connecticut. We can have fun there you know, it's not like I'm moving out of the country."

"Well, when you get settled, I'll come visit."

"Bet. But, I have to get off this phone. I will call you later."

"A'ight Syd. Be safe. Love ya girl."

"You too boo." Sydney hung up the phone, picking up a few more items before heading home. Once home she stopped at the mailbox. She tossed the mail in her grocery bag. Sydney walked over to her bathroom, opening up the pregnancy test. She took both pregnancy tests, placing them on a napkin, awaiting the results. In the back of her mind she wanted to avoid the test all together. She washed her hands going to retrieve the mail from her bag. There was a few pieces of mail for Gavin and a Priority Fragile envelope addressed to her from Miami. She read the sender information it said Natalia Garcia. Sydney smiled opening the envelope pulling out the contents. It was three, eight by ten professional photos of Natalia.

"Oh my goodness. Look at my Tati." Said Sydney with tears in her eyes. One picture she was laying on her back with her arms placed behind her head, her beautiful curls spread out around her face. She was dressed in her Dolce & Gabbana rose print dress. Another was a face shot with her fist under chin and a bright smile on her face showing her dimples. She looked just like Chris in that picture. Her hair was in a ponytail and out in the back. She had a cute pink diamond ring on her finger and diamond bracelet on her wrist. The last picture she was sitting on a miniature gold throne, in a pair of Cazal's, black skinny jeans and black top, Timberland knee boots on her feet. With a crown cocked on the side of her head and her body leaning in the seat. She looked like a miniature boss. She had her own diamond chains on her neck. Sydney knew that picture was all Chris' idea. She placed the pictures down reaching into the envelope there was a disc and card inside. Sydney took out the disc placing it inside of the television. The video started with Natalia trying to get focus on the camera. "Hi mommy!" she replied sweetly as she came into focus. She was dressed in a white shirt, denim shorts and Buscemi white croc sneakers on her feet she waved to the camera. "Wait a minute, mama." Said Chris as he took the camera from her not showing his face, keeping the camera on Natalia. What do you have to show your Mommy?" Natalia smiled as she popped up as if she was preparing for a routine. Chris put on the music. Natalia began to shake her hips, and clap her hands as Silento's- Watch Me. Natalia began to do the dance, Sydney began to laugh. It went to a montage of clips of her doing random things such as in the pool, playing in her room, and in a ballerina tutu dancing. At the end of the video Natalia came back on the screen. "Happy Mommy Day. Mommy. Amo! She blew kisses at the screen. "aww... she heard a woman's voice say at the end.

Sydney reached into the envelope reading over the mother's day card. Which brought a smile to her face. It was sweet that although their relationship had ended in the worst way possible he thought of her to put everything together. She walked over to the bathroom to check over the pregnancy tests.

The Results both displayed Pregnant.

"What the fuck am I going to do? Another baby?! I'm not even with Natalia! This is not fair to her!" Sydney began to cry, she took the tests results wrapping them in a paper towel and disposing them in the garbage can. "This is fucking crazy this cannot be happening!"

In Miami, Tatiana had arrived late to Reign and had stopped by the mall and picked up Chris' favorite cookies. Almond Chocolate chip. Chris was working the register when Tatiana walked in wearing a Bob Marley tank with distressed skinny jeans which showed off her every curve paired with her Christian Louboutin sneakers. Her hair blown out. Natalia was behind the counter, with her toy banging it against the glass. She ran her hand across Chris' back to announce her presence he immediately smelled the cookies.

"Yo, you got me some cookies? Good lookin' out." He attempted to take the bag from her hand.

"Um… no these are not for you. These are for me and Natalia." She smiled. She reached into the bag breaking up a piece for Natalia. Natalia dropped her toy coming over. Tatiana blew on the cookie before handing it to Natalia. Chris gave her side eye. "Really? You gon' come in here and give my baby my cookies and not me?"

"Yeah. It's not always about you boo." Said Tatiana with a playful smile. Tatiana leaned over the counter eating a cookie in his face. Chris watched her eat it, she laughed knowing he wanted them. He quickly jumped up grabbing the bag from her.

"Chris! Give me my cookies!" She jumped on his back as he hovered in the corner trying to take out a few. Her face was pressed against his as she reached over his shoulder trying to retrieve her bag. He took two out of the bag, handing it back to her. Chris sat back down on the stool behind the register. He grabbed Tatiana's waist pulling her over to him. "We still on for the movies later?"

"Of course. She replied looking into his eyes, his hand was placed on her ass.

"Can you get my phone for me, on my desk?" said Chris with a smile.

"What do you say?" said Tatiana.

"Right now." She rolled her eyes, folding her arms.

"I'm fucking with you. Please, right now."

"Yea, I guess I can." She walked past him walking to his office to get the phone. Chris watched her body as she walked down the hall. Once she returned, Chris looked over her body again. "You getting a little thick back there… what you doing? Don't tell me you getting shots ma?"

She laughed out loud, hitting him on the arm. "This is au naturel. Don't try me."

"Well see eventually huh…" Chris replied with a smile. Tatiana walked away to the back room. He unlocked his phone checking his messages. Preme had replied to his earlier message saying that he would watch Natalia. Chris slid his phone in his pocket as a group of people walked in the store. It was Angel and her crew, she immediately searched the store for Chris. Once located him at the register she walked back. Natalia began to whine and wanted for Chris to pick her up. He picked her up cradling her in his arms. Angel approached the counter with a smile on her face. "What's good boo? How are you and your princess?"

"We're good. What's good Angel."

"She's adorable. Anything new baby?" Angel flipped her hair over her shoulder, showing off her breasts in her bikini top. Tatiana had come from the back room, and saw Angel's blatant flirtation with Chris. Tatiana folded her arms across her chest.

Meanwhile, Sydney was going over her recent news. *"I cannot deal with another baby right now."* She typed in abortion clinics on her phone. Once finding an address she called the number. *"I can't keep this baby. It's definitely Dominic's. Me and Chris haven't touched in weeks. I can't. You are making the right decision."* She looked at herself in the mirror, to reassure herself again. She couldn't look at herself. After answering questions over the phone, and brief conversation. Sydney scheduled her appointment for the following day. She went into her bedroom, she laid on the bed thinking of Natalia. A million thoughts in her head. She heard the front door open, she hopped up wiping the tears from her face. She couldn't deal with Gavin's judgement. She would never tell a soul.

Gavin walked over to her room door, tapping lightly. "Come in." Sydney replied.

"When are you planning to move with Ingrid?"

"Next week."

Gavin nodded his head. "You know you are stupid for dropping those charges against that asshole. You are going to be just like these other hood girls. A house full of kids in the projects, holding drugs for some idiot. We raised you better than that Sydney! Ever since this asshole you have lost your mind. Wake the fuck up!"

"I am not in the mood to hear this bullshit today. If that's what I become that's what I am. I would still be a better parent than you."

"How's that? You don't even have your own child."

"Neither did you. So, let's not go here today. I promise you won't win. Now can you please leave out of here?"

Gavin left out of the room. Sydney looked over her items she had begun to pack. She glanced over Natalia's items in the closet. She began to think about random moments with Natalia and Chris. Their family outings and random laughs at home. She began to think about how Chris would make her laugh by having Natalia do the strangest things. She reminisced on when Natalia was about three months old and Chris had to take her temperature with a thermometer. He didn't want to place it in her rectum. To see him that vulnerable and nervous was hilarious to Sydney. Although, she tried to shelve her feelings in past weeks. She missed him. Sydney pulled out her phone calling Reign. It rang three times before a woman answered. "Thanks for calling Reign. Tatiana speaking."

"Hi, may I speak to Christian?"

"Hold on. One moment please." Tatiana placed the phone down. Chris was over in the VIP section with Natalia who was singing to him. "My baby gonna be a star. Don't hate on my baby falsetto." John laughed out loud.

"No one understand what she saying."

"Don't hate son. You sing mama." Tatiana walked over telling him that someone was on the phone for him. He picked up Natalia walking back to his office. Sydney waited patiently. She heard Natalia's voice singing, she smiled. "Hello." Said Chris.

"Hi Christian. It's me." He knew immediately it was Sydney. She was the only person that called him Christian besides his mother. He was speechless.

"Who is this?" said Chris, as he sat down trying regain his composure.

"It's Sydney."

"Oh a'ight. What's good?"

"I received the pictures of Natalia. Thank you. That was very sweet. She's getting so big."

"Yea, she's a handful. She gets in to everything."

"Yea. Replied Sydney. She felt awkward as if she didn't know what to say. A brief silence fell over the phone. So, what else is she up to?"

"Nothing much. She likes to dance. She says a few Spanish words you taught her a lot. She's learned no and she's pretty good with her numbers to five."

"That's awesome. You seem to be doing well with her. You are a great father to her. Thank you."

"I'm trying to raise her right. Said Chris. I'm planning to give her a birthday party in July. I haven't decided where or what yet. Thinking renting out somewhere. I was going to let you know, if you want to come."

"Of course. Let me know the details when you figure out what you want to do."

"Bet. Yo, do you want to talk to Natalia?"

"Yes. Chris handed the phone to Natalia. She perched it up to her ear. Hi baby! I miss you!"

Natalia smiled looking up at Chris when she heard her mother's voice. "Ma Ma." Said Natalia. Sydney smiled, tears filled her eyes. "I love you soo much Tati. Mommy, can't wait to see you again."

"Amo, mama." Said Natalia clearly. The tears began to flow down Sydney's cheeks. Natalia began to sing her song to Sydney. Sydney smiled, happy to hear Natalia's happiness. She knew she had made the right decision about charges. Natalia's happiness was all that mattered to her. "Blow your Mommy kisses Tubby." Said Chris. Natalia began to make kissing noises into the receiver. Chris got back on the phone. "Hello." Natalia began to cry wanting the phone back, Chris told her no. She began to fall out on the floor. Chris told her firmly to get up. He handed her a cup she crawled up into his lap, resting her head on his chest.

"Well... I was just calling to check on you and Natalia. I guess I will speak to you later."

"A'ight Syd."

"Bye." Chris hung up the phone. Sydney laid back on the bed thinking of calling Dominic now. Hearing Chris' voice made her flashback to their good times. When she never had to want or worry for anything. She looked at herself again in the mirror, she would have to get herself together again.

That night around seven, Chris dropped Natalia off to Preme's. He came in to make sure she was settled. Once she was in her room, and in her pajamas. He walked down to kitchen with Preme. "So, what's going on with you and Sydney?"

"She called today. I don't know what to say. I mean, I'm trying to be civil with her for Natalia. She must have dropped the charges. I'm definitely not trying to be with her, n'ahmean."

"So, you're done?" said Preme as he motioned cleaning his hands.

"Hell yea. I may let her see Natalia, supervised. She has to gain my trust back to ever let Natalia be alone with her again. I mean that shit."

"I feel you. You still want me to get the lawyer on the custody."

"Nah, not right now. I think we good. She won't bring the court in this shit I won't either." Chris glanced over his shoulder seeing a woman coming down the stairs in a silk robe. She had to be in her early thirties, coke bottle figure which was illuminated in the light. As she walked into the kitchen she saw Chris. She attempted to close the front of her robe. "Oh... baby... I didn't know you had company. Wait, is this Christian?"

"I'm Eve." Chris reached his hand out to shake her hand. She stretched out her arms for a hug. "We are family." Chris looked at her his face saying otherwise, he reached in giving her a hug. She walked over to the fridge heading back upstairs. Preme glanced over her backside. Chris looked at Preme.

"There's a lot I can say right now... but I won't. A smile across his face. But, don't forget Natalia birthday coming up."

"Really? You gonna come at me like that? Here. Happy Birthday." He placed a stack of twenty g's in Chris' hand. Chris looked at the money.

"That's all?" replied Chris with a smile. He hit Chris lightly. "Don't start no shit tonight. You know that shit is a fuckin' joke to me."

"I know pop. Be easy. I'm just fuckin' with you. But, appreciate the birthday spending money." They both laughed.

"So, when you going to Connecticut?"

"In June. I wanna check on mom situation while up there. I may stay up there for a few weeks. Set up meeting with Domino."

"A'ight. That's cool. I just don't want you nowhere in New York right now."

"Got you pop. Chris looked down at his phone. I gotta go. You want me to pick her up tonight or tomorrow morning."

"You can come get her tomorrow morning. She'll be okay."

"A'ight." He walked upstairs one last time to check on Natalia before leaving out the door. He walked over to her on the bed kissing her face. She reached up for him kissing his face. Chris left out of the room, he knew once she realized he was leaving she would possibly have a fit. Preme met him in the hallway. "I got a surprise for Nick's ass. I told him no fucking slip ups what I fuckin' meant." Chris hugged Preme one last time before heading downstairs and out the door. He felt no remorse for whatever Preme had in store for him.

Chris walked out to his car and in moments was heading out of the drive way. He called Tatiana, and she told him she would be ready and chastised him about not being late as he had been before. Chris hurried home, hopped in the shower and placed on a black Ninja Shield Rock Smith shirt, Givenchy pants and Jordan sneakers. He placed a Black Yankee fitted over his head and placed a diamond chain on his neck. He headed out to the Mercedes S Class Sedan, which was blacked out as his other cars. Once he arrived to Tatiana town house, he walked up to her door knocking twice. "Who is it?" "Chris." She looked thru the peephole. Her neighborhood was decent, and secluded. She opened the door wearing a black jumpsuit with So Kate Python Rosette Christian Louboutin stilettos. Her hair wand curled and sexy. Chris looked over her body. "What's good ma?" He reached out for a hug. "Hi. You're on time." She replied as they embraced. Chris realized the back of her jumpsuit had a keyhole accent. Which showed her flower vine tattoo down her spine. She turned to lock the door. "Look at you trying to be sexy for me. Thought we were going to the movies."

She laughed out loud. "Whatever Chris. Open the door." she walked ahead of him as he admired her backside in the jumpsuit. "That's a good look on you." She looked over her shoulder at him with a smile. She slid into the passenger seat as he walked around to the driver's side. As they headed to the movie theatre, listening to Teyana Taylor's "Do Not Disturb." Tatiana couldn't help but look at Chris out the corner of her eye. She didn't want to come off as thirsty, but she was definitely feeling him. She looked over his lips, and strong hands. *He's just so fuckin' sexy.* She thought as she bit her lip. She looked through her clutch for her iPhone. She was trying to act as if she was checking her messages and was going to snap a picture of him. Chris was focused on the road, she figured this was perfect time. She made sure her flash and sound was off. She aimed the phone in his direction, he looked over at her. "What you doing?"

"Nothing… drive." Said Tatiana.

"You trying to take a picture of me. Don't front." Said Chris with a smile.

"Maybe…"

"Well, don't take a fucked up one. Hold up." Chris massaged his chin, checking his face in the rear view mirror. He leaned back in the seat. "A'ight." Tatiana turned her flash on snapping the picture. Chris continued to pose, or not pose for the camera.

"Don't crash us."

"I got this. Take another one." Tatiana shook her head what had she begun, it was the beginning to an amazing night. The movie lasted an hour. They embraced during the movie, Chris placed his arm around her. Tatiana had ordered a soda which Chris drank all of, and popcorn which he said was wack and left the bucket on floor. After the movie, they walked outside of the pavilion in which the theater was located. There were a few stores and restaurants. The Florida humidity although it was night was sweltering, Tatiana wanted ice cream which was located beside the theater. As they walked in, Tatiana placed her body on his arm. Vani and her date were leaving out the theater. She immediately spotted Chris smiling with Tatiana on his arm. Her cool quickly faded, as she had to know more. Her date gently pulled her in his direction, and she decided to let them be, for now. They walked inside and Tatiana ordered a Strawberry sundae, which Chris paid for. Chris declined anything. They sat down at an empty booth. Tatiana sat across from him enjoying her sundae.

"I gotta go to Connecticut soon." Said Chris breaking the silence.

"Really... she replied as if she was saddened by the news. Are you taking Tati?"

"Yea, she's going with me."

"How long are you going for?" She replied, licking the ice cream seductively from her lips. Chris knew it wasn't intentionally, but it was definitely sexy watching her tongue play with the spoon.

"A couple of weeks. I've been putting it off for a while now. I need to go handle some business."

"Well... you be careful. A'ight."

"Aww... you worried about me? That's sweet."

"Of course, I'm worried about you. She replied defensively. I care about you." She pulled her hair out of her face. She wanted to kick herself for revealing her feelings to Chris. A part of her was overjoyed to finally tell him, but the battle in her mind kept telling her Chris had baggage, and feelings for him would be disastrous. She was willing to take that risk.

"I'll be good. Good looking out." Tatiana smiled. She looked into his almond shaped hazel eyes. "Here try this." She fed him some of the ice cream. He licked his lips. "Not bad. But me and tubby fuck with cookies and cream. Tatiana laughed. What are you going to be doing while I'm gone?"

"A few modeling things lined up. I stay booked boo. I may go see my family in Boston. They have been asking me to come this summer."

"That's good." Chris replied as he nodded his head.

"Are you going to stop thru there to see your family while in Connecticut?"

Chris began to stretch out his arms, his nerves were about to get the best of him. He knew where the conversation was about to go, and he wasn't sure yet if he wanted to let her in on the sacred part of his life. He sighed looking into her beautiful, angelic face. "I don't have any family there anymore. Well, my mother is buried there."

Tatiana dropped her spoon. Her eyes wide and confused. "Oh Chris, I'm sorry. I didn't know."

"It's a'ight."

"If you don't mind me asking, how did she die?"

Chris took a deep breath. He looked around the restaurant it was only them two, besides the cashier. "She was murdered, and I found her body."

"Oh my goodness! That's horrible! And you don't have any siblings?"

"Nope."

"I can't even imagine… what you went through. I'm so sorry to hear that Chris." She looked as if she was going to cry. Chris smiled. "It's been rough, I'm not going to lie. But, I'm good. Life is good now. I won't complain."

"That's a good way of looking at it. You're a great father, with an amazing business. You did good kid. I'm pretty sure your mom would be proud."

"I hope so. I'm not perfect, well close to it. He massaged his chin with a smile, trying to lighten the mood. I know I definitely have skeletons in my closet."

"Of course. We all do. No one is perfect. Besides, your mother is everything. A mother's love is unconditional." Tatiana slid the cup to the side. Chris looked over at her, her positivity definitely moved him. Something about her spirit in that moment intrigued him, in a way he had never been stimulated before.

"You ready to go?" said Chris as he got up from the seat. "Yes. I'm full now." She stood up adjusting her jumpsuit. She walked out in front of Chris he hit her on the ass. She turned her head to glance back at him. "Don't go there. When you know you can't win." They walked out the restaurant towards the parking lot. "What's that supposed to mean? You threatening me?" said Chris playfully.

"I'm saying, don't be hitting me when you know you're not ready for these hands." She punched him in the arm quickly, attempting to run towards the car. "Really? Tati." He tucked his chain in his shirt, chasing after her. He gained speed catching up to her, he picked her body up over his shoulder. He began spinning around in a circle in an attempt to make her dizzy and sick. "Chris! You make me sick! I'm going to throw up!" Chris laughed placing her down. Her head spinning she almost fell over in her Louboutins. "I just want to say I hate you! She replied trying to get her balance. She placed her hand on the back of the car, awaiting the dizziness to subside. Chris laughed at her. "How can you hate me? Look at this face." She smiled at his perfect white smile, which could bring any woman to their knees. She loved his arrogant candor, in the time they spent together it had become the characteristic she loved the most. Tatiana hit him on the arm. "So conceited. But, it's cute." Chris grabbed her arm, pulling her body into his. He grabbed her chin kissing her lips. The initial kiss was short and sweet. The second she let her tongue dance with his as he placed his arms around her body. When they separated, both looked into each other's eyes. Tatiana immediately felt awkward, after months of hinting around it had happened. What would their working relationship come to? A million thoughts rushed through her head. Chris walked around to the driver's side of the car, as she walked over to passenger.

The drive back to Tatiana's had been awkwardly quiet. Tatiana had been fantasizing about his body on top of hers the whole drive, contemplating had she made a mistake in kissing him. Chris parked in her driveway, dimming his lights. "So, what's good? Because I kiss you, we can't talk?"

"I mean... it's just awkward. I mean don't get me wrong, I do have a few reservations being our professional relationship. But... I definitely fuckin' want you papi... Tatiana bit her lip. Come inside." She slid off the seat walking over to her front door. Chris got out of the car, placing the alarm on, following Tatiana inside her home. She turned on the light, seating Chris on the couch. "I'll be right back." Tatiana went up the stairs, Chris looked around her living room. It was spotless, pictures everywhere of her family. "Chris... come here..." she replied from the stairs. Chris walked up the stairs. He followed the scent of candles, when he reached the room door there stood Tatiana top less in a black LaPerla Brazilian Brief panties and her Python Louboutins. Chris looked over her thick, curvy figure which was waxed to perfection. She took his hand leading him to her queen sized bed. Once he was laid back on the bed she removed his shoes and took her time caressing her hands over his body. She mounted him, looking into his eyes wanting him to take in every part of her body. She began to kiss, lick and suck all over his chest as she eventually took off his shirt. She saw his stab wound she began to lick over it gently. Tatiana could feel his bulge rising under her. She smiled as she lifted herself off of his body, unbuttoning his pants, she placed her hand inside of his Dolce and Gabbana boxers, pulling out all of his girth. She smiled, as she immediately placed it inside of her warm and full lips. Chris grabbed hold of her hair, wrapping it in a bun. Her gag reflexes and head game, was superb as she took in every inch of him. She reached into her nightstand, she pulled out a box of Magnums. She smiled showing him it had never been opened. She opened the package handing it to Chris. "I want you to take me papi and do whatever the fuck you want to do with me." Tatiana laid back on the bed. "Any and everything is fair game tonight." Chris looked over on her dresser there was whips, chains, handcuffs, muzzles, chocolate, and hot oils. Chris smiled who would've known Tatiana was a freak. He could definitely get with this.

Two hours later, exhausted and out of condoms. Chris had gone to sleep, Tatiana had drifted off herself for a second after their fuck fest. His arm was around her body. She looked into his face, running her fingers over his waves. "Chris... get up. Chris." "What." He finally mumbled. She sat up on the bed. "Look at me. Wake up." He opened his eyes looking over at her. "Yea. What up?"

"Where do we go from here? I mean where does this leave us? We clearly can't stay the same." She replied.

"What are you trying to say Tati?"

"I want to know how do you feel about me? What are we? I normally don't like labels and titles, but the way we just fucked I feel I've got to know."

"I mean, I'm feeling you that should be fuckin' obvi. I like being around you and shit. You're sexy, smart and we always wild the fuck out when we together. I just don't want none of my shit to fuck up anything... n'ahmean. You good people."

"Chris, I'm really feeling you. I mean I don't want to ruin our friendship we have over this, but I can't help how I feel about you. There is definitely something, I'm willing to explore. But, I'd rather know now where we stand." She placed her hand over his chest, kissing his lips.

"We don't need no discussion. You're mine." He grabbed her face kissing her lips. She mounted him again, placing the duvet over both of their bodies.

A week later

Sydney had her procedure and had been beating herself up silently over it. She knew she couldn't show any signs of distress with her father, so she tucked it away in the back of her mind, as if it never happened. Sydney had arrived in Connecticut today. Ingrid was picking her up from the airport. Ingrid stepped out the car in a DVF signature dress and pumps. She immediately hugged Sydney tightly before helping her place the bags in the trunk. "Let's get inside." They both got in placing on their seat belts. "Ma, I missed you so much!"

"I've missed you too honey. I'm happy to have you back home. So, what are your plans?"

"I'm thinking of taking some classes. Try to find a decent paying job, not in retail. Try to stack my money up, so I can get my baby."

"Yes, that's priority number one. Get Natalia back. But you are a smart, beautiful strong woman I raised. I want you to start acting like it."

"I know, mommy. It's just that I did get a little dependent on Chris, taking care of me. You know that was what he wanted. I never had to worry for anything and I just played my position."

"That's why you have your own Sydney. Never let a man control you. You hear me. Have your own shit so when shit comes to an end, you know you are good."

"I hear you mommy." Once they pulled into the driveway of their home, Sydney hopped out to get her bags out of the trunk rolling them inside. Once everything was brought upstairs to her room she came back down to where her mother was seated on the loveseat. She handed her the pictures Chris had sent her of Natalia. "Aww... look at boo boo. She's so adorable. Que linda. All of that hair!"

"I know. I miss her so much. But, I know I have to get myself together before I bring her into another situation."

"Exactly. You need a new car that Nissan sat out there so long I don't think it runs anymore." Said Ingrid at her own displaced joke.

"Well, I'm thinking of maybe getting a newer reliable car. You know that car always had issues."

"I can get you a newer car. But, this time you need to get your priorities straight. You are no longer a little girl, Mommy and Daddy won't always be here to help you out. You understand?" Sydney sat beside her mother, taking in all of her unsolicited advice. Although, she didn't want to hear it, she needed her help right now. She bit her tongue taking everything in. Over the next week Sydney had a new car which was a Lexus IS 200t which was metallic silver. Ingrid also got her a secretary position at an associate's law office. Fulltime, with benefits and weekends off, Sydney felt this was perfect for her. Today was Friday, and Sydney was to receive her first check. She checked her bank account for her balance, she had two thousand dollars in her bank account and she still had money in cash she took from Chris' safe in Miami. She hadn't done any retail therapy in a minute, she decided to pick up Natalia a few things for her upcoming birthday.

Dressed in her work attire a simple lace top, with pencil skirt and Jimmy Choo red pumps on her feet to match her Mac Ruby Woo lips, she entered the mall. Everyone at the office loved her fashion, they had dubbed her Miss Vogue. She picked out a few outfits designer outfits and shoes for Natalia, she mentally figured out her budget. Her phone rang interrupting her thoughts, it was Dominic. A smile immediately formed on her face. "Hello."

"What's good beautiful?"

"Nothing, just stopped by the mall after work. Can you give me a few hundred?" She said testing him for a response, although she did want the money. She had calculated her budget and she was slightly off thanks to the Dolce & Gabbana item she had just picked out for Natalia.

"Okay, I'll come down today and bring it to your house."

"Okay. Replied Sydney with a smile. What time?"

"Around eight."

"That's great. I appreciate it babe, I'll see you when you get here, call me when you're on your way."

"Of course, I will."

"How is your recording going? How's work?"

"I'm good. Just finished up two songs today. It's been a long day."

"Aww... have you been in the studio since Wednesday when you called?"

"Yep. But what Diddy say *Sleep is Forbidden*. He said with a chuckle. But, I'm good. I've missed you."

"I missed you too. I haven't seen you since I got here. What's up with that?" said Sydney defensively.

"Come on Syd, don't do this. I asked you if you wanted me to drive down on Monday night and you complained you were exhausted."

"Yea, but you could've surprised me. Just because I was tired doesn't mean I didn't want to see you."

Dominic sighed. Trying to understand women was something he still never caught on to. "Well, I will see you tonight. I have to get back in the studio."

"Okay, see you later." Sydney ended the call sliding the phone down in her purse. She looked up making eye contact with a woman walking in her direction with a baby on her hip. Sydney was immediately drawn to the baby boy. He was wearing a white t-shirt, True religion jeans and a pair of Timbs on his feet. His skin tone was mocha, bright eyes and a smile that would one day make any woman weak. As she got closer to the woman and baby she realized she had been staring when the woman gave her the ice grill, it was Persia. Sydney rolled her eyes at her, placing her focus back on the baby who had to be Maino's. He was definitely his twin, the boy looked over at Sydney a smirk on his face as his mother quickly made her way out of the mall. Sydney looked over at her once more before walking into another store.

Her phone rang it was Nadine. Sydney hadn't spoke to her in a while, and not returned her texts. She knew she would be pissed, so she answered. "Hello."

"Well, hello bitch! What's good?"

"I know. I'm sorry I haven't called or responded it has been crazy lately."

"Why didn't you tell me you were back in Connecticut?"

"I'm sorry girl. I've been busy working fulltime now, trying to get everything together."

"Get things together? Working? Girl, what the fuck going on?"

"A lot. To sum it up, Me and Chris are done. It's been a minute now." Said Sydney the words stung a bit as they left her lips.

"Wow... so y'all never got over the club shit."

"No, that started it. Well, I think we both had some underlying shit we needed to deal with. We became too much, situation was toxic. So we separated."

"Damn. What about Natalia?"

"He has her for now."

"Wait, you mean she lives with him and you are living here?" She knew Nadine wanted to say, *Bitch, what the fuck? Why are you here and your baby is in Miami.* Sydney found it funny everyone had an opinion, until their ass was going through the same thing. Then everything is justified. This was the part she began to hate to repeat to her family and friends. It was as if everyone was saying I told you so. I knew y'all wasn't going to last. She inhaled deeply, sitting down on a bench in the store.

"Yes, Chris has Natalia. It is the best thing for her right now. I want stability for her while I figure out the next move for us."

Nadine sighed, sensing maybe she hit a nerve in her friend. She quickly decided to change the topic. "Why didn't you tell me you were back? You should've called me."

"I know. I'm sorry. Between work and talking late night to my new boo. I'm exhausted."

"Oh, so you have moved on for good huh? What are you doing after you leave the mall?"

"Yes, we are done. Getting my nails done."

"Well, stop by my house so we can chat."

"You still with your fam?"

"Girl, no. I've got my own place. I'll text you my address."

"Okay, cool. Talk to you later." Sydney ended the call heading over to the nail bar to get her manicure and pedicure. After stopping by to get her brows threaded she headed home. It was after seven-thirty. Ingrid called asking her to dinner, she declined telling her that Dominic was coming by today and she was exhausted. Ingrid decided to call up her friend to meet her for dinner. Dominic sent a text saying he was in town and that he would be by shortly.

Back in Miami, Chris was at Reign. Tatiana had come in today at noon. Their new relationship definitely shifted the mood in the store. Although, they hadn't told anyone or displayed PDA, everyone could sense something was up. Tatiana's demeanor had changed. When Chris' groupies would come thru flirting with him, she tried to smile and act as if it wasn't affecting her. She made sure to assist them, so Chris would have no interaction with them whatsoever. Tatiana was dressed in a dark denim long sleeved, two pocket top with matching skinny jeans, and a pair of Aqua Jordan eights. She came up behind Chris placing her arms around his body. She caressed him gently, kissing him on the ear. The store was empty. He turned around, pulling her body over to him, with a kiss. "What's good? Where you coming from?"

"I went to do a swimsuit photo shoot."

"How did it go?"

"It was good." She went into her purse pulling out her phone, showing Chris the pictures. Chris leaned on the counter scrolling through the pictures. "So… you didn't have a top on a few of these huh?" Chris zoomed in to see if he could see anything.

"Don't be nasty. You can't see anything. Perv!"

"Well, let me get a copy of that. Text me that pic."

She laughed out loud. "Send it to yourself. Here." She leaned over his shoulder showing him how to send the picture to himself. Chris was not the most tech savvy, seconds later Chris felt his phone vibrate in his pocket. Tatiana hugged Chris' body, placing her face against his neck so she could smell his cologne she loved. He turned around on the stool, holding her in between his legs. "I missed you this morning." She replied as she looked up into his eyes. He ran his fingers through her exotic wild curls, her beauty was breath taking.

"I missed you too. Making me breakfast, these last few days.

"Oh, is that all you miss me for, is cooking for you?"

"I'm fucking with you. You know I like being around you." He kissed her neck which he knew was her spot. He began to work his way around her ear lobes. She squirmed, as her lips parted softly. "Babe... stop. You remember what happened on Tuesday."

"I don't care, this my shit." He smacked her gently on the ass. She laughed. "Are we still going to the Keys before you go to Connecticut?"

"Yea. You just make the reservations and shit. I'll handle it."

"I'll look online and set everything up. She looked into his face again. You know I'm going to have to stop working here soon."

"I knew that was coming."

"I mean... I want you to have your space and I have mine. I don't want our working situation to conflict with our personal any more than it has to. Besides, every time I look at you I'm wanting to kiss your punk ass." She said with a smile.

"I can't help it I'm a lovable nigga." She hit him, before giving in and kissing him again. Chris had his arms cuffed around her ass. John walked up, they broke apart. Tatiana ran her fingers thru her hair grabbing her purse.

"Y'all don't have to hide shit from me. I already knew." Replied John. Tatiana walked past him, heading to the back bathrooms. "Must be nice… you and Tati huh?"

"I'm not discussing this shit with you my nigga. What's up?" said Chris with a smile.

"Well, Nathan called in today. I'm not in the mood to deal with his bullshit today. He got into a fight last night."

"They must've fucked his ass up. They both laughed out loud. I'll deal with his ass." Said Chris.

In Hartford, Sydney arrived home to find Dominic waiting out front in a Yukon Denali. He got out of the car walking around to her at the steps as she waited on him to exit. "What's up beautiful?" "Hi baby." They embraced, before kissing each other. Dominic reached into his pocket pulling out a rectangular jewelry box. Sydney looked at the box anticipating seeing what was inside. He opened the box revealing a diamond bracelet. "Just a little something I saw and thought of you."

"Aww… thank you. It's beautiful. Please put it on me." She kissed him again before holding out her wrist. Dominic slid the box back into his pocket before placing on her wrist. Sydney smiled looking at the bracelet as it illuminated on her wrist. They continued into the house. "Where is mom?" replied Dominic, not wanting to intrude.

"She went out to dinner."

"What? And you didn't go with her?" he replied with a smile.

"What are you trying to say?" she replied defensively, hitting him on the arm, before locking the door. Dominic walked around looking over the house. "You have a nice house." Sydney thanked him, before sitting down on the recliner taking off her shoes. Dominic walked around looking over the baby pictures of Sydney all over the living room, he went over to the shelf. There was a picture of Sydney and Chris with a newborn Natalia. Sydney was lying in bed holding baby Natalia, with Chris' arm cuffed around the both of them. His diamond chain hanging from his neck with a white tee. The look on their faces was pure love, anyone could see it. Sydney looked as if she was glowing and Chris although his demeanor screamed he wasn't to be fucked with, his smile said that she was the love of his life. Dominic felt uncomfortable. "So... this is Natalia's father?" Sydney walked over to see the picture.

"Yea, that's Christian." She couldn't help that a smile instantly came upon her face. That was one of the greatest moments of her life, shared with the man she loved. Her greatest creation and achievement. Dominic interrupted her thoughts.

"Look at you. I bet you were beautiful pregnant."

"No, I wasn't. I looked like a huge penguin, bowling ball tummy with cankles." She replied with a smile.

"I don't believe it. I know you were sexy with child." Sydney began to feel uncomfortable, immediately thinking of the procedure she had in California. She quickly changed the topic, placing the picture down. "You want a drink?"

"Sure... bring me anything." Dominic went back to looking over the pictures on the shelf. A picture of Sydney and Chris at graduation, another of them and baby outside of a beautiful house with palm trees, and another of Sydney and Chris at a nightclub. Sydney came back with a bottle of Vitamin Water which she knew Dominic loved. "You were really into him huh?" said Dominic.

"Huh?" replied Sydney.

"I'm saying you and him really cared about each other. There is definitely something deep here." he said pointing over the picture.

"I mean, yes when we were together, I cared a great deal for him." said Sydney nonchalant.

"The question is, are you over him?" Sydney immediately became defensive, cutting her eyes at him.

"Why are you asking me these questions? Me and Chris are over! I'm always going to have love for him or love him, because he is Natalia's father."

Dominic placed the picture back down on the shelf, taking a seat on the sofa. "Hmm…" he finally replied.

"You say that to me like you don't have an ex- girlfriend that you still have feelings for."

"I mean, I care about them. But, that's it." said Dominic as he took a sip.

"So, you are saying that you don't love any of them anymore? That is bullshit! Maybe, because you don't have any children attached you can be immature to say that the love just goes away." As the words left Sydney's lips a part of her regretted it.

"Let's just drop the conversation. I didn't think you would get this pissed over it. Just conversation."

"You brought it up!"

"A'ight, Sydney. Let it go." Said Dominic his voice raised and stern. Sydney looked over at him thinking, *did he just raise his voice at me?* She smiled inside thinking she would let him for now think he ended the conversation. Sydney sat back down on the recliner.

"So, are you going to give me the money or not?" said Sydney.

"Is that what I am to you?" said Dominic defensively.

Sydney smiled. "Are you fuckin' serious?"

"I drove here to see you and spend time with you. The only thing you can say to me is where is the money? It's fucked up!"

Sydney stood up from her chair. "I never ask you for a fuckin' dime, my nigga! So, don't make it like I'm all about your fuckin' money!"

"You're always talking about money!" said Dominic as he threw his hands in the air.

"Really? If I was all about money, I wouldn't be fucking with a DJ!" shouted Sydney. Dominic's demeanor shifted. Sydney stood her ground ready for whatever, did he not know who she used to deal with. King of insults.

"What's that supposed to mean?" said Dominic calmly as he sat the water down on the table.

"I'm used to fucking with niggas who take care of me and I don't have to ask for pocket change!"

"So, you're used to selling ass for cash?" said Dominic.

"I can't believe you said that to me. You're a fuckin' joke."

"Fuck you Sydney. I'm out."

"Fuck you too!" shouted Sydney. Dominic headed towards the door. He was heated and he had never put his hands on a woman and he wasn't going to start today. Sydney continued to shout behind him. "Look at you walking out like a little bitch! Get the fuck out!"

"Sydney, shut the fuck up. Fuck you!"

"Fuck your mother!" shouted Sydney. Dominic hesitated before walking out the door. Everything in him wanted to react, but he immediately thought of his own mother. He walked over to his car, speeding off into the night. Sydney went back into the house, furious she took a deep breath sitting back down in her seat. She immediately thought of Chris. She had vented the way Chris would to her. Not caring about the hurtful things he would say. The roles had been reversed she was Chris and Dominic was her. She knew that Dominic was too much of a gentleman to hurt her, so she had went off of him. She immediately regretted her actions, how could she bring the same toxic energy to this beautiful man who didn't deserve it. She pulled out her phone calling Dominic.

"What!" he answered angrily.

"Baby… I'm sorry. Come back." She replied sweetly.

"You said some foul ass shit to me, Sydney."

"I know. I'm sorry. I was tired, frustrated and you said some foul things put me on the defensive. I apologize for taking out my frustrations on you."

"Sydney, I didn't drive here for this."

"I know. Come back." She replied again seductively. Dominic ended the call. Sydney went upstairs to change into a pair of leggings and tank. Ten minutes later she heard a car door outside, she met Dominic at her door. She hugged him tightly. "Dominic, I'm sorry. That conversation went left. But, in my defense I felt you started asking me questions about Chris as if you were jealous. As if you felt he was a threat to our relationship."

"Why would I be jealous of him? I don't even know dude."

"I'm only expressing what I got from our conversation."

"Sydney, you know that I am not about drama. I'm not about to argue with you about some other nigga or what you are used to. I'm used to different shit as well, but I don't expect that from you. I accept you as you are. As far as money is concerned I don't care about that shit. Anytime we are together I make sure you are taken care of and everything is handled."

"I know. She interjected. She kissed his lips. Do you forgive me?"

Dominic looked down into her eyes. He couldn't resist her. "Yes. I forgive you. Don't do that shit again." Sydney smiled kissing him again. She jumped into his arms, he wrapped his arms around her body. "Take me upstairs." Dominic carried her up the stairs, she began to bite and suck all over his neck. He began to swell in his pants. "I don't know what I'm gonna do with you." He replied.

Hours later they lay naked in Sydney's bed together. Dominic got up out of bed, to use the bathroom which was located in her room. "Syd, you should come with me to New York for the weekend?"

"New York. I don't know..." She replied as she covered herself with the sheet.

"Come on. I want to show you the studio, take you out in the city. Have you ever been to New York?"

"Of course. I lived there."

"Oh word, when?"

"Some years ago." Said Sydney, not wanting to relive the discussion from earlier.

"So, you down or what? Dominic walked back over to the bed climbing on top of Sydney parting her legs. Say yes." He began to kiss all over her body, sliding his finger in between her moist lips below. Sydney smiled, as he gently stroked her clitoris before sliding his fingers inside. Sydney let out a soft moan. "Okay, I'll go." She replied as she began to breathe harder. He removed his fingers, kissing her on the lips. "Get dressed." Sydney slid off the bed her pussy now throbbing, feenin' for round three. She threw on a shirt and leggings to tell her mother that she would be leaving for the weekend. Dominic walked into the bathroom, once relieving himself he went over to wash up. He looked at his reflection in the mirror. On the medicine cabinet, there was a wallet sized professional picture of Sydney, Chris and Natalia. Dressed in all white, smiles on their faces and Sydney sporting a huge rock on her hand as she cradled their baby. Dominic placed the picture back, Chris and Sydney were the past. He had no worries.

Ingrid was sleeping peacefully and Sydney decided not to awake her. She left a note on her mother's vanity mirror stating her whereabouts. She walked back upstairs to her bedroom, Dominic sat dressed on the bed placing on his socks and sneakers. "You tell your mom?" He replied.

"I left her a note. I just need to take a shower and pack up a few things and we can head out." Sydney grabbed a few things from her closet tossing them in a Louis Vuitton bag. After taking a shower she dressed in a pair of jeans and an On The Run Tour Shirt, she placed on a pair of socks and a pair of black Jordan three sneakers. Dominic grabbed Sydney's bag. He leaned in kissing her lips. "What was that for?"

"I just like kissing you. Being around you."

"Really? Even when I'm a bitch." Replied Sydney with a smile.

"You're not a bitch. You're just spoiled." He smiled. Sydney ran her fingers through her now wild hair. "I'm not spoiled." "Yes, you are but I'm not about to argue with you about it."

"Well, I'm ready." They headed downstairs and out to the SUV. Sydney locked the door behind her as Dominic placed her bag in the trunk. He walked around opening up her door for her, before walking around to the driver side of the vehicle. As he placed the key in the ignition he looked over to Sydney. "My sister is supposed to come thru tomorrow. Maybe you two can go shopping or whatever. I have to go to the studio early."

"Is that why I'm really going to babysit your sister? Are you going to be in the studio all weekend?"

"No, you're not coming to babysit my sister. I just thought you two would hit it off, because you two are similar, high maintenance into fashion and shopping. I'm only going to be at the studio tomorrow morning. After, I'm all yours."

"Okay. I thought your sister lived in Baltimore?"

"She does. She's doing a little bit of modeling now, so she's often in New York." Sydney reclined her seat, zoning out to the soft voice of Jhene` Aiko playing on the radio as she drifted off to sleep. When she opened her eyes, Dominic pulled into a parking garage. Her mind immediately went to Chris and their past. This was their city, so many memories flooded her mind. She raised her seat, Dominic had gotten out and had opened her door. "Have a good nap?"

"Yes, I did." She stretched her arms and legs before getting out of the car. They walked over to his building and were soon inside of his cozy Upper East Side loft. Dominic turned on the lights, giving Sydney an impromptu tour. Before showing her back to the bedroom and they both crashed immediately drifting off to sleep. The next morning around nine-thirty she heard Dominic moving around. She got out of the bed walking over to the kitchen where Dominic was standing over stove fully dressed. He was wearing a black shirt, jeans and Hermes belt, Timbs on his feet. "Good morning sexy." She walked over kissing his lips, looking over the breakfast he was preparing. Bacon and eggs, and bagels. "Good morning beautiful. I'm about to head out of here. My sister will be here around eleven.

Your breakfast is in here." He lifted plate revealing a bagel sandwich.

"Thank you. That was very sweet of you. Have fun in the studio, and make a few hits!"

"Thank you for being supportive. You keep me going."

"I know you will do well. Your work is great baby, don't forget it!" He kissed her lips again before leaving towards the door. Sydney grabbed the sandwich he had made for her, looking around his place. It was definitely a man's crib, no female influence anywhere, except the plug ins which had the scent of some Hawaiian fragrance that she knew Dominic hadn't picked. Once finished she took a shower, washing her face. As the hot water hit her face she had a brief thought about the abortion. She quickly turned the water off, stepping out of the shower. She looked down at her stomach. *You made the right decision.* She thought to herself, she slipped into a black bra and panty set, looking over her choices. She settled on a Bebe printed shirt dress, with belt and a pair of Giuseppe Zanotti over the knee black boots. She went into her jewelry box looking for her hoops which would go perfect with her outfit, she found her engagement ring. She looked over the ring in her fingers which once symbolized everything to her. She thought about the phone calls from Chris while pregnant and the hateful words he said to her. She tossed the ring back into the box grabbing the earrings. Sydney went to the mirror to apply her makeup, the door buzzed. Sydney walked over to reply. "Who is it?" "It's me." said a female voice. She soon heard heels clicking down the hall as they approached the door. There was two knocks at the door. Sydney walked over looking through the peep hole, all she could see was the back of the woman's head. Which was long black hair, with a round derriere. Sydney opened the door. "Hi." Said Sydney, prepared to extend her hand. The woman turned around. "Hello…" Her smile quickly faded as she looked into Sydney's face. It was Roxy. Sydney looked her body over in her tan crop top and matching pencil skirt. Her face was beat, her lashes and brows flawless. She had to be a 32DD, small waist, and ass that looked like balls stuffed in her skirt. She looked like a Barbie doll. She smirked at Sydney. "Your Nic's new girlfriend, huh?" Roxy looked her over as if she wanted to laugh out loud. She walked into the apartment. Sydney locked the door behind her. "So, how are you?" said Roxy as she sat down on the couch.

"Fine and you?" said Sydney as she walked back over to the bathroom.

"I'm fabulous. How long you and Nic been together?"

"About two months now."

"Oh, okay. He's told me a lot about you." Said Roxy.

"Oh really, too bad he didn't tell me anything about you." Sydney replied with an attitude.

"No need to get an attitude boo. I don't even know you." Said Roxy defensively as she snapped a selfie of herself. Sydney walked out from the bathroom.

"Seems like I know too much about you. Are you still eating bitch's box?"

Roxy smiled. "First, of all who said I ever ate a bitch box. However, I have no problem letting a hoe eat mine. Anyway, I'm dating only men again. That was a trial thing." Sydney rolled her eyes to her response.

"What happened to you and Chris?" said Roxy seductively.

"We separated." Said Sydney defensively.

"Oh, what happened? You seemed so happy before. Where is your baby?" said Roxy with a smirk on her face.

"With her father. What's with the twenty questions? But, since you want to ask questions. How long were you with Chris?"

Roxy smiled. "I mean, we were off and on, you know. Why?"

"Because I want to know. That's why."

"I mean, do you want to know if we fucked? Yes, absolutely. Numerous times. He was great, that nigga had ah-mazing fuckin' pipe game. Well, you know you had him." Roxy began to run her fingers through her hair, unbothered by Sydney's questions. Sydney on the other hand was fuming thinking of the fact that this bitch had a piece of her. She tried to calm herself, but it took everything in her not to slap the shit out of Roxy. "So, do you and Dominic have the same mother and father?"

"Yep. We do. So how did you meet my brother?"

"Out shopping in Cali. Are you ready to go?" said Sydney as she grabbed her purse. They headed downstairs to the car service which Roxy had waiting at the curb. Sydney decided today she would have to be the bigger person and not let Roxy get the best of her. Sydney at first looked out the window wanting to ignore Roxy, but she could feel her looking at her. "So, what are you doing with yourself?" said Roxy as if she already knew the answer, but wanted to see if she could catch Sydney in a lie.

"I am a secretary. Dominic told me you are modeling now right?"

"Yes, it pays my bills and keeps me living out of my suitcase, but I love it." Sydney looked over at Roxy, she remembered seeing her in the club all over Chris. Sydney couldn't get it out of her mind that they both had sex with Chris. It was getting under her skin. They headed over to Saks Fifth Avenue. "So, who's older?"

"He is." Said Roxy.

"I still can't believe you two are related. You two look completely different."

"We get that a lot. But, I'm told I take after our mom." The driver pulled over to let them out Sydney got out first, Roxy followed behind. They both had the same idea of looking for shoes. "So… what is Chris' sexy ass doing? Hopefully, staying out of trouble."

"He has his own business and is doing well." Sydney replied, trying quickly to end all Chris talk.

"Ooh… that nigga had thee best D. His head game… he still gets me wet." Said Roxy with a smile. Sydney stopped abruptly. "Don't make this shit worse a'ight. It's bad enough I'm trying to be nice to your bitch ass. Don't push it!"

"Why are you *trying* to be nice to me? I haven't done shit to you."

"Don't play stupid. You slept with my man. You came to my baby shower with my ex bestie, kissing each other. You even tried me at the Apple store when I was with Chris. To be one hundred with your hoe ass, I don't fuck with you. I will never be cool with a triflin' ass bitch like you!"

"You mad huh? Well, you mad with the wrong one bitch! I did not force Chris to fuck me. I did not even approach his ass, he wanted me! Maybe you should have been doing your job, so I didn't have to."

"Bitch, please. You were just a fuck for him. We have a family hoe, we were engaged. Didn't see your ass with a nine carat ring."

Roxy rolled her eyes. "But, you're not with Chris. You are with Dominic, my brother. So, Chris is free." Sydney looked at her, she bit her lip nervously, she swung slapping Roxy across the face. "Fuck you bitch!" Roxy swung back, store security came over breaking them apart. He had called back up and now both were being held. "Fuck you stupid bitch. You can believe that Dom won't have anything else to do with you! You're done bitch!" shouted Roxy as they pulled her out of the store.

"Fuck you! You won't have Chris again either!" Both were escorted out of the store. Sydney caught a cab, just wanting to clear her mind.

Back at the studio Dominic had been working with a new Def Jam rap artist, going over ad libs. His phone rang he stepped outside to take call. It was Roxy. "Hello."

"Hey Nic, I just left your slut ass girlfriend at Saks."

"Why she gotta be all that? What happened?"

"Me and her shared the same nigga Nic. Bitch, started talking out the side of her mouth and we got into it."

"What?"

"Her baby father, Chris and I were together while he was with her. I guess she mad now..."

"Word." Dominic was speechless.

"Yea. You need to watch out for him though. He is crazy as hell. Has connections with people everywhere. He's got money."

"What you saying?"

"Chris is a high level drug dealer. He carries at least two guns. Rumor has it he's bodied a few niggas. When we were together he would be carrying around like forty g's as pocket money. He has a crazy rep. I only tell you this because being dealt up with her, who knows what her shiesty ass is into. She's bad fucking news, she's a gold digger and she's only after your money. Be careful."

Dominic scratched his head. He took in what his sister was saying, he couldn't believe Roxy had confirmed what he had been thinking a few times. He had feelings for her so he often pushed it aside not wanting to believe it was true. It had to be Roxy had a past with Chris, which confirmed she knew them personally. His mind began to race. "Anything else I should know about this Chris? He ever put his hands on you?"

"No. basically, be careful. He's crazy as hell. I'm not saying you can't defend yourself, because I know you can. He's the type to shoot first, and I know for a fact he's been shot over five times."

"A'ight Rox. Good looking out. I love you."

"Love you too Nic. Be careful with that bitch, if you need me to come thru to handle her. I will."

"Bye." Dominic slid his phone in his pocket trying to digest everything that Roxy had told him.

Sydney had the cab to take her over to Junior's on Broadway, she paid before exiting the cab. Her phone rang it was Nadine. "Hello."

"Yea, before you chew me out. I'm sorry about yesterday. Dominic came to town and asked me to come to NY with him for the weekend. But, bitch I have some tea to give you. Guess who his fuckin' sister is?"

"Who?"

"Roxy."

"Girl... shut up! What did you say?"

"He told me his sister was going to be in town and we could go shopping. I was like cool. Girl, then this hoe arrives at the door titties and ass out. I tried to be civil, but then she wouldn't shut the fuck up about Chris. She kept bringing up slick shit about their sex and I lost it, popped her in her shit."

Nadine laughed. "Girl, I don't blame you. I couldn't be hanging with some bitch that have the history y'all have. Especially with my baby daddy."

"I know. It's crazy, I'm so over Chris. But, seeing her made me jealous again."

"Or maybe you're not over Chris. Maybe you still want him back. You and Chris were engaged, y'all have history. It's something I don't think y'all will ever be able to completely end."

"I mean don't get me wrong I still care about Chris, at times I think about him and miss him. But, I don't want to be with him. I just don't want that bitch to have him. Sydney laughed out loud. Is that bad?"

"Nah, it's honest. What about Dominic?"

"I'm feeling him. The sex is good. He's a great guy. But, I do feel there is something missing between us. I enjoy spending time with him, but I don't know."

Nadine shook her head. "Girl, seems like you don't know what you want."

"I mean, honestly Nadine, I just want to be happy. Genuinely happy."

"Well, I'm sorry boo. You're going to have to figure that out yourself. Who makes you genuinely happy, or if you need more time to be alone. I don't think you will get the answer you are looking for overnight."

"You're right. But, I will be back tomorrow. I will see you then."

"Okay. Love you girl. Be safe." Sydney walked into the restaurant sitting down looking over the menu.

In Miami, Chris and Tatiana were stocking the new inventory on the shelves. A group of five men walked in. Chris looked up looking over at them. "What's good?" said Chris as they walked in the store. "What up." a few of them replied. Chris looked over seeing Nick in their group. He didn't respond he glanced over at Chris rolling his eyes as he walked over towards the shoes. "What's good?" said Chris walking over to Nick.

"Oh… what up." said Nick dryly.

"That's how you gonna come at me, at my business my nigga, like I did shit to you?" Nick looked over at Chris, he knew that he was furious.

"Well, we said we would do our separate shit. You said we wasn't cool no more, so I was trying to give you your space."

"Fuck that shit. You pissing me the fuck off trying to play me like a joke. You see what your fucking slip ups did to my fuckin' stomach? Chris lifted his shirt. But, you gonna bring your bitch ass to my shop, and not acknowledge me? I oughta punch that shit outta your bitch ass." Nick threw his hands up. Chris immediately punched him in the face, knocking him to the ground. Tatiana ran over to Chris, pulling him back. "Chris! Don't do this, not in front of your baby. Remember what you said." She pulled him off of Nick. His friends picked him up, some reaching in their waist. Chris lifted his shirt again showing the piece he had on his waist. "We can take it there my nigga. Get this pussy out my store before I end this shit."

"Leave now! Get out!" screamed Tatiana. Nick and his crew left out the store. Tatiana locked the door behind them, the store was clear. "What was that?" she shouted, fear in her voice.

"I don't feel like talkin' about this shit. Fuck that nigga."

"So, we can't talk about this like two adults. You can't talk to me?"

"That's what I fuckin' said I don't want to talk about shit." Tatiana threw her hands in the air grabbing her purse and keys leaving out the front door. Chris went to his office picking Natalia up out of the playpen. She smiled at him. He kissed her forehead.

Back in New York, Sydney was now standing outside looking for a cab. She heard a man yell out "hey boots." She ignored. She looked down at her phone, checking the time. A man approached her. "Damn, I remember you." Sydney looked up looking the man in the face. He was brown skinned, nappy wild hair and overgrown beard, about 125 lbs. His lips black and could tell he used. She rolled her eyes. "You don't know me."

He smiled revealing his gold teeth. "My name Reese, known as Dollar. I remember you from the flower store."

"Okay…" said Sydney with an attitude. She remembered buying a floral arrangement for Dre and him harassing her. He definitely had fell on hard times.

"You still with that clown? Or did he pass in that fire?"

"And who would that clown be?"

"What the fuck that nigga name?" He reeked of weed and kept running his fingers over his crusty nose. Sydney was disgusted, she frowned up her face. A woman came storming over to them. "Who the fuck is this bitch Reese?!" shouted the woman as she looked over Sydney's attire.

"Yo, chill Nia it's not like that baby." Sydney looked over the woman. She was skinny, with bright red bobbed wig and gold teeth as well. She was wearing a body con dress that fit like a t-shirt on her petite frame. She looked a mess. "I know you wasn't sweating my fuckin' man."

"Girl, it's not like that. I do not want your man." Nia looked over Sydney's face. "Don't I know you?" "Um… no." Sydney quickly replied.

"That's Cash old lady." Said Reese.

"My cousin Chris. Her face lit up. How is he doing?" Reese grabbed Nia by the arm pulling her away. "Let's go." Said Reese angrily. "See you later." Said Nia. Sydney turned away, today had been too much she was ready to return to Hartford. She caught a cab back to Dominic's. She called him and he told her he was on his way there as well. She was exhausted. Within twenty minutes Sydney had arrived at Dominic's he came up behind her grabbing her waist. Sydney jumped, before seeing Dominic's face. "Don't scare me like that!" she shouted hitting him in the chest. He smiled kissing her cheek. "I apologize." He opened the door. Sydney walked in heading over to the sofa taking off her shoes, massaging her feet. "I didn't know Roxy was your sister." Said Sydney deciding to begin the necessary conversation and get it over with.

"Oh, so you know her?" said Dominic.

"Yea. I'd say we won't be hanging out or being friends."

"Oh yea. Why?" Dominic sat across from her looking into her eyes.

"So, she didn't tell you that she fucked my man!" Sydney felt a bit of resentment after the words left her lips. She placed her head in her hand.

"Your man? I thought I was your man."

"You know what I mean. Point is I don't like your sister never have never will."

Dominic looked at Sydney. His face cold and emotionless. "Do you want to be with me or am I honestly just another bank for you?" Sydney lifted her head, shooting him a piercing gaze.

"I am so fuckin' tired of talking about money with you! What do you think I am some gold diggin' bitch? Huh? I'm some groupie who is looking for backstage passes and a Birkin? Because just to make sure we are clear, and to be one hundred with you, I've been there and fucked that! I've had my own Mercedes, Lamborghini, and access to a safe full of millions, diamond rings, diamond bracelets and been on shopping sprees around the world. I've had all that shit before and I could have that all again if I wanted to! I'm tired of you coming at me like I'm desperate for your DJ money and little industry bullshit. I could care less!" Sydney stood up walking over to Dominic mooshing him in the face. "Don't put your fuckin' hands on me!"

"Or what? What the fuck are you going to do?" Sydney stood in his face. Dominic looked up into her face.

"You got some issues ma. Real talk." He stood up walking away from her. She pulled his arm back. "Don't try to flip shit like you didn't start this shit. When I know that your petty ass sister told you about our fight today."

"I wanted to hear your fuckin' side. I thought I could talk to your crazy ass, cause I'm tired of feeling used."

"Really? I'm using you? Shut the fuck up! Don't even flatter yourself!" Sydney brushed him with her shoulder as she walked past him to the bedroom.

"You act just like one of these niggas out here."

"Oh yea, well suck my dick!" Sydney shouted as she walked into the bedroom slamming the door. Sydney locked the room door, walking over to Dominic's walk in closet. The tears began to stream down her face. She knew what it was, she missed Chris. Ever since the day he had sent the video in California, she had thought of him. Many times she had wanted to call him and tell him about something funny she had seen on television, or just to hear his voice, and Natalia. She didn't want to admit that Chris over the years had become her best friend.

He was the one who knew all of her moods and how to make her laugh. The one she could argue with and the next minute make passionate love with. She had become accustomed to arguing just to make up. The game she and Chris knew all too well, Dominic would never understand.

Back in Miami, Tatiana had come back to Reign. Her makeup was smeared, and you could tell she had been crying. Chris was at the register taking out the money, placing in a deposit bag. As she walked past him, he grabbed her arm. "Look… when I'm mad just let me be. I know I say some fucked up shit at that time. But, when I'm heated nothing you can say gonna help, just let me be. Give me a moment to chill."

"I can understand that. But, the way you talked to me. It was downright disrespectful, Chris. I have never had anyone talk to me like that."

"I apologize. You forgive me?" said Chris as he pulled her over towards him.

"Yes. I forgive you." She replied turning away from him.

"Come on ma. You can't be mad at me." He kissed her face. Tatiana tried to turn her lips away from him, he kissed her on the lips. "I'm mad at you Chris stop!" said Tatiana. Chris placed the deposit bag on the stool. He picked up Tatiana sitting her up on the counter. He began to kiss over her chest and lips. Although, the store was locked Tatiana felt awkward knowing there was cameras all over the store. Her body became warm as Chris unbuttoned her shirt. She smiled grabbing her shirt closed. "Chris…" He smiled, "If you kiss me for real, I will stop. Although, I know you don't really want me to." He continued down to her pants. "Okay, she squirmed, she brought his face up to hers. She kissed him, she slid her tongue into his mouth. Chris pulled her closer, before lowering her from the counter. "Was that hard?" said Chris.

"You had me soo pissed with you."

"I know, I'm an ass sometimes. But it's part of my charm." Tatiana smiled walking towards his office. "Come on, let's get out of here. Before, I fuck you on the counter." She replied seductively.

Sydney had finally come out of the closet. She went to the shower. Rico Love's "Days Go By" was playing in her head as the water trickled down her face. She and Chris loved that album, TTLO. Sydney began to sing in the shower: *"I thought the craving stopped, but I still want you. When it's real it never goes away, it only grows much stronger."* After drying off and changing into a pair of Victoria Secret Pink sweats and tank. She laid across the bed. Dominic came into the bedroom. "Are you good now?"

"I'm fine. "

"Do you want to talk?"

"No, maybe another time." Sydney replied. Dominic got up from the bed walking out to the kitchen. Sydney pulled out her phone, she went to her bag she had dropped on the bed pulling out a piece of cheesecake. She sent out a text. Sydney grabbed the matching hoody to her sweats and slid her socks and sneakers on her feet. She decided to take a walk down the block. "Where are you going?" said Dominic seeing her fully dressed. "Just for a walk. I will be back."

"Are you good?"

"I'm fine. Just need some air."

Chris was sliding in the driver seat waiting for Tatiana to back out in her car. He heard his phone chime. It was one of his old business phones he rarely used. It displayed Wifey across the screen, he unlocked the phone reading the text.

"It's crazy. That I've been thinking of you this much. I miss my boo. I miss my family. Even if we never get together again... I miss you as a friend. Can we be friends Christian?"

He chuckled reading over the text a second time. He looked back at Natalia who was looking back at him, a smile on her face. He started the car turning up the air as Rico Love's "Somebody Else" came thru the speakers. "I never knew you considered me a friend. I guess, we can try being friends, because of Natalia. We need some common ground between us."

Sydney walked down the block reading his reply. She responded. "That's fine. I've realized you're about the only friend I've had that stood by me, thru anything. I didn't want to lose that."

"I appreciate it ma. But, we'll see what happens. We can work on a friendship."

Sydney smiled reading the message, replying "Remember, TTLO."

"Yo I was just listening to that joint. Listening to Somebody else. Lol." Sydney placed the phone inside her jacket realizing she had ventured further than she thought. She turned around to head back to Dominic's. Although, the block was crowded she felt she was being followed. She picked up the pace, someone pulled the back of her hoody. She turned around looking up at the dark figure, who she couldn't see which was hidden behind their hoody. "Guess who's back, bitch!" The man took down his hood revealing his face. It was Eric. His face was unshaven and over grown, he was wearing dark jeans and Jordan hoody. He had put on some weight, his face and hands dirty, he looked grimey. Sydney gasped. Sydney turned to run away, he grabbed her by the hair. "Oww! Please let me go!" Sydney tried to twist her body to break free. His grip was too tight and with every movement felt like her hair was ripping from the root. He leaned over to her ear, his breath hot and reeked of alcohol. "I'm gonna hurt that bitch like he did my family! Where the fuck is he?" Sydney finally was able to elbow him in the nose and punched him in the face. She took off running towards Dominic's frantic, tears flowed down her face. She didn't dare turn around, once she approached his building she nearly fell trying to make it to the elevator. She rushed out of the door, banging on his apartment door frantically. Dominic opened the door slowly and confused. "What is..." Sydney pushed him out of the way, locking the door. She fell to her knees, trying to catch her breath.

"What is going on Sydney?"

"Oh... my... God!"

"Are you okay?"

"Hell no... I'm not okay."

"What's wrong? What happened?"

"This. I can't do this. I can't do this with you." She finally worked out.

"What are you saying Sydney?" said Dominic frustrated.

"I just went through a traumatic experience. That I can't even explain to you. Even if I did, I don't think you will get it."

"What happened? Someone touch you?" replied Dominic concerned.

"I can't do this. Sydney pulled herself off the floor. I'm never going to be happy." She replied solemnly.

"Why not?"

"I haven't been happy for quite a while now and now I know why. Today, proved it to me. This is not me. I cannot be this basic bitch. I've tried, tried to be polite and not let my issues from my past ruin my present. But, I can't... my past is me. Good, bad or indifferent, trying to change has made me uncomfortable and insecure. To be honest Dominic, I'm too damaged for you. You deserve a woman who can appreciate your chivalry and your mid class existence. No disrespect. But you can't fix me." Dominic looked over at Sydney, his eyes said everything he was hurt. "My heart belongs to Chris. She continued. I still love him. She took her hand out of her pocket, revealing her engagement ring. He's always been my one. The tears soon flooded her eyes. She wiped them away. I'm sorry Dominic. But, I cannot be with you." She attempted to take the bracelet from her wrist, it unhooked and she placed it inside of his hand. She walked over to the bedroom, grabbing her bag, picking up her items from the floor. Dominic tossed the bracelet to the floor. He walked behind her into the bedroom.

"So, that's it? We're done."

"Dominic, I cannot do this anymore. I love Christian."

"So, what about my feelings? What about how I feel about you?"

"You can't possibly care about the gold digger that was only after your money. That's not me. I've always had money and been around the world as a child. I don't have to prove myself to you or your dumb ass sister. I don't need your money."

"It's not about the money Sydney. It's never been about the money! I care about you." Dominic shouted.

"Dominic, if you genuinely cared about me. Money never would have ever been an issue." Sydney picked up her bag heading towards the door. "Where are you going?" Dominic replied solemnly. "Back home." Dominic grabbed Sydney's arm. "We can't talk about this. I don't understand what did I do?"

"This?! It's not me. I'm loud, at sometimes I am a bitch. I think it is too much for you. I'm used to some extent being controlled, and now that I look at it. I like it. With you, it's like I control you, and I don't like it."

"So, you're saying that me being a gentleman to you and respecting you is wrong?"

"I'm saying that no matter what you do. It will never compare to Christian to me. We've been together too long to throw it away." Dominic was hurt. He sat down on the bed placing his head in his hands. He got up from the bed walking over to the closet pulling down a gift bag. He handed it over to Sydney.

"Dominic, please don't make this any harder."

"Take it. I made it for you." Sydney opened the bag, inside was a cd case and jewelry box. She opened the jewelry box it was a pair of diamond hoops. "K. Michelle came thru the studio today and I had her record this for me, for you."

"That is really sweet. You didn't have to do that for me."

"I wanted to." He smiled thinking maybe the gift had changed her mind. She walked over, hugging him.

"Thank you, Dominic. I hope one day you will find a woman that is just perfect for you." She kissed his cheek, turning away walking back towards the door.

"Sydney…"

"Take care Dominic." Sydney replied not turning back as she walked out the door. Sydney caught the elevator, before closing. Dominic soon ran after her, catching the next elevator. Sydney walked through the lobby adjusting her bag on her shoulder. "SYDNEY!" He shouted. She ignored continuing towards the exit. He ran over grabbing her arm. Sydney pulled her arm away from him. "Dominic, we are done! Leave me the fuck alone!" He dropped her arm, his eyes filled with rage and embarrassment, as patrons stared at him in the lobby. He stared into her eyes. "You are going to regret this shit! You will regret this!" Sydney rolled her eyes walking out of the door. Sydney stood on the curb, a cab was pulling along the curb. She looked at the crisp summer air, thinking how happy she was with her decision. Gun shots rang out in the night air. Sydney fell down to the ground. People began to run screaming. The cab driver hopped out of his car, to assist Sydney. "Ma'am are you okay?"

He attempted to pick her up. Her body was lying in a pool of blood, her body began to shake. "Someone call 9-1-1!" He shouted. Within fifteen minutes paramedics rushed to the scene. EMT rushed Sydney on a gurney, as onlookers crowded the scene. Sydney was unresponsive. "Let's get her out of here. Quickly."

*　　　　*　　　　*

The next morning Sydney woke up confused. She realized she was lying in a hospital bed, in a gown. She looked around her room, no one was there. She tried to remember why she was there. She began to check over her body seeing dressing on her hip. A nurse walked into the room. "Hello, Miss Cruz. How are you feeling?"

"What happened to me?"

"You were shot last night. You don't remember?"

"No. I don't even know where I am?"

"You are in New York City. Your mom has been notified and is on her way."

"Am I going to be okay?"

"Yes. The doctor will be in shortly. It was removed last night you should make a full recovery."

"How long am I going to be here?"

"Maybe a few days. Police will most likely be by later." Sydney looked away thinking of the thought of police being in her room. Sydney looked on the floor seeing her Louis Vuitton bag, her iPhone was beside the bed on the table. She picked it up two messages, one from Nadine. "Are you okay?" The second from Dominic. "I love you Sydney." She quickly erased both messages from her phone, as she looked up to see the doctor entering the room. The doctor was a Caucasian woman, early fifties she presumed, brown shoulder length hair, hazel eyes. "Hello... Miss Sydney how are you feeling?" she walked over to the side of Sydney's bed shaking her hand.

"Sore."

"Yes, unfortunately my dear you will feel that for a few days. I have you on Lortab's and your pressure concerned me a bit. Which is typical in these situations, however I want to make sure we can get that down before you're discharged in a few days. We were able to remove the bullet, now just the healing process. I have a nurse coming in shortly with your meds."

"Okay."

"You are going to be just fine. Get some rest."

Sydney laid her head back on the pillow looking up at the ceiling.

Chris was home cleaning up the living room. Natalia was walking behind him pulling down pictures off the tables, laughing to herself as she caused a mess. Chris looked over to her. "Tubby, stop!" shouted Chris pointing his finger at her. She looked over to him with a smile on her face, throwing another picture frame to the ground. Chris walked over to her, popping her on the hand. "I said, stop. Don't try me." Natalia began to scream, her eyes flooding with tears. She reached up for him. "Da Da!" He looked down into her eyes unbothered by her tantrum. She tugged at his pants, he finally picked her up. She laid on his chest, caressing his back. The house phone rang he walked over towards the kitchen counter answering the call. "Hello."

"Yo son, I got something to tell you." Said Preme.

"A'ight, what's good pop?" He could tell by his tone it was something serious.

"I just got news from people in New York... Sydney been shot."

Chris mouth dropped, he almost dropped Natalia. "What?! Is she a'ight pop? Yo, tell me she's a'ight!"

"She's good. One shot, in the hip. Be easy, a'ight. Chris let out a sigh of relief. She's at Lenox Hill."

"A'ight. We are on our way."

"You going to New York? Did you forget what I said to you?"

"You're trying to tell me I can't go check on her? You got me fucked up pop!"

"Chris, you cannot go up there right now. She will be out in a few days and you can go see her in Hartford. She's back with her mother."

"Syd, is laying up in a fuckin' hospital and you telling me I can't go to make sure she's good? I'm not even hearing that bullshit you spitting. How the fuck that make me look to be sitting here while she's in a fuckin' hospital! Chris raised his voice which startled Natalia in his arms. Fuck this shit! I'm out." Chris ended the call, walking upstairs to his room pulling down his luggage. He placed Natalia on the bed as he went into her room pulling down her Louis Vuitton luggage, tossing a few of her new outfits inside. He quickly tossed items in his suitcase, going over to his safe taking out a few stacks. He carried the bags downstairs, Natalia followed behind him. His phone rang in his pocket, it was Tatiana. "Hello."

"Hi baby. What are you doing?"

"Not in a good fuckin' mood right now. Syd was shot in New York."

"Oh my goodness. Is she okay?"

"I don't know. They said she's a'ight, but I want to know for myself."

"I understand. Anything I can do?"

"Nah, I'm not in a talking mood right now. I will call you back later."

"Okay. Be safe."

Chris placed the alarm on the house, walking out to the Range Rover. He placed Natalia inside starting the ignition, to get air circulating through the car. He placed their bags in the trunk. He looked down at the end of the driveway seeing a Bentley pull in. Preme entered the code driving up the driveway. Chris looked in his direction, not trying to hear whatever reason not to go Preme was going to debate. Preme stepped out the car, in a white t-shirt and linen pants. Chris could tell he had dressed hastily. He would never walk out this way. Ferragamo shoes on his feet. "Where are you going?" Preme demanded.

"You know where I'm going. I'm not about to debate shit with you Pop."

"Listen, Chris. There is a lot of shit going on in the city since you fuckin' left. You have liabilities listen to what the fuck I'm saying right now."

"I'm not trying to hear anything you saying right now. Fuck those niggas! I'm going to see what's up with her."

"So, because you in your feelings over some pussy. You going to throw everything you have built away. You going to just walk the fucking streets up there with Natalia with no protection or shit. You have to fuckin' think."

"Pop, I'm going." Chris replied calmly. Chris took his keys out of his pocket, as he walked around to the driver's side of the car. "So, you going to disobey me?" Chris rolled his eyes as he slid behind the wheel. Preme followed behind him. Both were stubborn and set in their ways both not willing to back down. Preme bit his lip as he took in a deep breath. "If you're gonna go over me and do this dumb shit, at least do it right." Chris looked over at him, showing he had his attention. Take my jet. I'm going to have someone go with you."

"I don't need a fucking bodyguard Pop."

"Listen to me! You are not going alone. Stop being so fuckin' hard headed. Preme shouted. His eyes were damn near red.

"Who's the dude?"

"Come get in the car with me. I'll take you to the jet. Chris looked over at him hesitantly. I'll take you to the fuckin' jet. The fuck I gotta lie for?" Chris turned the car off. He got out of the car walking around to the backseat to take Natalia and her seat out.

Back at the hospital Sydney had been given her meds through her IV again, and was sleeping. She had been sleeping over two hours. She awoke to see Ingrid beside her bed, running her fingers through her hair. Sydney smiled, happy to have her mother present. "Hi mommy." Said Sydney her voice raspy.

"Hi, my baby. She bent down kissing Sydney's forehead. How are you feeling?"

"Sore and exhausted mostly. But, I feel better than earlier."

"Do you remember anything that happened?"

"No. not really. Sydney adjusted herself in the bed, sitting up. She wiped her face. Her mother grabbed her hand looking over the huge rock that sat on her left finger.

"What is this?"

"Oh… it was my engagement ring from Chris, from a while ago. I always loved it."

"Engaged? You didn't tell me anything you little sneak! It's gorgeous."

"It's a Tiffany." Said Sydney with a smile.

"You had to throw that in there didn't you? Ingrid smiled. So, what is the last thing you remember?"

"Well, I remember breaking up with Dominic. I was outside waiting on a cab that was it."

"So... bazaar. Why would anyone want to shoot you? They didn't take any of your things. I checked into your purse your wallet and cards are still present. And obviously you still have that expensive rock on your finger. Where the hell is Dominic? Has he been here?"

"I don't know. I haven't seen him."

"Well, he has definitely rubbed me the wrong way. Although, Chris and I don't see eye to eye, he would have been here for you. Did you tell Chris?" Said Ingrid. Sydney looked over at her mom shocked she took Chris' side on anything. But, she was right Chris would have been there, within a New York minute.

"No, because I know he would be furious. I don't want him to get caught up in any trouble, when he has been doing so well. I'm hungry. This food is horrible."

"What do you want honey? I will go get it for you."

Sydney told her mother she wanted McDonald's. Ingrid gathered her bag and told her she would be right back with the food. Sydney texted her the meal she wanted. Sydney looked out to the window, thinking about what her next plan would be. There was a knock at the door. "Come in." she replied hesitantly. She grabbed the remote control as a weapon, for whomever was about to enter her room. In walked Dominic with a dozen long stem roses and a teddy bear. He looked over to Sydney as if he was in pain seeing her lying in the hospital bed. He walked over towards the bed, attempting to kiss Sydney's face. She quickly turned her face away from him, rejecting his advance. "Where were you last night Dominic?"

"What, do you mean? I came here as soon as I could. There was so much commotion last night I didn't even know what was goin' on!" He placed the flowers and bear on her table, remaining standing as he looked over her.

"So, you're telling me you were inside of the same building that I was popped outside of, and you didn't know shit?! This is why we're done. I can't rely on you, and you're not the type of man I want in my life."

"Sydney, how can you say that shit? I've always supported you! In everything!" He replied defensively.

Sydney held her throbbing head in the palms of her hands. "Dominic, please. I'm really not in the mood to argue with you. My head is killing me."

"Are you okay?" He replied concerned, rushing over to her side.

"I'm fine. I'm just hungry and my mom is getting me some food."

"Anything you need me to get for you?"

"No, I'm good. You can have a seat, if you'd like." He walked over to the chair, sitting down. He kept his eyes glued to Sydney as she flipped through the channels on the flat screen television.

Chris was in the backseat of a Yukon Denali as the bodyguard, Carl, Preme had approved cruised the street. Carl was six foot four, muscular build, hot tempered, mid-forties. Could tell he was an OG, Chris still felt some sort of way to have come with his assistance. But, he wasn't about to argue with Preme about him, so for now he would let it ride. He thought about ditching him blocks ago, but he knew Preme had people watching his every move and he had Natalia with him. He couldn't be reckless. Chris placed a Givenchy hoody over his chest, brushing off extra lint. He looked down at Natalia who was in his arms. He smiled at her checking her diaper to see if she was wet. He immediately changed her. "What hospital is she at sir?" said Carl.

"Lenox Hill."

Carl nodded in the rear view mirror as he turned the music back up. Nas' "Where's the Love" blasted thru the speakers. Chris looked out the window, taking in the blocks and niggas on the corner. He reminisced as the hook bumped thru the speakers, he thought of all the lost ones, the glory days when his team was everything. The days when he and Money were the Kings. A vision of Dre came to his head, he immediately shook his head thinking of his fallen homie. Life had been good to him since he had been in Miami, he smiled wondering what Dre would think of him now. The song ended switching to "Summer on Smash", Natalia placed her hands in the air as she bopped her head to the music. Chris looked down at his twin as her head moved from side to side. He smiled brightly, she looked over to him for his approval. Carl parked, they all hopped out heading over to the hospital entrance.

In Sydney's room, Dominic had gotten up wanting to talk things over to salvage their broken relationship. "I just don't understand, why can't we be together?"

"Dominic, please don't do this. There is nothing to discuss about us. We are not on the same page anymore."

"So, you and the thug Chris are on the same page? You and the nigga who pounded on you!"

"I am, so not about to debate who is right for me, right now with you. The point is Dominic, it's not you. Also, nothing can explain why you weren't there last night."

"I didn't know…"

There was a knock at the door. Sydney sat up looking towards the door, nervous who was next to visit. "Come in…" She hesitantly replied. Dominic looked at the door standing guard ready for whomever was at the door. Sydney leaned to the side trying to see who was opening the door. Four fingers appeared clutched to the door. She smiled seeing the caramel skin tone, clean nails, she immediately knew it was Chris. Her face immediately lit up. Chris walked into the room with Natalia holding on to his pants leg, two bouquet of white roses in his hands. Sydney smiled from ear to ear not being able to contain the smile on her face.

"What up Ma?!" said Chris with a smile. Their energy was definitely magnetic. Dominic sized Chris up as he began to walk over to her bed. Chris placed the flowers on her table.

"How… what are you doing here? I mean, how did you know, I was here?" said Sydney stumbling over her words.

"You know I got my ways. I know everything going on everywhere…" Chris smiled again flashing his bright white smile and dimple. Chris looked over realizing Dominic was in the room. "What up?" said Chris followed by a head nod. Dominic's face immediately went cold and emotionless.

"So, this is him huh? Your fuckin' one!" said Dominic. Chris immediately looked over to him, pointing his thumb back at him. Chris picked up Natalia placing her on the bed with Sydney.

"Who the fuck is this?" said Chris. Sydney ran her fingers thru her hair nervously.

"He's um… he is um…"

Dominic scowled watching Sydney fumble for words. "I'm the nigga she fucked for money!"

Sydney's mouth dropped. "Dominc?!" She shouted.

"What? You chose this pussy ass nigga, over a genuine man, who loved you. How the fuck am I supposed to feel? You can't even tell this nigga who the fuck I am?"

"Who the fuck you callin' a pussy? I don't think you know me, muthafucka." Said Chris as he pointed his finger in Dominic's face.

"I know enough about you. I know, you're a bitch ass nigga who beats on fuckin' women."

The room was silent you could hear a pin drop. Chris looked into Dominic's eyes with a smile, before dropping him to the floor. Dominic was out cold. Chris began to pound on him as he lay unconscious on the ground.

"You got more words to say, fuck nigga? I hit niggas too, muthafucka."

"Chris! Please stop!" shouted Sydney from the bed. Carl came into the room, pulling Chris off of Dominic. Chris was on a thousand at this point there was no bringing him down. Dominic came to, confused to where he was, blood covered his face and shirt. Chris smiled at him. "Get your weight up pussy nigga, before you start speaking on shit you ain't ready for! Get his ass out of here!"

Carl escorted Dominic out of the room. Chris took off his hoody, adjusting his chain on his neck. He looked at his reflection in the mirror. "Who the fuck was that?" said Chris.

"An ex- boyfriend."

"You fucked with that clown?" Chris shook his head, wiping his face with a paper towel. Not a drop of blood on his face. Sydney sat up in the bed trying to adjust herself.

"Chris, that's not important. He is of the past."

"A nigga just try to rush me in your fuckin' room and you're going to tell me he's not important!" replied Chris his voice echoed in the room. Sydney looked over at him, then down at Natalia who was playing with Sydney's blanket.

"Look Chris, I don't want to argue with you. My head is throbbing and I'm happy to see you two. Come here." Chris sighed deeply, walking over to her.

"How are you feeling?"

"Better. Tired and sore."

"Where were you hit?" Chris lifted the blanket looking over her body. "In my hip." Sydney lifted her gown so he could see, her bandages. He touched her hip affectionately, as if he was taking away the pain. He pulled back down her gown, tucking her back in under the blanket. "Damn, I can't believe this shit happened to you. Who the fuck would try you, knowing the repercussions."

Sydney looked down at Natalia. She sat up pulling her up towards her. "Hi, my love. I've missed you." Natalia played shy, hiding her face in Sydney's chest. Sydney kissed her cheek, moving her curls from her face. "So, what do you remember from that night?" Chris pressed.

"I don't remember anything. I blacked out. Woke up and was lying in this bed."

"Fuck." Replied Chris angrily.

"It's okay Chris. I will be fine. Doctor said I will be okay. I'm alive and didn't get hit in vital organ."

"Point is, no one should've fucked with you. Period. What were you doing here anyway? I thought you were living in LA?"

"I moved back to Hartford recently to live with my mom. I came up here for the weekend to spend time with him."

"Why would you come back here with that pussy nigga knowing what we had goin' on when we left? What the fuck was he going to do?!" Chris threw his hands in the air. He walked over to the chair. "How long you in here?"

"A couple of days. I guess, doctor hasn't been back." Natalia finally looked up into Sydney's face with a smile. Sydney smiled back at her. "Hi Tati. I love you." Natalia laughed, placing both hands on Sydney's face pressing her cheeks. "Ma Ma." She replied. Sydney beamed with joy, hearing Natalia's voice. Natalia repeated it over and over, bouncing on Sydney's chest. Natalia planted a juicy kiss on Sydney's lips. Before climbing down off the bed running over to Chris' legs. She sat on top of his feet.

"So how have you been?" said Sydney

"Been a'ight. A few setbacks. But I'm good."

"That's good to hear, you are doing well."

"What are you doing in Connecticut?"

"Secretary at a law office. Great benefits. Trying to save money, so I can get myself back on track for Natalia."

"So, what is your plan? Are you going back to school?"

"I can't. I don't want to ask my parents for money for Miami. I was thinking of taking a few classes at the local college, but I don't want to have to take anything over. Work is the best option right now, to secure some type of stable environment to get back on track."

"Don't let this shit fuck up your plans. Go to school. How much you need? I got you."

Sydney smiled, thinking about the last argument she had with Dominic and how money was always an issue. It wasn't the fact about how much money she would need. The fact that he willingly offered it touched her. Which was what she loved the most about him. Outside of his crazy tempers, outburst and possessive ways he had the biggest heart. "I don't know…Chris." She finally replied hesitantly.

"Look, if you need me to handle the school situation for you. I got you. We may have our issues, but I want you to achieve your dreams, ma. You're smart. I want to see you achieve that goal."

"I haven't decided yet. I'm going to take some time off. To regroup. I need to decide if I'm going to stay in Hartford or come back to Florida. I just want my next move to be my best."

"I hear you. Whatever, you decide though. I got you, a'ight?" Chris looked over at her waiting on her response. Sydney smiled looking into his eyes. "I know you do." She replied.

The room door crept open, in walked Ingrid with bags of food and cup holder. Chris stood up, Natalia moved from his feet, shying away from Ingrid. Chris took the items from her hands setting them up on Sydney's table. "Thank you Chris. How are you?" Sydney pulled the table closer to her as she looked inside the bag.

"I'm good." Said Chris.

"Oh my, is that my little cutie hiding over there?" Ingrid walked over to Natalia, bending to pick her up. Natalia looked over at Chris, her eyes saying *daddy, don't let her pick me up.* "Hi Natalia! It's nana."

Chris laughed at Natalia's awkward look on her face. "Don't act like that tubby. Give your grandma kisses." Natalia kissed Ingrid on the cheek quickly. Ingrid hugged her. "Aww thank you. Look at these cheeks. She's so adorable. I love you." Natalia smiled, pointing over to Sydney. "Ma ma."

"Yes... that's your mommy. Ingrid glanced down at the diamond bracelet, necklace and studs that illuminated when she turned her body. Wait a minute, is this real? Look at all the bling she has on. Is she on fleek? Isn't that what you guys are saying now?" Chris and Sydney both laughed at Ingrid's comment, trying to seem hip.

Sydney laughed. "Ma, you've never heard me say that. No more reality shows for you. But, of course it's real, look at Daddy over there." Sydney began to stuff her face with fries.

"Don't put me on blast greedy. What about that rock you sporting on your finger?" Sydney immediately hid her hand, forgetting that she had her engagement ring on. Ingrid placed Natalia down, she bolted over to Sydney with her hand out for fries. Sydney bit off the tips handing her a few. Ingrid looked over at Chris her smile fading. "So... Chris, I'm wondering what is going on between you and my daughter?" Said Ingrid bluntly her arms folded over her black Donna Karan sweater.

"What do you mean Mrs. Cruz?" said Chris with a smile.

"Oh, you're good. Charming. You know what I mean, custody of Natalia. What are you two going to do? You two are parents now. Putting your hands on each other, it's very childish. You two need to come to a resolution like adults."

Chris' smile faded, he looked over at Ingrid. "We definitely have some issues that we need to wrap up. But, we are not about to have this conversation with you. Because the issues don't involve you. Sydney knows we have things we have to clear up before we move on."

"When is this supposed to happen?" Ingrid interjected.

"Ma! We haven't had a chance to talk yet. They just got here! Besides we can handle this on our own."

"Hopefully, you two are mature enough to handle this on your own. It's getting ridiculous. I will take the baby downstairs for a while, for you two to get somethings settled." Chris looked over at Ingrid as she picked up Natalia heading to the door. He knew she wasn't crazy enough to take her, leaving Sydney within arm's reach. Chris sat up in the chair.

"I'm not gonna ask why your fam always making me out to be this fuckin' crazy ass nigga. Like I beat the shit out of you every day. I mean if I was all that shit why the fuck we been together that long."

"Chris…" Sydney replied sympathetically.

"Why you always telling everybody our business? You've done some fucked up shit yourself. That was one of my biggest problems with you." Chris stood up fuming. Sydney knew any moment he was about to go to a thousand, and there was no turning back. She patted the side of her bed, asking him to sit beside her.

"Come here, please." Said Sydney softly. Chris walked over to the bed, sitting beside her. He positioned himself sideways with one foot planted on the ground. He looked into Sydney's face. "I didn't tell my mom anything about what happened in LA. I'm pretty sure my asshole father did that for me. I'm sorry that we have to continuously bring up our past, and I apologize for everything. She adjusted in the bed, sitting up. I'm going to put myself out there. I love you, Chris. I know that we have our issues… but, I want to be with you. This last month I've been thinking of you and Natalia, my family, my heartbeats, like crazy. In the end, I see us together baby. You and I raising Natalia together. Giving her what we both always wanted, that love and structure we never had growing up."

Chris looked away, he scratched his head. He was not expecting Sydney to hit him with that information. He turned to her making sure to look into her eyes.

"You know how I feel about you. I will body any nigga for you. But, you can't turn your feelings off and on, when it's fuckin' convenient for you. I know, I have my own issues. I own at times I'm crazy as fuck, I spaz the fuck out and have no chill. He raised his right hand. I own that shit. But, I did everything for you! You wanted to go to school. Done. You want exclusive thousand dollar dresses. Done. You felt like going away for the weekend, flew to fuckin' Mexico. I'm not bringing this shit up to be petty, cause you know I don't care about that shit. Anytime, you ask me for any fuckin' thing to this day, I got you. But, even after all that, you shitted on me. Didn't give a fuck about how I felt. You took the one thing in this world that means the most away from me. Sydney felt the tears welling in her eyes as her chest became heavy. The tears soon trickled down her face unto her gown. She wiped them quickly, trying to keep a straight face.

"So... what are you saying Chris?" She finally replied, her voice trembling.

"I'm saying, I love you Syd. You know I do, I always will. No matter how fuckin' vexed you make me. You're my world. But, I can't go there with you right now." Chris shook his head as if he was disgusted at even the thought of reconciliation. Sydney immediately placed her head in her hands as she began to sob uncontrollably.

"I'm so sorry, Christian. I don't know what to say." Her voice muffled as she covered her face in her hands, too embarrassed to show her face. Chris placed his arm around her body pulling her into his chest. She removed her face from her hands, burying her face in his chest. Her tears continued to fall, as she sobbed hysterically. "I love you, Christian. What am I supposed to do? You're everything to me. I'm sorry."

Chris caressed her back as she cried into his chest. "You said we were friends right Syd? Be my friend ma."

"But, I love you, baby."

"I know, ma. I love you too. But, I'm not going there with you. I can't do that shit." Sydney cried until there was nothing left in her. Chris held her until his shirt was soaked. She finally lifted her weary eyes from his chest. She wiped her eyes, feeling her engagement band rub roughly over her eyelids. She looked down at her ring, and up into his eyes. She immediately thought of all their fights and arguments, which quickly disappeared in a collage of all the times they made love. Their random jokes, laughs and she thought about the picture that she had found in his pocket.

"So, where do we go from here?"

"We'll just take it one day at a time. We can't plan anything as far as custody until you are settled in a location. I also want to be real with you… I'm with someone." Sydney quickly moved his arm off of her body.

"What?!"

"I'm with someone right now."

"Who?" said Sydney.

"Tatiana." Sydney smirked, wiping the last remaining tear from her face. "Girl, from the whore store. Has she been around Natalia?"

"Yea, she's been around her, she works at the store. But, you know I just don't let anyone around Natalia like that."

"How serious are you two?"

"I mean, we good." Said Chris bluntly. Sydney worked out a fake smile, through gritted teeth she finally replied. "Well, I'm happy for you."

Ingrid walked back into the room with Natalia in her arms. Chris' phone rang, he stepped outside to answer. Natalia smiled with a book in her hand. Sydney forced a smile so her mother couldn't see that she had just been balling her eyes out. Ingrid placed Natalia on the bed. Sydney looked over at her baby, who was her father's twin. The same complexion, facial gestures and mouth.

"So, did you two talk and come to an agreement?"

"Mom, I love him and he just told me he's done with me! Sydney immediately began to sob. And he has a new girlfriend." Natalia looked at her mother, she immediately came over to her, wiping the tears from her eyes. Ingrid sat down on the bed.

"Sydney, stop crying! This is the time to get your shit together. This is the time to prove you can make it on your own and be the best parent you can for Natalia. Get out of your fucking feelings! You don't need him to make it."

"But, mommy this isn't just any one. This is or was the love of my life. He is Natalia's father. My everything, I love him."

"Sydney, stop it. Pull it together. It is not about him or his fucking girlfriend. This is about Natalia. You need to get it together to be there for her. So, you won't miss precious moments of her childhood. That is *your everything*. Fuck him."

"Mom, I'm sorry I can't be a fuckin' brave heart right now. He broke my fuckin' heart! I'm allowed to be hurt. I can cry because I want my family back and not strive to be a bitter single woman!" Sydney snapped back. The nurse walked into the room asking how Sydney was feeling she explained she was in pain. The nurse whisked away to get her a dosage. Sydney was given a dosage into the IV in her arm, within thirty minutes Sydney was sleeping. Chris walked back into the room seeing Natalia laying on top of Sydney's legs sleeping. He closed the door quietly. "She finally got some rest." Ingrid signaled for him to have a seat beside her.

"I understand that you two supposedly talked about something. But, I want to know myself. What are you and Sydney planning to do for custody?"

"I mean, I of course don't want to be too far away from Natalia. So, for that to work Sydney would have to move back to Florida."

"Okay, and what about arrangements?"

"If she moves closer, I was thinking of placing Natalia in day care and she can take her to school, possibly a few days a week. But, I'm definitely not letting Natalia move up here without me. If that is what you're getting at."

"What about what Sydney wants?"

"Look Mrs. Cruz, I really don't want to get into this with you, because it's not your business. But, what Sydney wants is really not my concern. See, everyone always want to make me out to be this crazy ass nigga. But, your daughter has done some shit that I cannot forgive at this moment. Ingrid looked confused. Sydney kidnapped Natalia and went out to Cali, and lied to me. She knew that Natalia is everything to me, and out of spite, she did that petty shit. So, I'm not trying to hear how hard it is for her. The bottom line is she has to gain my trust. Natalia is not going anywhere without me. Chris stood up picking up Natalia's baby bag and picking her up off the bed. He cradled her in his arms. We're about to head to our hotel. Tell Sydney we will be back tomorrow." Once Chris was out of the door, Ingrid looked over at Sydney. A part of her shocked of what Chris had told her. Ingrid's phone vibrated in her pocket. "Hello."

"How is she?" replied Gavin.

"She's doing okay. She's sleeping right now."

"What did they say? She's going to be fine right?"

"Yes, she will be just fine."

"Does she know who did this? Probably one of that bastard, low life asshole baby father of hers goons."

"Sydney, doesn't remember anything. However, I don't think it has anything to do with Chris."

"Everything has to do with him! He's been bad news since the day she met him. He's a fuckin' disgrace."

"Not all of him is horrible, Gavin. He gave us our sweet Natalia."

"The one good thing that's come from his fuckin' existence." Gavin barked into the receiver. Chris wasn't on Ingrid's good side at the moment. But she wasn't about to have this roasting session about Chris with Gavin today. He never brought up the good things about Sydney and Chris at times that began to annoy her. She quickly ended the call.

That evening Sydney awoke to a quiet room. Ingrid was lying in a recliner beside her bed. She looked around the room for Natalia and Chris. Nowhere in sight. She immediately replayed Chris' rejection. It still hurt, to think her family would be separated forever. It couldn't be. She had no choice, but to let it be.

Chris and Natalia had settled into their hotel suite, which was located on the Upper West Side. Although, Preme demanded he get a room in upstate New York or Jersey, Chris promised to stay low key while there. Natalia was exhausted stretched across their King sized bed. Chris could hear Carl on the phone he figured with Preme doing a checkup. He decided to lay down. Carl paced around in the room listening to Preme's demands.

"You keep a fuckin' watch on my son! Not one hair on his or my granddaughter's head better be out of place! Or it's a wrap for you. You heard?!"

"I got you, boss. I got you." Said Carl nervously.

Chris looked over at Natalia, kissing her cheek. His phone rang and Tatiana's picture flashed on the screen, which she saved under her number in a bikini. He smiled. "What's good Tati?"

"Hi baby! How's Sydney?"

"She's good. She's going to be a'ight."

"That's good. That's amazing news. How long is she going to be in hospital?"

"We don't know yet. But, I'm going to be staying here for a few days. Just to make sure everything good, n'ahmean."

"No worries. Take long as you need babe. I'm good."

"Good looking out. So, what you been up to?"

"Nothing much. Been at the store. I closed up today, so I'm exhausted. I was thinking of making some lasagna, but I decided to wait until you come back since we know how much you love it."

"Damn, don't tease me and shit. You can make it, I won't trip."

"Nope. I will make it for you later and serve it to you naked."

"Don't do that. Getting me harder than a motha… right now. Chris replied with a smile. You know I'm going to Connecticut and other business when I leave here, so I may not be back for a minute. Natalia began to move in the bed. But, I guess Tubby giving me hints I need to shut the fuck up while she trying to sleep. So, I'll hit you up later a'ight."

"A'ight babe. I'm going to send you something. Goodnight." The call ended. Chris turned over in the bed reaching for the charger he had plugged into the wall. His phone chimed alerting he had a text. He unlocked the phone, opening the message. It was a picture of Tatiana lying in her bed naked. Chris smiled, his dick rising in his sweats. *Damn.* He thought.

The next morning Sydney was determined to get up out of bed. She struggled out of bed, looking at her arm she realized that her IV had been removed. She limped over to the bathroom with help of a walker, placed beside the bed. Once finished in the bathroom, she walked over to her bags, looking for something to change into. As she sifted through her clothes she found the gift bag Dominic had given her. She tossed it into the garbage, not caring about the contents. She found an YSL t-shirt and pair of leggings. She hobbled back over to the bathroom. A nurse walked into the room seeing her in mid stride. "What are you doing beautiful?"

"Hi... um trying to wash off and put on these clothes."

"Okay, let me give you a hand. She helped Sydney into the bathroom again. Once she had washed up she helped her into her clothes. Was that your gorgeous baby that was here yesterday?"

Sydney smiled. "Yea, that's my princess. Ooh, I think I need to lay down." The nurse helped her back to the bed. She made sure Sydney was comfortable. "She looks like you and the father. Good mix."

"A lot of people say she looks just like him. You made me happy to think she looks like me."

"She does. But, her presence in a room is all you mama." Sydney smiled, her mind drifting to her conversation with Chris yesterday. She asked the nurse to bring her an orange juice and she would skip breakfast. The nurse insisted on bringing her fruit as well, saying she needed to eat. Ingrid began to stretch in her chair as the nurse left out the room. She sat up looking over at Sydney.

"Good morning, Syd. How you feeling?"

"Good. I saw the doctor earlier. I am going home tomorrow."

"That's great. Ready, to be home in my bed. Ingrid replied with a chuckle. Have you decided what you are going to do?"

"Well... I'm going to work and save money, get me a place. Chris said he would pay my tuition, but I don't know. I'm seriously thinking of moving back to Florida so I can be near Natalia."

"With Chris?"

"No, not with Chris. He's with someone. I was thinking Fort Lauderdale area. You know, I can be close to Natalia yet have my own space."

"Well, Sydney you know what you want to do. I am behind you. I will help you if you need me to get you back on feet with school." Ingrid began to check messages in her phone. She excused herself walking out of the room to take a few phone calls. The nurse brought back the fruit and orange juice. Sydney ate it and drank the juice. She began to jot down on her notebook her plans and possible moving expenses. She flipped thru the channels nothing was on. There was a knock at the door. "Come in." In walked Chris and Natalia. Natalia was dressed in a white Armani Junior shirt with a heart design on front, a pair of distressed denim shorts and a pair of Dolce & Gabbana jelly sandals. Her hair wild and untamed. Chris was dressed in a plaid short sleeved shirt, a pair of jeans, Timbs on his feet. Sydney couldn't help but glance at his biceps in shirt. "How you doing ma?"

Sydney smiled. "I'm good. What's going on with my child's hair?" Natalia tried to climb up onto the bed. Sydney reached over pulling her up. "I tried. She wasn't having it today. So, I said fuck it. I tried though. See that curl pattern I hooked up there." Sydney side eyed him as she looked over Natalia's hair, she could tell he had wet her hair and brushed it into this now afro of curls. Which humidity had amplified. Sydney laughed. "Okay, daddy. No shade. But, can you hand me my toiletry bag in the bathroom. Chris walked over retrieving the item handing it to Sydney. Sydney placed Natalia on her lap as she pulled out her comb and brush to tame her hair. Chris took a seat on a chair in the corner. "So, did you decide what you are going to do yet?"

"Yes. I'm going back to Hartford and working. So I can save money before deciding to move back to Florida."

"What do you mean you have to save money and all that shit? I told you I got you. I'll put you in a place and handle school for you."

"No, Chris. I'm going to save and do this myself. Natalia's birthday is coming up and there are things I want to do. What are your plans for her birthday?"

"I was thinking of Disney you know. We can take a family trip for the weekend." Sydney placed Natalia's hair in ponytail in middle and left her hair out in the back.

"That sounds nice. Are you inviting me?"

"Of course, I'm inviting you I said a family trip. Just me, you and tubby."

"Okay." Replied Sydney with a smile. Thinking of spending a weekend at a resort with her two loves.

"Yea, so don't get any ideas. It's a family trip. Don't be trying to push up on the kid." Replied Chris with a flirtatious grin.

"Whatever Chris." Replied Sydney with a laugh. She handed Natalia a mirror so she could see her hair. "Look at the pretty baby." Natalia smiled looking at her reflection in Sydney's compact mirror. Natalia began to pucker her lips as if she was doing duck face, one of Sydney's signature selfie poses. Sydney immediately burst into laughter. "Check you out." Chris looked over at her. "Ay, don't be doing no kissy face. Stop that." Chris playfully scolded her. Chris walked over to the bed to pick up Natalia. Sydney patted the bed for him to sit beside her. Natalia climbed down from the bed, as Chris laid back on Sydney's stomach. She looked down into his face as he looked up at her. "I'm thinking of placing Natalia in daycare. I've been researching some places."

"Really?" replied Sydney.

"Yea. You know me and pop gotta inspect everything. But, she's getting too big to be at the store with me and I have a few other ventures I'm working on."

"Like what?"

"In due time… definitely some big moves Tubby can be set. Chris looked up into her eyes. She looked down into his face. He smiled at her. I've missed you, Syd. It's good to spend time with you." She blushed, looking at the man she loved. She tried to keep a poker face and not reveal her love of him, since she had been previously shut down. They were just friends, and she didn't want anything to ruin that.

"How long are you two going to be here?"

"As long as you are here." He replied with a smile sitting up on the bed.

"Well, the doctor said I should be leaving tomorrow."

"That's good. Well, we're all leaving tomorrow." He replied sarcastically. Natalia walked back over to Chris asking him to pick her up. He picked her up getting up from the bed. He walked over to Sydney's table to see what food she had on her tray. "What you eat today?"

"Only some fruit and orange juice. You know this food is disgusting."

"Syd, you have to eat. What you want?"

"Maybe Chinese food. Fried rice and sesame chicken? Please."

"I got you. He handed Natalia over to Sydney who was now rubbing her eyes as if she was ready for a nap. I'm going to leave her here with you. Can I trust you to not run off with our daughter?"

"Really Chris? Where the hell am I going? She replied sarcastically. Besides, should you really be out and about in the city?"

"To your first question, let's not forget your Cali kidnapping, and secondly, I'll be straight I got someone with me. I got a bodyguard. Carl!" shouted Chris. In walked Carl, all six foot four inches and solid. His presence was intimidating, he looked as if he had spent a few years in the pen. Sydney thought to herself. "What's good chief?" said Carl.

"Nothing. I just wanted Syd to see you. So she could know that I'm good. See, Syd I'm good. I'll be back, you be here with Natalia when I come back." He replied half seriously. Chris headed behind Carl out of the room. Sydney looked over on the bed realizing that Chris had dropped some money out of his pocket on the bed. She picked it up counting over the money it was folded four hundred dollars. She slid the money over to her table under her bag to give him when he returned. Sydney flipped the channel to cartoons and called the nurse to bring Natalia some apple juice. Thirty minutes later Chris and Carl returned with bags of food. Carl brought in a bag placing it on the counter. Chris walked over to Sydney's table with her drink and plate. "Oh thank you, Christian. It smells good."

"You're welcome. You the only one who call me by my real name."

"Well... that's your name."

"And you always say that. I got a pint of fried rice, not that she'll eat it." He looked over at Natalia who was now sleeping beside Sydney. Chris set up the additional table in the room with his plate of beef, broccoli and white rice, before sitting down. Sydney flipped thru the channels again before settling on the movie, Soul Men which was on. Sydney began to tell Chris about how everything in New York reminded her of their past. They both shared a few laughs as they stuffed their stomachs. "Oh, I saw your cousin Nia. She looked bad. She looked dirty, gold teeth, this bright red hair, and crater face. I barely recognized her."

"Word. Damn, I heard she was out there. But, who would've thought she would've just fell off like that n'ahmean." He shook his head, thinking of the beautiful girl he once remembered.

"Yea, she was with this guy named Reese."

"Oh word? She with that clown now..." Chris cringed as he thought about how Reese had betrayed him. He never got a chance to clap back at him, he pondered if he should pay him a visit. He finished off his plate tossing the garbage inside. He belched loudly excusing himself as he caressed his stomach. Sydney finished her plate as well lying back on her pillow. She smiled caressing her full stomach. "I think the itis has set in. I'm sleepy now." They both laughed.

"I know. You need to move over so I can lay down with y'all."

Sydney laughed out loud. She extended her index finger telling him to come on. She pulled Natalia on top of her chest and pulled back the blanket for him to lay down. Chris quickly stepped out of his Timbs walking over to the bed. "You knew I was dead ass right?" Chris climbed into the bed, laying on his side, facing Sydney. Sydney rested Natalia in between the both of them. Chris stared into her eyes, a smile on his face. "What? Said Sydney.

"You got food on your face."

"What? Get it off."

"No." He laughed placing his fingers on her face wiping away the sauce from the corner of her mouth. "Thank you." She mouthed as his thumb caressed her lips. He removed his hand from her face, as he stared into her beautiful face. Which gave him some of the best and worst memories of his life. The same face that he spotted across the mall, which was the most beautiful, angelic face he'd ever seen. She looked back at him her eyes looked as if she had been thinking the same things. As if she was in deep thought.

"I remember. I meant to tell you that I saw Eric." Said Sydney nonchalant.

"WHAT?"

"The night I texted you. He tried to attack me. I was walking back to Dominic's building, and he came out of nowhere and grabbed me by the hair. I panicked and immediately elbowed and punched him. Then I took off running."

"Was that the same night you were shot?"

"Yes. Chris' smile faded, his brow lowered and the look in his eyes was piercing. Sydney knew that look all too well. He didn't even look like himself. He looked bummy, in a hoody, he has a beard now." Chris turned away from Sydney looking up at the ceiling, fuming inside.

"He say anything to you?"

"Chris, it's really not important, I'm safe."

"Did he say anything?"

"No. Don't worry about him. We're good." She caressed his face gently with her hand. Minutes later, Sydney began snoring softly with Natalia. Chris looked over at the both of them, he climbed out of the bed, slipping his feet back into his boots. He walked out of the room seeing Carl sitting beside the door. "Let's go." Said Chris. Carl hopped up following him down the hall, and within minutes were downstairs and inside of their car. Chris looked down at his Cartier it was two-thirty. Carl slid behind the wheel, waiting on Chris to give him directions. "Head to The Bronx." Carl nodded starting the ignition. He pulled into traffic, Chris sat in the back seat loading his guns which he had hidden under the seat. As they pulled up to E 86th and 3rd, Chris glanced out the window eyeing a man crossing the street in jeans and a t-shirt. Middle aged and medium build as he turned his face, Chris realized it was Lewis. "Pullover." Carl quickly pulled along the curb. Chris tucked the gun in the small of his back, pulling his shirt down getting out of the car. "Lew?! What's good my nigga?" Shouted Chris. Lewis stopped in his tracks turning around to see who had called him. Chris met him halfway and they embraced. "Lil' Maria! Damn, how you doing?"

"I'm good. Can't complain. But look at you my nigga? What the fuck you doin' over here?"

"Man just got off from work, hustlin' like a muthafucka. He replied with a laugh. Working at this restaurant, doing little delivery gigs in between. How you doing? You still in the game?"

"Nah. I'm done with that shit now. Just raising my shorty, you know."

"Wow, that's what's up. You look good though, don't look like that wild nigga I met a while back."

"Look at you! You clean?"

"Yep. About a year now. Got me a little place in Castle Hill, but I'm happiest I've been in a long time. I got my own shit n'ahmean. Where you at now?" Chris smiled. He extended his hand to shake Lewis', he was so proud of the changes he had made.

"I'm down south. But, have you seen Money?"

"Money? I was at his barbershop, in Brooklyn earlier today, and I heard them say that he was coming around three today, for a cut."

Chris glanced down at his watch again. "Good looking out my nigga. I'll see you. A'ight." Chris reached in his pocket, as he dapped him up for the last time he slid money into his hands. Chris quickly hopped back into the backseat, and told Carl to head over to Fulton St. in Brooklyn, he pulled out his phone looking at the time. His phone rang he realized it was Sydney. He forgot he had texted her asking her what drink she wanted at restaurant earlier. "Yo."

"Hey. Where did you go?"

"Out here handling business. What's good?" he replied bluntly. Sydney sat up in the bed. "Christian... do not do anything crazy, okay?"

"What are you talking about?"

"I know you are looking for him."

"Nah, just putting some business together. I'm good."

Sydney could tell by his demeanor, he was on a manhunt for Eric. "Chris... I'm begging you, please, don't get back into this."

"Oh, I'm not. I'm good." He replied calmly. Sydney sighed looking down at Natalia. "A'ight Chris. Be safe." Sydney hung up the phone. She tapped her finger nervously on her locked screen. She scrolled thru her contacts locating Preme.

"Hello."

"Hi Preme. It's Sydney. Chris is here in New York with me and I think he is looking for Eric to do something crazy. I don't want him getting himself in trouble."

"Why he going after E?"

"Because he attacked me before I was shot and could've possibly been the shooter. Please, if you can get thru to him. He's not listening to me. I'm worried."

"Fuck. A'ight, no worries. I'll handle it." Preme hung up the phone immediately dialing Carl's number. He answered on the second ring. "Hello."

"Where the fuck are y'all?"

"In Brooklyn."

"Get Chris from over there now!" shouted Preme.

"I got you boss." Carl abruptly bust a U-turn in the middle of the street a block from the barbershop. Chris looked out the window. "Where the fuck you going?" "We need to head back."

"I told you to go to the fuckin' barbershop! Turn the fuckin' car around." Carl ignored Chris, just as he began to accelerate they were stuck at the light. Chris was furious. He glared out the window, glancing at the faces of everyone walking the street. Eric appeared just as Sydney described his beard unshaven and resembled James Harden. He was dressed in all black. Chris quickly grabbed his Yankee fitted which was sitting on the seat, placed it on his head, placed his gloves over his hands and another gun from under the seat. He hopped out gun cocked, firing in Eric's direction. Eric ducked trying to pull out his own gun. People began to run and scatter out of the street. Eric fell onto the street, Chris ran closer letting off two more before retreating to the vehicle. Carl sped off down the street. Both not saying anything as Chris reached into the backseat looking for his bag that he had left inside. He took off his shirt placing on a white t-shirt. Carl turned up the radio. *"Just in... Man shot in apparent ambush in Brooklyn. An unidentified man was rushed to hospital with three apparent gunshot wounds. We will have more as this story progresses."* Chris slid the guns back under the seat, as they headed back to the hospital. "Get rid of the car... meet me back here with a new one.

Once back at the hospital, Chris brushed himself off before entering the room. Sydney was changing Natalia's diaper. He smiled touching her face as he walked into the room. "What's good?" said Chris as he looked into Sydney's worried eyes.

"You tell me. What did you do?"

"Nothing. I'm good." He sat down on her bed picking up Natalia. Sydney looked over his body to make sure he had no bruises or evidence of his transgressions. He was spotless. "You do realize you have something to live for? I don't know when you will finally get it. But, I want you to think about that." Said Sydney.

"What are you talking about?"

"I just want you to realize you have a reason to live and to not be reckless like you were years ago. You have a reason to live, sitting in your arms, it's about her now, not you." Chris looked down at Natalia who was playing with his watch. He laid back on the bed, into Sydney's lap. Natalia laughed as he tossed her in the air and made raspberries on her stomach. Sydney looked down at him, as he lay in her lap. "I'm not playing with you Christian. Maybe your new girlfriend doesn't care whether you live or die. But, I do."

He looked up into her eyes again. "I appreciate it. I'm glad you do."

That night Carl came back to take Chris and Natalia back to their suite he had copped a new Hummer, courtesy of Preme. The news had reported that it was indeed Eric who was shot and was in critical but stable condition. Chris had saw the news report, he decided he would go see Sydney first thing in the morning and be on his way to Boston.

The next morning Sydney woke up around seven. Ingrid was sleeping in the chair. She had freshened up and changed into a maxi dress and Chanel sandals. She was happy to go home, and saddened that this would be her last day with Natalia and Chris. Ingrid got up and began taking her items to the car, and said she would pick up Starbucks on her way up. Around eight,

Chris and Natalia arrived. Chris was dressed in black Trapstar signature tee, Dolce & Gabbana distressed jeans and Jordans on his feet. Natalia was dressed in a white tank and a pair of paisley print harem pants, with gladiator sandals. Chris had placed her hair in a decent top knot and headband, Sydney was pleased.

"Hey ma? What you doing up so early?"

"Excited to be out of here. Look at my baby, her outfit is adorable. What are you guys doing here so early?" Sydney picked her up kissing her face.

"We're about to get on road to Boston. Just wanted you to see tubby before we leave."

"Why are you going to Boston?"

"To see ma and check on her case, supposedly new information."

"Oh, they reopened it that's great baby." Said Sydney with a smile.

"Yeah, it better be. But, maybe when I leave Boston we can stop in Hartford to see you, before we head back to Florida."

"That will be great. Call me." She kissed Natalia lips again before placing her down. She extended her arms for a hug to Chris. "Come here." Chris looked over at her crazily, before walking over to hug her. They embraced, Sydney placed her lips to his neck, breathing deeply wanting to take in his scent and cologne she loved. "Be safe, Christian. She kissed his neck gently, before placing both hands on his cheeks. Take care of our baby. Thank you. She kissed him gently on the lips, he naturally went with it as they kissed each other passionately. As they separated, Sydney looked into his eyes again. I love you, if no one else does, know that I always will." She placed her hand over his heart. They both smiled.

"You take care, ma. I'll be calling you about the birthday at Disney."

"Okay." Chris reached in hugging her again. He held her tightly in his arms as he kissed her neck. "Be safe Syd. I love you." Natalia came in between them she began to tug at Sydney's dress for her to pick her up. Sydney picked her up placing her in her arms. "I love you too. Mommy will see you real soon." Sydney kissed her lips as the tears soon began to fall from her eyes. Natalia began to wipe her tears, Chris knew soon Natalia would have a fit to leave. He took her from Sydney's arms. "A'ight ma, we're gonna go. I'll get at you." Chris headed out the room and was soon on his way to Boston. Sydney sat on the bed drying her tears watching the news she saw the news report about Eric, she gasped knowing that Chris was responsible. The nurse came in and informed her they would be getting her discharge papers soon. She walked over to the bed to make sure she had all of her items in her bag. She sifted her hand through the bag, feeling something. Sydney removed the clothes on top of bag finding two stacks of money. "What?" She knew it was about twenty five thousand dollars. She immediately smiled. "He didn't have to do this." She slid the money back in the bag covering it with her clothes. Ingrid soon came back with two caramel Frappuccino's, Sydney's favorite. Within an hour Doctor came in and Sydney was given crutches and her discharge papers, as well as follow up instructions and they were on their way back to Hartford.

Meanwhile, Preme called Carl's phone. He dreaded answering the phone. "What the fuck happened yesterday?!" Barked Preme into the receiver.

"I was just doing…"

"Put the phone on fuckin' speaker. Chris, what the fuck happened yesterday?"

Chris sighed. He was not in the mood to hear one of Preme's lectures. "What happened is I was handling business. Nigga, must've lost his fuckin' mind to put his hands on Syd!"

"Who told you that?"

"She did! She told me the night she got popped she had seen him and he put his fuckin' hands on her."

"How do you know he fuckin' shot her?" questioned Preme.

"What's with all the fuckin' questions? Whether he popped her or not he should have never put his fuckin' hands on her for that he got checked." Preme shook his head, taking a sip of Dom Perignon in a Baccarat flute.

"Every time I think you've changed and let go of this petty bullshit. You come back with some mind boggling bullshit like this. You don't fuckin' listen to me."

"Pop, I heard what you said. But, no one gonna put their hands on my fam. I'm not having that shit."

Preme sighed, knowing his lecture was falling on deaf ears. "Where are you now?"

"On our way to Boston."

"Don't start no shit. Keep shit low key. And Carl you remember what the fuck I said." Carl hung up the phone feeling a wave of uncertainty, one thing he didn't want was the wrath of Preme.

Sydney and Ingrid had arrived back in Hartford. Ingrid had assisted Sydney up to her room. She was unpacking her things, and clearing away any memory of Dominic. Nadine called and said she was going to stop by. Just as Sydney decided to sit down and take a quick breather she heard Nadine's loud voice downstairs, talking to her mother. Nadine knocked on her room door before creeping in with balloons. "Hi boo. How are you?"

Sydney got up to hug her. Nadine motioned for her to stay seated and she placed the balloons down with the weights attached to it before hugging her friend. "I'm good. A little sore. But other than that I can't complain." Nadine sat on the ottoman at the edge of her bed. Nadine was dressed in a pair of black leggings and a Cocaine and Caviar shirt, Chucks on her feet.

"That's good. Do you know who did it?"

"No I don't remember shit. I blacked out."

"Girl, you weren't freaking out when you found out?! I would've been spazing out! Damn. I know Chris would've went zero to a hundred real quick on those niggas!"

"I mean, I wasn't so much worried about myself once I knew I was okay. And as far as Chris, girl he was. He came to the hospital."

"What?! Ooh... girl tell me what happened?"

"He brought Natalia. He was asking what happened, it was almost sweet. Well, I told him how much I loved him and that I wanted to be with him."

Nadine set up getting excited at the thought of them reconciling. "So, y'all back together?"

"No. he's with someone else now. But, that doesn't mean we are done forever, ya know? Replied Sydney, trying to be optimistic. It was a lot going on. He knocked Dominic's ass out. It was crazy."

"Shut up! Ooh... girl I would've loved to see that shit!" They both laughed out loud.

"Girl, it was messy as hell. Point is, I love Chris and I know he loves me. Unlike, the other times when shit went left, I'm going to do shit differently... I'm going to wait for him." replied Sydney proudly.

"Bitch, what the fuck are you saying?"

"I'm saying I'm closing down shop. I'm going to be celibate, until we are back together." Nadine looked at her shaking her head.

"Girl, you are crazy as hell. No dick?! 'Til you don't know? Kudos, to you bitch. Hope you have that rabbit still in here somewhere, 'cause I can't do it. I'm going to need a deadline, time frame or something bitch!"

Sydney laughed out loud at her outspoken bestie. "No, but for real. I can wait for Chris. I know we will be back together. Besides, I love him and when you love someone… you can wait."

"Well, I'm happy for you taking a stance this time. But, I have something to tell you."

"What?" said Sydney sensing a seriousness in Nadine's voice.

"I'm pregnant!"

Sydney screamed. "Stop lying! Bitch, you are lying?!" She jumped up from the bed hugging her. "I'm serious. I found out last week."

"Oh my god! Natalia's going to have a cousin! I'm so happy for you. What about the Daddy? What'd he say?"

"Oh he's excited. He said that he's going to do whatever for the baby, talking about getting a bigger place."

"That's great. When am I going to meet him? Yo, you have to let me throw the baby shower! I'm not asking you I'm doing it!" replied Sydney.

"That's fine with me. Between you and Tori, y'all figure that out. You will soon. He's out of town, he'll be back next week."

"Cool. Now about Tori, I don't have time for that bitch. But, for you and my new niece or nephew I will tolerate her if she wants to be involved. She come with that bullshit I'm kicking her ass to the curb."

Chris and crew were settled in their room at the Hilton. He immediately hopped into the shower, bathed Natalia as well before ordering room service. After eating he was going to head over to the Police department. He had Googled news articles to find out who was handling case. Although, he was leery to present himself in a police station, he knew this was the only way to get definite answers that he needed. First Chris asked Carl to ride past the cemetery and he wanted to confirm there had been any change in his mother's grave. When he saw the construction around her grave site he felt satisfied. Once they arrived at the station, Chris instructed Carl to go in first to see what response he received before entering. Carl walked inside feeling nervous as hell. He stepped up to the reception desk who was a young Caucasian female, blond hair pulled into a neat ponytail, attractive but slender. "Can I help you?" She replied attitude spewing from her lips.

"Yea, I have a family member here for the Maria Garcia case. I need to see Detective Rugero. I called and they said he was available?"

"One moment please."

The receptionist picked up the phone, dialing the detective. "I have a family member in the Maria Garcia case." He instructed he would be down. In minutes the detective stepped out from the elevator to the desk. Carl sized him up middle aged, Italian, he was already disgusted as he saw the gun in holster on his waist. "I'll be right back." Said Carl. He walked outside to retrieve Chris. Chris walked into the station, after a quick search, checking his surroundings walking into the station. The detective was now standing at the desk talking with the receptionist, once she saw Chris, a smile formed on her face. The detective turned to face him. "Detective Nicholas Rugero and you are?"

"Chris Garcia." Everyone looked over at him as if silence fell upon the station.

"You are Christian Garcia? We've been looking for you. May I see identification? Chris flashed his Florida driver license. The detective looked it over, Chris smirked at the officer as he examined the address which was a fake. Come on up." The detective led him to his office making small talk along the way. "We've been looking all over for you. How have you been?"

"Good." Chris replied. Once in his office the detective closed the door instructing Chris to have a seat in the plush chair at the end of his desk. His office was nice with a nice view. Chris observed the family pictures on his desk, he had two daughters.

"Well, Mr. Garcia, as far as your mother's case goes. We've been getting new leads as well as new evidence. He pulled out folders laying them on his desk. Originally, we were told, autopsy report as well, that Maria was cut ear to ear which caused her demise. We have found now that she was also shot first. We have some pictures here, wasn't sure if you were aware we have exhumed her body for evidence. If you are able to look at them I will go over them with you."

"Yea. I'm good." He pulled out a couple of eight by ten photos from a folder. There his mother lay on an examining table, her body looked as if was the same except the y incision on her body. He flipped to another picture which showed her back and showed a bullet wound near her under arm. Chris looked over his mother's discolored skin. Chris couldn't help but feel the tears form in his eyes, but he was not about to cry or show any weakness in front of Detective Rugero. "The new tips we are receiving they are saying that she knew the attacker. When we looked back over the initial crime scene photos here. He pulled out one showing the bloody bathroom. The water was on, there was no forced entry. Looks as though she opened the door let the person in and decided to take a shower. When we go back over items on the floor we see there was a struggle in the hallway. We believe that the attacker had an accomplice, and that they were the murderer. Do you know anyone who your mother trusted like that who would have set up something like this?"

"My mom didn't have a lot of friends. She kept to herself. A few neighbors she associated with. But, no one who could've had some beef to do some shit like this."

"We have a witness saying that there was a man over that day. Did she have a boyfriend?" Chris immediately sat up.

"What man?"

"Witnesses say that it was a man dressed in a suit. Possibly African American or Spanish, clean cut, driving an SUV." Chris looked over the pictures, making a mental record of the details the detective was giving him about the man. "How long y'all had her out for?"

"A few weeks."

"Can I see her?" replied Chris. The detective looked at him, seeing the pain in his eyes. He remembered looking over the evidence and seeing the picture of a boy with tears in his eyes and blood drenched over his clothes as he held onto his mother's body. That picture touched him, he had always wondered what happened to him and here he was. "I'll see what I can work out." Chris looked over the evidence pictures as the detective called the medical examiner's office to see if he could come by. After being transferred and placed on hold, he finally confirmed that he could go visit Maria's body. Only if he was present, of course. Chris told him he would meet him outside because he had his daughter waiting in car with someone and they would follow him to medical examiner's office.

Chris headed downstairs with detective. He climbed into the backseat informing Carl to follow the detective. Once they were on the road, Chris looked over at Natalia, who resembled his mother so much to him. Once they arrived at the medical examiner's office, Detective Rugero waited for Chris at the door. He stepped out of the car walking over to him. He smiled at Chris. "You look a lot like your mother."

"A lot of people say that." They walked inside and he led him back to an examining room. Chris looked in thru the windows, he could see a body covered in plastic sitting on the table. The examiner began to remove the plastic from the body, detective Rugero placed his hand on his shoulder. "You can go in. I will remain out here." Chris walked into the room, the examiner proceeded out of the room. She had been placed back on her white burial dress. Chris looked over her decaying nails, her long black hair which was so beautiful to him was still intact. He walked closer to the table looking into her face, tears began to well up in his eyes. He soon was crying uncontrollably, he touched her face. "Damn Mommy... Fuck! This is bullshit! Chris looked over her lips, nose and cheekbones. Ma, I gotta find out who did this to you. He placed his hand inside of hers, although it was cold. He immediately felt warmth. I love you mommy. You are everything. He looked at her chest and he could see the incision which it pained him to see, he blocked it out. He reached over kissing her forehead. I miss you. You have to see Natalia ma, she looks just like you and me. I hope I've made you proud." He wiped his eyes letting go of her hand. The examiner soon walked back in and the detective came over to the door. The examiner showed Chris where he could wash his hands, he refused. "Chris, look here is my card. If you find out anything."

"Yea. Replied Chris dismissively. When are you reburying her?"

"This weekend."

"I want her body to be moved. Somewhere better"

"You can get with a funeral home and set that up if you'd like." Chris looked back at his mother one last time before she covered her again with the plastic. He walked over kissing her cheek. "Love you Ma." Chris' face and eyes were now red, and his face wet. He walked outside to the car. Carl looked back at him as he slid in the backseat.

"You good?"

"Yea, I'm fine. Let's go." Carl quickly sped off headed back to the hotel. Chris looked over at Natalia as she slept, he thought of his mother. His phone rang interrupting his daydream, he looked at the screen it was Tatiana. He was in no mood to talk to her right now. There was only one person he wanted to speak to. On the way back to the hotel Chris picked up some food for Natalia, he hopped in the shower. Once out he fed Natalia chicken nuggets and fries. Chris laid down on the bed his mind racing of a million thoughts about his mother. He picked up his phone, finally dialing a number.

"Hello…"

"Yo Syd. It's me. Can I talk to you?"

"Yea, what's wrong? Are you okay?" she replied concerned.

"I don't know. Chris replied his voice raspy. I just saw my mom Syd."

"What, at the cemetery?"

"Nah, in a morgue. They exhumed her body for the case and shit. I asked to see her, and it fucked me up ma."

Sydney sat up, holding her chest with her hand. "Oh my god! Baby, are you okay?!"

"Nah, she was just lying there in front of me. The same shit replayed in my fuckin' head when I found her years ago. I feel like I'm going crazy. I had to see her Syd."

"I know. She loved you babe. You were her everything. You know that was the physical there and her soul is in a better place. She's been with you this whole time guiding you to be the best man and father you can be. She wouldn't want you to tear yourself apart over this. You know that she's always been with you right?"

Chris wiped his eyes. "Yea, I know… but, I got some shit from my past. You already know… What she think of me?"

"I'm not judging you, neither is she. She is your mother she will love you forever. Only God can judge you, and you're changing trying to better yourself, is all that matters. Stop being down on yourself. You have a good heart. Underneath that hot temper and craziness, is a giving man who loves, and will give everything for his family. Think about who instilled that in you."

Chris sighed. "Man, looking at her she looked just like me and tubby."

Sydney chuckled a bit trying to lighten the mood. "Well, you do look like your mother. You guys are triplets and I'm just the ugly surrogate who carried her for nine months." Chris laughed. "Nah, she got some things from you. Her greediness and attitude, and the fact that she doesn't listen."

"Whatever! Why she have to get all her bad traits from me?"

"Cause she did! I'm not hard headed like that."

"You left yourself open for something real inappropriate there… but it's not the time. So, I will just say I'm not hard headed. They both laughed. So you will be okay baby."

"Thank you. I was so vexed. You know I couldn't do anything to bring her back."

"Did they find anything new?"

"Yea, they said that the autopsy before was bullshit. She was sliced and shot."

"What?! How could they not know that?"

"That's what I said. Bullshit! She was shot in the back."

"Yea, that's crazy. Whoever did the first autopsy probably purposely fucked up the documents. You need to look into who that was, and I'm sure that will lead you to answers you need."

"Look at you little detective."

"That comes from watching those The First 48 marathons with you."

"That does make sense. But, who would've had dough to pay someone like that? Why would they lie? Then her body was in decent shape n'ahmean. But, you definitely given me some shit to look into."

"Glad I can be of help. When are they reburying her?"

"This weekend I believe. I'm moving her to a vault I think. I want her somewhere nice."

"That should be good. If that's what you want to do."

"Yea, that's what I want to do." Said Chris snappily.

"Don't get smart Christian!" replied Sydney with a laugh.

"I'm only fucking with you. Thanks for making me feel better."

"You're welcome. Even though you made me feel like shit the other day." Chris laughed out loud shocked that Sydney said that. "Yo, you wildin' Syd."

"Whatever. I tell you how much I love you and you tell me, *I'm not fuckin' with your crazy ass.*" She replied in her best Chris imitation.

"Well, put it like this… we both crazy as hell, so don't get gassed over that shit."

"But, I am. You hurt my feelings. After all we've been through, you love me but you're not going there with me? Like I'm some random ass bitch, or groupie."

"Syd, you know what I meant. Besides, what about the shit you did to me? So, let's not get into this shit."

"Well, I'm sorry. I didn't mean to hurt your feelings. I love you and I hope everything goes well in your mom's case."

"A'ight Syd. I love you. Talk to you later."

A week later, Sydney had recovered from her hip wound and was no longer on crutches. She and Nadine were at the mall, both dressed in skinny jeans and crop tops which was done on accident. They were catching up making small talk and Nadine decided to ask Sydney about her plans to relocate back to Florida. "So, you're sure about going back to Florida? Your mom is gonna flip!"

"I don't care. I need to be close to my child. I appreciate all she's done, but I need to be a part of my baby's everyday life. I'm thinking of getting a condo or townhouse in Fort Lauderdale. I've been researching a few places online. I'm thinking maybe in a month." Nadine looked at Sydney almost sad that her friend would be leaving, now that she needed her with her pregnancy. But, she understood Natalia came first.

"Well... I am going to miss you. Who am I going to call if I have pregnancy questions? My baby shower?"

"Don't worry girl, I'm only a call away and besides I still got you on baby shower, no worries." Sydney looked into her eyes with a smile.

"You better bitch." They both laughed, walking into Nordstrom. Sydney immediately headed over towards the designer sunglasses. She peered into the glass casing pointing to the ones she liked. "I was thinking of how I wanted to decorate Natalia's room at my new place. I was thinking pink and black. What you think?"

"What difference does it make? She's going to be sleeping with you and Chris anyway."

"Me and Christian are not together. I told you he has a girlfriend."

"Girl, please. She is not you. Besides, y'all love each other, and have a beautiful baby, she's just a jumpoff."

Sydney laughed. "We are only friends. I'm cool with that."

"So what are you sayin?" said Nadine defensively.

"I'm not going to ruin his happy home. He likes it, I love it." The sales associate came over to assist them with the case. Sydney picked out a pair of Gucci Aviator lens sunglasses. She placed them up to her face. Nadine glanced at the oversized shades on her face. "Those are a little big for you."

"They're not for me. I'm going to get them for Chris." Nadine smiled. "Mmhmm. That's what you do for friends? Buy them nine hundred dollar shades. She handed them back to the woman to ring them up. She walked over to the register to bag it up, the store phone rang. She answered the phone, her voice quickly changed to distress. Another associate walked over towards the counter. "Oh, honey can you please finish this order for me my daughter is stuck at camp!" she nodded walking behind the counter, she looked over at the total on the screen and then at the customers. Nadine looked up staring into the woman's face, her face immediately cold. She rolled her eyes as she grilled the cashier. "Syd... she's ready." Nadine replied as Sydney glanced through the cases. Sydney reached into her wallet pulling out cash. She glanced at the register for the total, when she realized the cashier, was Persia. Once Persia realized it was Sydney she immediately folded her arms across her chest, sucking her teeth. Sydney stared at her. "What the fuck is your problem? I'm tired of every time I see your bum ass, your fuckin' grilling me! I mean it's not that serious, we've both had the same niggas! Big fuckin' deal!" Sydney shoved the cash into her hand. She snatched it throwing it into the register.

"You don't know what the fuck you are talking about! Chris tried to kill me! Fucking bastard! Fuck him!"

"Girl, bye. Chris is not worried about your stupid ass. Just give me my change." Sydney turned her head away with her hand extended in Persia's face. Persia slammed the change into her hand, throwing the bag on the counter. "Bitch... you must have lost your fuckin' mind. Don't you ever throw shit at me!" Sydney pointed her finger in Persia's face.

"Fuck you Sydney! You better tell your crazy ass man to get his shit right. Cause I'm pressing charges and his ass is going away for a long time with the shit I got."

"Bitch, shut up. What about Maino? He was innocent too. Don't come with that bullshit bitch. Consider this shit a fuckin' warning!"

Sydney and Nadine walked away from the counter. Nadine looked over at Sydney. "What the fuck she talking about?" "Girl, nothing. No one is worried about her bum ass."

*   *   *

Days later Chris had his mother moved to Forest Hills Cemetery in a beautiful secluded area. He purchased another tombstone which had an angel on top. He purchased a plot for himself beside her. He felt good about securing his mother a better resting place, and the thought of himself one day being beside her gave him comfort. His phone rang interrupting his thought, it was Tatiana. "Hello" he replied nonchalant.

"Hey. What's going on with you? You haven't called me in days?" She replied angrily.

"I've been busy. I've had a lot on my mind."

"Yea, that's obvious, and it's clear it wasn't me!"

"Look, I've been going thru a lot of shit. I don't have time for this bullshit Tatiana." Barked Chris.

"And what about me? I've missed you. I've been doing everything I can at the shop and you can't even call me, see if I'm breathing or not!"

Chris sighed. "I've been up here doing shit with my mother's case. I really don't give a fuck how you feel right now, n'ahmean! Don't be calling my phone with this petty shit!" Tatiana removed the phone from her ear, looking at the receiver. She ended the call. Chris looked at the receiver pissed she hung up. He called her back. "What?!" she shouted into the receiver.

"Don't hang up the fuckin' phone when I'm talking to you!"

"Chris, I am not about to sit here and listen to you fucking yell at me."

"Well, don't call me with no bullshit."

"Are you done?"

"Nah, I'm not done."

"I don't have time for this. Bye Chris."

"You better not hang up this fuckin' phone. Tell John to call me."

"Whatever."

"You tell him what the fuck I said." Chris ended the call, unbothered by the hostility in Tatiana's voice.

Sydney and the girls were planning to meet up at a tattoo shop. They had all decided to get their first tattoos together. Sydney hadn't confirmed she would get one, but she wasn't totally against the idea. Nadine had told her Tori was coming. Sydney hadn't talked with Tori since she spilled all of her dirty laundry in Miami. When Sydney thought about it, it still hurt. Sydney and Nadine rode together and sat inside the car waiting for the other's to arrive. Sydney's phone rang with an unknown number. "Hello."

"How are you?" a male voice replied.

"Who is this?"

"Oh… you forgot about me already? It's Dominic." Sydney sighed, becoming annoyed.

"What do you want?" she replied angrily.

"Why all the attitude? Why you acting like I don't mean shit to you?"

"Because you don't."

"So, did you get back with that punk? You know you almost got him bodied in the hospital that night."

"Look Dominic… me and you are done. We are not friends, we don't have shit to talk about. Lose my fucking number!" Sydney ended the call tossing it in the center console of the car. "Girl, Dominic just called you? What is wrong with him?"

"I don't know. I'm going to have Chris get the number changed. He's got some nerve to call me."

"I know right. But, you know Chris is gonna want to know why you want the number changed."

"Girl, I don't care. I just want nothing to do with his punk ass anymore." Moments later Tori's white Dodge Charger pulled up next to them. They exited the car, standing beside Sydney's car. Sydney walked around to the passenger side. Kiana and Tori soon exited the car. Tori had lost a little weight, Nadine had filled her in that she had been doing the waist training cinchers and some tea diet she had found online. She was wearing a pair of distressed boyfriend jeans, white tank showing off her toned mid-section and wedge heels. Her hair was dyed burgundy red and was shaped in a bold cut, which went well with her face structure. She hit the lock on her keys, looking over at Sydney. "Hey everybody. She replied with a smile. Hey Syd."

"What up Tori." Replied Sydney, with a hint of attitude.

Tori walked over to her. "Look Syd… we've been through too much together to let Chris come between us. I'm sorry, I shouldn't have went off like that in Miami. I was in my feelings about how you had forgot about us and never kept in contact with us about the baby. I mean some of the things I said was how I truly felt. But, it wasn't my place to say it in front of everyone. I should've brought it to you privately. For that I apologize."

"Well, I guess I never took into consideration your feelings about Chris. I mean there was so many things transpired after moving to Miami, I got caught up in my own world. But, I definitely don't think it's fair for you to always try to make me choose between you and Chris. Both of you are important in my life. I also apologize that I put you in the middle of our situation in Boston. I know you were only looking out for me. I'm sorry."

Nadine smiled caressing her stomach. "Did y'all bitches get everything out? Damn, let's end this lifetime movie so y'all can throw my baby shower." Sydney and Tori both burst into laughter. "So, we cool?" said Tori.

"Come here bitch." Sydney extended her arms for a hug. They both hugged each other tightly, tears in both of their eyes. They wiped their eyes walking in to the shop. Samples and skulls lined the walls. There was five tattoo stations and the speakers were blasting House of Pain's "Jump Around" when the receptionist saw the women walk in she quickly changed the station to The Weekend's "The Hills". "Can I help you ladies?" She replied standing up behind her oval desk. She had both arms fully tatted and was beautiful, she looked like a porcelain doll to Sydney. Her olive skin, black hair and red lips, she resembled Dita Von Teese. "We are all getting tattoos. Just need a few ideas." Answered Nadine as she looked at the pictures. "Okay, I'll have the guys come over to help you." The artists came over to help the girls with ideas and one by one started heading over to stations to work on stencils. Sydney was still undecided. A tattoo artist came out of the backroom, immediately making eye contact with Sydney. He was Italian, spiked black hair, green eyes and tattoos everywhere. He had a beard like rapper Rick Ross. "Hello beautiful. What are you interested in today?"

"Hi, I'm a little undecided but… I think I have an idea."

"Okay. I'm Gabe."

"Sydney."

"And are you of age?"

"Of course." Sydney pulled her Florida license from her wallet. He glanced over her license, escorting her back to his office. Which was secluded in back and nice. Sydney looked around he had celebrity pictures and clients on the wall she assumed he must be the owner and this was a VIP suite. He sat on a stool pulling up one for her to sit on. "Come talk to me Sydney. He patted on the chair. What are you thinking?"

"Well I was thinking of on my lower abdomen here. She caressed her fingers over her flesh. Maybe going towards my hoohah. She laughed. I want a crown and it to say in a pretty script Christian. So it says King Christian, maybe a few hearts. She pointed to a script tattoo on wall. The writing like this."

"I got you. Going to make it hot for you." He turned around and began sketching. "So who's Christian?" Gabe replied with a smile.

"My baby." She replied with a smile.

"Sweet. For your little one or…"

"My man. She finally responded."

"I should've known a beautiful woman like you was taken."

Sydney blushed looking over his design. It was coming out amazing. "I want another tattoo on the upper right side of my back. Maybe an angel for my daughter Natalia. She mimicked her hand to the size she wanted which was about the size of the palm of her hand. Twenty minutes later he came back with stencils of both of the tattoos. Sydney approved. He placed down protective paper over the bench and allowed Sydney to lay down. She lowered her bottom so he could lay the stencil down. Gloves on his finger he immediately turned on the power supply Sydney said a quick prayer as she felt the needle press into her skin. The initial contact made her want to punch Gabe, after a while she became numb to it. Two hours later, Gabe was finishing up her angel tattoo on her back. "I added a few extras but I think you're going to like it. I added some color for you." Her phone rang, Gabe handed it to her as she lay on her stomach. "Hello."

"What's good ma?"

"Hi baby. Sydney replied seductively. I'm getting a tattoo."

"What?! Where?"

"On my back."

"I don't believe you. You a wild girl now?"

"Whatever. You kept telling me I should get one, so me and the girls came and I'm doing it. But, how's my baby?"

"Yo, I gotta see this. I know whatever you got is sexy. But, she's good, sitting here eating all my grapes. But, I will be in Connecticut possibly Monday."

"Okay. Oh, I also need you to have my number changed."

"Why? What up?"

"Dominic has been calling me and I'm over it."

"Damn, that nigga didn't learn from the chin check I gave his ass. Nah, let that nigga keep fuckin' with you, I'll make sure he don't do it again."

"Chris... please change the number."

"A'ight ma, I got you. We'll see you Monday."

In New York, Eric had been released from the hospital days ago. He was at Ben's house until he got better, but Ben wasn't helping his anger. He knew that Chris had shot him, because he saw his face and that infuriated him. He had the balls to blast him in broad daylight. His mother was there as well acting as his nurse. Ben knocked on his room door before walking in. Eric was sitting on the bed. "How you feeling son?"

"Good. I'm ready to go merk that pussy ass nigga."

"It's good. No worries Money, we'll end that coward. It's not just about ending him, we have to end his power. His higher force."

"Who the fuck is his higher force?"

"His bitch ass protection! Without Preme, there is no punk ass Chris. Nigga can't act alone he needs Preme's muscle." He replied sternly.

"So you saying we go after Preme. Do you know what kind of war we'll start with that shit pop?!"

"I don't give a fuck. Fuck them! Why the fuck are you questioning what I'm saying to you?! If you don't end Preme those niggas gonna end you."

Eric took in what Ben was saying. He still had reservations about Preme. "Preme was my nigga and all until Chris came into the picture. I don't have no ill will towards that nigga though. I want to dead Chris ass."

"What the fuck got into you? You think that nigga gonna let you end his bitch ass fam without bodying you first? To get to Chris listen to what I say, you need to break down his walls. That's going for Preme, you knock that down, that bitch ass nigga gonna crumble."

Eric soaked in what he was saying. Ben was making sense, his adrenaline pumping and blood racing, he looked over at his father. "Fuck it. Let's go to war. End all those niggas." Ben glanced over at his son with a smile.

*   *   *

Sydney's tattoos were finished he placed some A & D ointment over them before handing Sydney a mirror. She stood up first looking down at her abdomen. She smiled looking over the fine script on King Christian, and the hearts and four leaf clovers which led towards her happy trail. He handed her a hand held mirror so she could look at her back. "This is beautiful! Thank you." She stared at the angel which was on her shoulder, a halo over her head kneeling in a garden of flowers. Her face towards a sky with a shade of light coming out of the clouds. The artwork was detailed, Sydney was amazed. She looked below it said Natalia. She immediately became overwhelmed with emotion thinking about her beautiful daughter. "Can you take pictures of both for me?" She handed Gabe her iPhone and he snapped the pictures for her, before he covered them with the protective paper. "Keep this on for a least two hours, gorgeous."

"Okay. How much do I owe you?"

"For you one fifty."

"Are you serious Gabe?" She replied with a smile.

"For you, I'll give you a discount. You're beautiful it was definitely a pleasure." He placed his hand over his chest. Sydney reached into her Chanel purse, for her wallet she handed him, four hundred dollars. Which was about all she had left in cash today. She checked to make sure she had her credit cards. "No you didn't have to do this."

"No, you did an amazing job. Thank you." Sydney headed back towards the front with the others who were already done waiting on her. Everyone was waiting to see what Sydney had gotten. "So, what you get?"

"I can't show it. But, here is the picture." She showed them the paper on her back, before handing over her phone to Nadine. "Aww... Sydney this is dope! Everyone agreed in unison. Nadine began to flip thru the pictures seeing the King Christian tattoo. Bitch! You didn't?!"

"What?" replied Sydney innocently.

"You got Chris' name tatted on you! It's cute! He's gonna spaz out when he sees this shit. King Christian huh?" Sydney laughed out loud, lowering her bottom so they could see the paper on her lower abdomen.

"Wow. Said Tori. Y'all better get married now. It's a wrap after that shit." everyone laughed.

"Okayyy! Said Nadine. Wait 'til mama Ingrid see it, she's gonna beat your ass!"

"Whatever. Chris is my boo, father to my child, if I want him on my body that's my business."

"Okay. Don't get all sassy with us bitch. Just call me when he sees it. I know the dick gon' be everything that night." Everyone laughed slapping hands as they showed each of their tattoos. Tori had gotten a flower on her right arm, Nadine had gotten a vine of flowers going up her foot, Kiana got cherries in her inner thigh. Everyone decided to go out for dinner afterwards, Sydney decided to head home instead. She stopped by a store and picked up A & D ointment. Once home she headed upstairs to her bathroom and quickly hopped into the shower. She was in almost fifteen minutes before her mother was knocking at the door before entering. Sydney quickly grabbed the shower curtain. "Hey, your father's on the phone. He wants to talk to you."

"Ma, I'm in no mood to talk to him. Tell him I left. I'm going to bed."

"Okay. I'm making one of your favorite's chicken parmesan and mushroom risotto."

"Sounds good, ma." Ingrid left out of the room. Sydney turned off the water, exiting the shower. She wrapped a towel around her body. She threw on a London flag tourist shirt and a pair of Chris' boxer shorts she had saved. She rolled them over so they could fit on her waist and give her tattoo room to breathe. She laid across the bed checking the time. It had been two hours. She removed the protective wrap, applying the cream. She removed it from her back as well, she washed her hands lying down calling Chris. He answered after two rings. "Hi, it's me."

"Hey *it's me*. I know it's you, I got caller id." He replied.

"Whateva smart ass! I was calling you to ask what else I can put on my tattoo. This ointment shit is greasy."

"Well, I use Lubriderm lotion sometimes. It helps the peel. That shit be looking crazy when it peels. How big is it?"

"It's a pretty decent size. How often can I put the lotion on there?"

"Whenever it's dry. I can't believe you got a tattoo. I gotta see this shit. Send me a pic."

"Um… no. I want you to see it in person. Remember when we met?"

"When we met at the mall? When you were wearing that sexy ass skirt." said Chris confused about the change in conversation.

Sydney smiled reminiscing to her outfit that day. "Aww… that's sweet you remember. You remember what you said to me?"

Chris laid back on his bed beside Natalia. "I said you're mine."

"Yea. You know back then. I didn't believe it, or see it happening. I just didn't see us ever seriously being together."

"What was wrong with me?" said Chris defensively.

Sydney laughed. "You were hella cocky and conceited. I don't know, I just didn't see it."

"So you weren't feeling me huh?"

"I'm saying when I met you, I didn't see us having a future together. I never thought we'd come this far. We've been through a lot together. Good times and the worst."

"Yea, we've definitely been through some shit. You're the only girl I've been with this long. Gotta stand for something right."

"Right. Aww… I'm special."

Chris laughed. "You already know that. You gave me my baby."

"So… if I didn't give you Natalia would I still be special?"

"Come on. Don't go there. I already told you, I love you, that shit is forever. You always gonna be special to me." Sydney let the words sink in. She envisioned him lying next to her, Natalia in between them. So what time are you going to be here Monday?"

"In the afternoon." One of Chris' burner phones began to ring loudly. Sydney heard him answer and speak to his father. He came back on the line and told her he'd call her back. Once off the line he went back to Preme who was chewing him out about everything that had transpired in New York. He informed Chris that Eric had been released from the hospital and would be looking for him. In true Chris fashion he explained he was unbothered by Eric. Preme's last words were he demanded Chris return back to Miami by Wednesday, he felt it was too hot on the east coast right now. Chris being as reckless as he was would lead to another situation, and he wouldn't allow that with his granddaughter involved. After ending the call Chris was furious, Preme was too cautious. *I'm good,* Chris thought, *fuck that nigga*

Sunday came and Sydney had been up downstairs and eaten a bowl of cereal. She had plans to get her nails done, body waxed and her hair blown out. Nadine was to hang with her today and she was going to pick her up and finally see her place. Sydney pulled on a pair of black skinny jeans, white rayon crop top and Giuseppe Zanotti jeweled thong sandals. Saint Laurent Black monogram chain bag in tow. She quickly applied moisturizer to her face and gloss to her lips and was on her way to Nadine. She turned up Rihanna's "Work" as she coasted thru the streets. Once in her parking lot she called telling her she was outside, she gave her the door number. Sydney glanced at herself in the mirror once more before getting out of the car. She set the alarm, walking to the door. Nadine met her at the door. "Hey girl. I gotta finished getting dressed, make yourself at home." Sydney walked around the living room, looking over her chocolate and teal microfiber furniture. Not her personal taste, but it was cute nevertheless. "Your place is nice girl!" shouted Sydney as she glanced over the pictures on her shelf.

Many of Nadine in school and club pictures, she stopped on the last picture which was of Nadine and a man booed up at the club. Sydney's mouth dropped as she looked over the man. "Is this your baby daddy?"

"Where in that club picture, of me in the white? Yea, that's him."

"What's his name?"

"Tarik." Sydney immediately placed the picture on the shelf. A million thoughts running thru her head. She wondered what the status of Chris and his friendship was. What a small fuckin' world. "So, where is he now?"

"He's in New York, visiting his family." Shouted Nadine from the bathroom. Sydney knew it had to be him. She wondered if Nadine had told him anything about her and Chris. Too many thoughts in her head. Nadine was one of the realest bitches she knew. She had nothing to worry about.

After spending all day getting pampered and she was flawless from head to toe. All she wanted to do was take a breather, in her bed. She took off her sandals stretching out across her bed. She looked at the time on her phone it was nine thirty. Her phone rang displaying Chris' picture. "Hey."

"What up ma? What you doing?"

"Laying across the bed. What are you guys up to?"

"We're here."

"What?!" Sydney sat up.

"Yea, come by the room Hilton #1210."

"Okay, give me about thirty minutes."

"A'ight." Sydney smiled jumping up from the bed. She hopped into the shower quickly picking out her La Perla set and she pulled out her new Herve Leger A line black bandage dress she had been saving for tonight. She slid her feet into a pair of Jimmy Choo Rosanna ankle tie pumps, embellished in Swarovski crystals. She headed over to her mirror to apply her makeup, once finished she grabbed the gift bag for Chris and was out the door.

Once she arrived at the hotel, she checked her makeup once more before walking inside. She glanced at her phone it was midnight. She couldn't believe she had taken that long. She walked thru the lobby all eyes on her as she breezed past and on to the elevator. Once she reached the door she knocked twice, Carl opened the door. He opened gawking at her appearance, he could feel himself rise in his pants. He immediately walked over to his own suite. Chris walked out of the bedroom to the door, after hearing Carl. "Hey."

"What's good ma? Damn, look at you." He looked over Sydney's body as she twirled in her dress. He extended his arms for a hug, he hugged her tightly. Becoming amassed with the scent of her perfume. "Damn, you looking good Syd." He whispered in her ear. Sydney could feel his lip on her ear lobe, it sent a tingle down her spine. He kissed her cheek. "Thank you." she finally replied as she glanced over his body. He was wearing a pair of jeans and white t-shirt. His body insane underneath. He led her back to the bedroom where Natalia was laying. Sydney handed him the gift bag as she walked over kissing Natalia on the face. "What's this for?"

"Just something for you. I figured you would like." He smiled opening the bag he dug down pulling out the case when he saw Gucci on the front he immediately smiled. He opened the glasses eyeing them over. "Yo, these are fly Syd. Thank you." He placed them on his face, walking over to the mirror to check his reflection. "Thank you. I appreciate it." He hugged her again. "You're welcome."

"So, how's your hip treating you?"

"It's good, not bothering me."

"That's good. He looked over at Natalia. She tried to hang in there miss thirty minutes, but she tapped out."

"Oh... I'm sorry. She leaned over the bed again kissing her face, running her fingers through her wild hair. Chris glanced at her ass which was shown peeking out of her dress as she bent over.

"You hungry?" said Chris as he sat on the bed.

"Nah, I'm good." She walked over towards him on the bed.

"So where is this tattoo?"

"Oh that. I thought you'd forget." Chris looked over at her his face saying really. She sat beside him on the bed moving her hair over to the side. Showing her angel tattoo. Chris looked over the detail, a smile on his face. "That's hot Syd. Did a good job, a lot of detail in that shit." He caressed his finger over it. Sydney looked into his eyes. "I got another one."

"What? You got two in one day?!"

"Yea. It's something special to me. I hope you like it." she replied with a smile.

"A'ight where is it?" Sydney turned her back to him. "Unzip me." Chris smiled unzipping her dress, he looked down her spine to the lace thong in between her soft peach. She turned facing him her dress covering the front of her body. She slipped her arms out of the dress. Chris couldn't help getting turned on by her impromptu strip tease. She released the dress letting it fall to the floor. She lowered her panties, showing him her abdomen. A wide grin crossed his face. "Yo..." He replied covering his mouth. "I love you baby. I told you, you're my one. You're my king." Chris couldn't contain the smile on his face or his dimples peering thru on his face "I can't believe you did that ma." Sydney smiled sitting on his lap. He placed his arm around her body. "Wow."

"Do you like it?"

"Are you serious? I fuckin' love that shit! He looked into her eyes as he cuffed her chin. You really love me huh?" said Chris with a smirk on his face.

"I do."

"Come here" He pulled her into him kissing her lips. Soon their tongues were dancing in each other's mouth. Sydney became wet, she mounted herself on top of him. Laying him back on the bed. "You know what this mean." He replied as he looked up at her body sitting on top of his throbbing shaft. "What?" she replied seductively as she bit her lip.

"You are mine forever. No one better ever see this shit except King muthafuckin' Christian Garcia." He replied with a smile.

"No one ever will." She bent down kissing his lips again. "So, would you get a tattoo of me?"

"Of course I would. You my woman of course. She bent kissing his neck and ear lobe. He grabbed her ass. "Damn... I fuckin' missed you ma." She began to kiss over his neck softly as she slowly grinded on his body. She sat up, abruptly stopping. "Before this goes where we both know this is going... I want to know what's going to happen between you and me. Because as much as I want to fuck the shit out of you right now. I love you too much for this to be just a physical thing. I told myself I was going to be committed to you and only you, until this was right."

"What you mean?" said Chris.

"I want to know are we back together exclusively. Do you only want to fuck me? Where is this going? What about your girl in Miami?"

"My girl... I'm done with her."

"You broke up?"

"No. You want me to break up with her?"

"Yes. I don't want to be your mistress or jumpoff. I should be your one and only." Sydney replied with a confident smile.

"Fine. I'll call her." Chris reached over grabbing his phone off the nightstand.

"Chris! Are you serious?" She slid off of his body. He scrolled thru his contacts dialing Tatiana's number placing the call on speaker. "Yes… Chris." Said Tatiana dryly.

"Yo, it's over."

"WHAT?" She replied angrily.

"You heard what the fuck I said. We're done. You can keep your job at the store if you need it. But, to be one hundred I don't need you there either." Sydney hit him on the chest. "Don't be so mean!" she mouthed to him

"What you leaving me for that bitch?" She shouted.

"That's not important. The point is I'm done fuckin' with you." He ended the call placing the phone on the nightstand. "See. Handled."

Sydney looked over at him, shocked the way he talked to her. "Chris… you were so mean!"

"I don't give a fuck."

"I can't believe you did her like that. I mean… low-key, It kind of turned me on. But, rude as hell."

"I got some shit I want to get out before we go back down this road. This shit has to be about the best move for Natalia. Meaning we in this shit one hundred. You need to stop beefing about the petty shit when I'm out. Know that I'm only fuckin' with you at the end of the day. I need you to hold me down one hundred like I ride for you. Lastly, stop being so fuckin' jealous." Sydney nodded her head taking in his demands.

"Okay, I agree. But, you need to come talk to me instead of yelling and cursing when you're angry."

"I can't guarantee that shit. You know I have a temper. I have no control once I'm at a hundred." He replied with a smirk.

"No, Chris you can control it. Say that you will change." Chris looked into her eyes. "I will change..." She leaned in kissing his lips slowly. "You better never talk to me like that." "I didn't care about her the way that I do you. I love you." They kissed again. "I love you too baby." She sat on top of his lap removing her bra. She kissed and sucked gently on his neck, moving up to his ear again. "Come on and give me that King dick papi." Chris smiled, lifting her off the bed, she wrapped her legs around his body as he carried her into the adjoining room.

Hours and numerous orgasms later, Chris and Sydney lay winded at the end of the bed. Sydney laid her head on his chest. "I can't believe you got me tatted on you. Sydney smiled. I know your fam was vexed about that shit. Since, they hate me." They laughed.

"My mom hasn't seen it. They don't hate you. Well, my dad does. My mom likes you. I mean, I think she feels safe knowing I'm with you. The first thing she said at the hospital was *if you were with Chris, he would've been here.*"

Chris smiled as he ran his fingers through her hair. "If you were with me. It would've never happened."

"So what happened with your mom? Did you get her a better grave?"

"Yeah. Peaceful spot off by herself. I bought myself a plot next to her."

"Aww, baby that's sweet." She kissed his lips.

"So, how long I'm gonna have to wait before you come home?" said Chris as he looked into her eyes.

Sydney sat up. "You want me back in Miami now?"

"Yea. I want you to come home." Sydney looked around, immediately thinking of her parents. How angry they would be, all the sacrifices they had recently made for her.

"I don't want to leave so sudden. My mom brought me a car, and got me this decent job. I don't want them to think I'm always dropping everything to be with you."

Chris sighed. Not pleased with her answer, but willing to compromise. "What do you want to do?"

"I will stay here maybe a month longer. Get my things packed. I told her I would be moving to Fort Lauderdale, and maybe break the news to her later."

"A'ight. Whatever you want to do. But, I need to let you know... I threw out all your clothes and shoes." Sydney gasped at the thought of some of her rare pieces and bags that were now garbage. "Baby?! You were that mad at me?"

"I was gone. If you were near me, I would've fucked you up. But, that's the past. I'm changing. Don't worry about that shit. I will buy you all new shit."

Sydney's eyes lit up. "You're going to take me on a shopping spree?"

"Yea. You already know I don't care about shit like that. Wherever you want to go Paris, California, NYC we'll make it happen." He kissed her cheek.

"Well, tomorrow I want to spend the day with you two. We can go to the mall, maybe the park. I just want to spend time with my two loves."

"We can do that. Come on let's get in the shower before we get in bed with tubby." He smacked her across the ass as they hopped into the shower. While in the shower Sydney forgot about she had work the next day, fuck it she thought, she could miss one day. Chris and Natalia were more important. Once out of the shower Chris threw on a pair of Polo pajama pants. Sydney wrapped herself in a towel. "What am I to put on?" Chris slid into bed, help yourself. Sydney went thru his luggage. She threw on a Jordan shirt of his and a pair of his Dolce & Gabbana boxers. She slid into bed next to him and Natalia, he placed his arms around her body. The feeling felt surreal and warm, she felt at home, a feeling she hadn't felt in a long time. They soon drifted off to sleep.

The next morning Sydney woke up first. She went out to the couches to watch television. An hour later Chris woke up looking around for her. He heard the television in the other room. He walked out to her. "Good morning." Said Chris as he bent down to kiss her face. He sat down beside her placing his feet up on the coffee table. "Good morning. She replied. Tati sleeping?"

"Yep, she'll be up any minute." Seconds later like clockwork, Natalia began to cry. "In here mama. Come here." replied Chris. She climbed down from the bed walking out in her Hello Kitty thermals. She walked into the room, wiping her eyes, seeing Chris. She ran over to his legs. Natalia looked over to Sydney as Chris picked her up. "Hey boo. He kissed her cheek. Who is that?" he replied pointing to Sydney.

"Mommy." Natalia replied with a smile. Sydney smiled at her opening her arms. "Come give me kisses Tati." Natalia quickly left Chris' arms reaching for Sydney. She hugged her, kissing her lips. They decided to order room service and after would head out to the mall. First stopping by Sydney's house so she could get dressed. She changed into a hooded grey jumpsuit with a low V-neck which exposed her breasts. It looked painted on her body. Jordan thirteen edition custom black and grey sneakers on her feet. Chris gave Carl the day off, so they could enjoy their family day. They headed on their way to the mall.

Chris received a call from John. He answered. "Yo, what's good?"

"What up boss. Everything good with you? Tatiana just left out early today. She been spazing out all day, pissed."

"She'll be a'ight. I broke up with her ass yesterday."

"Oh wow. That's why shorty in here acting a fool." John replied with a chuckle.

"Yea, if she continues with that bullshit fire her ass."

"A'ight. We doing good in here. Got the website up and going that shit doing well. Got some things for you here, but you can deal with it when you return. Enjoy your trip."

"A'ight." Chris hung up the phone, turning up the volume. Pandora was playing and Sydney had changed it to the John Legend station, while he was on the phone. He placed his hand on her thigh as he began to serenade her along with John. "*My head's underwater but I'm breathing fine. You're crazy and I'm out of my mind. Cause all of me...*" Sydney looked over at him with a smirk on her face, thinking it was cute he wanted to serenade her, but upset he was butchering one of her jams. Natalia chimed in from the backseat with her baby gibberish. All you could understand was me and all. Sydney shook her head. "Why you have to ruin a beautiful song?"

"Stop hating Syd. I sound just like him. This my shit." He replied with a smile. Sydney side eyed him as she turned to look out the window. As they stopped at the stop sign she saw the tattoo shop on the corner. "That's where I got my tatts done."

"Oh yeah. We should stop in there."

"What?"

"Yea, I may get a tattoo."

"Are you serious? You're lying. You're not going to get a tatt." Chris pulled the car into the parking lot. He turned the car off, and slid out of the driver's seat. Sydney got out of the car opening the back door and picked Natalia out of her car seat, walking behind Chris as he walked inside. The receptionist saw Chris immediately, she ran her fingers thru her hair. Chris ignored her walking over to the samples on the wall. Sydney took a seat at the bench located by the door. Gabe walked out of the back, not seeing Chris. "Hi beautiful. How's your tattoo's healing?"

"Good. Thanks for asking. Hey babe, this is the guy who did my tattoos, Gabe."

"How you doin? Chris." They shook hands.

"What are you interested in?"

"I want a tattoo on my forearm. He extended his forearm, to show where he wanted it. I want a portrait piece of my wifey."

"Did you have a picture I can go off of?"

"Nah, you can base it off of her. Right?" Gabe looked over to Sydney. "Come back to my office." He led the way and Chris made sure he walked behind Sydney to make sure no eyes followed her. Gabe sat down at his desk. "How do you want her to be positioned?"

"I want her naked, or topless."

"Baby, don't get me naked." Gabe smiled.

"We can have your arms or hair covering your breasts. But, I would need a picture of you, to draw the sketch."

"Okay, replied Sydney nervously. So, I would have to take one now with my top off?"

"Yes." Said Gabe nervous of Chris' reaction to his request. Sydney sighed handing Chris Natalia. "You're lucky I love you." Gabe showed her to the bathroom which was located back in his area. She slid down her jumpsuit. Luckily today she was braless, because of the low V-neck on the jumpsuit. She ran her fingers through her hair applying lipstick to her lips. She walked out covering her breasts. Gabe pulled out a Polaroid. Chris looked over to him. "You know I want these pictures when this is done."

"I got you. Would you like her to be kneeling in the tatt?"

"Yea." Sydney kneeled on the bench as Gabe snapped away. "Okay. I should have the sketch done in a couple hours. When do you want it done?"

"In a few hours."

"Okay. He handed Chris his card. Sydney went back into the bathroom to fix her clothes. Once done they said a few words to Gabe and were headed out the door. Once down the road Sydney looked over at Chris, shocked that he was serious about this tattoo. "I can't believe you are going to get a tattoo of me on your arm."

"It only makes since. I got ma, and tubby. Only a matter of time before I put you on there."

Sydney smiled. "That's very sweet baby. Now you can always look at me." She reached over kissing his lips.

"Yea, and I can always see these." He reached over grabbing her breasts. She hit his hand. "Don't be nasty."

"What? I do like looking at your tits. Especially when they sitting out like they are today. You got on a bra?" He began to fondle her chest.

"No. She shooed him away again. I love your chest and abs but you don't see me being nasty about it."

"You frontin'. I'm not."

"Whatever, I'm not about to debate who is the nastiest with you."

"You know it's a losing battle." She laughed.

In Miami, Tatiana had cooled off and returned to Reign. She was still pissed, but she said she wasn't going to let everyone see her crack, since she broke up with Chris. Last thing she wanted was the gossip to go around the store that Chris had left her and she was heartbroken. The thought pissed her off, she began to second guess if coming back was a good move. Brandi had come in to cover her shift and Nathan was in as well. Tatiana had been throwing things in place and slamming things down since her return. Brandi had enough. "What the fuck is your problem?" shouted Brandi as she cleaned up the VIP section.

"Who are you talking to? I know you're not talking to me. Dirty bitch!" shouted Tatiana, she had been waiting all day for someone to press her buttons. Brandi picked the right one. Brandi placed the broom down, walking over to Tatiana. "What was that dumb bitch? What you in your feelings cause Chris probably ain't fucking with you no more?" As the words left her lips, she slapped Tatiana across the face. Tatiana picked up a vase on the table, throwing it at Brandi's head. It missed and shattered as it hit the ground. John came in between them, Nathan came to his rescue, and he grabbed Brandi. John held Tatiana's hands behind her back. "Fuck that basic ass bitch!" Screamed Tatiana.

"You the basic hoe. Mad cause Chris hit your weak ass pussy and left you alone. Step your cookie game up boo boo, so next time you can keep a nigga." Tatiana lounged at Brandi again, breaking free of John's hold she picked up a sign from a display throwing it at Brandi. "Tatiana... calm down." Said John.

"Fuck you! Fuck Chris, fuck this store!" She began to kick the clothes off the displays. John escorted her towards the door. "Tatiana you're fired! Brandi go home deal with you later!" The store was clear he locked the door picking up the items. Nathan escorted Brandi outside to her car, once clear he came back in to help John. John shook his head pulling out his phone, snapping pictures before calling Chris, his phone went to voicemail. He sent the pictures to him, caption said Hurricane Tatiana.

Chris and Sydney were walking through the mall. They stopped in Nordstrom's. Sydney followed Chris and they ended up in the children's section. Sydney immediately began to pick out Natalia a few Burberry pieces. Chris walked over to look over the glasses. Sydney grew tired of carrying Natalia. "Babe... Natalia is killing my arm." He smiled, "Hand her here and go pick out a stroller. I'm not going to carry her either." Sydney walked over looking over the strollers she spoke to the associate and said she wanted to pay for it and have it put together. They helped her put it together and brought the tag up to the register. Sydney came back with the stroller which was priced around three hundred dollars. She picked out a blanket to go inside of it. She walked back over to Chris he was picking out sunglasses. Sydney took Natalia placing her inside. "You see any you like?" replied Sydney as she approached him wrapping her arms around his stomach. "Yea, I got two. You see these women's ones look like the ones you got me. He pointed to a gold pair of aviators. You want em?"

"Yes, you can get them. We can have his and hers." She smiled at him. He told the associate he was ready to check out. She escorted him over to her register. He handed her the clothes, and tag for stroller and blanket. The order came up to over four thousand dollars. Persia walked over to her station, where the associate was bagging up their items. He handed her cash, Persia immediately spotted Chris. She became nervous, yet curious at the same time. There was no doubt, Chris was still sexy and had that presence that demanded every woman's attention. She flashed back to the sex they had in the club parking lot. Persia bit her lip. Her gaze shifted to Sydney who was on his arm, with their little one sleeping in the stroller. Persia quickly left from the counter, acting if she was straightening merchandise out of their view. Chris placed the bags under the stroller. "Syd, you hungry?"

"Yea, where you want to go? I could go for Cheesecake Factory?"

"That's cool with me." They headed to a few more stores, before leaving. Once in the car, Sydney stretched out reclining her seat as Chris drove. She yawned loudly. "Damn, you that tired."

"A little."

"Yea, I have the effect." She reached over hitting him on the arm. "Whatever. So, do you want me to keep Tati tonight so you can have a break?"

"You can if you want to. Only if I can trust you with Natalia." Sydney looked over at Chris. "I'm not taking Natalia from you. The only reason I went to LA was to get away. I was so angry with you. I don't want you always bringing that up either. I'm not going to kidnap our daughter."

"A'ight Syd. She can stay home with you tonight."

After eating, Chris stopped by the hotel so that Sydney could get her car and some of Natalia's things. Chris placed her car seat in Sydney's car. Once they were buckled in and ready to go, Sydney rolled down the passenger window. "What are you about to do with your free time Daddy?"

"Go get my tattoo. And those pictures."

"Are you serious? You have to come by and let me see it tonight."

"Maybe…" He replied. He rested his arms on the inside of the door. Natalia now up looked at him.

"Chris, you better come by!" Sydney pointed at him. "A'ight… bye tubby. Daddy love you, see you later." He reached in kissing her lips. Natalia grabbed his face, with a smile. He backed away from the car. "A'ight Syd. Love you, see you later." Sydney blew him a kiss before pulling away. Chris headed upstairs before getting Carl and they headed to the tattoo shop.

Sydney had given Natalia a bath and washed her hair. She sat in the bed in Sydney's lap as she read her a book. The Going to Bed Book by Sandra Boynton. Natalia smiled as she looked over the pictures. Sydney heard Ingrid come in downstairs. Minutes later she was at her door. "Sydney!"

"Come in." Ingrid walked in seeing Natalia in her pajama set. Natalia hopped up seeing her. "Hi nana's princess! Come here." Natalia ran to the end of the bed to Ingrid's arms. She began to kiss and hug Natalia. "When did you get here?'

"Chris is in town for a couple of days. Oh, you have to see the cutest Burberry things I got for her at Nordstrom today." Sydney went over to the closet showing her the outfits. "They are adorable Syd. So, what's going on with you and Chris?"

"Nothing. We're friends. Why you ask?"

"Because you know it's not unusual for him to come back and you fall back into his arms again." Sydney smirked.

"No, we are friends. But, I am still going forward with my plans to move down to Fort Lauderdale."

"Okay, and where are you going to stay? Job?"

"Ma, I will have a great plan and have that all figured out before I leave. But, my mind is made up. I need to be near my child."

Ingrid sighed not buying Sydney's reasoning. "Don't get too carried away with this Syd. Really think before you leave here. I don't want to hear Gavin's mouth about you and Chris."

"I don't care what he has to say. He ran out on us when we needed him. So, he is the last person who should be giving parenting advice."

"Sydney, all I'm saying is to think. You're a smart, beautiful woman. Use your head, not your parts." Ingrid picked Natalia up from the bed carrying her out of the room.

"Where are y'all going? We were having story time."

"Whatever. We are going to have a snack and she is going to chill with me."

"Fine, leave your mommy by herself." Natalia waved bye to Sydney. Sydney's mouth dropped. "Traitor!" Sydney laughed laying across her bed drifting to sleep. Several hours later Sydney woke up refreshed. She looked over at her phone screen which was lit up and stating the phone was ringing. She forgot it was on silent. She answered the phone it was Chris. "Hey babe."

"What's good? What y'all doing?"

"I just woke up and Tati is downstairs with my mom, around here somewhere."

"I'm going to stop by there in a minute. See you in about fifteen."

"Okay baby." Sydney slid off the bed ending the call. She rushed over to the bathroom to relieve herself and brush her teeth. She ran her fingers thru her hair and changed into a silk chemise, and robe. She walked down to her mother's room to check on them. They were knocked out. Natalia's feet and arms stretched out over Ingrid's body. Sydney tip toed back out of the room, looking at the clock on the cable box stated that it was eleven o'clock. Her cell rang again. She answered. "I'm at the door. Come in."

"Your mom in there?"

"She's sleep with Tati. Come in." Sydney opened the door seeing Chris walk up with a Givenchy hoodie on and a pair of jeans. As soon as he approached the door, she wrapped her arms around him kissing his lips. She locked the door behind them. "So did you get the tattoo?"

"Nah... that guy was lame. I'll wait until I get to Miami." They headed upstairs to her bedroom.

"Where are the pictures?"

"I kept them for me." Once inside her room Chris sat on the bed. Sydney was up placing Natalia's clothes in the laundry basket. Chris took off his hoodie, he glanced over at Sydney's ass as she bent picking items from the floor. "Syd... come here."

"Huh?" She walked over towards him, his demeanor serious. She stood in front of him. "Have a seat." Sydney sat on his lap. She looked into his eyes, ready for whatever he was about to say to her. He smiled staring into her face. "I love you Syd. So don't piss me off, and I have to cut my fuckin' arm off."

"What?" Sydney replied with a smile.

He placed his right arm down in front of her. "Oh my god! Squealed Sydney as she looked down at herself on his forearm. She was positioned seductively on her knees, naked, with her curls covering her nipples. Surrounded by exotic flowers all around her and one positioned in her hair. The detail was amazing, it looked just like Sydney. She looked like a goddess. "It looks just like me!"

"That was kind of the point ma." Replied Chris sarcastically. Sydney hit him "I fuckin' love it! I love you. I'm speechless." She turned kissing his lips passionately, he placed both arms around her hugging her body. Her body now mounted on his lap. Chris began to loosen her robe. He kissed her breasts gently her nipples hardened beneath her chemise. He kissed them thru the fabric, her body became warm all over. "Babe...

stop." She replied softly thru parted lips. As she leaned back on his lap. Chris grabbed her legs placing them over his shoulders. Sydney bit her lip anticipating, the initial contact of his tongue in her walls. Panty less, he made contact without interruption. Sydney grabbed onto the blanket as she tried to muffle herself from shouting. As his tongue ventured into every crevice of her pussy she unbuttoned his jeans placing his shaft into her mouth. She soon climbed down from his shoulders and mounted herself onto his dick. Balancing herself as she rode him her hands in her hair, she began to moan as he went deeper. Chris threw her to the bed, as he mounted her in doggy style position. Sydney buried her face in the blanket as she began to scream louder as Chris pounded in her backside. He began to moan with her as he pulled her hair in a ponytail. Which turned her on even more, she began to claw her nails into the bed, as she erupted into ecstasy.

An hour later, Sydney laid on top of Chris. Both naked, Sydney cuffed his body. He looked into her eyes. "Damn Syd, you did that shit tonight." He kissed her lips. "Don't I deliver every time?"

"Nah, that was some other shit, I'm not complaining. Need some of that shit when we get back to Florida." Chris chuckled as he smacked her on the ass. They embraced a moment longer. Sydney opened his arm, looking at the portrait of herself. "Babe, I still can't believe you got this."

"Yea, we getting married mos' def now."

"You think so." Replied Sydney sarcastically.

"I know so." Said Chris firmly. He kissed her again attempting to climb out of bed. Sydney pulled him back down. "Where are you going? Stay."

"You know I gotta get out of here. Your mom catch me in here she gonna flip. I don't need those problems while I'm in my boxers." He sat up on the side of the bed. Sydney placed her arms around his body, her breasts pressed into his back.

She kissed his ear. "I don't care. Stay." She whined. She pulled
him back down again, he gave in laying back down with her for
twenty minutes. He had almost dozed off. "I better go ma. I'll
see you in the morning when you drop off Tati." He got up
from the bed, walking over to the bathroom, naked. Sydney
watched him, thinking of what he had just done to her body. He
emerged placing his clothes back on. Once dressed he told
Sydney to walk him to the car. She threw back on her chemise
and robe. Chris led the way downstairs and out of her front
door. "A'ight ma. Give me some love." Sydney sulked over to
him, placing her limp arms around his body. He smiled,
knowing Sydney wanted him to stay. Shit, he wouldn't mind
going another round. But he decided he needed to go, he wasn't
in the mood for Ingrid's bullshit, on her turf. He picked Sydney
up. She smiled wrapping her legs around his body as he kissed
her lips. He lifted the back of her short robe as he palmed her
ass in his hands.

"Baby, stop... I don't have on any panties."

"Even better." He slid his finger into her warm wet box, she
shivered, biting her lip. He began to move his finger in and out
as she squirmed in his arms. "Oh... she moaned seductively.
Stop. You're not about to do this to me out here. Sydney
released her legs from around his body. Chris ran his finger
over her clit, with a smile. Sydney shuddered. "You play too
much! She hit him standing on her feet. She saw that the
interior lights were on in Chris' car. You had Carl in there the
whole time? Bye." Sydney turned to go back in the house,
Chris grabbed her arm pulling her in for one last kiss. He
walked over to the back passenger door, sliding inside. Sydney
quickly covered herself back up heading back inside, she
locked the doors walking upstairs with a pleased smile on her
face.

As Carl made a right down the next side street, he sped down
the road, merging onto the main road. As soon as he stopped in
the turning lane three police cars emerged from each direction.

Sirens blaring "Fuck." Replied Chris. He quickly reached under the seat, grabbing the floor paneling revealing a secret compartment. He tossed his gun inside, he closed it firmly with his hand. The windows were dark, he knew they could not see him in back. Officers swarmed around the car. "We need you all to step out of the car, hands in the air." Shouted one of the officers. Another officer on the passenger side flashed a flashlight inside the car. Carl rolled down the window slowly. "What's the problem officer? Said Carl with his hands placed in view over the steering wheel.

"I need you out of the car with your hands up!" he demanded.

"For what?" shouted Chris from the back seat.

"Get out now!" shouted the passenger officer. Chris looked over his shoulder realizing they were surrounded. He went to open the door, Carl proceeded to open his at the same time. Carl was out first his hands raised above his head, he bent his knees, slowly lowering himself to the ground. "Get on your knees!" shouted an officer with a gun pointed at Carl's head. Chris emerged from the car, rebellious, not wanting to place his hands above his head or get on his knees. "Get on your knees!" an officer shouted at Chris.

"Fuck that. I'm not getting on my knees for what. Fuck y'all." Shortly several officers rushed Chris slamming him on the car to frisk him, as the officer placed cuffs on his wrists. "What the fuck goin' on?" shouted Chris.

"You're under arrest for an outstanding warrant, Mr. Garcia." Replied an officer with a smile.

"This is bullshit. Fuck y'all!" They quickly escorted Chris over to a squad car alone. Carl in another. As they rode to the precinct Chris attempted to dial on his phone in his pocket. After he was fingerprinted and processed, he was brought into an interrogation room. Chris looked around the fluorescent lit room, it reeked of piss and coffee. Chris looked at the wall wondering what of the many things he had done, had given him the warrant. He wasn't going to let them see him crack, no matter what they brought his way. A white officer led the way in the room. He was about five foot eleven, dark brown hair, early forties with something to prove. Chris' face immediately shifted to a cold ice grill, as he placed his cuffed hands on top of the table. "Good Morning, Mr. Garcia. My name is Detective Clayton. Are you aware of why you are here?" His voice piercing and echoed throughout the room.

Chris rolled his eyes, looking into his face. "Do tell me… why the fuck am I here."

"Outstanding warrant for a battery charge. *Battery? Really…* Thought Chris. Don't remember huh? Persia Rodriguez ring a bell?" *That bitch!* Chris remained calm as he looked into Detective Clayton's face which was now positioned inches from his.

"Lawyer." He solemnly stated.

"Oh, come on you remember. The beautiful woman that you beat, tortured and left for dead over a year ago!" He pounded his fist on the table. Chris looked over at him again.

"Lawyer."

The officer became furious, scooting his chair back. "We know it was you asshole! We have evidence! The victim has fully identified every detail of you, your name and whereabouts. Chris remained stoic and calm as the detective went into a folder which he had placed on the table. He rose to his feet as his opened it, placing the contents on the table. "Do you know who this is?" He placed a crime scene photo of Maino dead in the car in front of Chris. Chris didn't flinch once to look over at the picture and show concern.

"Lawyer." Chris replied solemnly again. The officer smiled feeling that he had sparked a nerve in Chris. He pulled out another picture, of Chris and Maino out on the block together.

In the picture Chris was holding a drink a smile on his face in a conversation with Maino.

"Streets say you two were close. Shared the same girlfriend...partied together. Homies right? He circled around Chris. You were shot weren't you? He leaned over Chris' shoulder inches from his ear. Word on the street is you wanted revenge. He walked over to the side of Chris staring over at him, taking pride in every moment. Detective Clayton smiled at Chris. We have witnesses who say you were at the restaurant when Shaun Douglas was killed!" Chris placed his head in his hands acting as if he was going to sleep. "I'm glad this is amusing you, Chris. I have witnesses willing to put you away for life. Hope you make yourself at home, cause you won't be leaving here for a long time, handsome." He smiled at Chris, revealing his yellow stained teeth. He left out of the room and another officer walked in removing Chris from the room and walking him over to a holding cell. Once he was able to make a phone call. He called Preme's burner line, which was in case of emergency. Preme answered on the second ring. "Hello" Preme replied, as he glanced down at his watch it was six am.

"It's me. I'm in jail in Hartford. Get me a lawyer."

"What? They set you bail?"

"Not yet. Outstanding battery warrant." "A'ight, got you son." "A'ight." Chris hung up the phone, walking back over to his seat.

Sydney rolled over turning on her phone. She stretched her arms out as she waited for her phone to power on. She felt Natalia's little feet in her back. Sydney turned over to face her, kissing her cheek as she slept wildly. Once her phone was on and displayed no messages she walked over to take a shower, leaving the bathroom door cracked. When she got out of the shower, Natalia was now awake and rubbing her eyes. Sydney slipped into her bra and panties, as she dialed Chris' phone. It went to voice mail. She changed into a retro Jem & the Holograms tee, a pair of distressed skinny jeans and Giuseppe Zanotti snake skin sneakers on her feet. She changed Natalia into a white Burberry heart print tee, jeans and Jordan sneakers. She braided her hair into a side French braid which rested on her shoulder. After feeding Natalia breakfast she decided to call Chris again, no answer. She was concerned. She paused, to gather her thoughts as she checked her texts. No messages. *He would've called by now.* She gathered their things, Natalia in her arms and on their way to the hotel.

Once there she went up to his room, Natalia on her hip. She knocked on the door three times. She could hear the whizzing of the air conditioning as she pressed her ear up to the door. Silence. A surge of panic rushed through her body. She headed to the elevator and to the desk to check to see if they had checked out. Once she was informed they had not, she exhaled a sigh of relief as she took a seat on the plush black chairs. She glanced over at her phone again, debating her next move. Natalia rested on her chest, drinking water. As the lobby doors opened she glanced at the door, seeing Carl, hurriedly walking in. She immediately hopped up, walking over to him. "Carl!" He looked over in her direction, relieved to see her face. He met her halfway. "Hi Sydney. Have you spoke with Chris?"

"No. where is he? I have been calling all morning." Carl signaled for her to follow him up the room. She followed his lead, once alone on the elevator he finished his conversation.

"We got pulled over last night after leaving your place. Chris is in jail."

Sydney's eyes widened. "What? For what?!"

"They're saying he had a warrant."

"How long are they holding him? Is he getting bail?" said Sydney frantic. A million thoughts rushing though her mind. Carl touched her shoulder gently. "I don't know anything mami. I'm just getting out myself. I came back clean and was released. Figured, you want to come up get his things and wait."

"Yea, I can do that." Once they reached their room. Carl unlocked the room door, Sydney quickly walked over to his room. She placed Natalia on his bed, as she went into the closet. She grabbed his Louis Vuitton bags, snatching his clothes from the hangers folding them neatly in his bags. She knew that he had his travel safe with him, because he never traveled without one. She searched around the closet, finding it buried under his jeans, and placed it inside as well. As she glanced around the room looking for any other item of his. She walked over to the bathroom. Her phone began to vibrate in her back pocket. Unknown number. "Hello."

"What up ma?! How you doing?" said Chris his voice chipper and upbeat. Sydney smiled, placing her hand over her heart.

"Hi baby! How are you doing in there?"

"I'm good. Here with my lawyer. You didn't get my text?"

"No… when? I had turned my phone off last night. I'm sorry."

"It's a'ight. I may be getting out in a few hours. I got money in my safe, I need you to come get me."

"Okay, I got you. Are you going to be able to call me back?"

"I should be able to. This is my lawyer's phone. Hit it back if you need to. Where are you?"

"I was at your room. Packing up your things, I got everything."

"Good looking out ma. Get my phones out the nightstand. Let me get off this shit, and see what this judge talking. I'll see you soon, a'ight."

"Okay. We love you baby."

"Love y'all. One." The call ended. Sydney grabbed Chris' phones as he instructed placing them inside of his bags with charger. Carl soon came in to help her carry items down to her car. He stated that once the truck cleared he was leaving.

Chris was awarded a bond. His lawyer Grant Vaciani informed him that he would be in contact with him tomorrow. Grant contacted Sydney and informed her the conditions of the bond and that Chris release papers would be issued shortly after her arrival. Sydney rushed over to pick him up. She stopped by to pick up wings and fries he loved. Natalia was strapped in the backseat, playing with her Hello Kitty toy as Sydney sung along to the sounds of Adele blaring through the speakers. Once she arrived and met with the lawyer, everything was set, she sat outside awaiting Chris' release. She sat on a bench looking down at Natalia who was smiling at her. She stood her up on her lap looking into her eyes. Thinking of having Chris near her and how they were going to beat this situation together. Natalia began to jump up and down, Sydney smiled interrupting her own thoughts. "Why are you so excited mama?"

"Sup ma." Replied Chris' voice from behind her. Sydney turned quickly seeing Chris walking over to her. She hopped up from the bench, running over to him with Natalia in her arms. She immediately kissed his lips, as he placed his arms around her and Natalia. He kissed their faces. Sydney looked into his eyes examining his face. There was a few scratches on his face and neck.

"What happened?"

"Fuckin' cops. I'm good though. Happy to see y'all." Chris took Natalia from Sydney's arms. Chris followed her over to the car. He strapped Natalia in the backseat, as they were out of the parking lot and down the road. Sydney began to talk. "So, what happened?"

"Outstanding warrant, bullshit! That bitch Persia pressed charges!"

"What happened?"

"What happened is I beat her fuckin' ass! Trifelin' bitch!" said Chris angrily.

"Why?"

"That bitch was there when that pussy ass nigga popped me." Sydney glanced over at Chris thinking about her last encounter with Persia. "So, that's why she threatened me last time I saw her. She said that she was going to make sure she put you away and all this shit."

"Oh word. That's what she said?" Chris picked up a Styrofoam cup which was filled with lemonade. "This yours?"

"No, it's actually yours. I got you a plate as well on the backseat." He reached back picking up the plate. His stomach growling. He opened the plate seeing the fried wings and fries, he smiled. "Thank you ma." He reached over kissing her face as he dug into the food.

"You're welcome. Where do you want to go?"

"I'm gonna have to leave out of Hartford. If I stay here any longer I'm going to pop that bitch. Take me to New Haven, to get a room." Chris took out his phone calling Preme. "Yo Pop, what's good?"

"Yea, I heard from the lawyer that you were out. What you doing?"

"Headed to New Haven. Probably heading back to Miami tomorrow. I can't be up here right now."

"Yea, that's what you need to do. Lay low. Will get into details when you get here."

"A'ight pop. I'm going to call you back later." Chris ended the call placing the phone in the cup holder as he continued eating his chicken. He looked over at Sydney her eyes looked heavy as if she was worried. "What's good ma? Why you so quiet?"

"Just thinking. This whole situation. Every time we are happy some bullshit comes in and fucks our whole world up. I mean, I feel this situation is going to blow up into a shit storm. I don't want you to miss out on any of Natalia's life. I don't want this shit to break up our family. It's always something." Sydney hit the steering wheel. Chris wiped his hands off in the napkin, before caressing her thigh gently.

"Don't worry ma. We're gonna be good. I love you. We will be okay." The tears began to stream down Sydney's face as she stopped at the light. Chris placed his plate on the floor. He leaned in grabbing Sydney's face towards his, as he kissed her lips. "Look at me. We are good. When have I ever given you a reason to doubt my word?" She looked into his eyes, the man she loved with every ounce of her soul. The man she had created life with and saw her future with. As words came out of his mouth all she could do was cry. Her stomach in knots and in her heart she knew that this situation was far from over. The thought of him leaving her again was unfathomable.

In Miami, Preme had just arrived downstairs in his club. He was to meet Martin to go over business. His head of security, Loco, was to meet with him first. He walked down the steps dressed in all black Dickies, his signature style for years. Loco, government name Phillip Clark, was forty years old, brown skinned and medium build. He was a people person, charismatic, who people in the community adored. However, his charm was never to be mistaken for weakness, his reputation had always preceded him and young niggas respected him. Preme had met him as a teenager after his family was brutally murdered, he quickly became like a younger brother to him. Loco walked over to Preme seated at the table. They embraced, Loco sat down in front of him. "Hey boss. What's good?"

"Same shit. What's good in here?"

"We good. No complaints. Oh, this young cat I heard been asking around to get on with you. Name um... Yogi?"

"Yogi? Who the fuck is that?" said Preme disgusted someone had the audacity to speak his name in any capacity and he didn't know them.

"He's a small time nigga in Broward. Little shine... no threat. He's been asking to get with you for a minute. We could use some soldiers in Overtown. I've been watching his movements before I brought his shit to you. What you want to do boss?"

"Bring me his sheets and all. Pictures. Mama address, phone numbers and I'll see if he can be involved anywhere in my organization. I need all his records."

"A'ight. I'll have it for you tomorrow or the end of week." Martin came in thru the back entrance door, dressed clean as always in Ferragamo shoes. Armani suit and duffle bag in tow. He embraced Preme before sitting across from him at the table, resting the bag on the floor. Loco acknowledged Martin's presence before leaving upstairs to give them privacy. "How are you Preme?"

"I'm good. But, let's cut the bullshit and get to it. He adjusted himself in his seat, staring directly into Martin's eyes. This conversation has been long overdue, about Nick fucking up when I was away. I told you Mart keep your punk ass son in check. I don't want to have work done on your boy. But, he's leaving me no options."

Martin sighed, running his hand nervously over his head. "I will talk to him." He finally worked out.

"You do that. Before I have to. Chris has a little situation, I'm going to need DA Morrison information. Martin nodded his head. Definitely set that up. Also, Loco brought up a nigga name Yogi?"

"Don't know that nigga. But, I will look into it for you." Preme stood up from the table walking back behind the bar. He poured himself a drink, the door opened Loco came down with a duffle bag in his hand, handing it over to Martin. He left his duffel on the floor. He stood to leave not once opening the bag. "A'ight. I will get back to you."

"A'ight, talk to your boy. Replied Preme sternly. I don't want no shit. You heard?"

"Yea, but we can't get involved in that shit. They have to work that shit out."

Preme walked from behind the bar, approaching Martin in the face. "If my son handles this shit, your pussy ass son gon' be in a box. Ain't a damn thing you can do about it, 'cause you touch my son... I'm *touching* you. You feel me?"

Martin gulped as he looked into Preme's face. He looked around at Loco who was inches from him, who he knew was armed. He knew to cross Preme his days would be numbered, he would definitely get Nick in check.

Sydney and Chris were at a Hilton hotel. Chris had taken a long shower and was knocked out. Natalia was on her way next, she lay on his chest. Her ear perched on his chest listening to his heart beat. Sydney's phone rang, the screen displayed Nadine. She answered the phone. "Hello stranger."

"Whatever. How are you? How's the baby?"

"It's fine. I'm supposed to see a doctor soon. But, may be postponed Tarik talkin' about going to Virginia for a few months."

"Why?"

"Girl, I don't know. He was like it's too much going on in Hartford right now for the baby and we need a bigger place. He found a good deal there."

Sydney rolled her eyes. Tarik's reasoning did not sit right with her. What was Nadine thinking to go along with it? But, who was she to judge about being a fool in love. "You can't run forever. It may be a new city, but eventually the bullshit will follow."

"Yea, I don't really want to go. Because, my family is here and with the baby I want them to be involved." Replied Nadine sadly.

"Do what you think is right boo. I can't make that decision for you. It's about your family."

"I know. What's up with you though? You sound down."

"Just a little stressed. I'll be good. Probably going back to Florida in a few weeks."

"Really? What about your job? Did you save enough?"

"I will be okay. Chris will help me. It's just what I have to do, to get my family right."

"I hear ya girl. Nadine yawned. I'm always so fuckin' tired with this baby."

"Probably because you are carrying triplets." Said Sydney jokingly.

"Girl, don't say that! I mean really can you see my loud ass yelling at three kids. Bitch, I'd stay on the bottle." Sydney laughed out loud. Chris began to move in the bed, Sydney looked down at his face.

"Hey, let me talk to you later girl."

"A'ight." Sydney placed the phone on the nightstand. Chris moved Natalia from his chest resting her on his pillow. He sat up looking over at Sydney. "What's good ma?"

"Hey… I'm good." She replied dryly. Chris laid his head back in her lap.

"What's good? You seem upset?"

She sighed. "Baby… I guess I'm just worried."

"Why, you worrying? You don't see me worrying about this shit." Sydney looked down in his eyes. "I'm always worrying about you. That's just me. I care about what happens to you. Even though sometimes you don't. I don't want this to blow up into anything more, ya know."

"It's not because we're going back home tomorrow. You coming home with me?"

Sydney's mouth dropped. "What? I don't know baby."

"Syd, I need you there with me. I'm not gonna be able to stay fuckin' calm without you being there."

"What?"

"You know how I am. You the only one keep me sane. If you not there with me, you know I get reckless, do crazy shit. I already know."

Sydney caressed his face. "How do I stop you?"

"You just do. I know with you and Natalia there… I got a fuckin' reason to be here. I do some of the shit I do, for us, to be a'ight. I don't want tubby fuckin' struggling or you to be workin' just to get by. I keep us set so we never have to worry or want for shit. Having you there with me makes it worth it." Sydney looked down into his eyes again. Those eyes and smile that always made her melt, her mind telling her one thing and her heart another. She removed her hands from his face. "I feel like I'm betraying my family to be with you. I mean a couple months ago, I didn't have shit baby. I don't want to bring up the past, but you left me cold with nothing! I had to crawl back to my parents for help, do you know how embarrassing that was. Having them ridicule me and say that they knew it would've never worked. Not only that, precious moments that I've missed out of Natalia's life. How do I know this time is different? Because for me to up and leave this time, my support system will be done. I would have once again chosen you over them."

"This time is different because I have you fuckin' inked on my arm, and I'm on you. That's forever. I mean we have our faults, yea I've fucked other women. But, none of them mean shit to me. We're going to have issues and arguments Syd. But, at the end of this shit I'm with you. I don't see myself with no one else but you. Raising our family, taking her to dances, plays and shit. Giving our baby something we both never had, that family shit we both said we dreamed about."

Sydney reminisced over the many talks they had about their dreams and goals for their family. She thought of holidays and birthdays they would share together. Everything inside her mind said no, don't do it. But her heart, almost felt like it would burst out of her chest when he touched her. The way he said her name, the scent of his cologne, and debating television with him. Everything about his perfect imperfections made her love him, and as she looked down into his face again, she had made her decision.

"I will go home with you." She replied with a subtle hint of resentment as the words left her lips. A wide smile formed on his face. "Yo... come here." Sydney bent down kissing his lips. He slid in a little tongue which made her smile. Once they separated, Chris slid off the bed heading over to the bathroom. Sydney shook her head. "Ma, is going to hate me." That night Chris decided that they would leave for Miami before sunrise. He decided that they would drive. He called Preme after Sydney was sleeping to inform him of his plans and he informed him to call once they stopped in North

Carolina. Chris got a few hours of rest, waking up and throwing on a pair of joggers, hoodie and Jordans. Around one thirty he woke up Sydney. She quickly got up, throwing on a pair of leggings and thermal. She put Natalia on her jacket and sneakers. Sydney carried Natalia to the car as Chris came down with their bags, after checkout, Chris got behind the wheel. "I have to go by my house for some things before we leave."

Chris nodded. Once there Sydney crept thru the house, she could hear her mother snoring in her room as she past the door. She quickly ran upstairs grabbing her suitcases, throwing clothes and pictures in them. She rushed over to her desk penning a quick letter to her mom which she left on the fridge. Chris came to the door helping her with her bags, as she looked back on her house once more. A wave of guilt filled her body, she quickly rushed over to the passenger seat, sliding in as they sped off into the night on their way to Miami.

That afternoon they arrived in Asheville, North Carolina and got a room at a Sheraton. Minutes after they were settled in their room, Sydney rushed into the bathroom to shower. Chris called Preme and let them know their location and update. He placed Natalia on the bed under her blanket, before creeping into the bathroom. He stripped off his clothes, before stepping into the piping hot shower. Sydney was washing her hair, her back to the shower head covered in suds. Chris smiled admiring her body. He placed his hands in her hair to assist her. She jumped. "You scared me!" She shouted playfully hitting him in the chest. She quickly wiped her eyes. Chris smiled. "Are you going to wash me?"

"No. You nearly gave me a heart attack."

"My bad. He replied as he kissed her neck. Sydney smiled as she looked at his manhood, glistening as the water trickled over every inch of him. She turned away from him, squeezing more Dove body wash into her washcloth. Chris moved closer to her body again, kissing her earlobe, sent a sensation through her body. "Stop Baby…" She finally replied.

"Why?" He replied.

"Because, I'm trying to clean myself. Natalia is a wall away."

"Really? He replied with a smile. Never stopped us before. Anyway, when you gonna give me another baby?"

Sydney turned quickly looking him up and down as if he was crazy. "What?" He looked into her eyes again, not one bit affected by her side eye glare. "You heard me! When are *we* going to have little Chris?"

Her glare gave way for a smirk as she took in what he said. "You seriously want another baby?"

"Yea. I want us to have three kids." He smiled kissing her lips. "Three kids? You play too much. We'll see."

"Nah, we gonna work on number two right now." Chris picked Sydney up. She clasped her legs tightly around his body as he pinned her under the shower. The steaming water cascading down their bodies. Hours later they lay in bed eating room service as Natalia lay beside them. Sydney was sitting on top of Chris in his white t-shirt and Victoria's Secret Pink boy short panty. Chris was in a white t-shirt and Dolce & Gabbana boxer briefs. "I love you so much." Replied Sydney as she looked into his eyes.

"Why?" replied Chris with a smile on his face, he wrapped his arms around her body.

"I love everything about you. All of your crazy, the way you love me, the way you make me feel. These last few days showed me that again. What I grew to love about you in the beginning. Showed me why I can only be with, and love you. You love hard, and I love that."

"I love looking at you." Chris replied as he looked into her seductive eyes.

"What?"

"Your face, your lips, your hair when it's all over the place like right now. I love to see you smile. That was the first thing that drew me to you."

"Really?" Sydney replied almost squealing, as she pulled her hair out of her face.

"Yea. After looking at all of this. He cuffed her ass in his hands. Your smile was a wrap after that." She leaned over kissing his lips, Chris slid his hands up the back of her shirt. His touch sent goosebumps up her back.

Early that next morning, Ingrid got up to turn on her Keurig. She walked upstairs to check on Sydney and was greeted by her empty room. She retreated back downstairs, sending Sydney a text. She went to the pantry getting her cup, and walked over to the refrigerator to grab cream cheese for her bagel. She saw a note hanging on the fridge under a Miami magnet. She pulled the note from the fridge leaning over the counter to read it.

Mommy,

I know you are probably wondering about me, by the time you find this. But, I am fine. Me and Chris are back together... and I decided to go back to Florida. I know you are upset. But, I love him. I don't see myself being complete without him. So, if you and Dad don't want to talk to me. I understand. I feel I need to make this right for Natalia. She deserves a family, and I deserve to be with the man I love. All I ask is that you don't hate me. I appreciate all you've ever done for me mommy. I really do ☺ don't worry about me. I'm fine. I will call you soon. Don't hate me.

Love, Syd

Ingrid took the letter ripping it to shreds. Tears soon flooded her eyes as she tossed the paper in the air.

"I can't believe her! She's not going to be fucking satisfied until he drags her and that baby to the bottom with him! I don't know why she keeps going back to that asshole! Uggh!! I hate him!" Ingrid shouted. She picked up her phone, quickly dialing Gavin to inform him on the news.

In Miami, Preme met up with Loco, at his office at one of his premium liquor stores. He had files with pictures of Yogi's family members, addresses and a picture of his toddler son who lived in Hialeah, with his mother who was a stripper. Preme looked over the pictures of Loco, shaking his head disgusted. "He looks like a loud, cocky ass nigga."

"Yea, he is cocky. He's done a few jobs down here. Remember Buggy and Smoke?"

"Yea, niggas out of Broward. Night clubs or some shit, fucking with pills and shit."

"He handled that. Niggas tried to set him up on a deal."

"Oh yeah. Preme looked over his information. I'm gonna call Mart have that nigga meet me at the club this afternoon at four. My time is not to be wasted he a second late, it's over."

"A'ight. Will do."

Preme looked over his driver's license information. Javon Mario Wright. He was twenty three years old. Preme placed the information back in his folder. He placed items in his briefcase signaling for Loco to check to see if his appointment had arrived. Loco took the elevator downstairs seeing Carl standing outside nervous. Loco brought him up to Preme, once inside the office. Loco stood guard outside the door. He walked over to Preme's immaculate desk which was black and shined. He removed his hat looking over at the television screens which lined the walls of different cable channels. He extended his hand to shake Preme's. Preme looked at him ignoring his gesture. "What happened in New York?" said Preme bluntly as he pulled out a cigar.

"Um… I was following orders… sir. He told me to drive to the Bronx on the way there he saw a guy named uh… Lewis. He then switched his plans and said we were going to Brooklyn. I, got your call and I tried to switch up. He lost it, jumped out of the car, letting off shots. I tried to get him out of there, Preme." He replied almost stuttering.

"What was your job?"

"To protect him. Make sure he didn't get hurt."

"Did you do that? Carl sat nervous, silent. Did you do your fuckin' job?" Preme barked.

"No, sir. But…"

"Shut the fuck up. You didn't do what the fuck you were told! He stood up from the table, walking over to Carl. Carl began to shake his leg nervously, awaiting the wrath of Preme. He took his lit cigar, placing it to the side of face. Carl screamed out in pain. Preme walked over to his filing cabinet, he pulled out a hammer. What did I tell you?"

Carl's eyes widened seeing the hammer in his hands. "Preme please, I did all I could do! He wouldn't listen to me."

"Do I look like a fucking joke to you? Do I look fuckin' stupid?! Place your hand on the fuckin' desk. Carl shook his hand nervously raising it to the desk. The other day you let Chris and Sydney go fuckin' shopping, alone. Was that doing your job?" Before Carl could answer Preme wacked his hand with the hammer, he let out a blood curdling scream. I told you, you would be handled. Put your other fucking hand on the desk…"

Chris and family had been on the road. They were now in Georgia. Sydney was behind the wheel, with Pandora blasting through the speakers. Chris was sleeping his hat low, covering his eyes. He woke up hearing Sydney singing, Beyoncé's "Blow"

"Can you lick my skittles… that's the sweetest in the middle… Pink…." **She** sang loudly as she looked back in the rearview mirror at Natalia, who was sleeping her head leaned to the side of her car seat. She looked over to Chris, startled as he stared back at her with a smile. "What are you doing up? You scared me." Sydney held her chest.

"What, you listening to? He looked at the screen. Bey, get down like that? You can't wait for me to turn that cherry out huh?"

"Why you have to make it so nasty? She laughed. I was just singing the song."

"Nah, I saw you. You was doing more than singing, ma. It was sexy though. Where are we?"

"We are almost in Florida. I saw a sign that said we would be approaching welcome center soon."

"A'ight. We need to stop there go to the bathroom and change. Then I will take over again."

"No, I want to drive." Sydney whined. "Well at least until we get to Orlando."

"A'ight, until Orlando." They stopped at the next rest area Sydney took Natalia into the family bathroom, changing her diaper and clothes. She changed her clothes to a crop top and leggings, Chucks on her feet. Natalia was in a pair of tights and a shirt which said Billion Dollar baby, Buscemi pink 100 mm on her feet. When they headed back to the car they met Chris at the vending machine buying two of everything.

In Miami, it was just before four, Yogi had gotten the message and had been waiting at the bar. He was nervous, sweat trickled off his forehead as he looked around the club. There wasn't any girls on the stage yet, but he was set on making the best first impression. A waitress offered him a drink, he declined. He looked around wondering which door the legendary Preme would walk out of. He turned back forward and was greeted by Loco. "Let's go." Yogi hopped up from his seat, following behind Loco and another man. Both looked intimidating and non-conversational. He followed them downstairs to another bar setting. Before escorting him over to a table, the other man quickly hemmed him searching his body for weapons. He wasn't stupid enough to come into Preme's business strapped. Once he was cleared, they instructed him to sit at a corner booth seat. A door beside the bar opened in walked a brown skinned man, middle aged, in a Versace linen shirt and pants. Although casual his presence demanded attention, and to be respected. Yogi looked up knowing this had to be the legend he had heard so many things about, who everyone in Miami feared and loved. He was speechless. Yogi slid out of the seat realizing he was being extra, but was determined to show this legend the utmost respect. As he approached Yogi, Yogi extended his hand out to him. Preme looked him over with his cold almond shaped eyes, rejecting his gesture before sitting down. Loco stood beside the table. Yogi looked around the room realizing it was armed men at each exit. Yogi gulped before returning to his seat. His heart immediately racing.

"So, let's get down to it. You have been looking for me? Why should I let you work for me?" Preme clasped his hands in each other as he stared into Yogi's eyes. Yogi tried to keep the same intensity in eye contact but he was distracted by the diamond bracelet on his wrist and ring that sat on Preme's pinky finger.

"Because I can get shit done. I grind and get shit done by any means. You feel me?"

Preme looked at him with a scowl as if he was somewhat disgusted by his response. "I don't care about that fuck shit you rehearsed to make your punk ass sound like a fuckin' man! What the fuck can a broke nigga like you do for my team? Enlighten me."

"Mr. Preme, I come from the fuckin' bottom. Everything I got, I did my way. Why you should put me on because I am these streets."

Preme placed his hands down on the table. His silence was deafening. "Looking at you, right now I'm not impressed in the slightest. A part of me feels I should place two to your dome for even mentioning my name. But, some of your work has preceded your pussy ass presence. Since I'm in a decent mood today, I'm gonna give you a chance. Because for you to mention my name, look for me knowing the consequences you must be serious about this shit. What I will do is start you on a probationary period at the fucking bottom running errands. I got your numbers and all your information. I will have my second, watching your moves. He tell me one fuck up or bullshit it's a wrap for you. From this day your side fuck shit you came in is over until you have passed everything. You understand?"

"I got you." replied Yogi.

Chris and family arrived in Miami around two thirty in the morning. Exhausted, Sydney sulked into the shower with Natalia. Chris walked over to the shower opening the glass door. "I'll be back I gotta go see pop." Sydney looked at him with a glare which said *you got me fucked up*. She quickly sponged Natalia off who was in her arms. "Baby, it is two thirty in the morning."

"I'll be right back ma. I'll be back no later than four thirty I promise." He leaned in a little closer to her. "Okay. Be safe." She kissed his cheek, he quickly closed the door rushing out of the room and down the stairs. Sydney turned off the water, bundling Natalia up in a towel. She went over to her room changing her into a black and pink pajamas set. Sydney poured some warm milk in her cup she quickly drifted back to sleep. She walked to her own closet to find something to slip in. Her side was completely bare. Her designer shoe collection was gone, rows of Chanel, Dior, Christian Louboutin, Buscemi, and Giuseppe Zanotti to name a few were now bare. She couldn't believe Chris had seriously threw all of her things away. She reached into her bag finding a chemise throwing it over her body, lying next to Natalia.

Chris arrived to Preme's house around three. He had called on his way and Preme was waiting for him at the door. They embraced for a brief moment before Preme walked over towards the kitchen counter. "What's good son?"

"Nothing much. Good to be home and fuckin free."

"I hear you on that shit. I spoke to your lawyer. You are going to need to set up shit with him. They don't have any evidence on that murder bullshit. But, for that bitch they trying to pin attempt murder shit. Possible battery charges."

"Yo, fuck that bitch. What am I looking at?"

"Working shit out but may be no time at all. Work some things out with my people."

"Word."

"I saw Carl. How he do that week?"

"He was a'ight. But, a nigga like that can't handle a nigga like me. You should know that pop." They both laughed.

"Yea, you right. Oh yea, I'm testing out this new nigga to possibly be on my team. I want you to watch him and let me know what you think."

"A'ight, you know I got you." Chris leaned on the bar stretching out his arms as he yawned he was exhausted. Preme saw the new ink on his forearm. "What's that?" Chris smiled, opening his arm so Preme could see. "You know, Sydney my wifey." Preme looked at the detailed tattoo of Sydney on his son's arm. He shook his head as he smiled. "You sprung my nigga? It's a wrap now. You might as well make it official and marry her now. Shit."

"Yea, I'm thinking of getting her a new ring and we try this shit again. Try this shit one more time for our family. N'ahmean." Preme smiled at his son, proud of his growth. Preme had some reservations about Sydney, but he respected his decision to try to make it work. "I'm proud of you. Stepping up, doing shit for your family. How my baby doing?"

"She's good. Getting into everything. I'm going to start looking for a daycare for her. She's getting too big to be home. She needs to be around other kids."

"I'll have my people look into the best ones down here and get her set up." Chris nodded looking down at his watch it was three thirty. "A'ight, pop. I better go. I told Syd I would stay out of trouble, and stick to a curfew." They embraced once more. "A'ight son. Call me tomorrow." Chris headed towards the door and out to his car. He arrived home at ten after four. He stripped out of his clothes to his boxers, climbing into bed and curling up behind Sydney's ass. She moved her body arching her back so that her ass brushed against his dick. He kissed her cheek. She opened her eyes looking at the clock sitting on her nightstand. It was thirteen minutes after four. He cradled her body in his arms as she drifted back to sleep with a smile.

A month later. Chris had taken Sydney to Paris and London for a shopping spree. To replace all the items he had thrown out and more. Many of the things she had purchased were still being delivered to their home. Her closet was quickly back to its old self. While in Paris, city of love, Chris proposed again giving Sydney a bigger diamond than the last. She in turn gifted him another ring of his own. Chris had spent time with investors working on the design of his bottle as well as skype meetings with Preme for direction of marketing. Chris was excited, it was coming together and another bankable income for him which would be legit that he could if need be clear some ends through. It was now July, Sydney and Chris had become home bodies working on bettering their relationship. Chris hadn't been up to Reign, and Sydney hadn't seen Dana or Vani. They both were content being in their own little bubble. Sydney had considered it getting back to the basics, something they had never truly done since each time they reconciled a third party was always involved.

Sydney left the house today for her annual doctor visit. She laid down looking up at the fluorescent lights, her breasts were tender and she was horny. Nothing she wanted to discuss with her doctor as she had her fingers inserted in her vagina. "I've been really bloated, tired and spotting during my last period. It was very irregular it was on for two days."

"Hmm. The doctor removed her hands placing the gown back down over Sydney's body. She removed her gloves washing her hands. Sydney sat up. "Well... Miss Sydney you are perfectly healthy to be pregnant." Sydney flashed a stink face glare at Dr. Naveen.

"What?!" Sydney finally blurted out.

"You heard me. You're pregnant mommy! I'd say about four weeks. How do you feel?"

"Wow. I don't know what to say. For once, I'm speechless."

"You will be just fine. I mean, that is good news right?" Dr. Naveen replied sensing uncertainty in Sydney's voice.

"Oh yes, of course." Once dressed Sydney was given a card with the time for her next appointment. Sydney walked out of the building feeling as if her legs weighed a ton. The thought of another baby was overwhelming. They had just started working on potty training Natalia, and the thought of nine months of her body looking like a penguin, sent Sydney's mind racing. She hadn't been sick this pregnancy, she immediately thought of her parents a large lump began to form in her throat. She arrived home, greeted by Chris and Natalia in the driveway. Natalia was in her Black Benz AMG ride on. Nicki Minaj blasting from the speakers, with her shades over her eyes. Sydney walked over to them. Blowing a kiss to Natalia before kissing Chris' cheek.

"So how'd it go?" said Chris, as he folded his arms over his chest.

"Um... good. I'm fine."

"That's good news. Do you feel better now?" Chris caressed her arm.

"Baby...I'm so in my feelings right now about this. But, I'm pregnant!"

A smile immediately spread across his face. "What? You serious?"

"I am so fuckin' serious. I am pregnant!" Chris grabbed Sydney in his arms immediately picking her up. He hugged her body tightly. "Yo!! This is my little boy. I'm claiming this shit already!" He hugged her body again, spinning her around in a circle, kissing her lips. "That spin made me a little dizzy. I am going to take a nap. I feel so exhausted right now."

"You good ma?"

"Yea, I'm going to lay down."

"A'ight, we'll be in, in a minute." Sydney kissed Chris again before walking towards the house. "I'm having another baby. Wow." Sydney replied solemnly as in to assure herself. Once inside the house alone she shouted. "Mommy is gonna kill me!" Sydney changed into a Bo Knows Nike shirt and pair of leggings. Just as she laid back in the bed propping her feet up on top of a pillow, she could hear Natalia stomping upstairs. She ran over to the bed with a small bag of Cheetos Puffs. She reached for Sydney to pick her up. Sydney pulled her up onto the bed, waiting for her Daddy to appear. He came in shortly after taking off his shirt tossing it on top of the ottoman. He collapsed onto the bed beside Sydney. "We having another baby!" He shouted as he caressed her stomach, he lifted her shirt kissing her stomach. Sydney smiled looking into his eyes. "Are you ready for that daddy? Remember I wanted cheesecake all the time, cravings, mood swings and the penguin."

"Yea, I'm good. So, when are we getting married? I know you wanted to get shit together for this year. But, I don't want it to seem like we rushed shit n'ahmean."

"Yea, and I don't want to walk down the aisle with my gut sitting out in my Vera Wang. I want to be flawless, babe. We can plan while I'm pregnant and set the wedding for when the baby is about two months. I should be snatched back by then. A spring wedding?"

"Sounds good to me."

Sydney sighed. "Nine months of penguin. After this baby I'm getting on a pill, shot... something."

Chris laughed. "I can't help my pipe game strong." Sydney side eyed him, tilting her head to Natalia's presence. "Uggh... you make me sick. We haven't been out and about in a while. You going to Reign?"

"Yea, I was thinking about checking in there today. You want to ride?"

"No, I'm tired. Me and Natalia will stay here, and take a nap. When I wake up I may make chicken lo mein."

"A'ight. I'll call you and see if you need anything while I'm out." He reached over kissing her lips before walking into his closet changing into Ralph Lauren Black label, jeans and Giuseppe Zanotti sneakers. He climbed into the Lamborghini Aventador, speeding off down the street. Elated with the news of another baby and the good weather he felt great. Nothing could ruin his high today.

Sydney and Natalia slept for three hours. Once up she changed Natalia's diaper and started on dinner. She placed Natalia in her playpen in living room with television on while she was in the kitchen. Sydney thought about Dana as she looked at a picture of them on the fridge, she sent her a text saying she was back in Miami and to stop by. She immediately responded, On my way bitch! Sydney smiled placing her iPhone down on the counter. In twenty minutes Dana was at the gate, Sydney let her in walking over to the door to greet her. Dana looked amazing as always. She was dressed in a pair of distressed jeans, tank and jeweled sandals. Her hair up in a top knot and diamond hoops in her ear. "Hello Stranger! I've missed you." Sydney hugged her tightly, before closing the door behind them.

"I know. I'm sorry. After I had my number changed, me and Chris had been focusing on rebuilding our relationship. Home bodies." Dana nodded listening to her friend.

"Mmmhmm… where is my baby?" Sydney pointed to Natalia who was in the playpen playing with her talking Minion toy. Dana walked over to her picking her up out of the playpen, kissing her cheeks. "She's getting soo big. Looking like her daddy!"

"I know, it's sickening right?" said Sydney sarcastically as she walked over to the kitchen. Dana placed Natalia back in the playpen. Sydney now in a crop top, backed away from the pot as she stirred the noodles. Dana took a seat at the counter. "So,

how have you been? When did you two get back together? I
need the tea honey!" Sydney smiled placing salt and pepper on
the chicken in the skillet, and onions. She began to sneeze.
"Bless you." said Dana as Sydney sneezed repeatedly. Her eyes
began to water, she ran over to the garbage can spitting up.
Dana rushed over to her side. "Oh my god! Are you okay?"
"I'm fine. It's my allergies." Sydney finally worked out. She
spit again in the garbage, Dana rushed over to the fridge to
hand her a bottle of water. She took the top off handing it to
Sydney. She took a few sips of the water before wiping her
mouth with a paper towel. Dana looked at her concerned. "I'm
good Dana. I promise."

Dana stared at her, not buying the answer. Sydney
smiled. "I'm pregnant."

"You lyin?! Serious?"

"Dead ass. Natalia's going to have a baby brother or sister."
Dana hugged Sydney. "Oh my god! I'm so happy for you!
How far along are you?"

"I just found out today. But, about a month."

"How do you feel?"

"I mean, I'm happy. I do feel it was a little soon. But, maybe
God has a plan for me with this baby you know."

"Congratulations! When are you telling your parents?"

"When I'm giving birth. They both laughed out loud. My
mom is gonna flip! I'm not ready for her response. But, we got
back together after the shooting. I began thinking that I love
this man, he is my soulmate. I know he has his moments. When
I got shot all I could think about was my life without him, and
it was empty. He's the only one for me." Dana frowned as if
she was wiping tears from her eyes. "That's deep. Not
everyone can find their soulmate, you know."

"Then, I got this… which solidified it." She walked over to Dana lowering her pants so she could see the tattoo on her abdomen. "Girl! What did he say when he saw this? Was he there?"

"He came to Hartford with Natalia and I showed it to him. He went bananas. He loved it. Shortly after we were back together and engaged again."

"Congratulations girl! For everything, getting your man back and getting your life back in Miami. You glowing girl, you look happy!"

"I am. I have a wonderful home, healthy beautiful daughter, and a sexy amazing fiancé. I don't know why I was complaining before. I had everything. Blessed."

"Yes. So let me see this new rock on your finger?" Sydney walked over showing her ten carat rock on her finger. "I gave him one this time as well. So these groupies can know that, he's mine."

"This is gorgeous girl. So, can I plan your baby shower?"

"Sure, if you want. I don't want anything big like I had with Natalia. Small, with close friends and family. We are now planning the wedding after the baby comes."

"That's cool. I will get all this together and it will be amazing."

"Let's go out here, to sit down. Sydney led her into the living room. She propped herself up on the loveseat, Dana sat on the sofa. So, any new boo's in your life?"

"Girl, hell nah. It's been a drought. They both laughed. Between being at the salon, thinking of going back to school take some business classes. You know I want to own my own salon, get a celebrity clientele. My little cousins are putting my designs on social media, you know I'm not with that shit."

"It may be good for you. Marketing. I've been saying that I wanted to start accounts on social media shit, but I get sidetracked I don't have time. Besides, I can't deal with everyone in my business."

"Right. Especially with your man. But, maybe I can set up a page for my designs and no personal shit." Sydney's phone pinged, with a message from Chris, asking if she needed anything. She messaged back for him to bring fruit bowls from Publix.

At Reign, Chris received her message. He was in the VIP area working with DJ Best. Miami's number one DJ, who was syndicated on networks throughout the nation. He always stopped by Reign when in town, because he appreciated the love he always received from the staff and he told Chris he supported the hustle he had. He had one bodyguard at the bottom of the staircase. Chris walked over to the counter, as John prepared bags for DJ Best and his entourage. Vani and a group of women walked into the store, all scantily clad in bikini tops and denim shorts. Vani walked straight back to the counter where Chris was seated. She licked her lips before bending over the countertop. "Hi Chris. I haven't seen you in forever." She walked around to the side of the counter, extending her arms out for a hug. Chris looked over her body. Her breasts were spilling out of her bikini top and her shorts were unbuttoned with a piece of fabric bikini bottom covering her vagina. He hugged her briefly. She ran her fingers through her damp curls.

"How you been?" she replied with a smile.

"I'm good." He replied bluntly. He looked over the inventory book which was sitting on the counter as Vani scanned over his body. She started from the top of his head, biting her lip as she worked her eyes down his chiseled body. Everything about him was sexy. "Have you spoke with Sydney? How's the baby?"

"Sydney is good. Natalia fine as well." Chris replied with a smirk, which said he was annoyed by her questions. Her eyes stopped on the diamond band on his finger. She immediately became green with envy and furious. John walked over to Chris to tell him DJ Best and crew were ready to leave. He handed him a stack of cash. Chris went to the back with the cash, reemerging to tell his crew thank you, before he was to head out. As he shook each of their hands. John looked at him, once they were gone he questioned the new ink on his arm. "Is that Syd, my nigga on your arm?"

"I don't know what you talking about?" replied Chris with a smile.

"Bullshit! John opened his arm looking over the tattoo. That shit is hard man! Look just like her!"

"Yea, I had to get my mami tatted on the kid. It's a wrap now. We gonna finally do this shit."

"That's what's up!" They gave each other pound. "But, I'm about to be out of here. I need everyone here tomorrow morning for a meeting. No excuses."

"Got you boss." Chris headed over to the backdoor. Vani and her crew were looking over the clothes, when she saw John return to the counter she decided to pry the tea out of him. "Hey John. How you been?"

"I'm good. How you Vanessa? Still looking good as fuck." She smiled.

"Thank you. So, who is Chris married to?"

"Who else but Sydney."

"What? They are back together? That bitch hasn't called me in months. Wait until I see her ass."

On the drive home Chris stopped by Publix for Sydney's fruit bowls. Preme called as he got back into the car. "I want you to come by for a meeting tonight at the club?"

"A'ight. What time and what meeting about?"

"Around eleven-thirty. I want you to meet this nigga trying to be on."

"A'ight, I'll be there." Chris hung up the phone. Once home, he placed the bags on the kitchen counter looking around for Sydney and Natalia. "Syd?" "In Tati's room babe. But, yes we can go shopping tomorrow. I can get some birthday gifts for Natalia and pick out me some maternity wear." Said Sydney to Dana. Chris appeared in the doorway. "Hi baby. How was everything at Reign?"

"It was good. What up Dana?"

"Hey Chris. Congratulations on everything."

"Thank you." Chris replied with a smile. Any woman would find Chris attractive, he was without a doubt sexy, thought Dana. But, she didn't want Chris. She could appreciate his looks, but wanted nothing but the best for Sydney and if this was the love of her life, it would be what it is. Natalia came out of her closet hearing Chris' voice. "Dada!" she ran over to his legs. "Hey mama. He picked her up tossing her in the air, she grabbed his face kissing his lips. Let's go downstairs see what mommy made." He left out of the room with Natalia in tow. Dana got up deciding it was time to go as well. "I'm going to head out. But, I will see you tomorrow."

"Yea, text me in the morning." Dana laughed. Sydney walked Dana out to her car. She came back in and sat down at the dinner table with Chris. She made Natalia a small plate with easy mac which was her favorite and nuggets. Natalia sat in her high chair making a mess. "I've been thinking... how am I going to tell my mom that I'm pregnant?"

"What you mean? Just tell her. If you scared, I will tell her."

"No. I don't think that would be a good idea at all. You know you have no filter. But, I know when I tell her she's going to come at me with all her criticism and then she's going to tell my dad. I'm not trying to hear any of his bullshit."

"Yo, don't stress over this bullshit. When you ready to tell them I will be there. They can bring that shit to me and take it out on me. You know they don't fuck with me and I don't give a fuck what they think about me. We're getting married. We happy. They either with it or fuck em."

Sydney laughed at his blunt response. "Having a bad day?"

"Nah, I'm just tired of your fam bringing up old shit. Like I don't provide for my family, or like I need their fuckin' approval to handle my business." Sydney could see that Chris was getting heated by the conversation. She decided to end it, before it went any further. "Let's talk about something else." She replied.

"Oh yea, your cousin Vani came by store today."

"Oh, how is she?" replied Sydney with a smile.

"She's a'ight I guess. You need to watch her."

"What you mean?"

"She's always in my face and shit. Touching me. I'm telling you to watch her cause she is your fam, and you know how I get."

"She trying to get at you?! Hell no! Oh, I will have a talk with that bitch!"

Chris laughed. "Don't go throwin' hands with our little one in the oven."

"I can't believe her. My own fuckin' family. You can't trust nobody!" Chris continued eating his food. He looked over at Sydney who he knew was fuming inside. He touched her hand. "Don't worry about her thirsty ass. She's not the woman on my arm, or woman I'm going to marry."

"Aww... thanks baby" She kissed his lips. Sydney took Natalia out of her high chair and upstairs for her bath. After her bath she placed her in bed and read a bedtime story with her. It was after seven. She took the baby monitor in the room with her, turning on her night light as she crept out the room. Chris had taken a shower and was lying across their bed shirtless in a pair of drawstring pants. Sydney went into the closet to change into her lace gown. She walked over to her side of the bed sliding in. Chris sat up and she leaned on his chest. "I was thinking for our wedding wouldn't it be dope if it were on the beach. Beautiful exotic flowers, like a hundred people. No shoes."

"I like the beach idea. You in some sexy long shit. I can see that."

"Good we agree. I'm just coming up with ideas we both can agree on."

Chris began to run his fingers through her hair, something he often did when he was tired. He began to yawn. "Babe, I'm going to sleep for a few hours wake me up around ten-thirty."

"Really? Do you think I'm going to be up? Why don't you set the alarm on your phone?"

"Do you think I know where that is on this shit? Can you set it for me?" He handed her his iPhone and she set the alarm for him. She soon dozed off while he stayed up watching The Blacklist. When he drifted off to sleep, it seemed as if he was sleep for 10 minutes when the alarm went off. He was pissed. He thought of bucking the meeting but Preme needed him, so he climbed out of bed.

Once at the club he parked his Range Rover in the back. He was greeted by Loco. They immediately embraced and he was escorted down to the basement where the meeting was to occur. Once downstairs Chris immediately saw Preme, Martin and Darren seated at a table. Once they made eye contact with Chris they each got up to embrace him. "What's good son?"

"Can't complain. How you?"

"How's Syd and Natalia?" Darren interjected.

"Good. We got another on the way."

Preme eyes widened as if he couldn't believe what he had heard. "What?!"

"We having another baby pop."

"I'm having another grandbaby! This one is going to be a boy! Heir to the throne!" Chris laughed as he hugged Preme. "That's what I said. Chris took a seat at the table. The bartender came over asking if Chris wanted a drink he declined. The bartender was escorted out before any business was spoken. "Remember I told you I had good news. Well... I got with the DA up there and got some things worked out for your sentence."

"What am I looking at?"

"Working for no time, may have thirty days at most. Also got the best lawyer in that area. Trying to get trial set for October, or as late as possible."

"Nah, don't push it later. I want to get this shit over with. So when Syd ready to have the baby I'm here in case they come with any bullshit."

"I got you. Had some good things going on in the streets and good numbers. I was thinking when this trial is over and everything clear, letting you take over everything."

Darren looked over at Chris a smirk on his face. "What?!" said Chris shocked.

"You taking over everything."

Chris took in a deep breath. "I don't know pop. I'm not trying to have my kids brought up in this shit. You feel me? I'm trying to build shit to get away from this."

"So, that's a no. Do what's best for you." Preme replied bluntly. Although, Preme's face was cold Chris knew he was pissed. An awkward silence filled the room and when Chris looked at Preme he wouldn't have eye contact with him. "We good?" said Chris annoyed with the silence.

"Of course we good. You're my son. I'm always going to look out for you." Loco walked over to the table. "Boss, he'll be here in ten minutes." "Bring him down." Loco went upstairs. He came down fifteen minutes later with a man in a white t-shirt, true religion jeans and colorful Nike sneakers on his feet. Darren and Martin were now seated at a separate table which was facing him. "How you doing?" He extended his hand thinking it was the polite thing to do in their presence. He didn't know who they were but wasn't trying to disrespect anyone on Preme's team. They both stared at him blankly. "I don't like him. Clown ass nigga." said Darren. He saw Preme's back at a table behind them. He walked over to greet him. Loco pulled him back. Darren looked over at him. "What the fuck are you doin? You wait for him to address you then you walk your dumb ass over there." Yogi gulped hard, standing back in place.

"Come here, let my son look at you." stated Preme. Chris placed his arm across the back of the chair ready to see who had been recruited. Yogi walked around immediately making eye contact with Chris. He froze up. *Ain't this a bitch!* Yogi thought as he felt the sudden urge to piss. Chris immediately chuckled. "You gotta be kidding me right? Can't be fucking serious?"

"You know him?" Preme replied looking to Chris.

"Nah. But he know me and Syd right?" Yogi looked away, not wanting to speak. He knew nothing that could come out of his mouth at this point could save him in this situation. "You heard my son! You know of him and Sydney?"

"Um... I uh... know of Sydney." Chris stood up to his face. "Don't lie nigga. How you said you knew of her?"

"I met her at a club"

"Come on nigga spit that shit out. What the fuck you told me you did?" Yogi swallowed his spit. "What the fuck did you say?" said Preme standing up from his seat. Yogi backed up. "I said I fucked her." Preme punched him in the mouth, he immediately fell back holding his face. "I'm sorry! I lied. I didn't... fuck her. I didn't know he was your fam." Yogi stood to his feet He pleaded. Loco pulled out his gun. Darren, and Martin soon had theirs drawn as well.

"I told you I'm nothing to fuck with. Pussy nigga." Chris punched him in the face. He fell back again holding his jaw, it felt broken. Preme signaled for security. "You know what's coming right?"

"No, please! Please man!" Loco held Yogi in his arms as the other guards walked over. "Handle it." barked Preme. The guards grabbed Yogi by his hands and legs as he pleaded for his life. Security stuck a potato sack over his head. Carrying him out of the basement. Chris laughed out loud. "Pop, I'm not done with him yet. I got some shit for him to do."

"A'ight he'll do it"

"Need an errand boy at the shop." Preme buzzed security. Loco emerged to escort Preme to where they had placed Yogi.

He was bloody and they had started their first round of torture on him. "You know you've fucked up. First thing tomorrow morning I want you at Reign whatever time they open you have your punk ass there."

"Yes… sir" Yogi replied coughing on blood.

"From now on you take orders from my son. If you got a problem with that we can end you right now." Yogi shook his head no. "Do we have a problem?"

"No sir." Shouted Yogi loudly. Preme and Loco turned to walk back inside. Yogi pulled himself off of the pavement, quickly scurrying away to his car.

The next morning Sydney was up cooking breakfast. Waffles, eggs, sausage, bacon and grits which Chris would request. The house phone rang, she looked at the caller id seeing it was Reign she answered. "Hello."

"Good morning Sydney. Its's John. Chris there?"

"Good morning John. He's sleeping. What's going on?"

"Need to ask him about meeting and there is someone up here for him."

"Okay… one moment." Sydney walked past Natalia who was sitting up on the couch watching movie Home. Sydney walked upstairs into their bedroom, Chris was stretched out across the bed. She began to shake him. "Baby… get up." Nothing. She pushed him again. She climbed unto the bed sticking her tongue in his ear kissing his earlobe. He turned over, she smiled handing him the phone. "John." Chris sat up wiping his face. Sydney climbed down from the bed. "Next time don't wake me up like that, if you not going all the way." She laughed walking out of the room. "Hello."

"Yo, my bad for waking you up. Yogi been up here since nine. What you want him to do?"

"Tell that nigga to stand outside and hand out fucking flyers."

John smiled. "Until what time?"

"Until I tell him to stop."

"What about the meeting?"

"Let's reschedule that for the afternoon. I'm tired as fuck."

"A'ight. Three thirty, four good?"

"Yea." Chris ended the call, rolling over going back to sleep. When he awoke again it was after twelve. Sydney and Natalia were dressed. Sydney was in the mirror applying makeup to her face. Natalia was lying on top of Chris face. He awoke to her curls in his mouth, she smelled like Johnson's shea butter. He brushed her hair away from his face tickling her. She laughed, curling into a ball. "What are you doing? Got all your hair in my face." "Daddy!" She replied with a smile. He picked her up kissing her face, tossing her in the air. He placed her back on the bed as he walked over to the bathroom. Sydney was walking out. "Good morning ma." He kissed her on the lips. "Don't you mean good afternoon?"

"You know what I mean?" he closed the door behind him. He washed his hands walking back into the room. "Where you going?" He replied to her wardrobe. She was dressed in a black bodysuit, and jeans which looked painted on her figure. Christian Louboutin four inch pumps. Chris shook his head. "Going shopping with Dana."

"Not in those." He pointed towards the closet. "Really babe?" Sydney sat down on the ottoman removing her shoes. She walked back into the closet looking over her shelves of shoes. She saw a Givenchy pair of open toed, ankle strapped sandals with a three inch short heel. "Are these better, my love?" She replied sarcastically. "Yes. You carrying the prince can't be falling and shit." Sydney rolled her eyes. "Anyways...what time you get in last night?"

"Around five. I told pop about the baby. Had a few drinks."

"What he say?"

"He was happy. He claiming the prince like me. Don't forget to make the reservations for Disney weekend." He headed out of the room. "I will make them when I come home today." Chris headed to the kitchen, he saw the food was covered on a plate on the counter. He placed the plate in the microwave. He reached into the fridge pouring a glass of Simply Orange juice. He sat at the counter turning on the television in the kitchen, he rarely used. He could hear Sydney on her phone upstairs, he ate his breakfast and headed upstairs to shower and change. Sydney was in Natalia's room preparing her bag. The intercom buzzed Chris went to answer it. He looked at the screen in his room, seeing Dana at the door. "Baby, get that please it's Dana… and she has Vani with her."

"What?"

"Be nice. I'm going to handle her." Chris walked over to the door, and was greeted by Dana. "Hey Chris." "What's good Dana." Vani pushed her way forward, smiling in his face. She was wearing a crop top and pencil skirt which left little to the imagination being that it was nude and sheer. Her tan areolas were exposed through her top. "Hi Chris." She stated seductively. "Sup." He closed the door, walking away from them. They walked over to the living room taking a seat. Sydney walked down the stairs with Natalia in tow. She was wearing a Versace ruffled light pink print top, with a pair of leggings, and her favorite pink Dolce & Gabbana Jelly sandals. She ran off down the steps ahead of Sydney. "Tati, stop running! Hey ladies." "Hi." They replied in unison.

"Let me grab her drinks and snacks and I will be ready to go. You two want anything?"

"Nah, I'm good." Sydney went into the pantry grabbing snacks and juices for Natalia. Chris came down with his keys in hand. He picked up Natalia kissing her on the lips. She hugged him tightly. "Bye Dadda" Dana looked on admiring the relationship Natalia and Chris had. Chris walked over to the kitchen. "Ma, I'm about to go. She stepped out of the pantry and kissed his lips. You good? You got money?"

"I'm fine. Have a good day." He placed his hand on her stomach, before walking towards the door. "A'ight ladies." Vani couldn't help fantasizing about his body on top of hers. She bit her lip imagining him naked inside of her. Sydney and Dana headed over towards the door, with Natalia. "Vani... you coming?" said Sydney. She got up from her seat hurrying over to the door. Sydney locked up walking over to the Range Rover. "I figured I would drive being Natalia's car seat and everything is in car."

"That's cool. Let's use your gas." Said Dana playfully. She unlocked the door and everyone piled in. Sydney placed Natalia in her seat. Once down the road Sydney put on some music which was Tamar Braxton's latest Calling All Lovers. As the beat for Angels and Demons came thru the speakers, Dana threw up her hands. "This is my song!" Vani rolled her eyes. "So how are you and Chris doing?" said Vani from the backseat. Sydney glanced over at Dana. "We're good. Why you ask?"

"Just asking because after the club. Who would've thought y'all would have ever got back together."

"Yea. We had our issues, but what couple doesn't. I love him, he loves me, and we're getting married."

"Really?"

"As long as I'm invited." Dana interjected as she bopped her head.

"Of course. You will be in it boo." Vani looked out the window, hating the fact that they were engaged. What did she have that Chris couldn't stay away from her? "I wish you all the best cuz. I hope everything works out for you and Chris."

Sydney rolled her eyes, not buying one bit of her fake well wishes.

Chris arrived at Reign and it was busy. John greeted him telling how busy it had been all morning and that his groupies must have put out a mass message because they had been in all morning. Chris smiled. "I'm not worried about them. Where is flyer boy?" John pointed out the front window to Yogi who was standing on the corner in a hideous King crown, passing out flyers. Chris chuckled as he saw the sweat beaming down his face. He reached under the counter grabbing paper towels and Windex. Yogi was trying to flirt with a girl he'd handed a flyer to. When Chris appeared he sucked his teeth as the girl walked away. "Yo, I need you to clean the glass out front." Yogi cringed, snatching the cleaner and paper towels from his hand. "We got a problem?" "Nah."

"That's not how you address me." Chris replied sternly.

"No sir." Yogi replied solemnly. Chris walked back inside, watching Yogi march over to the store door angrily as he began to clean it. Angel and her squad of friends walked up to the door. She glanced over to Yogi cleaning, she immediately side eyed him. "Is this shit cool?" She stated sarcastically to her girls as they stepped past him. Angel ran her fingers quickly through her Malaysian bundles and adjusted her dress. She was wearing a white tunic dress, which barely covered her ass. Chris had been working on the men's display. Angel walked over to him standing in front of his face, making sure she got his full attention. "Hi Chris. How are you?" She flipped her hair over her shoulder as she placed a hand on her hip. Chris couldn't front her body was amazing in the dress, her hips thick and ass fat. "I'm good. How you?" he replied with his poker face.

"I've been good, but wondering where you been sexy?"

"I've been out of town, handling business." He placed a shirt on the mannequin. Angel licked her lips looking over his body. She inched closer to him placing her hand on his chest. "Where is your baby?" He removed her hand from his chest. "Don't touch me, ma. With her mother." Chris placed a belt on the mannequin, Angel looked over his arm seeing the fresh ink of Sydney. It definitely left a sour taste in her mouth that he had rejected her, and was serious about her. "So, when is the new shit coming out?"

"Friday." Angel licked her lips. "Maybe I'll take a quick look around."

Sydney and crew had been in the mall and were in the Gap. Sydney was looking for simple pieces for Natalia she quickly had a handful. Dana came back with a couple pair of jeans for herself. Vani came over looking at the items she had in her hand. "So, how are you and Mark?"

"We're okay. We are working it out, ya know." Vani replied nonchalant.

"Oh, okay, so I should have no problem with you trying to get at Chris?"

"What?" Vani replied defensively.

"I know you want Chris. But, I'm here to tell you and any other bitch, he's mine! This time I'm not playing games with you hoes. Y'all been taking my kindness for weakness, and I have to start checking you bitches. I'm going by any means about mine." Sydney replied looking directly into her face.

"Girl, nobody want Chris ass."

"Why the fuck you lyin? I see it all over your face. I see how you look at him. I'm just letting your triflin' ass know, stay the fuck away from my man!" Sydney walked away picking out a couple of flats for Natalia. "Who the fuck you talkin' to my nigga? I said I don't want Chris. Don't ever come at me like that, fam or not I will fuck you up Syd."

"Vani stop trying to play me. Just stay the fuck away from Chris. As of now, our friendship is a wrap. I don't need no fake ass friends on my team. Bye bitch." Sydney picked up Natalia walking away. Dana came over hearing the commotion. "What is going on?"

"Syd, about to get done in. Nobody want her cheating, lying ass nigga!" Sydney ignored Vani walking over to the infants section. Vani continued to yell out things to Sydney when store security finally came over and escorted her out. Sydney didn't even look in her direction. Dana came over once Vani was out the store. "What the hell is going on?"

"Chris told me Vani is always hitting on him. In his face flirting and touching up on him. I don't appreciate her smiling in my fuckin' face, and the whole time you wanting to fuck my man. So, I let her know."

"I can't believe she would do something like that. Are you sure?"

"Hell yeah, I'm sure. Chris would never lie about something as petty as this. Besides, I peeped the way she was eyeing Chris today while I was in the kitchen. I bet she was the one told Chris I was in LA. Fake bitch." Dana placed her arm around Syd trying to calm her down. "I'm done in here. Let's calm you down. Let's go over to the bookstore and get you some wedding and pregnancy magazines." Sydney smiled. "I need more than some books. I'd like a drink."

"Well, since you can't how about we get the books and then go pick up some Krispy Kreme doughnuts."

"Yass bitch. I'm down with that." They laughed heading up to the register to pay for the items. As they headed over to get the books. Dana's phone rang and it was Vani. "Hey, Mark is coming out here to get me. Tell Sydney I said fuck her dumb ass! Fuck Chris!" "Okay… bye." Dana ended the call looking over to Sydney. "That was Dana… Mark picking her up."

"Good for her. Fuckin' with me her ass would've been walking home today or in an uber." Dana shook her head.

Chris had Yogi doing chores all day. He looked at his watch and realized it was after six he was closing up. Yogi had finished the bathrooms, Chris dismissed him and told him to return tomorrow at the same time. Once he was gone and Chris and John locked up. Chris called John into his office. "What up Boss."

"Thanks. For looking out while I was away." He handed, him a stack of cash it was ten thousand dollars. John looked over the money. "Nah boss. You serious?"

"Dead ass. Consider it a bonus, you keep shit together in here. I want you to know I appreciate you. I'm heading out."

"Thanks boss." He dapped Chris with a quick embrace. Chris walked out to his car, John behind him. Chris headed home, once he pulled into the driveway he saw that Dana's car was still there. He sighed hoping Vani wasn't still there. He walked into the house, walking down the hall to the dining room. Sydney and Dana were seated looking over wedding magazines, with post-its. "Hey. What y'all doing?"

"Hi baby. Looking over wedding dresses and baby name books." He leaned over kissing her cheek.

He glanced over the book Sydney was looking in it was in pink and the first name popped out was Jayla. "I don't know why you looking up girl names. We're having a boy." Said Chris confidently.

Sydney rolled her eyes. "Baby, I know you want this to be a boy. But we don't know that yet, and I don't want you to get your feelings hurt if it is Natalia part two."

"I'll be good either way. But, I know it's a boy, trust me on this. Anyway, where is my baby?" Sydney pointed over to the playpen, Natalia was sleeping in. Chris glanced over a bride's dress which was opened. "That shit ugly as fuck. I hope you weren't saving that page." Chris pointed to the picture.

"No, but look it's twenty g's and it looks like shit." Everyone laughed at the dress which was a princess gown with lace. Dana looked over at Chris' tattoo inside his forearm. "Chris, what is your tattoo of?" Sydney smiled. "Which one?" She stated. Dana pointed to his forearm. Sydney opened his forearm so that Dana could see it. Chris stood in between them. "It's me!"

"Wow... that is so sweet. Look at the detail. It looks just like you!" Chris smiled.

"Don't be gassing her up. She don't need to be thinking she special." He replied sarcastically. Sydney hit him.

"It's dope though, Chris."

"Thank you."

"Well, lovebirds I'm going to be out of here. I'm tired and I've eaten three doughnuts sitting with you preggers." Sydney laughed out loud. "I told you we have the gym if you wanted to do some cardio. Thank you for everything today girl."

"You're welcome. Anytime." Sydney walked her out the door. Chris picked Natalia up out of playpen, placing her upstairs in her bed. Sydney came back in closing the door. She walked upstairs, checking Natalia's room before going into their bedroom. Chris had took off his shirt and was washing his face in the bathroom. "Yo, ma I got you something today." "Really I got you something too." Chris handed her a small black gift bag first. She reached into the bag pulling out a small jewelry box. It was a pair of Tiffany & Co 18k white gold diamond large hoops which she'd been drooling over on the website a few weeks ago. They were going for over eight thousand dollars. She told Chris how much she loved them, but he acted as if he wasn't paying attention. "Baby, I love them. Thank you! She kissed his lips. Now I feel bad about the gift I got you, but you said you wanted it. She went into the closet bringing out a black hoverboard, which resembles a skate board but has two wheels and moves based off body movement. Chris became ecstatic. "Yo!! He immediately picked it up, trying to stand on it. "Babe please don't fall and bust your ass." Once on he began moving all over the room. "Thank you ma. He rode over to her kissing her lips. Get on here with me?"

"Um… hell no." The house phone rang Chris rode over to the phone picking it up. "Hello."

"Hi, is Sydney there?" replied a woman.

"One moment." He handed Sydney the phone. She mouthed who is it? He shrugged his shoulders. "Hello."

"Well… hello miss Sydney. How are you?" Sydney realized it was her mother she immediately tensed up.

"Hi mommy. How are you?"

"Good. Did you forget I exist? Hmm? After you left out in the middle of the night."

"Mom, it was no disrespect. But, I've been busy."

"Too busy to call?"

"Look ma, it's not going to get us anywhere going back and forth. So let's drop it please."

Ingrid looked at the receiver, pissed by Sydney's response she held her tongue. "Fine. How are you?" Chris got off of the hoverboard walking over to Sydney, he motioned to Sydney to tell her mother the news. "I'm good. We are engaged again, I'm going to register for class…" Chris folded his arms across his chest waiting for Sydney to reveal her news. "Tell her." He finally stated out loud. Sydney sighed. "Ma… I'm pregnant."

"You're what?! Sydney! What the fuck is wrong with you? Chris leaned in to her to try to hear what Ingrid was saying. Why aren't you on any birth control? It makes no damn sense, you're out here screwing that ass hole, creating these bastard children. What are you planning to do?" Sydney was speechless, she couldn't believe the words which were coming out of Ingrid's mouth. She expected this from Gavin, not her mother. "Well... I "

Ingrid interjected. "You plan on sitting there and letting Chris toss you to the curb again? Are you crazy? Didn't I raise you better than this?"

"Ma, I don't have time for this shit! Sydney finally shouted. We are getting married and I don't want to hear all this bullshit!"

"Sydney, who the fuck are you talking to? I am not one of your little friends, okay? You are so stupid sometimes! What are you going to do if he leaves you again? You going to lug two kids across the country? You damn sure won't be coming here, I can tell you that. Another baby! You are not even twenty four yet! Hell you are not even married, or have a degree. Your father is going to flip. We are very disappointed in you!" Sydney couldn't take anymore, she broke down in tears, dropping the phone. Her mother's words hurt her to the core. Chris held her in his arms. "What's wrong ma? What she say to you?"

"What is that asshole saying? Put him on the phone!" Ingrid could be heard shouting from the receiver on the floor. Chris picked up the phone. "What's good?"

"Yes, this is Ingrid something you want to say to me."

"Ain't nobody scared of you, you don't have to put on this hard shit for me. I want to know why she crying?"

"Really… you're concerned with her tears now? How many times have you made her cry?" Chris bit his lip, feeling his temperature rise.

"Why you always bringing up old shit? Why can't you be happy for her? I think the problem is your bitter ass need a man!" Ingrid and Sydney gasped.

"I don't need you telling me what the fuck I need! What I need for you to do is stop stringing my daughter along having bastard babies!"

"Why is it bothering you? I don't ask you for a fuckin' dime, you don't fuckin' take care of em!"

"I don't know why I would think a bastard like you would understand any of this. You're not about to have my daughter stuck with two kids!"

"You got one more fuckin' time to call me or my kids out of our fuckin name. On everything I'll show you what this bastard will do. Don't call my fuckin' phone with this bullshit. Either you gonna be happy about the shit or shut the fuck up. I only wanted her to tell your dumb ass, 'cause I felt you should know. But, fuck you and your pussy ass husband!" Chris hung up the phone tossing it on the bed. Sydney sat on the bed speechless. "Did you hang up on ma?"

"Hell yea. Fuck her! She not about to be speaking on us or our kids like that. Calling the kids bastards? Nah." Chris shook his head.

"Well… I guess the good thing of this conversation… is that she knows?" Sydney replied wiping her face.

"Yea she knows, not to call here again with that bullshit." Chris walked downstairs with his hoverboard heading out to the backyard, he went into his office first to get a blunt. He felt he deserved a smoke tonight.

The phone rang again, Sydney picked it up. "Hello."

"Who the fuck does he think he is to talk to me like that? I have never…"

"Mom, I am not trying to argue with you. You cannot call people all types of names and talk to people crazy and think they are not going to respond."

"So you are justifying the way he talked to me?"

"I'm only saying you said some crazy things to him as well. Calling him a bastard, our kids are bastards? You're being ridiculous!"

"I called your father. He should be calling soon."

"I don't want to talk to him."

"I told him everything that asshole said so he will be calling. I can't believe you are going to choose that arrogant, loud mouthed, gang banging asshole over your own family! Your own blood! I'd love to know what magic potion he has in that dick of his, that keeps you stuck on stupid!"

Sydney gasped at her mom's comment. "I am not choosing anyone. I am doing what is best for my family! Christian is now my family, and yes we are having another baby. You and Dad can either get with it or get left behind. That's on you. But, you will not be in our lives saying this negative shit you keep spewing at me." Ingrid was speechless. She sighed.

"Sydney where do you see yourself in five years?"

"Happily married. Raising my babies, a registered nurse or business major."

"How do you plan to finish college with two children?"

"The same way I was able to with one. Chris does help me with Natalia, it's not like I am the only parent here."

"Whatever, Sydney. Throw your life away. Everything isn't easy out there. You don't want to listen to anyone or anything, but Chris and his magic dick so be it. After the way that asshole talked to me today, I'm done with him. You do not have our blessing to marry him! As long as you are with him, do not talk to me. You made this bed and you're going to lie in it." Ingrid hung up the phone. Sydney looked down at the receiver placing the phone on the table. Tears flooded her face again. Chris walked in from the patio, lit. His eyes low and he reeked of weed. Sydney looked at him. "Ma, called back."

"What she say now?"

"She's done with me. I don't have her blessing to marry you." She began to cry in her hands. Chris sat beside her cradling her in his arms. "Syd don't feed into her bullshit. She don't want us to be happy, fuck her. How could she say that shit about her own grandkids? A person like that, why would you even want their blessings? I love you. We are getting married with or without her presence, ya heard." Sydney wiped her eyes. "I love you too." She kissed his lips.

In Oakland Park, Yogi was at one of his homeboy's house having a drink. He had been angry all day after being forced to be Chris' bitch all day. "Where you been all day nigga? Been calling you and shit."

Yogi scratched his head. "I've been busy, can't really get into it, Doing shit for Preme."

"Word?!" said his friend Pop.

"Yea, remember when we were in Walmart that day and that red nigga started talking slick."

"Yea, the nigga they say own Reign."

"Yea him. How about that's Preme's son. I gotta work with him for a minute."

"Damn. That's crazy my nigga. You think they gonna put you on?"

"Trust. They gonna put me on. Stated Yogi with a mischievous grin. He blew the smoke from the blunt in the air. I got a plan."

"Ah, shit. Whatever you got planned my nigga don't do it. Preme team is fucking crazy. He got cops, judges, and niggas all over on payroll. I bet he got niggas watching your every move!"

"Fuck what he got. I got a plan, which will get me everything I want and more."

*   *   *

At the Garcia residence Sydney was sitting up in bed, paying for the Disney tickets and making the reservations for a suite at the Gaylord Palms Resort, once everything booked she pulled out her notebook. "Do you have any ideas or request you want for the wedding?"

"Nah, not really. I told you I was good with the white or ivory and gold. As long as we have seafood, steak, and chicken. Good fuckin' DJ, I'm good."

Sydney glanced over at him as she wrote his request in her notebook. "I mean location, how many guests, flowers it's a lot."

"Well, I don't know nothing about putting that together. Besides you're not gonna be able to handle all this while pregnant. You need to hire a planner or whatever who does that shit."

"We could've handled this. You just don't want to be involved."

"Syd, you are not going to be picking out all that shit when you start showing. You remember you were moody and tired. Hire a wedding planner and let them do that. Besides you know how picky you are, and they have experience with that." She nodded her head, a wedding planning was an excellent idea.

"I guess you're right. I will look into a wedding planner. But, you have to help. You can start by looking into this wedding vows book. So, you can make sure you have the most amazing vows to me."

"Why I gotta work on my vows to you? What about yours to me?"

"I'm looking up wedding planners." Chris glanced over the vow book reading a few lines and tossing it to the side, before picking up a bride magazine looking over reception pictures. Sydney began to Google wedding planners in the area. "I need to call my lawyer tomorrow."

"When is your court date?"

"August."

"You want me to go with you?"

"Nah, you'll be starting school. Stay here with the babies." Sydney looked over at him with a piercing side eye. "I don't care about classes! You're my husband I should be there supporting you!"

"I'm good ma. I appreciate you wanting to be there. But, I'm going to be good. I'll be back in no time. He smiled kissing her on the face. Now I'm hungry as fuck."

"Ooh what are you going to get? How about Chipotle and Subway cookies." Sydney replied with a smile.

"How is it I always get stuck going out for the food?"

"The baby wants it. I love you." Chris climbed out of bed throwing on a shirt, jeans, hoodie and Jordan sneakers on his feet. He headed downstairs to the car. Natalia began to whine from her bed, Sydney carried her to their bed. She narrowed her search down to three wedding planners whose portfolio attracted her: Marcella Gomenski, Geneva Roman, and the last was Monica G. Hansen. She wrote their numbers down in her notebook and sent them each an email. Chris ended up going to Chipotle, Wing Stop and lastly Subway for the cookies. After he climbed back behind the wheel of the G wagon, and sped off down the road. In his rear view he noticed there was a black sedan had been behind him. He switched lanes to see if the car would as well, but it pulled alongside of him at the light. Once the light turned green, he floored the pedal the car followed behind him. Now annoyed, there was no way he would let this car follow him home. He pulled into to a RaceTrac gas station, parked three spots from the store entrance. He walked inside the store, figuring he would get gum and a drink. He walked outside the car was now parked two cars from his vehicle, the car had dark tinted windows. He walked over to the driver side window, tapping on the glass with his glass Mistic bottle. "Why the fuck you following me?" The driver door opened, Chris quickly reached for his waist. Tatiana stepped out of the car, slamming the door. She was in a crop top and pair of skinny jeans, her body amazing, her hair was shaved on one side and now dyed blonde. "How dare you treat me that way? Like I didn't mean anything to you!" She barked at him.

Chris screwed up his face as if he was offended. "You didn't. You was a cool girl or whatever, but we was never going to be serious. You would never be my fuckin' wife."

"Why are you lyin' Chris? You loved me. If that bitch wouldn't have gotten shot, you would've been with me! Don't try to play me!" She began to wave her finger in his face.

"But, she did. I'm done with you. I ain't never fuckin' love you, so don't put words in my mouth. I cared about you, but never loved you. Don't get it twisted. He pointed in her face. Stop fuckin' following me, and if you come up to the store again I'm fucking you up!"

"Fuck you Chris!" She raised her hand back to hit him, he grabbed her arm. "You not fuckin' stupid." He began to bend her arm behind her back. Stay the fuck away from me." He pushed her body into the car before walking away. He walked over to his car. She picked up an empty beer bottle tossing it at his head. It missed shattering to the ground. He took the Mistic bottle he had in his hand, throwing it into her back window. The glass shattered. On lookers watched in amazement at her shattered window. Tatiana charged after him. Chris reached for his waist. His phone rang in his pocket playing John Legend "You & I" Sydney had placed that as her ringtone on his phone, and he hated it. They had played that song a lot once back together, but he got tired of everyone at Reign laughing when his phone rang. He took his hand from his waist and slid behind the wheel of his car. He answered the phone. The person in the car beside her backed up blocking Tatiana from his car. "What up ma?" "Hey... what are you doing? It's been over an hour?"

"Remember when I told you I needed you here."

"Yea... what's going on?"

"You just saved me from doing something reckless. I love you Syd. I'm on my way home. Give me ten minutes and call me back."

"Okay. I love you." Chris ended the call, backing out of the parking spot and speeding off into the night blasting John Legend's You & I all the way home. He arrived home fifteen minutes later as he pulled into the driveway, Sydney called back. "I'm outside. About to come in." He walked into the house setting the alarm. He walked up to the bedroom. Natalia was laid across Sydney's lap. Chris handed Sydney her Chipotle bag. She looked inside seeing that if he'd got the chips which she loved. "What happened?" Chris took off his clothes to his boxers. "That crazy bitch Tatiana was following me."

"What?"

"Yea, I stopped at the gas station to handle her real quick. She tried to hit me with a bottle, I threw a bottle at her back window. I was seconds from pulling out on her dumb ass, when you called and stopped me. Shit, I can't have any more cases right now."

"Proud of you, for thinking before you reacted. It shows you are growing." Chris pulled out his lemon pepper wings which he ended up having to share with Sydney. He handed her the cookies. "I try not to spaz out. But, you gonna just sit here and eat three of my wings from my ten piece. After you ate your chicken bowl in peace."

She laughed. "It's the baby. I'll make it up to you. What do you want for breakfast?"

"I want waffles, sausage, bacon and an omelet."

"Okay, babe I got you."

"That don't mean I'm sharing my plate with you tomorrow." She laughed laying back on the bed looking down at her belly which was now sticking out. She began to caress her fingers over her stomach. "Oh I found three wedding planners I contacted. Do we have a budget? I know will be the first thing they ask."

"When have we ever had a fuckin' budget?"

"I'm only asking. You know some weddings can be millions of dollars. I know we have it, but I don't want to spend everything on the wedding."

"Look I don't care what it costs. As long as our wedding is the best shit Miami ever seen." Chris got up taking the trash downstairs to the kitchen. When he came back Sydney was sleeping.

The next morning while she was cooking breakfast for Chris, Monica Hansen called her on her cell. "Hello"

"Hi, this is Monica Hansen. May I speak to Sydney Cruz please?" Sydney immediately picked up she had an accent. She was definitely Latina.

"Hi, this is her. I looked over your website and I liked what I saw. I was wondering if I can set up a meeting with you to discuss possibly planning my wedding."

"Well, Congratulations. When are you planning to get married?"

"Possibly April or May of next year. We haven't really given it much thought except colors and things like that. We need help with everything!" They both laughed out loud.

"Well, I am available today after one pm, if you want to stop by my office."

"Perfect. I will look up your location and see you at one."

"Great! I look forward to seeing you. See you soon."

"You too." Replied Sydney ending the call, Monica had worked herself up to the top of her list with her quick response to her inquiry and she liked her voice she seemed warm. Chris came down for breakfast he had received a text from John stating Yogi was back. Chris responded to have him clean bathrooms and sales floor. Sydney sat on the couch starting on Natalia's hair. Chris sat to the table Sydney had placed his plate at his seat. "We need to start looking into a school for tubby. She getting too big to be home."

"I agree. But, are you going to be okay with that?"

"Yea, of course I'm going to thoroughly check the place and I don't want her going all day. But, it would be good for her to be around kids."

"We can start looking into that. Oh, I got a call from one of the wedding planners I looked up. I'm going to meet with her at one. So, can you take Natalia with you and I will pick her up on my way home from meeting?"

"Of course, I'll keep my tubby today. Clear your plans sometime this week, were going out to the movies." Sydney smiled at his request. "Okay... Papi." She replied seductively. "Don't start, Syd." She burst into laughter. Natalia laughed wanting in on the joke as Sydney put her hair in a side braid. After her hair was complete, Sydney went upstairs to get dressed and pack her bag. She dressed Natalia in a Gap skirt overall with a black short sleeve tee underneath, and bamboo small hoops in her ear. Sydney placed Jordan sneakers on her feet, and let her play in her closet as she dressed herself. Natalia ran out of the closet to the bed, falling down she began to look under the bed, picking up an item from under the bed. She smiled running back to Sydney with her new discovery. "What you got mama?" said Sydney as she pulled her V-neck white shirt over her head. She looked down at what Natalia had in her hand, it was a hundred dollar bill. "What are you doing with this?" Sydney tried to pry it out of her fingers, Natalia began to scream. "Give it to me now!" Sydney popped her on the hand, she let go of the money falling out on the floor in tears. She began to kick her legs, her arms flailing. "Get up off the floor." Said Sydney calmly as she slid into her boyfriend jeans. "Dada!" she screamed. Chris walked into the room hearing her cries. "What's wrong with daddy's girl?" Natalia hopped up from the floor running over to Chris' legs. He picked her up in his arms, wiping her tears. Natalia pointed at Sydney, with a pout on her face. "I don't care tell your daddy. You're not playing with money!" Sydney handed Chris the money. "Where was this?" "I guess on the floor." Chris looked on the floor, three hundred more dollar scattered on the floor. "My bad. Must've been my pocket change from yesterday." Chris slid the hundred dollar bill in the back pocket of Sydney's jeans. He took the extra money placing it in his pocket. "Why I get the hundred?" Sydney smiled. "Really? Here. He reached in his pocket handing Sydney the money. What you gonna do with that? Get your nails done."

454

"I was only kidding babe. I'm good. She placed the money on her vanity counter. Oh, I meant to ask you a while ago, what's your relationship with Tarik?"

"We a'ight. What up?"

"He's dating Nadine now, and she's pregnant."

"Word."

"Yea, she showed me a picture of them together."

"Hmm… she still in Connecticut right?" Chris sat on the bed with Natalia in his arms who was still upset with Sydney. Sydney nodded in agreement as she applied blush and red lip matte lipstick. She slid on a pair of Christian Louboutin pumps and a white blazer. Diamond hoops in her ear. She walked over to Chris. "I'm out of here. Her bag is ready on the bed. Give me good bye kisses Tati." Natalia looked at Sydney turning her face away from her. Chris laughed. "Really? You are just like your daddy. Stubborn."

"Don't front Syd, you are too. Give mommy a kiss, tubby." Chris teased. Natalia looked at Sydney reaching in to kiss her, she kissed her on the cheek. Sydney laughed. "I want a kiss on the lips." She pointed to her lips. Natalia quickly turned away. Sydney picked her up. "No you didn't! She kissed Natalia on the lips, hugging her tightly. I love you Natalia. You love me? Natalia finally gave in kissing Sydney on the lips as she grabbed Sydney's cheeks. Aww… you forgive me." Chris received another text, he quickly got dressed. He and Natalia ended up leaving out before Sydney. She forgot her iPad and Monica's information. As she headed towards the door the house phone rang she went over to answer it. "Hello."

"Hi Sydney this is your father. What are you doing?"

"What do you mean?" Sydney sighed with a hint of aggression.

"Your mother told me you moved back with that asshole, and you're pregnant! What were you thinking?"

"That I love him. We're getting married, he's my soulmate."

"You think he's gonna marry you? He's just stringing you along until he's done using you! Why would he buy the cow when he's been getting the milk free?"

"You know what... you and Ma are both on some bullshit. I'm tired of y'all shit! I'm a grown ass woman, I don't need a lecture from you two on who and what I let into my vagina! I love Chris and he is who I want to be with, instead of being happy y'all want to keep calling me with your opinions. I didn't ask for 'em, to be frank I don't give a shit! You want to down him and his flaws like you have been a saint! We are getting married with or without you, and I have his name tattooed on my body. So, you can either put a smile on your face and shut the fuck up or you lose our fuckin' number!"

"Sydney, have you lost your fuckin' mind? You are sitting here defending this lowlife ass hole who has put his hands on you? God knows how many times! You want me to just forget that shit, you are my daughter I gave you fuckin' life!"

"Look we have moved on..."

"I haven't. You're making a huge mistake Sydney! I tell you that 'cause I love you."

"Don't try to act like you are this great father. How can you talk about someone else's sins? You left me and ma with nothing so you could live with some bitch! How can you fix your mouth to ridicule anyone?"

"Sydney, I am not about to go back and forth with you. You want to live like a lowlife and throw your life away, fuck it. But, last thing I'm going to say is you were wrong to let that bastard talk to your mother in that way. When I see him I'm fucking him up! I'm going to be helping a friend on a case in Connecticut, you should come up so we can see you and talk to you. Seems that weather down there is doing something to your brain."

"Well, was the weather fuckin' up your head when you cheated on your wife and moved in with your mistress?"

"Fuck you, Sydney. That was the past. Get over it."

"Not cool when we bring up your skeletons. But, I'm not coming to Connecticut. You want to see me, you know where I am. Good bye." She hung up the phone walking towards the door. The phone rang again, she ignored it as she set the alarm.

At Reign, Chris was in the VIP area talking with John as he dusted and cleaned up, changing out the magazines. He began to tell Chris about his new voluptuous jump off. Chris laughed not taking anything he said about this "goddess" serious. "I mean she's about five foot six, thirty-eight triple d's, ass look like two basketballs, Brazilian chick."

"You sure that ass real tho? Bitches fuckin' niggas for ass shots now. John laughed. Happy my baby one hunnid, without that shit." The door chimed as Chris and John headed back over to the register. John looked over seeing Tatiana strut in through the door. She was dressed in Adidas tights and tank, Jordan sneakers on her feet. "What up Tatiana?" said John trying to cut her off from speaking any further. "Move John. I want to speak with the owner!" Chris looked back seeing Tatiana. "What the fuck you doing in here? What did I tell you?" He pointed his finger over John's shoulder, who was standing in between them both.

"You broke my window, and you're gonna fix my shit!"

"I'm not fixing shit. You better get the fuck out of my store!"

"Fuck you" Tatiana reached over John mooshing Chris in the face. Chris retaliated punching her in the face. She fell back grabbing her face. John tried to hold Chris back pushing him back towards his office. "Come on son…" said John.

"You bastard! I'm gonna fuck you up!"

"Come fuck me up!" Nathan had come in early he tried to grab Tatiana from charging towards Chris. Chris let go of John walking over to the counter to sit down. "Get the fuck out of my store bitch!"

"Fuck you and this store! Pussy ass nigga! Shouted Tatiana as she headed for the door. Fuck you and your dead mother, fucker!" As the words left her lips Chris came charging over towards her, he knocked John over to the floor. Chris reached Tatiana choking her. He lifted her body in the air, with his hand. She began to swat at his hand for air. Chris pulled out his gun aiming it at her head. John and Nathan tried to subdue him. He tossed her body towards the front door her body crashing into a display table, as John and Nathan finally pulled him back. "Get that bitch the fuck out of my store, before I end her ass!" Tatiana peeled herself from the floor. "Fuck…" John came over escorting her out the door. "Let's go, Tatiana!"

"Fuck Chris! Bitch ass! He want to kill me, I want to see him do it! John took her by the arm guiding her out the door and onto the sidewalk. Fuck you too, John. That nigga put his hands on me. I'm going to get niggas to come in here and fuck his ass up!"

"Tatiana… don't make this shit harder than it has to be. You don't want fuckin' problems with Chris and his fam." Tatiana shrugged her arm away from his grip, she pulled her hair behind her ear, as she headed over to her car. Her heart shattered in a million pieces, how could he do this to her?

Sydney was seated at Dana's station her fresh manicure drying as they caught up with gossip. "Where's my baby?"

"She's spending time with Daddy today. I have a meeting with a wedding planner I found online."

"Must be nice! I know the wedding is gonna be everything!"

"Yea, we decided it would be easier to have a planner, with me being pregnant, I'll be moody I want everything to be right."

"What did your boo say about wedding?"

"Girl, he's like he wants everything big, extravagant. No budget, whatever I want. Where is Vani?"

"Yass... no budget! He has fucked up now! Dana laughed. Vani is coming in late today. She supposedly had to go to Orlando with Mark on a run." Dana shook her head.

"What? She is soo stupid! What if he gets cased up? There's a lot of road between here and I-4."

"I know. I try to tell her that shit, and you know she's all *I'm down for whateva...* Bullshit." Dana signaled for Sydney to remove her hands. "I don't know what's wrong with her anymore. She's on some other shit." Vani strolled in thru the back door, wearing a peach strapless romper which barely covered her derrière, Chanel sandals on her feet. She glanced over at Sydney, rolling her eyes as she walked over to her station. "Has Michelle been up here?"

Dana looked over to her. "Nah. Only Tiffany to get her brows done and Jasmine who went to hair store and Sydney." Sydney glanced down at the time on her iPhone. "Oh, I gotta go Dana!" Sydney reached down on the floor grabbing her Crocodile Phantom Céline bag. She reached inside placing the hundred dollars she got from Natalia earlier on her counter. "Syd..." She stood up adjusted her clothes covering her exposed midsection with her shirt. "Keep it girl. I need my toes done soon, but no time."

"Okay, call me and tell me how the wedding planner meeting went."

"Of course. Thanks. Oh yea, me and Chris are going out sometime this week can you watch Tati for us please?"

"Of course. You know I don't have a man! Text me, ahead of time though." They both laughed. "I will." Sydney hurried out the door not looking once in Vani's direction, which pissed Vani off even more. Dana began to clean off her station. Vani began to plug in her flat irons. "So… she really think Chris is gonna wife her now? She laughed out loud. What changed?"

"What you mean? They are in love. I mean madd love now. Bonnie and Clyde shit, tatted on each other's body. They are doing good."

"Shut the fuck up! He didn't get her name tatted on his body?!"

"She's got his name tatted on her, and he's got this big ass portrait of her on his arm. It's cute. I'm happy for them." Dana replied sensing hate in Vani's tone.

"That's stupid. Why she would get his cheating ass on her is beyond me. Everybody says he be fuckin' with girls in that store."

"Well, I can't speak on that, I can only speak on what I know. I have been around them together and he loves Sydney, you can see it in the way he touches her, looks at her. A bitch would be stupid as fuck to think he would leave her for them! Especially when he has a big tatt of her on his fucking arm!"

"Damn… calm down fan club… I'm only saying what's been in the streets."

"I'm only saying, Syd is my girl. Bitches fuck with her they fuckin' with me."

"It's like that, she's your bestie now?"

"Yea, you can say that. She good people. She has my back."

Vani rolled her eyes. "Whatever. Me and her are done, I don't appreciate her thinking I want Chris' bitch ass. We were besties, more like sisters and that's how she do me. Fuck her!"

"Well, someone had been telling her that you wanted him. You should've talked to her about it and y'all could've squashed it."

"Fuck Sydney. She should've never came at me like that. I'm not checking for that nigga."

Sydney arrived at Southwest seventh St, to the location. She looked up at the office building, checking her lipstick in the mirror before sliding out of the car. She walked up to the building once inside she was greeted by a receptionist and guard. Sydney proceeded over to the receptionist. "Hi, Monica Hansen, which floor is she on?"

"Hi, she is on the twentieth floor." Sydney thanked her before walking over towards the elevator. When the elevator stopped Sydney exited looking over the décor in the hall leading to the office mirror everything white roses in vases leading to the office doors. There sat another receptionist behind an oval desk, typing away at her Mac computer. Sixty inch televisions lined the wall, white leather seats. The receptionist, a Latina her hair in a top knot. "Hi, how may I help you?"

"Sydney Cruz. I had an appointment with Monica."

"Great! One moment I will get her, you can make yourself comfortable. Would you like anything to drink, water, champagne or fruit?"

"Um… no thank you. I'm good." Sydney took a seat on one of the single chairs, she glanced at the televisions which were displaying events she had done. Minutes later a medium sized woman appeared in front of her. "Hello, Mrs. Cruz, I am Monica." Sydney scanned her body, Monica was a cougar. She was five foot five, mid-forties, Latina, hazel eyes which with her contoured beat face looked like she was on the cover of a magazine. Her hair dark brown and curled hair layered around her heart shaped face, dressed in a DVF dress with Jimmy

Choo's on her feet. She extended her hand to shake Sydney's. "Nice to meet you." said Sydney.

"My goodness. You are beautiful. Cute shoes!" Replied Monica with a smile.

"Thank you." Sydney blushed. Monica motioned for her to follow her back to her office, which was enormous. She sat behind a glass top desk with black bottom. The room everything was white with little touches of black. Sydney scanned the pictures on the wall in the room. There was a painting of a Peruvian flag as well as a Degree on the wall. Sydney took a seat in the plush black chair. "I guess it is safe to say that you are Peruvian?" Sydney replied looking at the little souvenirs she had on top of her desk.

"Guilty… I guess I went overboard eh?" She smiled, exposing her perfect white smile. "What about you?"

"I'm Brazilian and Sicilian mix…"

"Wow, your complexion is amazing. Your skin is honey. I would have to get tan for that." Sydney smiled looking over her skin tone which was a smidge of a shade lighter than her. "Your skin is amazing too."

"Why thank you. Monica spun around in her chair handing Sydney a folder. I like to give all my clients or prospective clients some homework included with different events I have done to look over. I have worked with some of Miami's A list celebrities, hosted community events and more. I like to get to know my clients personally, and get a feel for the couple so I can help them achieve the best wedding to fit their love. Not one couple has the same love." Sydney looked over the folder contents she was excited after page two sprawling ice wedding, everything Monica did was big. Sydney's mind was made up immediately.

"I'm definitely interested. What would you like to know about me and my fiancé?"

Monica laughed. "Okay, tell me about your fiancé? How did you meet, his name?" Monica pulled on a pair of Chanel frames over her eyes, and her tablet. "Well... his name is Christian. We met at the mall about four years ago. The first thing he said to me was I would be his... and after a second meeting I was. Sydney smiled, thinking of their first time. He is sexy, cocky, hot tempered and my everything. Monica jotted down everything as she continued. We have a two year old daughter and another on the way." Sydney caressed her stomach.

"Wait, you're pregnant? How far along are you mami?"

"I'm only a month. We just found out. So, we wish to get married once the baby is a month or two."

"Got it. What are some of the ideas you and Christian have?"

"I really like the old Hollywood, The Great Gatsby opulence. Bling, diamonds, ivory and gold. Maybe with an urban... hip hop edge, if that makes sense."

"No, I got it. Good references to pull from. Reception any ideas? Are you thinking about a church wedding or location?"

"We are leaning towards maybe a location with beach view where it can play as wedding area outside and reception inside. Or venue where it can have multiple rooms."

"Great! You have definitely given me some ideas I can play around with and get some things put together for you to look over. I love the ideas you have, were off to a great start! I will need you and Chris to go over information in notebook and I would love to sit down with the both of you after you answer the couples information inside."

"Okay, great. When would you like to meet again?"

"How about Thursday? Is that good for you?"

"Sure. The morning would be better for both of us."

"Great. We can set it for ten. I will have some possible locations by then they may fit the look you are going for. Also here is a copy of my card in case you have any questions and need to reach me. anytime." Sydney skimmed over her black business card, which looked like an ATM card. It stated in bold script. Monica Garcia Hansen. "You are a Garcia too?"

"Yes, my maiden name. Divorced, but kept my name."

"I asked because my fiancé's last name is Garcia."

"Oh, he is Spanish?"

"Yes. Well, he is actually Peruvian and Black." Monica's face lit up with pride. "Nice. I can't wait to meet him." They both stood from their chairs. Sydney leaned forward to shake Monica's hand again. They chatted a few moments more before Sydney left out of the office. Butterflies in her stomach excited to be planning her dream wedding. She reached into her bag, for her phone. She couldn't believe it had been over an hour. She had two missed calls and texts from Chris, she called him back. He answered after the second ring. "Hey babe, what's up?"

"Where you at?"

"Leaving wedding planner, headed to Reign. What's wrong?"

"A'ight, I'll tell you when you get here. Love you."

"Love you too." Sydney tossed her phone on the center console anxious to know what had occurred which had Chris on edge. She arrived at Reign and parked in back. Yogi had been cleaning the passenger tires on Chris' car that Sydney didn't see him when she stepped out. John had stepped outside to take a phone call. Yogi gawked at her body as she embraced John with a hug. "What up Syd? Congratulations on the baby."

"Thank you. Chris told everyone huh."

"You know it. We all happy for y'all. We family."

"Appreciate it. Is he in office or at the counter?"

"Counter." Sydney walked in through the back entrance down the hall and out to Chris. Chris was sitting on a stool with his back to her. Sydney walked up behind him quietly, placing her arms around him and kissing his cheek. He immediately tensed up, turning his head sideways to see who it was. "Hi baby." "Sup ma. My bad." He kissed her lips. He turned his body towards her. "Where's Natalia?" "Over there in the mirror." Chris pointed to her with a pair of Dolce & Gabbana shades on her face, as she tried to dance. "So conceited, like her daddy." "I'm not conceited. He caressed his chin. I'm just that nigga, you feel me." "I can't with you today. Sydney replied with a smile. Chris pulled her over to his lap. The door chimed and in walked Angel and crew. Natalia took off towards the open door, Sydney rushed over to catch her. Angel saw her come in their direction and they blocked the door from her making an exit. She stopped in her tracks, looking up at the scantily clad women. "Hi Princess, where you going?" Natalia began to blush, twirling the sunglasses in her hand. "She's adorable. Is this Chris little girl?" replied her friend.

"Yea, look at her, she looks just like him." Sydney had finally approached them, Natalia saw her and jetted towards the door again. She began to pound her hand on the door. Sydney walked over to her picking her up. "What are you doing Tati?" Natalia pointed out the door. "Mama." "You want to go outside baby? Natalia smiled saying yes. Give mommy kisses and we'll go for a walk." Natalia grabbed Sydney's face kissing her lips. Angel and her friend had watched the entire interaction. Angel shifted her weight, placing her hand on her hip. "That's your baby?" She said pointing to Natalia. Sydney side eyed her, "Yes, this is my daughter. Baby, I'm taking her outside for a walk." Sydney shouted back to Chris. "A'ight." He replied. Sydney walked outside with Natalia. Angel made her way over towards the register. John walked in from the back. Chris stood up from the counter. "Yo, boss Jeanie from the Caribbean spot said that she'll have our plates ready in like fifteen."

"A'ight, I'll get it you watch the counter. Make sure that nigga don't fuck up my car." Chris walked past Angel out the door after Sydney. The heat him immediately, he looked down to the end of the sidewalk seeing Sydney and Natalia. It was almost ninety degrees, he wiped his face, walking over to them. "Damn, it's hot." "I know. Getting a little tan being down here. So, what happened baby?"

"Man, I fucked up. I fuckin' lost it. He punched his fist in his hand. Tatiana came by today on that bullshit and I flipped."

"What, is her fuckin' problem? What did you do?"

"Ma, you know how I get once I'm on a fuckin thousand, no turning back. I pulled out on her dumb ass!"

"Oh my god! Did you..."

"Nah, I thought about tubby being up there and shit. I got this case coming, I can't afford no bullshit right now. N'ahmean, working on this Vodka launch." Chris shook his head looking over to Natalia.

"Baby, you gotta keep it together. You have to control your anger. We have two babies to raise, which I know you don't want to miss out on, by catching a case for dumb shit as busting her stupid ass window. I'll handle this little situation, throw some money her way, to pay for her window so she can go on about her business. We have bigger things to worry about. We are building empires, we are not about to lose sleep over this weak bitch." Chris looked into Sydney's eyes, that fire that was behind them, calmed him. Sydney on her grind was a turn on to him, he loved her ambition. He sighed, nodding agreeing to let her handle Tatiana, she was right he wasn't about to catch a body over a window, with this other bullshit case looming over his head. Sydney kissed his lips. He picked Natalia up in his arms, kissing her face. "Come walk with me." he replied to Sydney.

"Where are you going?"

"To get this food, down the block." Sydney adjusted her purse on her shoulder following him over towards the restaurant. Ten minutes later they returned back to Reign with food in tow. Sydney declined a plate, Chris headed to his office to eat his and of course share with Natalia. Sydney decided to look at the new merchandise, she walked out on the sales floor. She looked over a few dresses, and tops. Angel who had just finished her purchases, looked over at Sydney with disgust. Upset that she was with her man. Sydney paid her glares no attention. Sydney heard Natalia running down the hall to the sales floor. "Come here baby." She carried Natalia up into the VIP area to sit down. Yogi came in thru the back door, as Chris was walking out of his office. "My shit better be fuckin' spotless." He walked out the door to inspect his car, Yogi followed behind him. Once he approved the car, Chris turned to walk back inside, not uttering a word. "Anything else you need me to do sir?"

"Take the trash out!" Chris walked back inside, Yogi followed inside to collect all of the trash. Chris acknowledged his customers before walking up to Sydney and Natalia. "What you about to do?" said Chris seeing the clothing in Sydney's hands. "I'm about to try these on. Can you open the doors back here?" He pulled out the key, escorting Sydney back to the dressing room. He picked up Natalia, standing outside the door. She tried on a striped crop top and skirt, which was made of a mesh material. Sydney looked over her reflection in the mirror, immediately feeling insecure about her midsection barely there bulge. "I look like a pig in this." She shouted over the door. "Let me see." Chris stepped back from the door, sitting down in the chair. Sydney stepped out placing her hand on her hip. "What do you think?" Sydney twirled around, her body looked amazing. "You look good, ma." "What? I don't look fat?" She caressed her hand over stomach which she felt was sitting out. "You're not fat. You're carrying our baby."

"Which is making me fat! I look bloated." She stood inches from his face. "You're beautiful, Syd. You're not even showing yet." She smiled, bending over to kiss his lips. She appreciated his support. Chris caressed his hand over her ass. Yogi stood in awe at the top of the steps. Mesmerized by her full breasts, and her thick derriere. As she flipped her hair over her shoulder with a smile, he couldn't help but smile, feeling his nature rise in his pants. Sydney turned away walking back to the fitting room not seeing Yogi standing in the distance. Once the door clicked locked. Yogi fell out of his trance. "What the fuck you looking at?!" He looked forward to see Chris standing inches from his face. "Uh..." Yogi stumbled to work out. Chris became furious, seeing the lust he had in his eyes for his woman. He grabbed Yogi by the neck hemming him on the wall. "Stay the fuck away from her. I don't want to catch you, talking to, looking at or anywhere near her fuckin' existence! I catch you eyein' her again, I'm cutting both of your fuckin' eyes out! You heard?" He tightened his grip on his neck. Yogi's eyes almost bulged out of his head. Chris released him, bashing his head up against the wall. Yogi gasped for air, trying to catch his breath. Sydney tried on a dress where the back was completely open and bottom barely covered her bottom. "Babe... come here!" She replied over the door. "What?" Chris replied bluntly. "I want you to come here. I don't want to come out with all of my business showing." Chris walked over to the door. Sydney opened the door. Chris took one glance at Sydney in the dress he quickly looked over his shoulder, to make sure no one else could see her. He blocked the door with his body. "Yea, get that. Get all of it. Don't try nothing else on in here... I'm not trying to have a situation." Sydney laughed. "Fine." Chris closed the door walking over to Natalia who was playing with his phone. Yogi remained on the floor, regaining his composure. "Get the fuck outta here!" Chris shouted to Yogi. Yogi scrambled to his feet, nearly falling down the steps. Chris eyes followed him as he walked out the front door. Chris picked up Natalia walking over the dressing room door. "I'm going over to the office to change Tubby." "Okay, I'll be out soon." Minutes later Sydney emerged with the items in her hand heading over to the register. John looked at her skeptically as he began to ring up the items. Chris walked out Natalia on his shoulder fighting to keep her eyes open. "What are you doing?" said Chris to

Sydney. "I'm paying for my things." "Really... Syd. He looked over the items sarcastically. John, don't ring up the shades." "I'm going to pay for it. Ring it up John." The total came up to over fifteen hundred dollars. Sydney reached in her wallet handing him cash. John bagged up her items and handed her the change. She took the bag, following Chris into his office. He placed Natalia in her playpen, she immediately laid across her pillow. "You have money?" said Chris bluntly. "Yes, babe. I'm good." "Let me see." Sydney pulled out her Givenchy wallet, she had chosen today which she had forgotten her credit cards. She pulled out the bills she had which was about five hundred dollars. "That was all I brought with me today. I'm good." "Where are you going after here?"

"Pick up a few things, for dinner and maybe drop by to see Dana." "Here." Chris reached in his front pocket, he pulled out a stack of five thousand dollars. "Baby... I don't need..."

"Take it. I'm not having you walk around with pocket change." "Fine. Sydney slid the money into her purse. How much longer are you going to be here today?"

"Maybe another hour or so." Sydney reached down in the playpen picking up Natalia who was still up. "Tell daddy, you'll see him later." Chris walked over kissing Natalia's cheek. "See you later mami. Daddy love you." He kissed Sydney on the lips. "Love you." said Sydney. Chris plastered a fake smile on his face. "Oh, you do?" "Don't be cute. You can't say it back!" "Why do I have to say it? You know how I feel about you." said Chris sarcastically. Sydney side eyed him, frowning up her face. Chris smiled at her. "I'm fuckin' with you ma. I love you. Don't have to hit me with the screw face." "Whatever. We're leaving we will see you later." She turned to pick up Natalia's baby bag. "You mad? You know you can't stay mad at me. He caressed his chin, the kid too sexy for that." Sydney laughed at him. "I can't with you today. Bye." Chris followed her to the door to walk her out, John stopped them telling him he had a phone call. Sydney assured him she was okay and he could take the call. She proceeded out the back door to the car. She unlocked the door, placing Natalia in her car seat. She placed the bags on the floor. As she closed the door, startled she clutched her purse seeing Yogi standing beside her. "What's up sexy?"

"What are you doing here?" said Sydney startled. She quickly looked over her shoulder for any bystanders, and Chris.

"I came to see you. He smiled. How you been?"

"Look, she pointed her finger in his face, stay away from me! Whatever, you thought we had, is over! I am with Chris."

"Fuck him! When you gon' stop fuckin' with that pussy ass nigga and fuck with a real one." He caressed her arm. Sydney smacked his hand away, raising her finger again inches from his nose. "Stay the fuck away from me!" "Look, I know you putting on for that bitch ass nigga. You gon' be with me."

Sydney felt her stomach churn, as rage built up inside of her. "If you want to live, stay the fuck away from me." She climbed behind the wheel, locking all the doors. Yogi walked over to his car, Sydney sped off down the road heading to Dana's.

Back inside Chris was on the phone with his lawyer Grant Vaciani. He was trying to get Chris to agree to come sooner so they could go over details in person, which Chris was not trying to make happen at all. "I'm not coming up there this month. Shouted Chris, maybe August."

"Chris, I need you up here as soon as possible."

"Yo, I've got a lot of shit to handle before I come up there. I've been paying you more than your fuckin' mouth is worth. You handle that shit! Make sure I'm not doing no time, before things get messy."

"Chris, they are trying to pin a lot of things on you. It's going to be almost impossible for you to not do anytime."

"Well, you got a fuckin' problem don't you. Make it happen."

"Okay, Chris, I will get this handled."

"Get it handled. I'll be there August 6th." Chris hung up the phone. He looked over their family picture on his desk, a million thoughts rushing thru his mind. He packed up his items and decided to call it a day.

Dana was out, and told Sydney she would meet her at Target. Sydney grabbed a cart placing, Natalia inside. Dana was seated in the front Starbucks café a caramel Frappuccino in her hand. "Syd!" She waved walking over to her. "Hey girl."

"Hey, what's going on? Your text had me like what the fuck." Said Dana.

"Girl… so much drama today. Tatiana came to the store today fuckin' with Chris. Yogi's crazy ass was waiting outside store for me… One hell of a day." They headed over to the air freshner section. "What the fuck? What was Yogi doing at the store?"

"I don't know what his dumb ass was thinking. But, I cannot have him lurking in fucking parking lots and shit."

"Right! What if Chris would have saw him?!"

"I know! That's why I told him whatever you thought we had is over, I don't want you! Thank God Chris got a call and didn't walk me to car, he would've flipped."

"I know! So what happened with the wedding planner?"

"Oh, I like her. She's cool, her work is amazing and Thursday we are supposed to look at locations. She's also Peruvian as well, which Chris will like. But enough about my drama filled day, how was your day?"

"I had a good day nonstop rest of day. Made about three grand today. Trying to save up for my own spot."

"That's good. Make that money boo."

"When are you going to Disney for Natalia's birthday?"

"Her birthday is Saturday. We will probably drive down Friday morning. Also, you can watch her for me this week right?"

"Okay, I'll bring her gift by Thursday. Yea, I can watch her, I told you just let me know the time. Shit, I need a man."

"Hmm... we need to get you a man. What about John at Reign? He's a cutie."

"He's okay, but I don't know. He seems like a big ass flirt."

"John is good people. I think you two would be cute together. He's funny, and he's got some coins. I'm going to hook you up."

"No, Sydney!"

"What's wrong with dinner and a movie? I'm not saying you have to marry him. It's just a date." Dana looked over at Sydney, who had a cheesy smile plastered on her face as if she was geeked she had made a love connection. Dana sighed, tossing popcorn into the cart. "Fine... I might as well go along with it. Because, you going to set it up anyway."

Sydney laughed. "You know it. Dana and John, you'll have cute little babies."

"Girl, bye. He is not getting my cookies."

"That's what you say now. It's been a minute, you may need a tune up." They both laughed.

Vani was closing up the salon, Yogi came thru the front doors. Vani jumped startled. "Hey, I'm closed."

"Nah, I'm good. I wanted to holla at you. You alone?"

"Yeah. What's up?" Vani locked the door after him. She walked over to one of the stations taking a seat. Yogi stood leaning on an opposite station. "How's your cuz, Sydney?"

"I guess alright I don't fuck with her." said Vani. Which he had already knew, since he had already sent girls into the salon to get info on Vani and had overheard her trashing Sydney.

"I got a proposition for you. It's about fifty g's in it for you." Vani side eyed him. "Doing what? And how did you get that money?"

"Hear me out. Look, I'll front you twenty g's in the beginning at the end you will receive the rest."

"What, you want me to do? What's the catch?"

"I need you to help me with a kidnapping." His eyes menacing and piercing. Vani looked over at him concerned.

"Who?"

"Chris' little girl."

"What?! Are you going to hurt her? What the fuck Yogi?!"

"Calm down. We not gonna hurt that bitch, just hold her for ransom. If it makes you feel better you can hold her until we get the money. You in or out?"

Vani began to ponder the situation in her head. Chris would be furious, and they would all be possibly sealing their own fate. She began to think how furious Chris would be if the kidnapping was Sydney's fault. He would hurt Sydney and her happily ever after would be over forever. Chris would be free, and that alone made her smile. She glanced over to Yogi. "I'm in. On one condition, we do this my way. It will only work if we do it my way, your way they will see it coming."

Yogi nodded his head he moved in closer to Vani. "Bet. They shook hands. I'll be in touch, to iron out details." Yogi headed towards the door, Vani followed after him to lock the door. Yogi stopped abruptly, staring directly into her eyes. "Don't cross me Vanessa. If you tell anyone of our plan…"

"You don't have to worry about that. I'm good. You just make sure you have my twenty g's." Yogi nodded walking out to his car. His plan would be perfect. He would pull this off, and when he returned Natalia he would look like a hero and receive Preme's approval. He would become one of Preme's trusted men and finally receive access to his connects. His plan was fool proof, Vani would be the perfect partner, he had it all figured out.

It was Wednesday, morning Chris had brushed his teeth and showered. He prepared breakfast for he and Natalia as Sydney remained sleeping upstairs. He was watching First Take on ESPN, while he bit into his sausage, and egg sandwich. Natalia sat in her high chair eating sausage and French toast which Chris had placed in the microwave and cut up into little pieces. Hours later Sydney had gotten herself and Natalia dressed, she was going to the school to drop off paperwork. She headed back downstairs. She placed Natalia on Chris' lap, Chris glanced over her outfit which was a Dolce & Gabbana body suit, denim skirt and gladiator sandals her hair in a top knot. Chris smiled at how cute she was with her diamond studs in her ear, and her diamond crusted name plate necklace on her neck. He snapped a selfie of them together. Chris glanced up at Sydney in her maxi dress and top knot with Chanel frames on her face. Her ass looked amazing in the nude colored dress. "Come here." He replied as he looked her over. Sydney walked over to him, once she was in arms reach he cuffed his hands around her ass. She leaned over him her breasts spilling into his face, he kissed her face. He motioned for her to sit on his lap, just as she positioned herself to sit her phone vibrated in her hand. She looked at the screen which read Nadine. She hadn't talked to her in weeks. "Hello."

"Hey...Syd... I lost the baby." Nadine blurted out as tears soon followed.

"What?! Oh my god! What happened? Are you okay?" Sydney stood up, holding her mouth.

"I don't know. I found out two days ago. I've been soo fuckin' angry. I just wanted to let you know before you plan anything."

"I'm soo sorry Nadine! Is there anything you need me to do? How are you?"

"No. There's nothing to do. I have nothing. She sobbed. Tarik left me... I have nothing." Chris sat up watching Sydney's body language.

"He left you?! Why?"

"We've been arguing a lot lately. He's got this case and new lawyer... he's never home. I've been stressed out, when I told him I lost the baby, he said fuck me and there is no reason for us to be together! What type of shit is that?! He supposedly loved me. Fuck him!" She sobbed loudly. Chris heard her through the phone.

"Nadine, fuck that pussy ass nigga! If he is going to treat you this way after you lost his child, fuck him! Pull it together hun. You don't need him. I cannot believe he treated you like this." Sydney shook her head.

Nadine cleared her throat wiping her tears. "Bitch ass small time motherfucker! You know he's been thinking he was that nigga since he came up on a little dough."

"Damn, I'm so sorry that happened to you. You didn't deserve for him to treat you like that."

"It just hurts 'cause I really wanted a baby you know. I had been planning baby names and shit." Nadine began to cry again. Sydney looked over at Natalia on the couch who was now playing with Chris' phone. Tears soon welled up in her eyes. Chris tugged at her arm, pulling her to his lap. She followed, needing his embrace right now. He cuddled her in his arms. "What's wrong?" said Chris which Nadine knew he had to be sitting next to Sydney.

"Nadine... lost her baby."

"Damn. Tell her I'm sorry to hear that. Sorry, for her loss." Nadine smiled hearing Chris. "Tell Chris, thank you."

"I will. Are you going to be okay? Do you want me to come up there for a few days?"

"No, I will be okay. Just taking it one day at a time. I keep telling myself that God must have a better plan for me."

"Right. It will happen for you, one day you will have a healthy, beautiful baby. Maybe right now wasn't the time, but it will happen. I want you to know I love you girl and any time you need me. I'm always a phone call and plane ride away."

"Thank you girl. It means a lot right now. I'm done crying, I won't ruin your day anymore with my drama. Let's change the subject, how is my little cutie doing?"

"Oh, she's fine sitting here now playing on her Daddy's phone. She gets into everything. She will be two this weekend. We are taking her to Disney." Sydney slid off of Chris' lap, he reached over taking his phone from Natalia she began to cry. "No, Daddy." Chris picked Natalia up walking out the room.

"Aww... she sounds soo cute, yelling at daddy. Take pictures for me at Disney. I'm going to take a shower. I appreciate everything. Luv you girl."

"Luv you too. You know I always got your back. Call me or I'm calling you! Be safe."

"Talk to you soon Syd." Nadine ended the call. Sydney looked down at her phone and her stomach. She couldn't bring herself to inform Nadine that she was pregnant with baby number two, after all that she had been through. Sydney walked back upstairs to their bedroom. Chris was in the closet going through his clothes. Natalia on the bed watching television. Sydney stepped in the closet entrance, Chris turned to her. "So, how is Nadine doing? She going to be a'ight?"

"Yeah, she is going to be fine eventually. It's going to take some time. But, Tarik's bitch ass just up and left her, like fuck you, I can't get over that shit!"

"Oh, word… That's fucked up."

"She said he's got a case and lawyer he's dealing with, he's been ghost a lot lately. I never saw him as being a dude who would do some shit like that, ya know." Chris made a mental note of the details Sydney had given him about Tarik's situation. He settled on a blue Ralph Lauren Polo shirt and jeans. He walked over to the center island, where his jewelry was encased in. "I love that color on you. Let's take a selfie." Said Sydney. She quickly hopped in front of Chris she placed the phone in the air and the timer on. Chris placed his arms around her body, kissing her on the cheek as she blushed. Sydney turned the moment into a mini photo shoot, eventually bringing Natalia into their closet to join in on the moment. "Yo, when you going to take the naked pictures with the baby?"

"Um… I'm shocked you want professional pictures like that." She smirked.

"No, I'm going to take the pictures." Chris replied with a smile.

"You're being nasty, and besides don't you have enough on your arm already?"

"Nope, I want pictures of you and the baby."

"Fine, I will let you take the photos only if you give me a nice massage afterwards"

"Bet. Chris looked down at his diamond Cartier watch on his wrist. Yo, I gotta go meet pop. See you later." He walked over kissing Sydney's lips.

"I love you. How late are you going to be at Reign today?"

"Probably late today, got a few things to handle.

"Okay, don't forget to free your schedule later and tomorrow meeting with wedding planner."

"I remember. Chris walked over to his shoes taking down a pair, Sydney gathered up Natalia's bag. Chris kissed Natalia before heading out the door. Sydney followed shortly after him with Natalia in her arms. She decided to take the S class, she strapped Natalia in her car seat before sliding behind the wheel. She immediately looked on the passenger floor. There was a La Perla bag on the floor, she picked up the bag pulling out the contents which were panties and lingerie. She looked over the receipt which was located inside, the total was over twenty five hundred dollars. The purchase was from two days ago. She smiled, knowing that Chris had bought the items for her. Sydney tossed the receipt back in the bag, and placed it back on the floor. As she started the car, ASAP Ferg's "New Level" blasted through the speaker. She glanced over in the passenger seat at a stack of mail. She browsed through the letters, which were paid bills. She stopped on a letter from Piedmont Hospital in Atlanta addressed to PO Box in Fort Lauderdale, Chris had set up under one of Preme's workers name which he rarely used. She looked over the amount said paid in full, ten thousand dollars. Sydney placed the mail in her purse, she definitely was going to confront Chris about this, she thought.

Chris and Preme were in his office chatting over Preme's morning coffee. Chris sat back in the plush chair, eating on grapes. "Where's my baby?" said Preme as he sat up in his chair.

"She's with Syd today."

"I got some information on a few top schools for her." He went through a few folders on his desk handing one over to Chris. "Good looking out pop." Chris placed the folder in front of him as he continued on his green grapes. "I also heard about you and that bitch at the store."

Chris sighed. "Bitch, trying to get at me, about a fucking window. Fuck that shit."

Preme caressed his chin. "With this case shit pending you don't need no extra shit right now. Throw some bread at that bullshit, or I'll handle her in my way."

"I got her. She will be a'ight. Grant telling me I might do some time. Not trying to hear that shit, but I need to make sure my fam is good."

"Chris you're not doing any time. Preme said assertively. If anything, it'll be consequences for that bastard. We not paying him for the bullshit."

"Yea, but if I do I need Syd to be good while I'm away. I'm ready for anything, n'ahmean. So, I need a favor from you." Chris placed the plate on the desk, sitting up.

"What you need?"

"I need some work, anything you need handled, pushed. I got you."

Preme looked at Chris knowing how much he had wanted to distance himself from the game. He could see the frustration in his eyes. "You sure?"

"Yea. I can't have Syd fuckin' struggling while I'm in a box. I want at least another two million stashed away. Planning a wedding, baby coming, this vodka company, and thinking of getting more property and store locations. I got too much shit going on right now, to give this case bullshit any of my fuckin' energy."

"A'ight son. If you need it, I got you. You don't have to worry about Syd and Natalia, they will be taken care of. As far as the wedding, I'll pay for the wedding."

"Nah, I'm a man. I have to take care of my own responsibilities. We're good now, but like you taught me, think ahead for the unexpected. These next few weeks I'll grind." Preme looked over at his son, he was definitely maturing. No longer that spitfire, going through life with no worries or giving a fuck. Now was an ambitious father and entrepreneur with the weight of the world on his shoulders. Preme stood up, exiting the room and returning with two duffle bags. Chris stood up taking the bags in his hands. "Thanks pop."

"No problem. Stop by the club and Loco will hit you off with another package. When you head up to Orlando, Darren will hit you off with things up there. Chris nodded in agreement. I'll give you a few contacts as well. Keep everything from all." Preme returned back to the desk, Chris sat down placing the bags beside him. "How is Sydney doing with the baby?"

"She's good. She not showing yet, but she thinks she's big and shit." Chris and Preme laughed.

"Typical female. I've told you before that you can bring the baby by sometimes. Maybe we have dinner or rent out somewhere for the night."

"Keep that in mind. We'll link up soon."

"You going to drop these off now?" said Preme.

"Yea, before I go to store."

"How that nigga doing at your store?"

"You don't need him on your team pop. He's a clown. I'm ready to get rid of his ass."

"Hmmph." Preme scoffed.

"You don't need pussy niggas on your team."

"Well, it's a wrap for him. Preme replied as he went to his phone." Chris interjected. "Not just yet Pop, let's wait until I get my court date and shit together. I got a few more things for that nigga." Preme put down his phone. "It's your call for now."

"Let me catch that nigga looking at Syd again."

"What?! He still fucking with her? I'll handle that. Get niggas to watch his every move."

"Yea. Nigga might think of stalking Syd or some shit."

"He must think I'm a joke. Dead that shit." Preme quickly dialed number, Loco answered after first ring. "What up?"

"Need you to find information for a party location for me, for the new hire." Loco smiled on the other end. "I got you." Preme ended the call looking back to Chris. "How long are you gonna be at Reign today?"

"Probably seven. I have a few things to handle. Syd want to have date night shit tonight so I may leave earlier."

"A'ight, hit me back later. I will have some things to go over with you."

"A'ight." Chris stood up carrying a bag in each hand as Preme followed him to the door.

Sydney had left admissions at school and was sitting in the car as she texted Dana to make sure she was still available to watch Natalia tonight. A surge of hunger rushed over her she reached in Natalia's bag grabbing a mini pack of Teddy Grahams. Natalia who was watching Inside Out on her iPad mini attached to the seat, quickly gave Sydney side eye for taking her snack. As she stuffed her face she received an email from Monica, the wedding planner, confirming their appointment tomorrow. Sydney quickly responded that they both would be there. After Dana responded she was free, Sydney drove away to pick up lunch.

Shortly after Chris left Preme met up with Loco at the club. "I got the crew ready to go. Fam is in Lauderhill." Preme looked around at his six goons dressed in black and bulletproof vests had handled situations for him in the past.

"A'ight, I want y'all to go in there, no mistakes, just in and out. Let them know I'm nothing to be fucked with." Each nodded in solidarity, before walking out to the black Yukon's parked in back. Loco waited behind for a final instruction from Preme. "Get eyes on that nigga's every move. Make sure he is nowhere near my daughter and law, anything come up let me know! I don't give a fuck what hour it is."

"Got you boss, I'll make sure he know what time it is." Loco walked out the door. Minutes later Preme headed home. Once the crew arrived on NW 31st street, ski mask covered their faces with gloved hands and guns in each hand. One car pulled outside of a cream brick home with missing grass patches, and a small garden in the home. The other pulled on street located behind it. Three in the back, three in front as well as Loco. Loco gave the signal and all three men headed towards the front door, shooting the door knob off before entering. The three at back door burst through the back door at the same time. A woman screamed falling to the floor dropping the pieces of fish she had been seasoning in pan. One of the men kicked the woman in the stomach as she screamed in agony. She was about one hundred and sixty pounds, brown skinned with a black silk bonnet on her head. Dressed in a shirt and khaki capri pants. The men began trashing the house as they checked in the other rooms.

In the guest bathroom, her nephew hopped from the toilet to retrieve his gun from under the sink. Panicked the gun was wedged too far behind pipe. A blast came thru door, he stared at the masked assailant in front of him. Immediately rushing towards him, the assailant fired one shot, wounding him in the stomach. He fell back into the tub. Hearing the shot, a teenage girl screamed from the bedroom the door flung open and a half dressed girl came charging down the hall a vase in her hand. Once she reached the end of the hall, she was grabbed by one of the assailants placing a gun to her head. She immediately burst into tears, trying to break free of his hold. He hit her with the barrel of the gun and she fell to the floor. As the others shot out televisions, they checked on the nephew he was dead in the tub. Loco walked in last looking over the scene he walked over to the woman in the kitchen. He picked her up from the floor. Trembling and wet face. "Tell your fuckin' son, if he don't want us back out here or worse, to stay the fuck away from Syd. You understand! She nodded her head feverishly. If we have to come back, we merking every fuckin' muthafucka in here. Consider this a fucking warning." She nodded her head again. He grabbed her by the bonnet bashing her head into the counter. She screamed out in pain as the men walked out of both entrances as they had come filing back into their cars and down the street.

Sydney arrived outside of Reign with a Bacon ranch salad and Happy meal from Mcdonald's for Natalia and herself and Chipotle for Chris. The store packed Sydney attempted to maneuver Natalia thru the store, thinking why she didn't park in back today. Chris was engaged in a conversation with a woman, most likely Latina in a bikini top and unbuttoned jean shorts which showed off her matching pink bottom. She had a plastered flirty smile on her face as well as her double d's in Chris' face. "Did you think the pants were cute on me?" she replied with her hand on her hip and garment in her hand. Chris smiled. "That's not for me to decide."

"Yes, it is. You're sexy papi, I'd like for you to see them on the..." Sydney walked up placing her hand on his back. "Hey." He turned around with a bright smile on his face seeing Sydney and Natalia. "What up baby?!" He replied as he kissed her lips. He reached down picking up Natalia. "Hey, I brought you some food. I'll be in your office."

"Thank you ma." The woman with the pants waiting patiently, taking in their encounter "Wow... is this your baby? She's adorable, she looks just like you!"

Sydney side eyed the woman. "Yea, this is my daughter and she is my wife." Sydney smiled smirkingly at the woman before walking back to the office. Sydney sat at his desk pulling out her salad and Natalia's cuties and nuggets. Chris soon followed behind with Natalia. He placed her in the playpen and Sydney handed her the cuties and her sip cup. Chris sat down digging into his burrito bowl. Chris reached into the mini fridge he had just installed he handed Sydney a drink and himself one as well. Halfway thru the salad Sydney closed the plate caressing her stomach. "So... what happened in Atlanta?" said Sydney bluntly.

"What?" Chris replied defensively.

"You heard me. I saw the letter from the hospital, I'm asking what happened?" Chris placed down his fork, looking into her eyes.

"You went through my shit?"

"You left it on the seat."

"So you opened my shit?" said Chris angrily.

"Yes, I opened your shit! Why were you in the hospital?"

"I had a situation I needed to take care of."

"What? Why didn't you tell me? What situation?"

"I wasn't fuckin' with you then. That was when your crazy ass bucked to LA with Tubby. I was stabbed."

"What?! Why did you get stabbed? What were you doing?"

"What you think? I got stitched up and left. No big deal." Sydney sat up leaning in to the desk.

"Why are you talking to me this way? I asked you a simple question."

"And I answered you! What the fuck you else you want me to say?" barked Chris. Sydney got up from the seat grabbing her purse. "I see where this is going and I'm not about to go there with your pissy ass attitude. Bye."

"What you talking about you leaving?"

"Yes I'm leaving. Because I know you're pissed about the fuckin' mail and you're about to blow up and I'm not in the mood for it."

"You mean, you are not in the mood for it? You went through my personal shit."

"We shouldn't have personal shit! I'm about to be your wife! What are you hiding?"

"I'm not hiding shit. What the fuck I got to hide?!"

"Boy bye!" Sydney reached down into the playpen picking up Natalia. Chris stood up walking over towards them. "Stay out of my shit Syd!" Chris barked. "As long as we are together anything that is in our house is my business. So you can go to hell." Sydney stormed out of the office and into the front of the store. Once at the car she started the ignition on the key so the air could circulate before strapping Natalia in. Chris soon emerged from the store, the scantily clad woman came out after him a smile on her face. "What the fuck do you want?!" shouted Sydney to the woman. "Excuse me…"

"Chris, you better get her! I have no problem dragging a bitch today!" Chris tried to console Sydney, she brushed past him to the driver's side of the car, peeling away from the curb. "What was that all about?" The woman said to Chris. Chris ignored her comment as he walked past the woman back into the store. John was posted at the counter, Chris walked over to him. "Yogi been up here today?" "Nah." Chris walked over to his office.

Meanwhile, Yogi was frantic after receiving a call from his mother to come to her house immediately. She didn't give any details, but he could tell from the despair and tone of her voice it was serious. He pulled up next to two remaining squad cars, police tape around his mother's house, blocking off onlookers. "What the fuck?" said Yogi out loud as he looked over his mother's bullet ridden door "Sir, you cannot go in here." stated the officer with his hand on Yogi's chest. "This my mama house muthafucka, this is my fuckin' family." A second officer was on the porch he walked over telling the officer to let him by. He immediately recognized his face from the portraits in the living room. "What the fuck is goin on here?" shouted Yogi to the officers. "Your family was attacked in an apparent ambush..." Yogi rushed past the officer into the house. He immediately saw the disaster which once was his mother's house, broken glass and bullet holes everywhere. Blood on the floor. "MA! He shouted as he walked back to her bedroom. She was seated with a detective, tears in her eyes. Yogi rushed over to his mother's side. He hugged her tightly, looking over her bruised face and black eye. He was furious. "Who did this to you? The fuck happened here?!"

"I don't know who they were they were looking for money. I couldn't see their faces... they killed Maurice." She sobbed. "What?! Fuck! Where is Brittney?"

"She went over to Marie's house, she was too shaken up. She's pretty banged up as well. Too afraid to go to doctor. I'm gonna take her to hospital. Once I try to pick up some things here."

"Ma'am I'm going to head out. Here is my card again, if you receive any information please give me a call." He nodded his head walking towards the door, Yogi had his hands over his head. He looked over to his mother again, the front door closed. She got up from the bed walking past Yogi disgust on her face. She walked over to the living room looking out the window watching all the officers and onlookers leave the road. Yogi followed out after her. "Ma.."

"Those niggas were after you! I told you about that shit! She punched him in the chest. They were gonna kill us, over your bullshit!"

"Ma... I'm sorry... what you mean I thought you said for money?"

"I told him that. They were looking for you! They mentioned someone's name, about six or seven of them, with guns. They had a gun to my head! Beat me up over your bullshit, Javon!" He walked over trying to console her again. She pushed him away. "No, I want you out of here. They are threatening to come back!"

"Did they say anything? His mother walked past him into the kitchen cleaning the broken glass from her kitchen floor. Ma! What did they say?!"

"Something about a Sue... Sin... I don't remember..."

"Sydney?!"

"Yea, they said to s tay away or something." Yogi became enraged. He immediately thought of Chris, his blood boiling. "I gotta go mama... go to auntie Jess house, you don't need to be here."

"Don't you worry about me! You just make sure you don't bring your ass back over here with this foolishness! This my fuckin' house I'm not going nowhere!" Yogi too upset to argue with his mother dropped a small stack of cash on the kitchen counter, before leaving out the door, heading over to Reign.

Once there he pulled up front strapped ready for war. He stormed into the store, John was seated at the counter. "Where Chris?" he shouted.

"He left already."

"How long ago he left?"

"I don't know why? What up?" Yogi looked over to John, he turned around walking back out the front door. It was six thirty when Chris arrived home, Sydney had just taken Natalia out of the bath laying her on their bed naked in her robe. Sydney massaged oil over Natalia's body before placing her in her pajamas. Chris walked into the room walking over to the bathroom, minutes later walking out taking off his shirt. Sydney picked up Natalia placing her in her room inside her bed. She walked back into their bedroom.

"Are we going to talk about this or are we going to ignore each other?" said Sydney

"What you talking about Sydney?"

"You walked in here and ignored me."

"You didn't say shit either." Said Chris angrily.

"Babe come on! I don't want to argue with you. Stop trying to make me angry." Chris walked over to the safe. "All I'm saying is stop going through my shit. Done."

"Chris what is the big deal. It was a hospital bill. We are a family. I let you in everything in my life. I've never kept anything from you since we've been back together. It pisses me off that your closing me out of something as petty as a bill, like I'm some random bitch." Chris glanced over to Sydney, silent, before walking out of the room and downstairs to the kitchen. Sydney messaged Dana asking if she could come to pick Natalia up. She responded yes, she told her it was an urgent as her and Chris had some issues they needed to clear up. Within twenty minutes Dana was over and Natalia's bag was ready.

Sydney grabbed her spare car seat which was in the garage. Once Dana and Natalia were gone Sydney locked the doors, heading up to their bedroom where Chris was. He was located in the safe counting money. "Baby... please come talk to me. You can't ignore me all night." Sydney slipped out of her robe, dressed in only her bra and panties. She walked over to Chris placing her arms around his body, resting her face in the center of his bare back. She decided being angry would get her nowhere with him, she decided to let him be and end the issue about the bill. She squeezed in between him and the safe, she began to kiss his chest softly as Chris placed the stack of hundreds back into the safe. She caressed his chest moving her hands over his frontal she ran her finger over a scar on the side of his stomach. There it was again. How had she missed this before? She thought.

"You were back in the game again weren't you?"

"Nah... I was standing in a store and a bitch got me." He replied sarcastically.

"You can be such an ass sometimes." She pushed him out of the way walking over to the closet to put on something. She walked out in a wife beater tank. "Why can't we have a conversation like two adults? Can you talk to me?"

"Syd, leave me the fuck alone right now. Can you do that?" He shouted sitting on the ottoman.

"No, if I want to talk to you, you are going to speak to me! You can talk to the bitch at the store with the silicone tits. But, you can't talk to the mother of your children?" Chris now beyond annoyed placed his phone down.

"You want to fuckin' talk Syd let's talk, so you can shut the fuck up! What the fuck were you thinking taking Natalia to LA? Why do you get on my nerves all the fuckin' time?" He barked at her.

"I get on your nerves? I wasn't getting on your nerves, when you were fuckin' me making babies was I?" She snapped back.

"You're a good fuck." Chris replied bluntly. Sydney was speechless, Chris could see the rage in her eyes.

"I can't believe you said that shit to me! Fuck you!" Sydney picked up a vase which was on top of her vanity mirror, aiming at his head. Chris ducked as the vase hit the wall, and white roses fell all over the floor, missing him entirely. She stormed out of the room, she returned five minutes later. Chris was laying across their bed watching television. Sydney walked over attempting to block the screen with her body. "You're going back into the game, aren't you? Every time you go back into this shit, you act like this. What's the reason you've come up with this time?" Chris ignored her. She powered off the television, snatching the remote from the bed throwing it towards the balcony. She climbed into the bed mounting herself on top of him. "Say it."

Chris looked away from her before looking up into her beautiful face. He sighed. "Do you realize what the fuck is going on? I'm a hustler Syd. I'm not no nine to five nigga working for a bullshit check. I have a court date coming up in a few weeks. I could possibly spend time in a box, you heard? What the fuck are you gonna do then? How you gonna be spending three and four stacks a day on purses and bullshit?"

A single tear streamed down her face. "You think that is all I care about is your fuckin' money?! After all the shit I've been through with you, you can actually say that shit to me! She removed herself from his chest. All of the hell I've gone thru and you can say that to me?! I was waiting on the reality to set in, I knew the honeymoon would be over soon and Mr. Cash the asshole, would find a way to rear his ugly fuckin' head." She shook her head trying to hold back the tears that was now flooding her face. She walked downstairs to their screened in pool. She sat on one of the deck chairs, looking over the Swarovski crystals she had begged to be placed in the bottom of the pool. Something about the night air and the crickets in the distance was somewhat calming to Sydney at night. Chris soon appeared at the door in his Polo drawstring pants. He walked over to Sydney sitting behind her in the chair, he placed his arms around her stomach. His lips perched to her ear. "I'm sorry ma... I'm stressed. I didn't have to go to a hundred about that bullshit, but I've had a lot on my mind." He kissed her ear and cheek softly. His touch sent a warm sensation over her body, and goosebumps formed on her arms.

"Why couldn't you just say that, baby? I love you. I am not against you. We are a team."

"I know, but you know this is hard for me. Trust is a big issue for me. You know that."

"I know. But, communication is everything. You can't just shut down and ignore me whenever an issue you don't want to talk about comes up. We have to talk."

"I hear you Syd. I'll try to do better. I'm sorry." Sydney smiled as she turned to face him and look into his eyes. She knew that was a big step for him to apologize, also growth that they partially communicated through a dispute. "Apology accepted." She replied genuinely. He laid back on the chair. Sydney laid on his chest. "I went to Atlanta with Nick to handle some drop-offs, nigga tried to rob me. Got one in on me."

"Baby, you have to let this shit go. You don't need that shit anymore. Reign is doing well, what happened to us investing and flipping."

"I know that's still a plan. I have moves I gotta make, I have this case coming I need to make sure you and Natalia are set."

"Baby, we are fine. If ever a time we aren't fine, I will make moves."

"No, I'm not having that. He kissed her face. He looked down at her bare legs. Are you out here in your panties?"

"No one can see back here." She replied with a smile.

"You never know who's a peeping tom. White people freaky like that." Sydney laughed out loud sitting up. Chris removed his leg from behind her standing up. He extended his hand to help her up. She placed her hand in his, standing to her feet. Chris pulled her in close, kissing her on the forehead. "You *are* a good fuck... but only with me." Sydney smiled as she kissed his lips. "I love you Christian."

"I love you too ma. He kissed her lips again. Come give me some of that bomb pussy." Sydney blushed, immediately turned on. "You're so nasty..." She began to bite gently on his neck, before they returned back into the house. Sydney hopped on top of the island in the center of the kitchen, removing the wife beater and bra. Although, she was pissed that Chris was considering the game, she'd rather he be honest than lying to her. She decided for now she would have to let it go. In this moment all she wanted was all of him inside of her. As he pulled her body over to his face, she closed her eyes with a smile.

Hours later they were laying in their bed eating Natalia's Halo's which she would flip if she knew they were eating. Sydney was laying back on his chest, looking at his tattoo of her on his arm. "What are we going to name the baby if it's a boy?" said Sydney as she stuffed her face.

"I mean he's already gonna be a little me like Tubby, so he doesn't have to be a junior. I want him to have his own identity... not attached to the crazy shit I've done."

"What about Cruz Garcia? After my last name?"

"It's a'ight, I'm not feeling that. I like King...or Cam."

"I do like Cam. King, no I don't need any of these thirsty bitches checking for my baby in school. What about Gavin, after my dad. Replied Sydney with a smile. Gavin Christian Garcia."

"It's not bad though. I low key fuck with it, but don't want my son named after your punk ass daddy." Said Chris with a smile.

"Whatever. I like Christian as the middle name. What if it's a girl?"

"It's not. It's a boy. I know."

"Okay... Daddy." Moments later they both were out.

The next morning Sydney felt the air on her face from the balcony. She panicked as the sun hit her face. She reached for her phone on the nightstand. It was ten thirty. "Babe! Get up! She shouted as she hit him. Where is Tubby?"

"In her room." Chris replied groggily.

"No... Dana has her remember." Sydney replied as she tried to unlock her phone.

"No. she dropped her off this morning, you were sleep." Said Chris.

"The wedding planner! Oh my god, I can't believe you let me oversleep. We have to go! Can you please get Natalia dressed for me?"

"What?!" said Chris.

"Please, come on I need you." Sydney rushed over to the shower. Chris got up angrily walking over to Natalia's room. Once out she quickly threw her panties and a black strapless body hugging mid length dress and a pair of Sophia Webster Lilico Underwater bootie heels she had been dying to wear. She quickly applied a little makeup to her face and MAC gloss to her lips. Chris walked back into their room. Natalia was dressed in a pair of distressed jeans, black top and a pair of Timbs on her feet. "Y'all head downstairs I'll meet you at the car in like ten minutes." He replied as he passed Natalia to

Sydney. Sydney grabbed her phone and purse, going down to the car. In about ten minutes Chris emerged in a slim fit Royal Blue Polo Ralph Lauren linen shirt and jeans, Timbs on his feet. He slid in behind the wheel of the Range Rover, Sydney looked over at him, smelling the Jimmy Choo Man cologne on his body. "You look sexy babe." Said Sydney she reached over kissing his neck.

"Thank you. Not one hundred, since you woke me out of my sleep." He looked to her with a smirk. Once there Chris pulled his diamond chain out of his pocket placing it on his neck, he helped Sydney put on her necklace. Chris carried Natalia into the building. Sydney walked over to the reception desk as she did before and signed in. It was eleven fifteen. Monica soon emerged down the hall dressed in a cute Roberto Cavalli sleeveless dress which was lime and pink, her hair out and Jimmy Choo heels on her feet. Sydney eyes scanned over her outfit, in her mind thinking. *Yass bitch!* She loved Monica's style. "Hello Sydney!" Sydney stood to her feet extending her hand for a handshake, Monica brought her in for a hug.

"I'm so sorry for being late."

"You're fine! I was running behind myself. She smiled looking over to Chris. So, this is Christian?" Chris stood up to shake her hand.

"Yes. This is my fiancée Christian Garcia and our daughter Natalia." said Sydney.

"Nice to meet you. You are very handsome, look at that face."

"Thank you. Nice to meet you." said Chris. Monica smiled and waved to Natalia before leading the way back to her office. Monica took a seat behind her desk, her eyes immediately drawn to Chris. She stared into his eyes and long lashes, she looked over his mouth and hands. Chris felt her staring at him, so he tried not to look in her direction. He quickly shifted his eyes around the room, seeing the Peru painting on the wall.

"So, you're Peruvian?" said Chris as he glanced around the room, refusing to make an awkward eye contact with Monica.

"Yes, I am. Sydney said you are as well right?"

"Yea, I'm mixed. My mother was Peruvian." He said looking her in the eyes.

"Oh okay." She smiled which caused Chris to naturally smile back. Monica instantly felt warmed by his smile. She couldn't help but to stare at him. "I'm sorry Christian to stare at you. You remind me of one of my family members. If I may ask where are you from?"

"New York. But, I was born and raised in Boston." Said Chris in a tone which gave off as semi hostile. Monica looked into his face again unsure if she should probe more questions. Sydney looked over to Chris' body language. She knew he was becoming slightly annoyed, it was early and only a matter of seconds before he grew tired of her personal questions. She looked over to Natalia, she went into her desk pulling out a picture, and she handed the picture to Sydney. It was a picture of a beautiful little girl playing on top of a bed, her wild curls everywhere.

"Oh my god, she's cute. She kind of looks like Tubby."

Monica smiled. "That's my daughter Isabella. She looks just like my sister. Looking at your daughter reminded me of her." Sydney handed the picture to Chris. He looked over the girl's face, she did resemble Natalia. Big bright eyes, dimples and a beautiful smile. The little girl was no more than two in the picture. Chris handed her the picture back. Monica looked off for a moment. "My sister died a few years ago. I hadn't heard from her in years before her death. Which is why I tell people family is so important. Monica looked over to Chris' face again, he now had his head rested on his hand. I'm sorry to bring it up."

"It's okay." Said Sydney. She reached in her purse pulling out the paper work she was to return. Chris placed Natalia down from his lap, and was holding her between his legs. She soon broke free running over to Monica's book shelf. Which had picture frames, awards and etc. Chris looked back at her. "Tubby get from over there!"

"It's no problem. She's okay." Monica began to look over the forms. Natalia picked up a heart shaped knick knack, which dropped to the ground. Sydney and Chris both looked back at her. She walked over to Chris with the item in her hand.

"So I do have a few locations, I would like to show you." Monica turned on her seventy inch screen which was located to the side of her. Sydney sat up ready to see what she had. Natalia dropped the knick knack in Chris' lap. He picked up the item looking it over, immediately freezing up his body tense. It was a small obituary picture of Maria. Sydney looked over to Chris, as Monica typed into her computer. "Baby... what's wrong?" Sydney whispered to his now shifted attitude. A snarl on his face. He sat up in his seat placing the item in the air. "How do you know her?" said Chris with an assertiveness which deserved an answer. Monica looked over to what was in Chris' hands, a smile on her face. "That's my sister, Maria."

Chris immediately screwed up his face, feeling his blood began to boil. Sydney looked over the picture seeing his mother's face. "Oh God." Said Sydney nervous for his reaction. Chris looked over the picture caressing his finger over her face.

"This is my mother." Said Chris somberly.

"Wait a minute... Pumkin?" Chris immediately looked into her eyes. Pumkin was a name his mother called him. Hearing Monica's voice, which reminded him of his mother, immediately sent a wave of emotion thru his body. It couldn't be. He said to himself. "Yea... it's me." Monica immediately burst into tears. "I knew it from the moment I laid eyes on you I said you remind me of Maria! She stood up from the desk

walking over to Chris hugging him tightly. Oh my god! I'm
your auntie Monica. Chris stood up overwhelmed with emotion
himself he embraced her. I haven't seen you since you were...
three years old. You are soo handsome, she touched his face,
and you look just like her. She loved you soo much. Oh wow.
Monica replied her hand on her face as she admired Chris. It's
a small world. We had been looking for you, no answers or any
information to where they had placed you. I cannot believe
this. I have to call mama." Monica pulled out her iPhone
placing it on speaker. After three rings a woman came over the
phone.

"Hola mamá. He encontrado cristiano! está vivo. él es tan
guapo!" Shrieked Monica. Sydney smiled interpreting to Chris
what was said "She told her she found you, you're alive and
handsome." She whispered.

"Gracias Jesús! Puedo hablar con el?" Monica handed him the
phone. "Mama would like to speak to you? Would you like the
phone on speaker?"

"Yea, that's fine. Replied Chris. Hello?"

"Hello? Christian? This is your abeula Isla. She spoke softly
in her broken English. How are you? estado buscando para
usted. Te amo Pumkin. Nunca dio para arriba en usted."
Sydney smiled translating to Chris. "She says that she has been
looking for you. She loves you, and never gave up on you."
Sydney caressed his back. A huge smile formed on Chris' face.
"It's all good. I'm good. Monica began to translate to her
mother. I had a baby girl, I'm engaged with another on the
way. I would love to see all of you."

Isla's voice lit up as she spoke to Monica. Chris could hear
she was excited and kept thanking Jesus. "I can't wait to see
you. Te amo Cristiano." As she continued to repeat she loved
him his heart immediately became full, he fought back the
emotion building inside of him.

"I love you too. I'll get with Monica to make arrangements to see you. I've been waiting for this day for a long time. He bit his lip. I will be in touch." Monica translated to her mother taking the phone off speaker saying a few more words before announcing she would call her later. Once she ended the call she sat back down looking into Chris' face intently, making a memory of all of her sister's features in her son. "How have you been? What happened?"

"A lot of shit has happened. I've had a rough life. But, I'm good now I own my own business, and home."

Monica lowered her head. "Chris, your mother's death was the hardest thing for our family. Mama took it the hardest. At the time we all, mostly me, used our savings to try and bring you with us. I flew mama and papa from Lima to Boston and I was to meet them there to help with custody. The day before I was to fly to Boston, a group of men came to my home and beat me. They threatened to kill me and you, if I became involved. I didn't know what to do. They told me if I went to authorities or told anyone, I would be dead. She began to cry. They had guns to my head. I was soo scared. I had to tell mama something came up with work and I wouldn't be able to assist. Mama called me once she arrived, and said when she arrived at the police station she was introduced to a family friend of Maria's, who said that he would assist her with a lawyer. Mama said he was friends with a few of the officers so he seemed trustworthy you know. He told her that the only way that they could guarantee to get you is to pay off the debt Maria owed as well as lawyer fees. He asked for over fifty thousand dollars! We didn't have that type of money. I couldn't get involved... Once Mama went through hoops with the friend with money issue, she heard nothing."

"What? Do you know friend's name?"

"Oh no, I don't. Mama could not tell me any information about the friend or the money was off the table. Chris placed his hand over his chin. It's just so amazing to see the man that you've become. I just wanted to let you know I never stopped thinking about you. I have a picture of you and Maria on my mantle, I kiss every day. I remember Maria telling me that you were meant to do something big. She had such big plans for you."

"Why did you and Ma lose touch?"

"I would wire her money all the time, and once she got back on drugs, she would use the money for a fix. I became angry and flew up to Boston to see you all. I reserved a room and she became angry that I wouldn't be staying with her, we got into a huge fight. She cursed me out and it became physical. She said she didn't want anything to do with me ever again. I hadn't spoken to her in years. You were around eight or nine when that happened."

"You know as much as I've heard about ma doing drugs, she never brought that around me. I never saw that. Ma was cool."

"Yes, Maria was cool, but she lived a crazy life. She was as sweet as can be, but if you ever cross her, there would be hell to pay. Always beautiful, her presence demanded everyone's attention. I always looked up to her."

"When did you come from Peru?"

"I came at sixteen years old lived with your great uncle Robert. I finished school and went to college. He passed about six years ago. Chris' phone rang interrupting their conversation, he looked down at the screen seeing that it was Reign. He declined the call. You two don't have to worry about the fee for your wedding. I would love to plan your wedding for free. I would also like to get to know you and your family Christian."

"I want to get to know you too. This is a lot to take in. you don't have to do it for free."

"No, I want to. I owe it to you. I know it won't make up for all that you have been through, but it's the least I can do."

"I appreciate it. It's gonna take me some time to process all that happened today. I have no problem with you planning the wedding."

Monica smiled bright. "I'm so honored to do this for you. Let's make this the best wedding Miami has ever seen."

"Let's do it!" said Sydney with a smile, as she wiped the tears from her face. Chris looked over to her a smile on his face. He leaned over kissing her lips. Natalia tugged at Sydney's leg asking to pick her up. She sat her on her lap. What are the odds he thought?

At the club Preme and Loco were having a meeting in the basement about the details of the pop up with Yogi's family. "We had one body boss."

"What?! What the fuck did I say?" said Preme as he slammed his glass onto the table.

"Nigga was trying to pull out, had to blast his ass." Preme shook his head. "Who was it?"

"Small nigga named Maurice, did a bid a while back on armed robbery, rat nigga."

"I'm gonna need full information on this Yogi nigga. Moe telling me he went by fuckin' Reign yesterday."

"I'll keep an eye on him. Have you told Chris yet?"

"Nah, I'm gonna tell him about it tonight. I want eyes on that nigga all day. Anything pop off it's your ass. Also I want phone taps on that nigga lines and messages. Chris and Syd expecting I can't have no shit going down while she's carrying my fuckin' grandchild."

"Got you boss. Tell Chris congrats on the baby."

"You just handle business. This nigga fuck with her livelihood, I will personally fuck up his."

At the salon, it had been fairly steady. Dana was cleaning her station and sanitizing her utensils. Vani came through the door yelling into her phone. Dana looked over to her curious to know who she was talking to. Vani slammed her phone down removing her purse from her shoulder. "Where have you been?" said Dana.

"Running errands for Mark's dumb ass. It's been busy in here?"

"A few people looking for you."

"I sent everyone messages telling them I wouldn't be in today and to reschedule." She replied with an attitude.

"Well, I'm going to be in late tomorrow, I need some rest. I'm going to drop Natalia's birthday presents off tonight."

"Aww, her birthday is coming up, I forgot. I should get her something. Just because her mom is a petty ass bitch, doesn't mean I should punish her huh?" Vani replied sarcastically.

"You should go and talk to Sydney. She's your family."

"Fuck Sydney. She chose Chris' cheating ass over me. We used to be best friends, and like that she said threw all that away. Fuck her!"

"Vani life is too short for bullshit. Dana grabbed her purse and phone off the counter. I'll see you tomorrow." Dana headed towards the door as she reached the exit, Yogi was at the door holding it open. She glanced over at him with a side eye and looking over to Vani. Yogi had an MCM bag on his back. Vani walked over to the door locking it behind her. "Yo.. we gotta…" Vani placed a finger up waiting to see Dana's car pull away from the curb. "What's up?!" She replied.

"We have to plan this shit now! ASAP! As in next fucking week!" shouted Yogi.

"Why? What's going on?" Vani sat down in her chair.

"Chris sent niggas to my fuckin' mom house. Him and his niggas need to know I'm not to be fucked with!"

"First off, where is my money?" Vani placed her hand in the air. Yogi looked over to her with a smirk, placing the MCM bag in her lap. Vani sifted through the bag counting the bands. It was twenty five g's. "You will get the other half at the pickup. We gonna go in and pick the bitch up from the store." Vani skimmed through the stacks making sure it was legit.

"Chris is not going to let Natalia out of his sight. It's not gonna work like that. The best move would be to wait until Sydney has the baby." Vani stood up placing the bag over her shoulder. Maybe when she comes to get her nails done again. I can tell Dana I want to see the baby and she will bring her through. As long as you don't fuck up my salon!" She pointed her finger at him. "You're not going to hurt the baby right?"

"Nah, I ain't gonna hurt that fuckin' baby. I ought to hurt Sydney! Fuckin' bitch!"

"So, when you want this to happen?"

"Well. I heard Preme is supposed to be out of town next Wednesday. We need to get her while he out of the way."

Vani stared at Yogi. "Preme? What does he have to do with this?"

"Preme is Chris' fam."

Vani's eyes widened. "What?!"

"Preme is Chris' fuckin' Pops. Ain't you and Sydney family? How the fuck you ain't know that?"

502

"Yea, but she never said shit to me about Preme. What the fuck? This can't be serious." Vani began to second guess this whole plan. Yogi began to sense her doubt. "I'll have it set up for Wednesday. You be in place. You got my money, no turning back now!"

"Whatever."

"Don't fuck with me Vani. Have Sydney and the baby here in the morning."

"You didn't say anything about Preme being involved. That's on some other shit! Fuck!"

"Have the fuckin' baby here! Don't worry about him." Yogi left towards the door. Vani unlocked it letting him out, before locking it back she let her back rest against the door. The thought of doing anything that could lead to Preme's retaliation had her shook. Although Preme was a person everyone in Dade County knew, he was rarely seen. His was notoriously known for murders in broad daylight, popping family members, no one was off limits. Everyone knew he was well connected with half of the city and beyond on payroll. He was a millionaire numerous times over. Vani imagined him finding out she was involved and having her killed her body flown to another country. "Fuck man..." said Vani in the dark.

After the meeting with Monica and getting a few ideas out there. Sydney was starving and begged for him to take her to Popeye's as they sat in the drive thru waiting for the food. "What do you think of Monica being your aunt?"

"It's crazy as hell. Ma, never talked about her it was as if she never existed. If she didn't pull out some of those pictures or call my grandma. I don't know if I would've bought it."

"Your mom *never* mentioned her?"

"Nah, I don't remember her saying she had a sister, I know she had a brother as well."

"Well, she did say that they had a feud maybe your mother disowned her. The woman came back to the window with the food. She smiled at Chris. Baby, get some strawberry jelly for my biscuits." Chris smiled at her request.

"Strawberry jelly. He passed the bag over to Sydney. Once the woman handed him the jelly, he passed it over to her. All I'm saying is I'm not letting my guard down, just yet. We don't know her." Sydney opened the box of food passing a few fries back to Natalia on a napkin.

"Fine baby. What time are we going to Disney tomorrow?"

"Probably around eight."

"Okay. I only have one last thing to say about Monica. You shouldn't shut her out, because maybe there is more to your past that she can help you with. You can't shut everyone out all the time babe."

"I hear what you saying. I'm only saying that I'm being cautious. I don't know who the fuck she is and who or what she knows. I have to look out for you and my babies, you heard?" "Okay baby." Sydney's phone binged that she had a message it was Dana saying she was coming over with Natalia's birthday gifts. Sydney informed she could drop them off, they would be home in twenty minutes. Chris looked over to Sydney as in to insinuate who you texting?

"That was Dana. She is going to meet us to the house she has presents for Tati."

"A'ight. I like Dana. She cool, n'ahmean."

"Really? You like her. You usually hate anyone I bring around."

Chris laughed. "I don't hate everybody. Only Mercedes, Vanessa and Persia."

"You know from what she told me, a while ago... you were feelin' every part of her..." said Sydney with a smile.

Chris looked over to Sydney, his face cold. "You think that shit funny?"

"What? I'm only saying you hit that. Didn't think it was a secret the way she was going around."

"Yea and you was fucking with some pussy ass nigga who let you get shot."

"Why can't you take a joke? It wasn't that serious." Said Sydney now becoming annoyed.

"I'm good. I got a joke for you though. In a few months, you gonna be big as fuck. Waddling around like a penguin. Chris smiled. They say after the second baby women don't get they shit back the same. I guess it's a good thing I got you on me now, cause after the baby you may be big mama." Sydney rolled her eyes looking down at her chicken now becoming disgusted.

"Whatever. You'll still be fucking this fat bitch." said Sydney glaring at him.

"May not be able to let you ride any more. I want to keep my good back. Chris laughed loudly knowing he had got under her skin. Now, that's some funny shit!"

"Fuck you." said Sydney as she hit him in the arm. Chris stopped at the light he leaned over kissing her cheek.

Once home, Dana arrived shortly after they arrived. Chris had went upstairs to bed and Sydney had placed Natalia in the tub for a quick bath. Sydney pulled Natalia out of the bath in her robe, Dana stood in the hall. Once Sydney walked out of bathroom she followed her inside of Natalia's room. Natalia smiled trying to see the bags she was holding in her hand which were metallic pink. "Stop being so nosey so I can put your clothes on." Sydney hurriedly placed on her diaper and a pink gown. She immediately ran over to Dana who was now sitting on the floor. "Hi muffin! Can I have a hug?" Natalia hugged her quickly before pointing to the bag. Sydney pulled out her phone snapping pictures. Dana helped her pull the items out of the bag. She had bought her stuffed animals Hello Kitty and Minnie Mouse, her favorite movies, sneakers and custom jeweled Timberland boots, and a few outfits. Natalia picked up the Minnie Mouse hugging it close to her body. "Baby!" She replied before running over to her bed. "Thank you soo much Dana. You didn't have to do all of this. We appreciate it!" Sydney hugged her, tears in her eyes.

"It's okay girl. You my ace boon, and I had to make sure my muffin set."

"No really, thank you. You've been such a good friend to me. You're always there for me. I wanted to ask you. Will you be a bridesmaid in my wedding?"

"Are you serious, of course I will. You have become one of my best friends."

"I feel the same. I'm so excited. Do you want anything to drink?"

"Sure, any type of juice." Sydney went downstairs to the kitchen, she came back with a glass of Simply Lemonade, handing it to Dana. Sydney sat down on the recliner with a bottle of water. Dana sat on the ottoman. Natalia grabbed her sip cup of the nightstand laying back in the bed.

"Oh girl I meant to tell you about Vani she's been buggin' lately. She's barely at the salon. She comes in late all the time."

"What?"

"Yeah. Tonight Yogi came in to see her as I was leaving. I was like what the hell is that about."

"Yogi?"

"Yes! He's been calling her and all. They were not that close in past."

"So, she's with him now?"

"I don't know. But, I'm going to find out. Mark hates Yogi and I know she's not trying to get bodied over Yogi punk ass."

"Yea, he's been harassing me too. But, I am not worried about him. All it takes is one call." Sydney stood up going over to Natalia's immaculate closet with its own little island inside. Sydney took down her Disney suitcase she had purchased days ago. She began to pack her suitcase. In about five minutes she was done. She wheeled Natalia's suitcase outside of the door. "We can finish talking in my closet." Sydney tucked Natalia in before turning on her nightlight. Sydney walked over to the double doors at the end of the hall. Dana had never been in their bedroom before. She looked over their immaculate room. Everything was white and gold, white roses, seventy inch television sat on the wall. Dana looked over Chris bundled up in the Versace print duvet. Sydney turned the light on in their closet as each casing lit up Dana looked on in awe and their closet which looked like a department store. Dana quickly took a seat on the chair seated in the back of closet. It was an antique Italian chair which was white with gold accents. "This is nice Sydney! Do you have every Louboutin ever?" Sydney laughed out loud. "I wish. She pulled down their Louis Vuitton luggage. I guess I'm going to have to pack his too. Sydney went to his side of the room and pulled out the rows of jeans, she began to toss a few items into his suitcase. "You never reminded me to hook you up with John."

"Girl… no. She looked over Chris rows of sneakers all brand new, hats, suits and shirts. Everything color coordinated and neat. Does Chris wear half of this, he has in here?"

"Yes and no. He can't wear anything twice, unless its pajamas or something like that. Other than that he will not wear it again.

His shoes it depends. He's petty girl." They both laughed. Sydney began packing her own clothes, they began to chat about Natalia's birthday plans. Once Sydney was done packing, she and Dana walked out of the closet. Chris moved in the bed coughing loudly, they both looked over at him. He grabbed a pillow placing it under his head before snoring again. Sydney rolled her eyes. "Imagine that and Natalia at one time." They both laughed walking out of the room. "Well, you all have a safe trip tomorrow. Take pictures of muffin and Mickey Mouse. Have fun." Dana hugged her. "We will. Thank you again girl." Sydney walked her downstairs to the door. Once she was safely out of the gate, Sydney went back inside locking the door, setting the alarm. Sydney grabbed some Oreos and strawberries before drifting to sleep.

The next morning everyone was dressed and ready for the road by eight thirty, after breakfast. Chris loaded all the luggage in the trunk of the Range Rover including his additional bags he situated for business that morning. He did one last check to make sure things were off in house before locking up. He slid behind the wheel looking back at Natalia and over to Sydney, who had a tan fedora over her head with a curve fitting maxi dress on. Chris' phone rang, it was Preme. "What up?" said Chris.

"Hey son. How are you?"

"Good. About to head down to Orlando for Tubby birthday at Disney."

"Oh a'ight. I wanted to let you know we had to handle some business with Yogi's fuck ass."

"What happened?"

"After you told me about him and Syd situation. I had to handle that, let him know I'm nothing to fuck with. Had some boys run in and do some work. But, you shouldn't have any problems out of that nigga anymore. I got people watching his moves. Tell Syd while this situation hot, to not be out in the streets. Especially since she carrying our boy right now." Chris glanced over to Sydney to see if she was eavesdropping on his conversation. She was looking through her phone. Chris focused back on his conversation, trying not to mention anything to alert her of what they had been speaking of.

"A'ight pop. Text me contacts."

"A'ight be safe." Chris ended the call, Sydney immediately changed the station on the radio as they headed up 95 north.

At the salon Dana came in late as she said she would. It was empty, Vani sat on at her chair sipping a Gatorade as she flipped through a magazine. "What's up? Isn't this a little early for you? I thought I would be opening although I'm late."

"I had a lot on my mind this morning. Dealing with Mark and his bullshit."

"Oh, I understand."

Vani placed the magazine down in her lap. "Do you know Preme?"

"Bentley Preme?"

"Yes, I mean have you ever seen him?"

"Nah, I've never seen him in person. I've heard he's crazy as fuck. Millionaire shit. You know what everyone says about him. What made you think of him? You dating him now?"

"No, I was talking with Trin last night about him, she was telling me about seeing him in a Maybach or some shit."

"Of course she would be sweating his moves with her trifelin' ass. Ain't he old enough to be her daddy though? They both laughed. I saw Yogi come in as I was leaving what was that about?"

"He just wanted to talk, nothing serious."

"To talk? Are you smashing him?"

"Hell no! We're just friends. He's been cool for years. Besides what's with all the questions?"

"Just asking. Why are you so defensive?"

"Whatever." Vani stood up from the chair organizing her counter as Dana began to clean her station. Vani began to pace back and forth as if she was nervous or anxious. Dana looked over at her again. "You good? What is up with you?"

"I'm fine. I told you I've been a little stressed lately! Damn!" Vani stormed back into the sitting area. There was definitely something strange going on with Vani and she was going to get to the bottom of it."

        Sydney and Chris had arrived at the Gaylord Palms resort. Sydney and Natalia were drained from the car ride. Chris said that he would go out and get some food and drinks. In reality, he had some drop offs to handle with a few connections Preme had sent which was the start of a good connection. Preme had made plenty of money with this sophisticated realtor tycoons, known as The Ivy Boys, who used flipping houses and their properties everywhere as a laundering playground. They began to fund their money into the drug game flooding their suburbs with the best white product out, thanks to Preme. Preme knew they would be a perfect fit for Chris, they were professional kept everything legit and Preme never had an issue with them or their teams. The Ivy Boys had crews in Florida, Georgia, California, Las

Vegas, New York and Chicago. As well as internationally. Chris was to meet them in Celebration at one of their vacation homes.

Sydney laid back against the pillow, preparing to take a long nap. Her phone rang loudly on the nightstand. She grimaced picking it up, she looked at the screen it said "Mommy." She rolled her eyes answering.

"Hello."

"Hello Sydney. How are you?"

"I'm good. Hungry and tired."

"Oh, sorry to hear that. How is Natalia? Tell her Happy Birthday."

"I will she's good. We're here in Orlando to take her to Disney for her birthday."

"Aww… take lots of pictures. I called because I had something to tell you. She replied her voice serious. Your father and I have been back together for about three months."

"What?! Why? Serious ma, where is this going?"

"Sydney…stop it."

"I mean, why would you take him back?"

"Sydney I didn't say we were getting married again or anything like that. We are just feeling each other out. He's been in town working on a case, and he is staying at the house. It's been nice."

"I don't know what to say. If you want to deal with his bullshit that's on you."

"Syd, you are being overly dramatic. It's not that serious."

"Fine, be with your ex ma! I just don't want him to leave you again and you are heartbroken."

"I understand what you are saying Sydney. But just like you had to go with your heart and go back to Chris. I have to do the same. I didn't want Chris to hurt you again, but I had to let you figure out your own path and pray for the best."

"So what are you saying?"

"I'm saying. I'm going to try to give Christian another chance, if you can give your father another chance. You know he is the only father you will ever have, on this earth."

"I know. But, I can't stand him. You can't tell him anything, everything always has to be his way."

Ingrid chuckled. "Just like you. You are your father's child."

"I'm not that bad anymore. Natalia changed all of that. Now it's whatever she wants goes… well with Chris." They both laughed.

"I'm really sorry Sydney. I was soo furious when you left here, after all I sacrificed for you. I felt you chose Chris over me and your father. But, I love you so much and I only want the best for you. So, if Chris is what you want I will have to accept it. I don't agree with it, but I'll deal with it. You are my only child. If it will keep you and my grandbabies in my life, I will put my feelings aside. I cannot live my life without seeing my babies grow, and watch you blossom into this beautiful, nurturing mother. So if Christian makes you happy, I can deal with it."

Sydney sat up in the bed, shocked by her mother's apology. "What brought this on? I'm happy but…"

"Life is too short. Your father said he doesn't care for Chris as well. But we are both willing to be civil so that we can have a life with you and the kids. So, we are coming down soon to visit."

"Really? That's great! You are more than welcome to stay at our home. I will have to let Chris know. But it'll be fine." Natalia turned over screaming in bed, as if she had a bad dream. "Mommy...Mommy!" she screamed. "I'm right here mama. What's wrong?" Sydney caressed her back gently. "Aww... is she okay?" Sydney handed her a sip cup she began to drink as she rubbed her eyes. "She's fine ma. Probably had a bad dream." "Oh, poor bella. Tell her happy birthday from me and her Papi. We love you both."

"We love you too ma. See you soon!" After they said their goodbyes, Sydney sat shocked at her mother's revelation.

Chris returned two hours later. He saw the room service plates on the table, as he walked in with Cheesecake factory and cartons of juice for Natalia. Sydney and Natalia were sleeping. Chris walked in placing the plates and drink down. He immediately stripped off his shirt, tossing it to the chair. He walked over to Sydney bending to kiss her cheek. "Wake up ma." He smiled at her as she wiped her face looking around confused. "Where have you been?"

"Had to go see unc and handle a few things. Store is not near here had to go out in the boonies."

"You should've told me we would've went with you."

"Nah, it's good you needed your rest. Sydney sat up in bed looking over to Natalia. She touched her diaper to see if she was wet, which she knew she would be. She reached over to her bag and began to change her diaper as she slept. Sydney's phone rang she looked at the screen it stated Monica. She answered the phone. "Hi Monica."

"Hello, Sydney. How are you? Hope, I am not interrupting you?"

"No, not at this moment. We came to Orlando to Disney for Natalia's birthday."

"That's awesome. I don't want to intrude too much. I found some locations I was going to ask you to come look at tomorrow, but that's okay, enjoy your vacation and I will send you pictures of locations."

"That's great. We will be back Monday. How about I meet with you Tuesday morning."

"Sounds good to me. How's Christian?"

"He's good. Taking it day to day. It's going to take him awhile to process everything."

"I understand. I'd love to talk to him whenever he wants. I have pictures and information I'd like to share with him."

"That's great. But, you will have to let Chris in his own time come around about Maria situation. That is a very sensitive subject for him."

"I understand. But, I look forward to meeting with you Tuesday. Enjoy!"

"Thank you." Sydney ended the call looking over to Chris who was looking to her as in who you talking to. "Monica, found some locations we may be interested in and she asked how you were doing. Sydney got up washing her hands. She went over to the bags of food. She began to warm up their plates. Chris walked over to the couch. Oh babe, guess what?! Mommy called and apologized!"

"What?! That's good for her acting like an adult. After saying all that dumb shit."

"Yea, that's not the half. Her and my dad are hooking up again..." Chris looked over at Sydney as if he was shocked. "I know. But, the crazy part is that they are supposedly coming down soon, so that we all can sit down and talk."

Chris laughed. "What the fuck we need to talk about?"

"I mean, I guess for us all to get along."

"Whatever. I can be cool with them from a distance for my kids. We don't have to be on this fake shit though."

"Well, you know that when you marry me, you're marrying them as well."

"Like hell. They are only the kid's grandparents and barely that. Your punk ass daddy haven't done one thing for Natalia. Regardless if he fuck with me or not, that's his fuckin' granddaughter." Sydney thought about it, Chris did have a valid point. He never called to check on her or ever bought her anything.

"Well, if that is how you feel, you can tell him that at the meeting."

"Syd, I don't care what they think of me. I take care of my family, keep a roof over your head and food on the table. Fuck them." Sydney brought his plate over to him, rolling her eyes to his comments about her parents. Chris' phone rang, he looked down at the screen, sighing before answering. "Hello Chris, this is Grant Vaciani am I interrupting you?"

"What up?"

"They are pushing the date up. Will need you to come here possibly by the second. There's another person of interest. Which should put you out of getting maximum time."

"What happened to no time?"

"Chris that may be impossible. I'm speaking with the codefendant's lawyer now. The sooner you can come the better. I need to talk to you."

"I will see what I can do. Right now, you interrupting dinner with my family with this bullshit! I'll get there when I can, you handle it."

"Ok…" Chris ended the call. Sydney looked over to him, as she began to blow the mashed potatoes on her fork to feed Natalia. "I don't want to talk about It." said Chris. Sydney rolled her eyes at him, feeding Natalia. The next morning around seven, Sydney woke up to use the bathroom. Chris and Natalia were both sound asleep. Sydney looked over his iPhone which was on top of the table. Sydney couldn't believe his phone was unlocked. She went thru his call log, tip toeing back to the bathroom. Sydney called the number back from last night. "Hello Chris?" said a male voice.

"No, this is his fiancé Sydney. I was calling out when is his court date."

"It's August fourth."

"What charges is he looking at this time?"

"I can't give that to you right now."

"How much time is he looking at?"

"Possible to have zero to two years at this point."

"Two years! Sydney shouted. I'm pregnant! We are supposed to get married next year."

"Calm down, ma'am. What I need is for Chris to get up here as soon as possible. August second at the latest, but he is giving me a hard time."

"Oh, I will make sure he is there a soon as possible."

"Thank you. I will talk to you soon ma'am."

Sydney ended the call, creeping back out to the room to place the phone back in its previous location. She looked over at Chris again to make sure he was sleeping. She walked back into the bathroom to take a shower, once out wrapped in a towel, she looked through the luggage for her bag. It didn't help all of the luggage was Louis Vuitton. She bent down unzipping the bags one by one: the first was Chris' clothes, the second Tati's shoes and toys, the third was full of money. Sydney picked up one of the bricks of money. *Why would he have all of this? This is over two hundred and fifty g's.* Natalia began to toss and turn on the bed, before waking up completely. She sat up looking around the room. Sydney picked up the last bag which she knew was hers. "Happy Birthday mommy's baby." Natalia smiled crawling over to the edge of the bed where Sydney was standing. Sydney picked her up kissing her face, she decided to order room service. She googled in her phone bakeries, and looked up some of their work she decided on a Publix Hello Kitty cake, which she insisted would have to be ready today. The manager ensured her they would make it happen. Sydney placed Natalia in the tub for a bath. Halfway thru her bath Chris woke up, Sydney gathered Natalia out of the tub, so that Chris could use the bathroom. "Happy Birthday Tubby." Said Chris affectionately as he kissed her cheek. She giggled playfully. Chris kissed Sydney's forehead as he walked towards the bathroom.

Sydney began to dress Natalia in a Minnie Mouse shirt, a pair of distressed jeans, and Jordan sneakers on her feet. She began to brush her hair up into a top knot. Chris walked out of the bathroom, walking over to the closet. He walked over to the bed where they were seated with a Tiffany & Co bag, which was robin's egg blue. Sydney's eyes widened as she saw the bag. "You didn't buy Tati Tiffany?"

"Why not?" Sydney took the bag from Chris opening the jewelry box. It was a platinum diamond charm bracelet with custom charms. One of the charms was Hello Kitty, Peruvian flag, a globe, and the Tiffany & Co logo charm. On the back of the charm it said: *To my Tubby, Love always Daddy.* "Aww... this is so sweet baby."

"Yea, it's got a key to it so no one can open it or take it off without it."

"Where are the keys?"

"One in the safe. The other on the end of my necklace." Chris took out the key which was attached to his necklace. He unlocked the bracelet, Sydney placed it on Natalia's wrist. Natalia smiled at how the diamonds illuminated in the light. "How much was this?" said Sydney.

Chris smiled. "Let's just say mami can trade this in on an E class."

"What?" Sydney looked over the bracelet again, thinking of the fact that her baby was wearing a car on her wrist. "That's my baby. I'll do anything for my princess."

In Connecticut, Tarik had met up with his lawyer at his office. His lawyer had informed him that he may be looking at serving some time, being that the witness was ready to testify. "Look... I'm not doing any fuckin' time! I'm not snitching on nobody that shit out the question."

"They are going to try to pin all of this on you. Pulling bigger charges such as attempted murder. We have to be smart here Tarik."

"I don't give a fuck! Fuck that bitch!" Tarik threw a book which was on top of the desk at the wall. His lawyer rolled his eyes. "Look Christian, is already pleading not guilty, one of you is going down. We have to make sure it is not you."

"Have you seen Chris yet?" said Tarik.

"No one has."

"Look Gavin... I don't give a fuck what you have to do! Eric and Ben told me you got them out of a lot of shit! You better do the same for me! Fix it."

"That was different. It was personal." Said Gavin as he adjusted his cuff links.

"Well, make this shit personal, I can't do no time!"

"You need to be logical here. They are going to put one of you away." Gavin placed his papers inside of his suitcase.

"All I'm saying is it better not be me. Bitch, deserved to be beat."

"Well, you need to figure out what you are willing to do. Chris and his team are willing to do whatever, to have this placed all on you."

"I'm not a snitch, nigga!" said Tarik defensively as he hopped out of his seat.

"You need to figure out what you are willing to do. I will be out of town for a week, visiting my daughter. I'll be in touch." Gavin got up out of his seat, ready to escort Tarik to the door. "You better fix this shit." said Tarik as he walked out the door. Gavin's phone rang he answered as he walked over to gather his things. "Hi, I spoke to Sydney. They are in Orlando at Disney for the baby's birthday. I told her that we were to come down and she said that was fine."

"That's good. I forgot about Natalia's birthday, can you pick something up for me. This case may take more time than expected, we may only have a few days down there to reconcile with her."

"That's fine, it'll be good for all of us to be together again. I will let her know. When are you coming home?"

"In about an hour."

"See you later hun."

Meanwhile at Disney, with the park hopper's pass, Sydney and Chris had been to Animal Kingdom and Magic Kingdom. They had rode the tea cups and carousel, as well as met a few of the big characters as they came off the trolley at the entrance. Natalia had eaten ice cream, soda and candy. She had a life size Mickey and now it was three-thirty she was exhausted. She was sleeping in her stroller. Sydney decided to leave the park to pick up the cake and get her toys she wanted to purchase for her birthday. She wanted to stop by Toys R Us, which Chris felt made no since. Sydney had wanted to get her a play kitchen and house. "Syd, why don't we go to the store once we get home, so we don't have to ride on the road with all these boxes in trunk?"

"Fine, I'll wait!" said Sydney with an attitude.

"What's wrong with you?" said Chris defensively. Sydney's phone rang interrupting their conversation.

"Happy birthday muffin! Screamed Dana." Sydney laughed out loud. "Thank you girl. She's in her car seat knocked out."

"Aww…Disney wore her out huh."

Sydney quickly switched over two lanes of traffic without looking in her mirror, after seeing a Walmart sign. "Where are you going?" said Chris angrily.

"To Walmart." Said Sydney as she made a u turn in the middle of the street.

"Do you need to get off the fuckin' phone 'cause you obviously can't do two things at once?"

"I'm good. I needed to make a u turn. Calm down."

"When are you guys coming back?"

"Probably tomorrow."

"Okay, enjoy your vacay just wanted to tell muffin happy birthday."

Sydney ended the call, glancing over to Chris who was holding his stomach. "Damn... fuckin' stomach bothering me." Sydney pulled up to the red light, Chris opened the door, vomiting on the pavement.

"Oh my god. Are you okay?" said Sydney as she looked over to him.

"Yea. He drank some water, swishing it around in his mouth before spitting it out as well. The car beside them, driver looked over disgusted, their window down. "What the fuck?" the women replied. "You got a fuckin' problem?" said Chris as he looked over to them. The women immediately faced forward, slowly rolling up their window. Chris closed the door, looking down at his shirt to make sure he was clean.

"Are you okay?"

"Yes. That damn salty ass pretzel I ate. I'm good, now."

In Miami, Yogi had stopped by Vani's salon to go over final details of their plan. Vani was now hesitant about now dealing with Preme and the repercussions. She was already leery of the wrath of Chris but now knowing Preme was his family, she was having second thoughts. The salon was clear, Vani locked up after him knowing the level of their conversation. "I've been thinking, we not going to take the baby from here. I think it will be better if we get her while she's sleeping."

"I've told you before that is not going to work. Chris' crib is like Fort Knox, it's not happening. I told you the best plan was to get her from here while Sydney has her! You can't keep changing the plan." Said Vani nervously. She didn't like that he was being sloppy.

"A'ight you make sure she bringing her here this week and I'll come scoop her up."

"I thought I was gonna keep the baby."

"You are. But, somebody got to kidnap the bitch. I got people in place to make this shit look official. All I need is for you to keep your end of this shit, by making sure she in place."

"I got you, said Vani."

"What up? Don't be backing out now. We in this shit together!"

"I hear you. I'm just worried about P, what if he knows? You didn't say shit about him when you brought this shit to me."

"Look, fuck Preme he'll be out of town soon anyway. He doesn't know shit! Yogi grabbed Vani's arm, tightening his grip. I thought you were a ride or die bitch! Get your fucking head together! Wednesday afternoon we doing this shit!" there was a knock at the glass, it was Dana. Vani nodded her head in agreement, before shrugging him off of her arm. Yogi walked over to the door, Vani unlocked it letting him out and Dana in. Dana looked over Yogi, seeing the grip he had on Vani from the door. Once Yogi was out of sight, Vani placed her hand up. "Don't ask me shit!"

"Why are you so defensive?"

"Because I know you're about to ask twenty questions and I'm in no mood for that shit today."

"I'm not saying shit, but how is Mark feel about this new friendship." "Fuck Mark." Said Vani hastily.

In Orlando, Sydney and Chris were in Walmart. Chris was still holding his stomach as if he was in pain. "Why don't you go over to the pharmacy section and get you some Pepto Bismol for your stomach?"

"Why don't you get it? You're my woman." Said Chris sarcastically. Sydney looked over to him rolling her eyes. They were a section over from pharmacy, Sydney walked over with the cart finding it and tossing it in the cart. "What's wrong with you?"

"I'm fine." said Sydney with an attitude.

Chris leaned in to her. "Are you mad about not going to the fuckin' toy store? If you want to go to the damn store, let's go. I don't want to see you pouting all fuckin' day."

"Don't start with me, Chris."

"I'm just saying you could've did that shit days ago. You knew when her birthday was, why wait until the last minute."

"Chris, leave me alone."

"Whatever Syd. I'll call you when I'm done in here." Chris had Natalia in his arms. Sydney looked over to him. "Leave her with me." "What?" said Chris. "You heard me." said Sydney defiantly. "Like she want to be stuck over here with you." Sydney walked over to Chris with her arms out. Natalia reached for her. She placed her inside of the cart. Chris looked over to her. "Bye." Said Sydney as she looked to Chris. "When I'm ready to go, be ready." Sydney walked back over towards the toy department, she picked out a few books, Frozen toys as well as a Minion stuffed toy Natalia had picked up herself. She picked up a few leap frog games as well. She received a text from her mother stating that they would only be staying a few days instead of the week. She went over to Electronics and ended up picking up the Sex and the City series. She immediately thought about Tori and Nadine, this was their favorite show. They would have sleepovers watching seasons back to back. She decided to call Nadine. The phone rang six times, when a man answered the phone. "Is Nadine there?" said Sydney.

"Nah, she not here right now. Who this?"

"Um… just tell her Sydney called."

"Sydney? How you doing ma?"

"Who is this?" said Sydney with an attitude.

"It's Tarik. Sydney froze. What are you doing with Nadine? I thought you left deadbeat." Replied Sydney bluntly.

He chuckled. "She told you that. hmmph. How Chris doing? You need to tell him to call me."

"Why does he need to call you?"

"Tell him to hit me up at this number."

"Bye." Sydney ended the call, tossing her phone in her Birkin. She walked towards the front thinking of getting some fruit. As she approached the aisle she immediately spotted Chris, looking over the grapes. There was a woman beside him in a pair of Adidas tights and tank. Sydney peeped the way she was leaning beside Chris trying to attract his attention. Chris reached for a bag of grapes. The woman leaned in to him. "Excuse me cutie. I need one of the half bags below you." "My bad." Chris backed up to let the woman move in front of him. She arched her back, bending in front of him. *Bitch.* Thought Sydney. She decided to send in reinforcement. She picked up Natalia. "Go get daddy Tubby." Natalia smiled as Sydney placed her down on the floor. She immediately took off towards his legs. Once she spotted him she hugged his legs, giggling. "Daddy!" Chris smiled looking down at who was on his leg. He picked Natalia up. "Hey tubby. Where is your mommy?" The woman looked over Natalia. "She's adorable." "Thank you." Sydney came over with the cart, she looked directly into Chris' eyes. "Are you ready to go?"

"Yea." Natalia smiled, looking at Sydney. "Mommy, cup?" The girl immediately sized up Sydney realizing their conversation was over. "Aww… baby I forgot your cup in the car. Mommy will go get one of the shelf and get you a drink." Sydney walked over to get the cup while at the register she picked out a Simply Lemonade Raspberry, she poured it into the cup handing it to Natalia. As they headed up to the register Chris looked over what was in the cart. "Why don't you ever get shit I like?" said Chris.

"What? I get things for you?" Sydney replied defensively.

"Nah, you don't. But, it's a'ight that's just you."

"What are you saying I'm selfish?"

"I didn't say shit. You did."

"That's what you are implying. I'm not selfish. I do a lot of things for you, some that I'm not going to mention in public."

"Go ahead we're adults."

"No, I'm not. I can't believe you said that about me." Chris' phone rang it was Preme. "What up pop?"

"Hey, we've been tapping that clowns calls. He got something going on with that girl who owns the salon, blonde haired on union."

"So what we doing?"

"I got a wire set up on that bitch car. We'll know something by Wednesday. I want you to stop by the club when you come back home. Also, I want you out of Reign for a while. I've been hearing niggas from New York in town and been stopping through the store. I only say that shit because you have the baby with you, can't have these pop ups."

"New York niggas? What you thinking?"

"You already know. Come by once you get here." Chris walked over to get a cold Sprite, he placed it on the counter. Chris handed the cashier cash for the order. Once out in the parking lot placing the bags in the trunk. Sydney placed Natalia inside the car in her car seat. "I can't believe you called me selfish." She walked over to him at the trunk. "You are selfish, when it comes to me. I do things for you all the time without you asking. I have to ask you."

"So, why are you with me if I'm so selfish and don't care about you? And if you say 'cause I'm a good fuck I'm going to slap the shit out of you." Chris smiled.

"Because I love your selfish ass." Sydney rolled her eyes walking over towards the passenger door. Chris pushed the cart to the side. He walked over to Sydney he placed his arms around her body, kissing her neck. "Stop. Why are you so mean to me?"

"I'm not being mean. I'm being honest. Why can't you accept it?"

"I'm not. What about the fact that you have issues?"

"I one hundred percent accept the fact that I have issues. I don't deny it." Sydney slid into the car. Chris closed the trunk, walking over to the driver's side. They stopped by to pick up the cake. That night they had a party inside the room where Sydney took plenty of pictures of Natalia with her cake.

The next morning Chris woke up early to stop by Darren's as well do a few drop offs and making new connections. He had gotten rid of all the keys he brought with him. He arrived back at the room around noon. Sydney and Natalia were in bed watching cartoons. Chris walked over kissing them both. "Where were you?" said Sydney.

"Had to stop by Unc's." Sydney looked over to him rolling her eyes.

"I'm going to take a shower." Minutes later Chris heard the water inside the shower. Natalia was laying back on the bed minutes from sleep herself. Chris walked over towards the shower stripping off his shirt. Chris came in looking over Sydney's naked body in the shower. She looked over hearing him come in. "Why are you in here?" said Sydney as she washed her legs.

"Why am I in here? Your mine, that's why I'm in here." said Chris with a smile. Chris stripped his clothes off before stepping into the shower with Sydney. "Where is Natalia?" "Sleeping." Said Chris. Chris began to caress his fingers over her body. Sydney turned towards him. "Baby stop…"

"Why?"

"Because, I said so." She continued washing herself ignoring his advances.

"So, you telling me you don't want me?" said Chris.

"I'm telling you I don't want you bothering me."

Chris smiled. "I'm bothering you? a'ight. I'll leave you alone. It's gonna be a long trip back to Miami." He quickly rinsed himself off before stepping out of the shower to allow Sydney to be alone. Chris changed into a pair of Givenchy joggers and white tee. Sydney placed on a maxi dress, Sophia Webster sandals. Chris was texting on his phone Sydney picked up Natalia placing her on a tunic and pair of leggings by DKNY. She began to brush her hair. Chris looked over at her. "Look at my princess. Looking just like her daddy." Chris reached over kissing her cheek.

"And I guess I was just the storage that carried her for nine months."

"You mad or nah? You might want to chill on that before the baby look like me too."

"It's not all about you Chris." Said Sydney sternly.

"Something you want to say to me Syd? What's good?"

"I think I just did. Everything is not about you!"

"I'm not hearing that shit. Cause there ain't another nigga like me. No nigga even part of my pedigree."

"Whatever. I'm not about to go here with you. Because all you want to do is talk about Christian Garcia and I will not entertain it today."

Chris smiled. "Ma, don't hate me 'cause I'm a fly ass nigga. You never had a nigga like me. All those punk fucks you were with never showed you the shit I did."

Sydney rolled her eyes. "What's that, a broken nose?" Sydney picked Natalia up allowing her to roam on the floor. "Why you always gotta go there with the low blows?" said Chris he reached over to hold her.

"Chris, please leave me alone."

"What's up? I can't fuckin' touch you. You don't want to talk to me. What is this your hormones? What's on your mind?"

"I don't want to fuckin' talk about it." Sydney replied mimicking Chris.

"Whatever Syd." Chris gathered the bags together to take them to the car. The vacation was definitely over. Sydney did one last check before packing up their last items heading over to the elevator. Chris said he would be at the desk checking out. Sydney and Natalia were on the elevator, as the door began to close two men stepped on the elevator. Sydney looked over at the two gorgeous muscular chocolate men, who were in tanks and shorts as if they were headed to the pool. One of the men looked over to Sydney his beard full, he had almond shaped brown eyes. He smiled at her. "How are you today beautiful?" Sydney looked away. "I'm talking to you. I'm definitely not talking to him." Sydney blushed. "I'm good." She replied pursing her lips. "Your little one is pretty like her mom. He extended his hand out. BJ." Sydney shook his hand. He looked at her waiting for her name. When he realized it wasn't happening. Are you from around here?"

"No… Connecticut."

"Oh okay. I'm from Philly. How long you here?"

"I'm leaving today."

"Well can we exchange numbers, and meet up sometime."

"You can give me your number." Said Sydney.

"Okay, here is my number and email, friend." He replied with a smile. His smile was bright and white as he handed her his business card. It said BJ Clark, Owner of a promotion company. "So, can I at least have your name?" The elevator stopped. Sydney smiled. "Honeydip02 at gmail dot com." Sydney exited out of the elevator a smile on her face. The front desk was located in front of the elevator. Chris had walked in and seen them all exiting the elevator and the smile which was plastered to Sydney's face. Sydney walked over to him. "Who's that?" said Chris.

"What?" said Sydney nonchalant.

"The niggas you smiling at on the elevator. Do I need to catch another case Syd?"

"I don't know. Do you?" Sydney walked past him. "Syd, dead ass… you know I will make a fuckin' scene in this bitch. Don't try me!" Sydney reached in the baby bag for a wipe to clean Natalia's nose. When she turned back around Chris was at the counter by the men from the elevator. *Shit.* Sydney played it cool walking towards the door. Chris was at the counter talking to the woman behind the counter. The men looked over to Chris. "What's good?" The men ignored him. Sometimes karma was a bitch, today it was in the form of an overzealous two year old. "Daddy! She screamed. Hi Daddy!" Chris looked back at Sydney. "Come here mama." Sydney rolled her eyes, she attempted to place Natalia to her feet so she could walk over to him. She began to curl her legs, climbing on to Sydney's arm. "No." She began to cry saying that she didn't want to walk but be carried over to Chris. Chris pulled out cash to pay for the room. Once Sydney approached him, he reached over to pick Natalia up. She kissed Chris' cheek. Sydney tried not to make eye contact with BJ and his friend.

Chris smirked. "You don't want to talk to your niggas you was smiling and shit with on the elevator?"

"Chris don't." replied Sydney.

"Don't what? What's good? Don't front like you wasn't cheesing and shit with these punk ass niggas." BJ looked over pissed at his comments. "There a problem nigga?" said BJ to Chris' outbursts. The clerk handed Chris his receipt. "Yea, I got a problem. What the fuck you gonna do about it?" said Chris as he stared into BJ'S face. Sydney came in between them. "Look... stop. It was nothing Chris. Let it go." She placed her hands on his chest. BJ looked over Chris with an ice grill. "A'ight ma. Get your friend. See you later." BJ then touched Sydney's chin. Chris eyes widened, he quickly bitch slapped BJ across the face. Sydney quickly grabbed Chris by the shirt pulling him away. "Chris let it go. You have the baby." "Touch her again bitch. What's good?" His friend jumped in between them, grabbing BJ. Sydney pulled Chris away. Once the friend got BJ out of the building pleading with him they had a baby, don't retaliate. Chris handed her Natalia. "Don't say shit to me Syd." Chris soon picked up his pace, to meet BJ out the door. Sydney realized Chris was looking for BJ to retaliate, the parking lot was clear. She exhaled, thinking the problem had been adverted. She looked over to Chris he was vexed. It would be a long trip back to Miami. Chris got behind the wheel, soon veering over into traffic.

"You better be fuckin' happy Tubby in this car. Because the way I feel right now, I should slap the shit out of you!"

"What? I didn't do anything! screamed Sydney like an angry child. The guy was only talking to me! You get so jealous, you can't try to kill every nigga that talks to me.

"Syd, shut the fuck up." Chris glanced at the cars to the side of him. A car slid in front of him causing him to slam on the brakes to avoid hitting their bumper. Sydney grabbed the dashboard. Chris blew the horn throwing up his finger. The car blew their horn back, as they merged into the turning lane. Chris pulled beside the car. The driver was a mixed woman early twenties, in a Nissan Altima, with their window down. Chris rolled his window down. "Watch where the fuck you going dumb bitch!"

The woman yelled something back. "What the fuck you say?!" Chris placed the car in park as he exited the car. The woman now scared, became silent. "Get out the fucking car bitch! Cut in front of me again bitch, blow the tires off this raggedy shit!" Sydney was so embarrassed. Chris walked back over to the car sliding in. "I can't believe you did that?!"

"Bitch, shouldn't have cut in front of me."

"Your temper is worst than before. You need to go to anger management."

"I don't need you telling me what the fuck I need!" Chris began speeding down the highway. Sydney immediately felt dejavu to the night of the concert. In hour into the car ride home, Chris had calmed down a bit. Sydney knew he was still furious. She lowered the volume on the stereo. "Why are you so angry with me? I haven't done anything to you."

"Don't come at me with that bullshit Syd! You've had a fucked up attitude all morning. The fuck you mean you haven't done shit!"

"Why are you still hiding shit from me?" said Sydney.

"Man... Syd, you can dead it with this fuck shit."

"How are we ever going to make it married if we can even make a weekend together?"

"Stop coming at me with the dumb shit. getting on my fuckin' nerves! You so fuckin' selfish and petty my nigga."

"How the fuck am I selfish when I try to talk to you. You push me away. I'm tired of having to baby you to get a fucking answer out of you!"

"Baby me? You play too much."

"Do you see me laughing? Sometimes, I don't even think you care about how I feel or what you say to me. You treat me at times like I'm just some random bitch for you to fuck."

Chris looked over to her. "That's how you think I feel?"

"Yes that's how I feel. See I can be open and talk to you." said Sydney.

Chris immediately smirked into a scowl. "Why would I just fuck you… there's plenty of bitches to fuck. What would make you think you were special?"

Sydney rolled her eyes, "Fuck you!" She shouted holding back the tears from streaming down her face. Nicki Minaj's "I lied" came through the speakers. She hated that he could always hurt her feelings with his heartless words.

"Fuck me? We already been there and done that shit."

Chris looked into the rearview looking at Natalia. Thinking about his pending case. He turned the music back up. Sydney wiped her tears, looking out the window. Refusing to give Chris any eye contact, she placed her Chanel frames over her eyes. She looked over the enormous rock on her finger. The ring in this moment meant nothing. As she listened to the lyrics of Nicki Minaj she drifted off to sleep. She awoke hours later realizing they were home in the driveway, and she was alone. She immediately became furious that Chris left her in the car until she heard him in the trunk. She removed the shades from her eyes, exiting the car. She stretched looking over to Chris. She walked over to the trunk, deciding to let their argument go and be the bigger person. "Babe, I'm sorry. I had a great time this weekend, and I apologize for being selfish."

Chris looked over to her. "Syd, you can't treat me like shit all day and expect me to just let that shit go."

"I know. I'm sorry." She walked over to him, kissing his chin and lips. Chris smirked. "Now you want me..." Sydney turned towards the front door going into the house. She had spoken her peace, she knew Chris would have to forgive in his own time, but she was not about to argue with him.

It was now Wednesday, Sydney had been up early to take Natalia to her doctor's appointment. She and Chris had sort of made up, they were speaking to each other, but no kisses or hugs. Sydney had planned something special for Chris tonight. They had arranged for Preme to keep Natalia tonight. She would pay for a top chef to come into their home and make them a romantic dinner. Her parents were coming on Friday, everything was set. She looked over to Natalia and Chris who were bundled up under each other. Sydney then thought what if Chris did time. How would that affect Natalia? She loved her Daddy, and he was world. They both were always connected to each other. Maybe Chris was right, she had been selfish. Only thinking of how situations would affect her. Natalia's well-being was the most important. If he did a year, what would she do? They had separated in the past but it was never for a period of months where she couldn't see or talk to him. She woke up Natalia getting her ready. Chris soon woke up as Sydney was in the closet. Sydney placed an outfit out for Chris which was inside of a Givenchy bag. They left out the door to the appointment, Sydney had a busy day. The doctor stated Natalia was fine and didn't have an ear infection. She had a few teeth coming in, which caused her to be more irritable. As she was in the drive thru at Chick fil-a Chris called. "Hey babe. She's good. Just a few teeth coming in."

"Oh that's good. Where are you?"

"I'm at Chick fil-a. You want something? I can bring it by before I go to meet with Monica."

"Nah, I'm good. I'll see y'all later."

"Okay. Ask Preme what time he wants Natalia."

Sydney ended the call and another call came through it was Dana. "Hey girl! What are you up to?"

"Getting some food. About to meet with wedding planner."

"Oh okay. Are you and muffin still coming up to the salon today?"

"We may. I'm so busy today, although I wanted a fill in on my nails. I have to get things together for me and Chris' romantic evening."

"Oh, no worries. Have fun do what you have to do. But, I wanted to tell you I have a new boo from Chicago named Devin. We have to talk girl! He's really sweet he brings me flowers to work. It's only been two weeks but he's a sweetheart."

"Oh my god! Girl, we have to go out to lunch tomorrow and you spill this tea! I'm so happy for you."

"But, call me later okay."

"Okay, girl." Dana ended the call. Vani sat in her chair on pins and needles awaiting her answer. "Is she bringing the baby by?"

"Probably not. She and Chris are busy. No biggie." Vani tried to hide her worried expression. If Sydney didn't bring Natalia by their plan would be ruined. Who knows what Yogi's next plan would be, she thought. "Oh man, it's been forever since I saw Natalia…" said Vani faking.

"It's okay she will probably be by this weekend."

Vani looked down at her phone it was Yogi. She looked over to Dana and walked outside to take the call. "Yea, we gonna come through around six."

"She's not coming today."

"What?! Don't fuckin' play with me bitch! We going over to his house!"

"You can't do that!"

"Fuck that. We going to that nigga crib at eleven tonight!"

"Yogi listen!"

"I'll be at the shop at ten thirty."

Vani sat shook. What had she gotten into?

Sydney and Monica had went out to look at a few locations. Sydney's mind was preoccupied with a million thoughts, she couldn't focus on wedding locations. The first two they had seen were not perfect enough for her or grand enough. She looked over to Monica thinking she should ask her questions now that the two of them were alone. "Why didn't you try to contact Chris after he left the home? Did you know he had been released or?"

"I wasn't able to have any communication with him. I sent a letter to him in the home and it was returned to sender. I tried to call and find information on his case worker and men were at my door the next day. I was petrified. Maria had kept Chris secluded from us. To be honest I didn't know if he was even receptive to having us in his life."

"Chris was a child! He needed family. He didn't have anybody. Do you know how that must have felt?"

"I know. I beat myself up for years for not trying harder. After the threats and thugs I was nervous, scared and paranoid. My life had been watched, every move they let me know they were on me."

"I understand what you are saying. But, please put yourself in his shoes he has the right to be hurt. He was abandoned. Lost his mother... It's heartbreaking." Monica nodded her head wiping tears from her eyes. They arrived at Fontainebleau, and Sydney immediately fell in love with the ballrooms, crystal chandeliers and lighting. She could already envision saying her vows on the secluded cabana over the pool. "Oh this amazing I want ivory everything and gold. Original invitations, flowers everywhere. Let me film this for Chris. We want this!" Sydney raised her iphone above her to try to take in all of the scenery. Dressed in a white v neck top and white low rise skinny jeans, her shirt began to raise as she tried to film. Her pudge showing slightly as well as her King Christian tattoo. Monica smiled seeing the top of her tattoo. "You really love Christian huh?"

"Yes. You know how you can love someone so much it hurts that's how I feel about Chris. I feel without him there is no me. He is the best and worst of me." Sydney smiled tears forming in her eyes. After jotting down a few notes they headed back over to Monica's Mercedes. She unlocked the trunk, walking over. "I have something here for Chris." She took the top of the storage box. Sydney glanced over the items inside. There was pictures, and letters inside. Sydney picked up one of the pictures of a five year old Christian. "There is some letters in here from the lawyers, and mama about the custody case. Maybe it can answer a lot of questions for Chris and he can make sense of it." Sydney looked at one of the pictures of a beautiful baby girl in the tub. "Wow. Is this Maria?"

"Yea, she was about two in that picture Mama said."

"Wow! Natalia looks just like her!" Sydney put the top back on the box, becoming excited to show the contents to Chris. "Thank you. I know Chris will love this." She hugged Monica before they got back into the car heading back to her office.

Once in her car Sydney stopped by Agent Provocateur, for the Darcia playsuit she had been wanting to wear tonight. She stopped to get a few oils and candles. The florist called and said the flowers were on their way to the house. She headed out of the store to the parking lot. A woman walked in her direction her eyes glued to Sydney. She looked up realizing it was Tatiana. "Hey girl! Don't stare you can at least say hello." Said Sydney with a smile. Tatiana rolled her eyes at Sydney as she approached her. "Fuck you. Your punk ass man broke my window. He is going to pay for it."

"Your right my man. But, why you so mad though? I thought you were some model, Instagram hoe or something? You haven't gotten that raggedy shit fixed yet?"

"Fuck you, bitch! If you wouldn't have gotten shot, Chris would have been with me!"

"Aw… that's cute, you mad. Sydney smiled again at her. See what you hoes seem to fail to realize is that dick was always mine, boo. Always have been and always will be."

"Oh really? If that was always your dick why was it fucking and sucking me?"

Sydney sighed. "You were renting that dick, I own it. How'd my kitty taste when it was all over your lips? Sydney reached into her Birkin. So, I'm only going to say this once. Stay away from my man and my store. She took out a stack of money. Here is some change to fix your bum ass window, your bitch ass life, those wack ass brows and last year's Loubou's on your feet. That should be enough to upgrade your life and that bum ass car you keep whining about." Sydney handed her the money. Tatiana frowned up her face. "Bitch, don't act like you can't use this to fix your life. Don't let your feelings fuck up your blessing." Tatiana took the money. "See, I can be nice. Just to think I was originally going to pop you in the mouth with it. Have a blessed day." Sydney walked over to her car Tatiana looked over the cash it was at least twenty thousand dollars.

Sydney looked at her phone it was after three. She headed home to let the chef and his team in. She realized she had enough time to stop by to get her hair done quickly. Dana said she could get her in, since Vani had just left. Sydney rushed into the salon. "Thank you Dana, for hooking me up real quick. Just want some old Hollywood curls to go with my dress tonight."

"Girl, you know I got you. When you coming to let me get those nails?"

"Saturday definitely. Look at my toes." Dana laughed. "Your toes are fine. Just swollen."

Chris stopped by Preme's to check on Natalia as well as talk to him about his plans. When he walked into the house and back into his office, he saw Natalia in her playroom which Preme had created downstairs. He peeked his head in. "What up mama?" Natalia smiled running over to his legs. He picked her up kissing her before placing her back down to play with her kitchen set. Chris walked over to Preme's office. "What up Pop." Preme stopped the tapes he was listening to. "Hey son. He hugged him, sitting back in his seat. What's going on?"

"Court date coming up. I'm flying out to Connecticut on Friday morning. I leave at eight and I haven't told Syd yet."

"Why not?"

"Because I don't want her worrying and stressing with the baby. I'll be good."

"Yea, I told Grant you better be good or it's his ass."

"Ready for this shit to be over."

"I've had Loco watching Yogi moves. He said nigga been staying low key and that he may be fuckin' girl at shop, haven't heard anything else."

"I need you to watch the house and keep an eye on Syd while I'm away."

"I got you. What are you and Syd doing tonight?"

"I don't know. I'm just supposed to show up at eight." Said Chris with a smile as he checked his watch. Preme stood up to walk Chris to the door. Meanwhile, Sydney's hair was done and she quickly paid Dana rushing home. The food smelled amazing as Sydney had the assistants to help with the flower display. The pianist came and set up on the grand piano which was located in their white room. Which was dimly lit with candles and white rose bouquets everywhere. Sydney went upstairs for a shower and got their bedroom ready as well. Once out the shower she changed into an Emilio Pucci black ruffled gown which fell off the shoulder and also accentuated her growing bump. Giuseppe Zanotti Crystal patterned sandals with four and a half inch heel. She placed her diamond earrings in her ear as well as jewelry on her wrists. She lightly bronzed her face, and applied Chanel Passion lipstick to her lips. She could smell the food and immediately became hungry. She walked downstairs, looking over the dining area to make sure everything was perfect. She looked over the bottles of 2006 Louis Roederer Cristal Rose' which was on ice. She looked over seeing Chris at the door, dressed in the Givenchy outfit she picked for him. The pianist began to play John Legend "You and I" Sydney walked over to the door to greet him. Chris looked around at their home which now looked like a white wonderland. He kissed Sydney's lips. "What's all this?"

"It's about you tonight baby." She led him over towards the middle of their beautiful ivory and gold marble floor. He placed his arms around her body. "You look beautiful ma." "Thank you. You look handsome as well love." Chris looked around as the music filled the room. He looked around the piano seeing the gifts stacked around the bottom of the piano. He smiled. After two songs and dancing Sydney led Chris over to the table. The chef poured Chris a glass of champagne, and Sydney some Orange Juice. He brought over the first dish which was a salad. The way Chris liked with Chicken, bacon and cucumbers. Sydney sat across from him caressing his leg with her foot as she gazed into his eyes. "I appreciate this Syd."

"No problem babe. Did you see the gifts for you under the piano?"

"Yes, I saw them. Thank you." The chef brought over the entrée. Lobster and Filet mignon with risotto which was one of Chris' favorite meals, green beans on the side. Once the chef placed the finishing toppings on the cake, Sydney dismissed him and the pianist, with a hefty tip. As Chris sat back after a second serving stuffed. Sydney brought over the strawberry shortcake to Chris. The chef had already sliced it and had prepared with ice cream whipped cream and strawberries. Sydney sat on top of Chris lap, feeding him the cake as she kissed his lips. Her gorgeous man, who made anything look sexy. She bit her lip watching as he licked the icing from his lips. "How is it baby?"

"Yo, it's good. Remind me of those nights when ma had got her stamps and cooked a big dinner, she would top it off with strawberry shortcake. I used to be so fuckin' happy." He smiled as he reminisced.

"I love you." said Sydney as she looked into his eyes. He ran his fingers through her curls. "I love you Syd." She kissed him passionately, their tongues dancing in each other's mouths. Sydney leaned over to his ear, biting on his ear lobe. "Come upstairs in ten minutes." She kissed his ear gently removing herself from his lap walking up the stairs. Chris poured himself another drink. He looked over the fridge seeing a picture of Natalia when she was a baby, another of them cuddled up at Sydney's graduation, and the last was a selfie of Chris and Natalia at the beach. Natalia was smiling in a bikini sitting on top of his chest. Chris sighed. What if he did time? How could he miss out on Natalia's life? What if he was sentenced to five years? He couldn't fathom being away from his children. What about Sydney, could she handle it? He couldn't leave her with two children for five years. Serving anytime wasn't an option for him at this point. He picked up the bottle placing it to his lips. "I'm Chris muthafuckin Garcia. Fuck that bitch." He replied solemnly. He walked upstairs to Sydney, who was sprawled across the bed in an Agent Provocateur, playsuit, Sydney climbed unto all fours. "Come take me Papi."

It was after ten forty and Yogi had been blowing up Vani's phone all night. She received a call from an unknown number, she knew it was him. She finally decided to answer the phone. "Hello."

"What the fuck going on? I know you seen my calls!"

"Look, I spoke with Dana tonight. She confirmed Sydney is coming to the salon on Saturday. It'll be a go, I promise."

"Saturday is the end of this shit. If I can't get the fuckin' baby we kidnapping Sydney's ass. I'm done with this fuck shit!"

"What?!" said Vani.

"You heard me! We gon' rape her bougie ass and toss her in a fuckin' ditch. Fuck her and that pussy nigga!"

Vani was horrified. "You said no one would be hurt. What the fuck?"

"That was before, now this shit is personal and I'm out of fucks to give. Fuck that bitch, fuck Preme, and fuck Chris bitch ass! Saturday it's done." Yogi ended the call. Vani immediately placed her hands in her hair. She did hate Sydney, but she didn't want her dead. What should she do? Should she tell Chris? She knew something was gonna happen and she needed to think fast. This situation was beyond her now, this was definitely goin to start a war when this took place. *Shit! What the fuck am I going to do?* Thought Vani.

Thursday morning, Sydney awoke to the sun gleaming on her face. She realized she was sleeping on their balcony, naked. She sat up realizing Chris was holding her in his arms caressing her stomach. He kissed her chest. "Good morning baby."

"Morning." Said Chris as he kissed her cheek.

"What's wrong?" said Sydney. He shook his head. "Nothing just thinking about the baby. What is he going to look like? Personality... children such a blessing you know." Sydney nodded her head. "I hope the birth is as easy as Natalia. But, we have a while for that. I remember seeing your face as I was pushing, you looked so happy."

"Yea." said Chris somberly. "Baby, what is up? Why are you so down?"

"I'm good. Just getting things together for this case."

"Do you want us to come with you?" Sydney leaned off of him attempting to peel herself from the floor. She realized she had roses stuck to her ass. Chris extended his hand to help her up. "No, I'm good. I told you to stay here with the babies. Didn't you say your parents would be coming soon?"

"Yes, they are actually coming in tomorrow for a couple days. I would've told you earlier but I didn't want you to be upset."

"Sydney, I'm leaving... to Connecticut tomorrow." Sydney looked at him as if she was broken in a million pieces. "What? Why didn't you tell me? When were you going to tell me?" "Tonight." Sydney walked over to him placing her arms around his body. "So today is possibly the last day we can see you for awhile?"

"Ma... calm down. I will be fine."

"How do you know that? What if they give you time? I'm not okay without you. Natalia will be crushed. We need you baby." She began to cry in his chest. Chris removed her face from his chest, lifting her chin. "Sydney..."

"Why didn't you tell me you were leaving? You're going to do time aren't you? Just tell me."

"Syd, I'm not doing any time. I will be back soon. I have the best lawyer, my court date is August fourth. I will be home that next week." He placed his hands on her face kissing her lips. "I love you. When have I given you a reason to doubt my word. We're good." She nodded her head. "I know, baby. I trust you." Sydney walked over towards the shower. She decided to suck up her tears to be strong for Chris. The gate buzzed Chris looked at the screen seeing it was Preme. He threw on a pair of boxers, Jordan shorts and Black shirt. He unlocked the door letting them in. Preme hugged him. Natalia rushed past him. "Daddy!!" Chris picked her up kissing her cheek. "Hey Tubby. Have fun with pop?" Chris locked the door behind them taking the baby bag from his shoulder. Chris placed Natalia down she took off towards the steps. "Mommy!" she screamed. Chris and Preme walked over to the living room. Sydney appeared at the top of the steps. "Hi Preme! Hi mommy's baby."

"How are you Sydney? How's the baby?"

"I'm good and you?"

"Can't complain." Sydney picked up Natalia walking over to the kitchen. Preme you need something to drink?"

"Nah, I'm good." Natalia pointed to her juice boxes. Sydney gave her one, retreating back upstairs to the bedroom. She pulled out her Macbook to check her emails. She had over a hundred emails. One email, stood out from BJ promotion. She smiled reading the email:

How are you Honeydip? Didn't think you would hear from me after that clown threw that cheap shot? It's all good, hopefully you dumped that clown. I would love to get to know you beautiful. I'm going to be traveling over the next few months up the east coast, I'd love to see you on one of my stops. Sydney immediately looked over her shoulder before gazing at the rock on her finger. She began to type simply.

"The guy in the lobby is not a clown, he is the love of my life and my fiancé. Take care. Best wishes." She heard Chris walking upstairs she quickly ended the email, he walked up to their bedroom closing the doors. Once back down in front of Preme, he sat up. "Pop, watch over my fam, while I'm away. I got over four million put away in the safe in the garage. I got some other shit in the safe inside of Tubby room."

"Syd know about these?"

"In garage, but not in Tubby room." Sydney pulled out the monitor, praying that the other was in the playpen in living room where she kept it. She turned it on, going into their closet, to eavesdrop. "Yea, in Tubby room safe there is a few keys a piece and about five million." Sydney's mouth dropped. *In Natalia's room?* The monitor began to beep saying the battery was dead she turned it off leaving it in the closet. She walked over to the bed turning on the television. An hour later Chris came upstairs saying that he was taking them to the beach to get ready. Ingrid texted Sydney their itinerary, she became excited to see her parents, especially now with Chris' looming departure. They spent all day at the beach in the sun, when they arrived back home Natalia was exhausted she slept the whole car ride home. Sydney washed her off before placing her in her gown in her bed. Chris and Sydney made love, trying to erase their pending separation. In the middle of the night Chris went to get Natalia from her bed bringing her to their bed. Around five thirty he awoke, checking over the safes and packing his bags. He hopped in the shower before going downstairs to grab a carton of orange juice and a muffin. He looked at his phone it was now six thirty. Sydney awoke looking over to him. He walked over to her sitting beside her. "Time to get up ma." "Uggh… sighed Sydney, she quickly hopped in the shower and threw on a black maxi dress and a fedora over her head, Sophia Webster Becky Gem slides, She brushed her teeth. She placed Natalia in a pair of leggings, floral print top and Ugg boots on her feet. Chris went down and placed his bags in the car. Sydney and Natalia soon came down. Sydney slid behind the wheel, placing her oversized Chanel frames over her eyes. She knew the tears would come, but she didn't want him to feel guilty about his situation. She tried to remain quiet the whole drive. Chris looked over to her. "Don't forget to keep the safe in the room locked. Keep the house alarm on." Sydney nodded in agreement. Chris placed his hand on her leg. "What's good mute?"

"I'm fine." Sydney replied. Chris smiled looking over to her.

"Who you fooling? I'll be back before you know it, Syd."

"Yea, I know." Replied Sydney with a fake smile. Chris reached over pulling the sunglasses from her eyes.

"I want to see your face." He held the sunglasses in his hand as they pulled up to the terminals. Sydney paid to park, since she would be waiting on her parents as well. Chris exited the car heading back to the trunk. The tears soon streamed down Sydney's face. Sydney sat beside him at the trunk. Once he had all his bags out, he closed the trunk. "A'ight ma. Come give me some love. He stretched out his arms to hug her. Sydney nuzzled her face in his neck kissing his neck gently. Trying to let his cologne seep into her nostrils. "I love you soo much baby. Be good and come home soon."

"I will. I love you Syd." They kissed on the lips long and slow. He walked over to the passenger door, to Natalia. "Hey mama! Daddy love you." He reached in kissing her face. Natalia smiled thinking he would take her out of the car seat. He touched her hand. Before closing the door. "Okay, ma let me go. I'll call you." Chris walked towards the terminal entrance. Sydney watched him walk away. A part of her wanted to run behind him and hug him again, but she knew she wouldn't let go. Once he disappeared through the glass doors. Sydney walked around to the driver's side. Her phone rang it was her parents saying that their flight had just landed. She told them which terminal she was outside of and they said they would meet her. Her phone beeped with a message from Chris. "Stop looking at my picture in your phone. I will see you soon. Love you." She smiled reading the message. "I can't help but stare you are my sexy baby." Minutes later she saw Ingrid and Gavin emerge from the airport.

She got out of the car to greet them. Once they were all piled in Gavin sat in the back with Natalia. On the drive to the house, Gavin began to talk about how big Natalia had gotten. "She's so adorable."

"Don't tell her that. She's just like her father into looking at herself in a mirror."

"Where is Chris?" said Ingrid.

"He's out of town for a few days."

"Will we see him at all?"

"Maybe." Sydney pulled up to their gated community using the remote, once they pulled up to their gate. Sydney typed in the code to their personal gate. Gavin looked around at the beautiful houses in their neighborhood. Ingrid looked around at the fleet of cars in the driveway. "This house is amazing Sydney!" said Ingrid. "Thank you ma." Sydney parked the car walking around to get Natalia out the backseat. The minute her feet hit the pavement she became shy, clasping Sydney's leg. Sydney walked up to the door unlocking it. "There are rooms downstairs and up, I wasn't sure if you were in the mood to walk but there is a guestroom upstairs and to the left."

"We will stay upstairs." said Gavin as he marveled at this beautiful mansion. Sydney walked over to the kitchen to fix Natalia breakfast. She placed her in the highchair placing French toast sticks and bacon on her tray. Ingrid walked over to her. "How is the baby?" She placed her hands on her stomach.

"It's good. I'm not ready to get fat yet." Ingrid walked around looking at the pictures on the mantle. She gazed over a picture she had never seen of Natalia which was in black & white. "Can I have a copy of this picture? She looks so adorable."

"Yea, let me check to see if I have any more in the office." Sydney left to the office, Gavin walked down the stairs looking over the pictures on the wall. There was a frame of Natalia's birth certificate, with her footprints. "I never knew her name was Natalia Maria…I thought she didn't have a middle name."

Sydney came back with the pictures she gave her three copies. One in an 8 x 10, and two 5x 7. Gavin continued looking over the mantle. He stopped at Chris' GED. "Christian Garcia." He read his name out loud. Sydney looked over what he was looking at. "I was very proud of him for getting that."

"Garcia? I thought his last name was Lopez." Sydney and Ingrid both shook their head at his remarks.

"Really Gavin? Where the hell did you get Lopez?"

"I thought that was what you told me."

"Well, guys I'm sorry to be a bad host, but I'm going to take a nap upstairs. Make yourselves comfortable, whatever is here is for your consumption." Sydney took Natalia out of the highchair carrying her upstairs with her. "Oh it's okay Syd. You're with child, we will be fine." Gavin walked around the house admiring the expensive vases and décor. Ingrid walked over to the fridge seeing the rows of Gatorade, orange juice cartons and variety of sodas. She picked out a bottle of Evian water. Gavin ventured over to the other rooms in the house seeing the office which was immaculate and their in home gym. How did Chris afford this? He pulled out his phone dialing Tarik. He answered on the second ring. "Hey, it's Gavin. I was looking for details in the case. Can you give me a description of Christian?"

"For what?"

"I just received information from witness. I wanted to confirm some of the details."

"Well… he is mixed. Spanish and black, light skinned, low cut, muscular he has tattoos on his arm one says Death Before Dishonor."

"Okay. I'm gonna check over her description I will get back to you. I'm out of town visiting my daughter. I will talk to you soon." Gavin walked back out to Ingrid looking over the pictures of Chris on the mantle, he tried to look on his arm to see what his tattoo said, and in one of the pictures he was on his phone. It was too dark, he couldn't read the lettering. He took off his coat sitting next to Ingrid.

Breaking News in Hartford, Connecticut. Persia Rodriguez and her toddler son were found burned in a Honda Accord, in an abandoned parking lot. We have been following this story since the story broke this morning. The car which was partially burnt was spotted by a resident who lives a few blocks from scene, said she was out walking her dog this morning, when she saw the horrific scene.

Chris checked into his hotel room and was headed upstairs when Grant called him. "Hi, Chris. Where ever you are stay there!" He said frantically.

"What? Are you on your way here?"

"Yes, I'm on my way." Chris hopped in the shower to rinse off the jet lag, changing into a Givenchy shirt and jeans. Ten minutes later he heard pounding on his door. "Who is it?" Chris replied angrily to the pounds. "Grant!" Chris opened the door, Grant walked into the room he immediately took in everything in the room seeing that Chris' bags were not unpacked and suite had not been touched. Chris closed the door behind him. "What up?"

"The witness, Persia, was found dead this morning."

"What?!"

"Burned to death, her and son. You know what this is going to look like."

"I didn't have shit to do with this."

"I know. We are going to have to divert some of this away from this case possibly her lifestyle choices. The other defendant is pleading not guilty."

"What other defendant?"

"Tarik… Logan. Witness said he was involved as well. He lives here in Connecticut. You know him, right?"

"You've gotta be kidding me my nigga." said Chris as he sat down on the bed.

In Miami, Sydney and Natalia had awoke from their nap sitting up in the bed. Sydney's phone rang back to back. She looked down at the screen seeing Nadine. She answered, "Hey girl."

"Hey! Girl guess what?!" she replied cheerfully.

"What?"

"Persia was found dead this morning girl!"

"What?! You lying?"

"Dead ass. Her and her baby burned to death in a car. Stupid bitch. Always was running her fuckin' mouth probably caught up to her. You know her thirsty ass had started stripping and selling pills."

"Oh my god! That is so sad. Her and her baby that is fucked up. I don't wish that on anyone."

"It's been on the news all fuckin' morning."

"Damn… I know you hated her bitch, but you being a little ruthless."

"Fuck her. I just wanted to call you to fill you in on that tea. I'm heading down to Virginia for a couple weeks. I'll speak to you soon."

"Okay. Talk to you later." Sydney immediately thought of Chris. She called his phone no answer. She became worried a million thoughts rushing thru her mind. Chris wouldn't do some crazy shit like that. Not to her child, and definitely not with his past. She changed Natalia's diaper heading downstairs to fix lunch. She began to cut up apple slices as she made Natalia PBJ sandwich. Gavin walked over to the kitchen. Looking over Sydney's attire a spaghetti strap tank and low rise drawstring pants she had rolled down which sat on her hip. Her phone which was on the counter rang loudly showing Chris' picture, she smiled rushing over to the phone. "Hi baby! How are you?"

"Good, just getting situated in my suite. How my baby?"

"Good, eating lunch. So what's going on?"

"I can't go into anything, but some bullshit going on right now." Sydney looked back at her father who was eavesdropping on her conversation.

"Watch her, please. Said Sydney as she walked towards the pool. Babe, I know what happened. I just want to know..."

"Syd, I didn't have shit to do with this bullshit." Sydney sighed, conflicted. Gavin stated he had to go to the bathroom and asked Ingrid to watch Natalia. Once finished, he walked out of the bathroom. He glanced to a frame in the center of the hall above a side table with flowers and candles. He leaned in looking over the obituary inside. He stood frozen as he looked at the picture inside. *"She leaves behind one son, her everything, Christian Garcia."* Read Gavin out loud. He gently caressed his finger over the picture. "Maria..." he replied softly. He heard Sydney walk in downstairs he looked back at the picture once more, before walking back down to Sydney. "Everything okay?" said Gavin as he looked over Sydney in the fridge.

"Yea, everything is fine."

"Good. So tell me about this Christian? What makes him so special to marry my princess?"

Sydney side eyed her father, thinking how awkward it would be to have a conversation with him about the man he hated. "Well first of all, I love him. He is the father to my children. He loves me completely, flaws and all, he takes care of me. I know that he would do anything for me, he is a great provider and amazing daddy."

Gavin looked around the kitchen. "This house is amazing, and I know this neighborhood or cars in the driveway were not cheap. I know that SubZero Fridge alone ranges at about sixteen thousand dollars. So what does Christian do?"

"Dad, we are not going there. I told you he owns a business and we are happy."

Gavin placed his hands in the air showing he would back off. "Have you met his family? What do they do?"

"Well... Chris' mother is deceased, but I'm good with his father, he and Natalia have a great bond."

Gavin's eyes grew wide. "You know his father?" Sydney nodded her head. "Yea, he and Chris are close." Gavin almost choked. He sipped on the water he had on the counter as Sydney made herself a Turkey sandwich. He saw the tattoo on her back. "Why did you get that ink on your body? Let me see." Gavin came over looking over the Natalia tattoo on her back "It's for my baby." He sighed. "I bet he talked you into it. I'm pretty sure he is full of tattoos."

"No he did not talk me into it. He wasn't there I was with my friends. And he doesn't have a lot of tattoos, only a few important ones." Said Sydney with a smile.

Back in Connecticut Chris was annoyed with being confined to his room. Grant had stated that it would be best for him to stay in while this story is hot. He had the local news and they were reporting the story all day. *"Persia was last seen leaving Tails gentleman's club where she worked as a dancer. Relatives say the victim came after two thirty am to pick up her son, which she normally did and would head home. Her car was found torched this morning, with her and her infant son's remains inside. Police are looking for anyone who has any information to please call the number listed on the screen at this time. We will have more as this story progresses."*

Chris decided he had enough he was getting out of the room he placed on a jacket and Yankee fitted over his head. His phone rang it was Grant saying he was on his way back, they needed to go in and talk to police. Back in Miami Gavin received a call from Detective Clayton saying that they needed Tarik in today by four. Although he pleaded for another day, detective stated he would issue a warrant for his arrest. He immediately stepped outside called Tarik. "This is Gavin, detective just called me the witness has been murdered! Are you fuckin' serious! Do you know how this looks?!"

"I didn't have shit to do with that." said Tarik nonchalant.

"They need you there by four. I'm out of town with my daughter."

"You need to figure out something because I ain't doing shit without you there." Gavin threw his hand up in the sky. "Alright, I will see what I can do."

"Yea, you handle that." Tarik ended the call. Gavin became furious punching the air, he regained his composure before walking back inside. Sydney and Ingrid were inside her bedroom. Ingrid was gawking over the beautiful Versace duvet on their bed. Sydney placed Natalia on the bed walking over to her closet. Ingrid looked at the picture of them on the nightstand. "This room is amazing Syd. This house is amazing." Ingrid sat on the bed, Natalia came over looking at the picture. "Thank you ma."

"Who's that Natalia?" said Ingrid pointing to Sydney in the picture.

"Mommy. She switched her finger over to Chris. Daddy! Daddy! Said Natalia cheerfully.

"Someone's a daddy's girl eh?"

Sydney laughed walking back out to them. "Yes, everything is daddy with her." Ingrid looked over the Tiffany charm bracelet on her wrist. "Oh, this is gorgeous. Are these real diamonds?"

"Of course. Daddy bought that for her birthday."

Chris was seated in the interrogation room, his lawyer seated beside him. One detective seated the other standing. "Hello Christian. How are you?"

"Good."

"Do you know why you are here?"

"I'm sure you will inform me." Chris looked directly in his face.

"You are here as a person of interest in reference to the murder of Persia Rodriguez."

"I don't have anything to do with that."

"Where were you last night?"

"At home with my fiancé and daughter in Florida."

"Where were you around eight this morning?"

"On a plane to fly here."

"When was the last time you spoke to Persia?"

"I don't know her like that."

"What time did you get here?"

"Around eleven thirty."

"Where did you go after you arrived?"

"To my hotel." The detective who was standing exited the room.

"Well, we have no more questions for you at this time. But as a person of interest you cannot leave the city of Hartford as a condition. If you leave you will be considered a suspect and a warrant for your arrest will be issued."

"Whatever. Are we done?"

"Yes we are done." Chris and Grant exited the room. In Miami, Gavin was able to get an extension and said he would be in first thing in the morning, he explained his dilemma with his daughter and expecting grandchild, which got him brownie points. Gavin and Ingrid were in the room exhausted after a day of food and shopping, he began to explain he had to go home. Ingrid decided she would leave with him. She walked over to Sydney's room. "Come in." Sydney had tucked Natalia in on Chris' side of the bed. "Hey…" said Ingrid solemnly.

"What's up?"

"Some things have come up in your father's case he is working and he is going to have to return to Hartford ASAP. I'm going to return with him. He needs me right now."

"What about me? I need you!" shouted Sydney.

"Sydney, you are fine."

"Yea, I guess I will be! You don't give a shit about me! You only care about him!"

"Sydney, please don't do this. Don't make me choose."

"I won't. Leave. Get the fuck out of my house!"

"Sydney... you will not talk to me like that!"

"Ma, get out of here! You've made your decision get the fuck out!" Sydney walked over to Ingrid pushing her towards the door. Ingrid knowing she was pregnant allowed herself to be pushed out instead of retaliating. Gavin came out of his room hearing the ruckus. Sydney locked her room door behind her. Ingrid was in tears. "What is going on?"

"Sydney is upset I'm leaving."

"Well, maybe you should stay with her and the baby?"

The door unlocked and Sydney appeared. "Maybe both of you should get the fuck out!"

"No need to be disrespectful Sydney. You are acting like a spoiled brat." Said Gavin.

"So what! I want you out tonight. You better call a cab or car service. Better yet you can drive back in that car you bought me because I don't drive that crap."

"Listen you ungrateful little bitch! Shouted Ingrid. I'm leaving. She threw her hands up. You're pregnant and my grandchild is here I don't want to make a scene but if you weren't with child I would slap that smirk off your face. I am your mother. Don't you ever talk to me like that!" Gavin pulled Ingrid back heading over towards their bedroom. Once Sydney heard them roll their bags towards the door, twenty minutes later she stepped out of her room to watch them leave. Ingrid looked back at Sydney as she walked down the steps. "I love you, Sydney."

"Bye ma. said Sydney bluntly. Ingrid headed out to the car. Gavin came back in for one last bag. He looked over to Sydney, he headed over towards her. "Why are you walking over here, you know me and you are not cool."

"Ever since that punk has come into your life, you've had this attitude with me. I am your father. The only one you have on this earth."

"Gavin, cut the shit, let's not pretend like you were this amazing father. Goodbye." He shook his head walking over to the car. Sydney stood at the front door watching the cab as it pulled out of the driveway. She immediately placed the alarm on the house walking upstairs to Natalia. She was furious, she walked into her closet, tripping over the box Monica had given her. She sat on an ottoman inspecting her toe. Her phone rang It was Chris, she answered. "Hey babe."

"What up ma? What's wrong?"

"Me and my parents got into a big fight. My dad had to handle something with a client so they are heading back to Connecticut. My mom acting like a fuckin' groupie saying he needs her she has to go too. Fuck outta here! So, I kicked them out."

Chris chuckled. "Well, you know your mom love your punk ass daddy. Don't worry about that shit. I love you, I got you. Your mom care about you, she just sprung on that nigga right now, cause she getting some d." Sydney laughed out loud.

"Babe, I don't want to think about them getting it on. I was soo furious. But enough about me. How's everything there?"

"I'm good. Got me stuck on this shit can't leave Hartford right now. Chris yawned. I called just to hear your voice before I go to sleep. So, kiss my baby for me. I will see you soon. Love you."

"Love you too." Sydney ended the call. She opened the top to the box. She quickly flipped through the family pictures on top before pulling out one of the file folders. On page one it said from the Office of Gavin Cruz, to Phillipe Garcia, Sydney's mouth dropped reading over the document which was on an official letterhead and in Spanish.

Phillipe,

This letter is in regards to Christian I have spoken with other offices to try to assist you in this matter. The only way you can receive him is to send twenty five thousand to cover rehoming fees as well as court fees. Also, asking for fifteen thousand a week for additional fees. If this amount is too much for you, I have contact numbers for people that can assist you. You have to know with the lifestyle Maria was living this is not going away, more as a warning. Best wishes

Gavin Cruz

Sydney was in shock, speechless. Her father trying to sell Chris? Was he trying to extort his grandparents? Why? Did he know Maria? She knew Chris would kill Gavin on site if he ever got his hands on these documents. She quickly tossed the folder back in the box closing it shut. *What the fuck? What the hell am I going to do?*

*   *   *

The next morning Sydney woke up around eleven thirty. Natalia wild curls blocking her face. She moved her to the side before reaching for her phone. She had numerous missed calls. One was Chris she immediately called him back via Facetime. Which she knew he always had a hard time using. Once he appeared on the screen she smiled. "Hey babe."

"What up ma. He checked out his face on the screen. This makes my nose look big as shit!"

Sydney laughed. "It's the angle that your holding the phone. I was calling you back."

"Oh, you texted me saying call when I get up so I called. What you and Tubby doing?" Sydney panned the phone over to Natalia who was smiling. "What up tubby?" She smiled placing her face in front of Sydney's "Hi daddy! Chris waved at her in the screen, pretending he was kissing her cheek. What you doing today Syd?"

"Well about to comb this hair of hers and then head over to the salon with Dana to get my nails filled in. what are you doing today?"

"Going to get a rental, get some food. Meet with lawyer."

"Okay. Well babe, I'm about to get dressed and I will call you when we come back from the salon. Be good. Love you."

"Love you." Interjected Natalia with a smile.

Chris smiled. "I love you both. Be safe."

Sydney ended the facetime texting Dana to tell her she would be in around four thirty if she was available. She texted back seconds later stating that she was. She placed Natalia's hair in a ponytail in center and her hair down in the back. She put Natalia on a Fendi denim romper with a floral print with her Sophia Webster Riko sandals. Sydney dressed herself in Givenchy black printed jersey tank and Hudson skinny ankle jeans and Sophia Webster Nereida sandals on her feet. Sydney sat down to apply a little makeup. She walked past the box again thinking about what she read, it made her stomach turn. She pulled another purse down from her closet transferring items to the purse she was carrying today. A Givenchy Antigona two toned leather satchel, which she had been wanting to use for a while. She grabbed Natalia's bag, with her following after heading down to the kitchen. Once all packed she headed out to the Mercedes, starting the ignition she slid Natalia into her seat. Beyoncé's "Sorry" came through the

558

speakers. Natalia immediately threw her hands in the air, dancing to the music. Sydney walked over to the driver's side and they were on their way.

Vani sat in her chair texting Yogi. "They are coming around four thirty. Come close to five." He texted back shortly. "Bet. I'm gonna hit you up when we on the way." She placed the phone on her counter looking over at Dana. Her nerves were on edge, her fingers twitching. She had been smoking black and mild's all day. Once she came back inside Dana looked over her demeanor. "What's up with you today Vani? You mad busy."

"I'm good. Just got a lot on mind today." Dana shrugged walking back to the bathroom.

In Connecticut, Tarik was smoking a Newport as he sat inside the interrogation room with the same detectives Chris has sat down with previously. He reclined back in the chair his posture cocky and arrogant.

"Do you know why you're here?"

"For that Persia shit"

"How did you know about that?"

"That shit has been on television all day."

"Where were you yesterday around eleven pm?"

"I've been home all night and morning."

"So, you haven't been anywhere at all?"

"That's what I said."

"When was the last time you spoke to Persia Rodriguez?"

"I've never talked to that girl. We weren't fuckin' friends, you feel me."

"So, you never talked to her ever?"

"I said we not cool or friends. I may have spoken to her in a club or some shit, but I don't know her."

"Well, Tarik at this time you are considered a person of interest you are not to leave Hartford under any circumstances. If you leave the city limits there will be a warrant issued for your arrest." Tarik rolled his eyes.

"We done?"

"Yes, you're free to go." Tarik got up slamming his chair back against the wall, before exiting the room with Gavin behind him. The detectives looked at each other. "We need to keep an eye on him. Did we get that information checked on the first one Garcia?"

"We have the footage being sent over from Miami airport as we speak. So far his story adds up with location and time frames he gave. We are awaiting the hotel footage. Let's not cancel him off as of yet, we need to wait until everything is one hundred percent."

"Get Leedmer to give us any information can find on autopsy reports.

Gavin and Tarik walked over to his car to chat. Gavin slid behind the wheel Tarik in passenger. "I'm going to need you to be on your shit next few days. They will be watching your every fuckin move. Associates, and anyone in your family."

"I know." Tarik looked out the window. Gavin reached into his pocket pulling out a picture he stole from the mantle in Sydney's house. Tarik's face instantly lit up when he looked over the picture of Chris holding Sydney's body kissing her. "Do you know who that is?" said Gavin.

"That's Chris and Sydney. Gavin looked over to him, upset he knew his daughter. Where did you get this picture?"

"How do you know the girl?"

"That's my homegirl Syd. We go back to New York. She's fuckin' Chris, that's his old lady."

"Is this Christian Garcia, from this case?"

"Yea, but I'm trying to figure out how you get this picture?" said Tarik angrily.

"Sydney... is my daughter." Tarik placed his hand over his mouth not believing the words which left Gavin's lips. He thought about the times that Chris had said he hated Sydney's pops, he knew Chris would flip when he saw him in the court room. "Wait a minute, my nigga. You fucked with Ben and them, knowing your ties with your daughter. You know you done got over your head my nigga."

"What do you mean?"

"Yo, you done fucked up my nigga." Tarik handed him back the picture. He glanced at Gavin once more, before exiting the car. Gavin looked down at the picture, disgusted with the way Chris was holding his princess. He hated everything about him. "Fuckin' punk." He stated out loud.

In Miami it was four twenty, and Sydney had just arrived in the salon with Natalia on her hip. She walked over to Dana's station placing Natalia on her lap. "Hi pretty girl." Said Dana as she smiled at her. Sydney placed her baby bag and purse beside her on the floor. "So how are you?" said Dana.

"Good. Planning this wedding, eating everything while praying not to become a whale." They both laughed. Vani walked out of the back seeing Sydney sitting at Dana's booth. A surge of panic rushed through her body. She looked over seeing Natalia sitting on her lap, playing with her phone. Vani's phone rang she already knew it was Yogi. She answered. "Hello."

"On our way."

"Okay. Damn, why do I have to get you some shit from Chipotle! Fine, I'm leaving now." Yogi ignored her diversion and ended the call. Vani walked over to Dana's station. "Hey that was Mark, I have to go get a burrito bowl for his petty ass."

"Okay, Niecy wants a sew-in when you get back." Vani looked over at Natalia. "Hi mama." Sydney looked over to Vani. "How are you Vani?"

"I'm good. You?" said Vani shocked she spoke to her.

"I'm good as well," Vani looked over at Sydney and Natalia one last time before walking out the backdoor. A black Yukon pulled up around back, she quickly pulled out of the parking lot driving towards the front seeing two more Yukon's pull along the front curb. Minutes later eight men dressed in all black, ski masks on their faces and loaded guns in their hands entered the salon. Three warning shots pierced the salon doors. Sydney immediately grabbed Natalia and shielded her under the table with her body. Three of the men stormed over to Dana's station while the others guarded the door with guns pointed to the women in waiting area. One of the men grabbed Sydney by her hair, pulling her off of Natalia.

"Oh my god! Please don't hurt my baby!" Sydney pleaded.

"Shut the fuck up bitch." He raised his hand slapping her across the face with the barrel of the gun in his hand, knocking her across the floor.

"Fuck no!" shouted Dana as she jumped up to hit him. The two men who were surrounding her pointed their guns to her face. She sat down. Blood oozed from Sydney's blonde curls as she tried to crawl back towards Natalia.

"Give me all your fuckin' money bitch!" He snatched her purse from the floor. "Mommy! Shouted Natalia as she attempted to run to her. One of the men grabbed Natalia by her hair.

"Oh my god! Please give me my baby! I will give you whatever you want!" screamed Sydney.

"Mama! Screamed Natalia as the man held her tightly in his arms. The man grabbed Sydney by the hair, punching her in the face. "Shut the fuck up bitch! Sydney fell to her knees. Dana jumped up, she was immediately pummeled by the two men surrounding her. Blood spewed from her face as they punched her repeatedly.

"Give me the necklace and the fucking rock." Sydney tried to quickly remove the necklace from her neck, her fingers were trembling so much she couldn't grip the latch. "Hurry up bitch! I don't have all day." Sydney handed him her necklace and engagement ring.

"Please, don't hurt my baby." Said Sydney as she wiped the blood away from her lip.

"No! Screamed Natalia as the man held her she began to kick and claw at his face. "Look little bitch! He quickly placed his hand around her throat placing his gun to her head. When Sydney looked up seeing the gun to Natalia's head she lost it. "Get your fuckin' hands off my baby! Motherfucker!" She rushed towards him, kicking him in the nuts. The men all piled on Sydney punching and kicking her. She screamed out in pain as gunshots rang out in the salon. She immediately blacked out becoming numb to the pain which filled her body. Her vision became blurred before she felt nothing at all.

Tires squealed onto the pavement, as the men rushed back to their vehicles. The salon looked like a scene out of a horror film. The floor covered in blood, bullet holes and broken glass everywhere. Two women lay dead in the waiting area. Sydney's motionless body lay in the middle of the salon. The sirens could be heard blaring in the distance as one last person walked through the salon. The masked person leaned over Sydney's body, pulling her tresses out of her face. "Yo' pussy ass nigga finally fucked with the wrong nigga. Sweet dreams beautiful." He leaned over kissing her face as he picked up the baby bag from the floor walking out of the backdoor. As the ignition started, a faint cough filled the air.

"Tati?"

*   *   *

www.ingramcontent.com/pod-product-compliance
Lightning Source LLC
Chambersburg PA
CBHW030536020726
47494CB00005B/1388